Danica

USA TODAY bestselling and RITA® Award-winning author **Marie Ferrarella** has written more than 250 books for Mills & Boon, some under the name Marie Nicole. Her romances are beloved by fans worldwide. Visit her website, marieferrarella.com

Also by Danica Winters

Also by Marie Ferrarella

Discover more at millsandboon.co.uk

A JUDGE'S SECRETS

DANICA WINTERS

COLTON 911: SECRET DEFENDER

MARIE FERRARELLA

MILLS & BOON

® and ™ are trademarks owned and used by the trademark owner and/
or its licensee. Trademarks marked with ® are registered with the United
K____ _____ _____ ____ _____ for Harmonization in the
Internal Market and in other countries.

First Published in Great Britain 2021
by Mills & Boon, an imprint of HarperCollins*Publishers Ltd*
1 London Bridge Street, London, SE1 9GF

www.millsandboon.co.uk

_____ Harlequin (UK) Limited
_____ and Company Publishers
_____ _____ 1 London Bridge Street
Ringsend Road, Dublin 4, Ireland

_____ © 2021 Mara V Wilson

Special thanks and acknowledgement are given to Mara Parlorbury ___ her _____

ISBN: 978-0-263-28346-4

0721

MIX
Paper from
responsible sources

FSC
www.fsc.org
FSC™ C007454

This book is produced from independently certified FSC™ paper to ensure responsible forest management.

For more information visit: www.harpercollins.co.uk/green

Printed and bound in Spain
by CPI, Barcelona

A JUDGE'S SECRETS

DANICA WINTERS

To all those who have stepped into the flames
and kept moving forward.

Chapter One

Secrets had a way of feasting on a person's soul. Their appetite was voracious, parasitic in their inability to stop consuming until there was nothing left of their host but an empty shell. Judge Natalie DeSalvo had witnessed this parasitic invasion time and time again, and would continue to do so as long as people walked the earth.

This week had been especially brutal for Natalie; just that morning she'd had a case centered around human trafficking. One of the kidnapper's victims had been subpoenaed and forced to testify. When the woman had slipped into the courtroom, she had held her trembling hands together in front of her, and her eyes had never left the floor. Sweat beaded at her hairline and her face had been a sickly white. No doubt the victim feared for her life.

Natalie had asked the woman to look at her on the stand and had gazed directly into dark, nearly black eyes. In those seconds it was as if the woman's penetrating stare had acted as a vacuum, pulling every shred of empathy and pity from Natalie until it threatened to ooze out onto her notes and smudge the ink.

Her entire body had hurt for the woman as she had

told her story of being taken to the streets of Las Vegas and sold. The secrets poured from her, faster and faster, as the lawyers pressed her, until finally, she no longer stared down at the floor. Soon, some of the life that had seemed stripped from her began to return, filling her until she changed from empty automaton to flesh-and-blood accuser. Her voice became stronger, and then—when she looked at her kidnapper—the world shifted.

The woman came back to life.

It was those moments of self-acceptance and that break from secrecy that made Natalie love her job. There were only a handful of moments that made her feel like she was doing what she had been destined to do. The rest of the time she felt as if she was just a cog in the wheel of the criminal defense system, a system she found to be broken as much as she felt it worked.

By the end of the trial, and after hearing all of the victims' testimonies about the atrocious things the man had done to them and their lives, she had sentenced the man to prison where he would serve twenty years, without the ability to seek parole. It was the maximum allowed for his crimes.

The sad truth was that, even if the trafficker spent the rest of his life behind bars, he could still get to this woman—even make sure she was killed if the mood struck him. Even doing everything Natalie could, the power she wielded as a judge wasn't enough to promise anyone any real safety.

It was no wonder that she was often hard-pressed for a good night's sleep.

Thankfully, the other district court judge, Steven Hanes, had been tremendously generous with his time and mentorship. Tonight she would need his ear and support more than ever.

She sighed as she packed up her things after the last trial of the day—one where a drunk driver had managed to get a jury of twelve to ignore his blood alcohol content and find him not guilty. That kind of thing was common. Often, there was someone on the jury who had gotten a DUI, or knew somebody who had, and comprehended exactly what kind of long-lasting ramifications came with a guilty verdict.

The man on trial had definitely played the pity card, talking about how he had been out of work and had just been trying to get out a series of résumés and applications when he'd been asked to have a drink with a potential employer. It was hard to know if the man was telling the truth or lying, but it was clear, based on his threadbare and too-small suit jacket, that he was down on his luck.

Little did the jury know, but the man had eight previous DUIs and this was nothing more than his best attempt to take advantage of the good nature of the people on the jury who only wanted the best for him.

He had walked away with the harshest consequence she could hand down—a warning not to repeat his mistakes.

Yes, this was one of the days she hated her job and the way that criminals so often knew exactly how to take advantage of others and the system.

She sighed and picked up her briefcase, slipping the strap over her shoulder, and the bailiff followed her out of the empty courtroom. She bid him goodbye with a nod and a small wave. Before she made her way from the courthouse, she stopped by Judge Hanes's chambers.

He'd had a DUI on his docket, as well, and he tended to take these kinds of trials harder than she did. His first wife had died as a result of a drunk driver when she was struck in the middle of the day while trying to cross a street. The accident had left him a single father of a rowdy boy who had become an even rowdier man.

Judge Hanes was at his desk when she stuck her head in. "Heard you had a heck of a trial. You doing okay?"

He sighed and reclined in his leather wingback chair, which sat behind his mahogany desk. "That was a tough day."

She smiled but felt a tiredness in her eyes that she couldn't blink away. "I'm sure you did what you could."

He waved her inside. "Why don't you come in, sit down? Or do you have somewhere to be?"

She loved hanging out with the age-wizened judge, and truth be told, she looked forward to their evening chats. Usually, he was like her, rushing about and needing to be somewhere, so it was a treat to receive the invite from the man she looked to as a father figure.

Besides, where did she have to be? Her house was empty and there was no one waiting for her at home. There hadn't been in four years, ever since she had kicked her ex-boyfriend to the curb. Since then, she had poured herself into her work and became the youngest female district court judge in Montana's history—some days, like this one, she wondered which had been harder, breaking up or being young and in power.

She walked into the office, clicking the door shut behind her.

"How did your case go this morning?" he asked, motioning to the chair across from his desk as he got up and went to the concealed side bar that was tucked away in the corner of his library beneath several shelves of law books. His lips were drawn into a tight line, and the creases in his brows were the deepest she had ever seen them. "Want a scotch?"

"Sure." She wasn't much of a drinker and she definitely wasn't a scotch drinker, but she always made the exception for Hanes. "I'm surprised that the man's lawyer didn't ask for a change of judge. If I'd been the lawyer on that case, it would have been the first thing I would have done. He couldn't have assumed a female judge would remain impartial in a case of trafficking women."

Judge Hanes scoffed. "You know public defenders. Most are so overwhelmed that they don't have time to tie their shoes let alone do the legwork required in high-intensity, emotionally riveting cases."

He opened a bottle of water and filled her tumbler halfway and then added a dot of scotch as though he was aware she was only going along with this for his benefit. He handed her the glass and then filled his own, the mixture more to his taste. As he sat down in his chair, he let out a long exhale.

She had seen him after many of these kinds of trials, but tonight he seemed more road worn than normal. "What's wrong?"

He chuffed. "That easy to tell?"

"I know you're a poker player, but tonight I would advise against hitting the tables," she said, hoping to lighten him up. "You want to tell me what's on your mind? I don't know how much help I'll be, but I'm willing to listen."

He took a long drink, nearly emptying his glass. This was unlike him. He wasn't a man about getting drunk;

he was a man about making a statement. Whatever was on his mind must have been eating him up inside, making her wonder if this was less about the trial and more about whatever was happening in his personal life.

He cleared his throat. "I've always appreciated that about you. You're good people, Judge DeSalvo. It is all too easy to fall into the darkness that comes with our position."

Yep, he definitely wasn't being himself. He normally used her first name when they were in private…why the sudden shift to her professional moniker? What was the significance?

"What's on your mind?" she pressed.

He closed his eyes and sighed as if he was trying to decide whether or not he really wanted to open up to her, and it made her feel for him. Finally, he looked at her and there was a pain in his features she had never noticed before. "I'm trying to clean up some trouble. And because of it, now someone wants me dead." He took a drink. "I'm used to this kind of thing, but…"

She sat in shocked silence, waiting for him to continue and not wanting to rush him even though she wanted to ask about the threat. She couldn't believe how calm he seemed. Yes, he was thrown off balance and worn, but not overly surprised.

Hanes opened up his top desk drawer and pulled out a photograph. "I'm having a hard time dealing with the fallout." He slid the picture across the desk.

Picking it up, she looked at the image. Hanes was standing at the top of the steps that led into the courthouse on the day she had been made district court judge. The picture had been on the front of the local paper the next day and was now framed in her office. There were several court clerks, the sheriff and the district attorney standing around them. Everything looked as it should except Hanes had been circled. His face was ex-ed out. A note in Sharpie had been scrawled on the bottom. It read: "Your death is coming. Soon. Turncoat."

She dropped the picture and it skidded out from her before lurching to a stop. "Did you report this to the police?" She looked back toward the door. "I could go and grab the bailiff. Maybe he hasn't left for the night yet."

He waved her off. "No. I don't want the police involved. I have a feeling that their digging into this would cause more harm than good."

Troubled by that answer, she ignored it for the time being. "Why did they call you a turncoat?"

He shrugged. "To the guilty, we're all turncoats."

"Have you told anyone else about this?"

"Just a couple people."

"What about your son, Sven?"

"Not yet. He doesn't need trouble. He's still trying to find his feet at the fire station, you know." He refused to meet her eye.

She didn't doubt Sven was still struggling, not for a second. It was well known the only reason Sven had gotten the job and wasn't in prison—thanks to his alleged drug possession and several assaults—was because of his father. "What do you think he would say?"

"Sven? He'd brush it off, probably say something about it having to do with one of my cases." He ran his hands over his face. "And he'd probably be right. You know how this world of ours works. There is always someone gunning for us."

She nodded, trying to come up with advice that would actually do some good. For now all she could think was that it was best if she gave him an opportunity to get things off his chest. Judges received threats from time to time, and most of them were empty blasts of anger meant to instill fear, but with no real follow-up. Hanes was a tough man and had enough security in place that he would remain safe. That wasn't to say someone couldn't get to him if they wanted him to be hurt, but they would definitely have to know what they were doing.

"Wait," she said, thoughtfully. "How did you get the picture?"

He emptied his glass before standing up, and this time just going for straight scotch instead of watering it down. "I found it on my desk this morning."

"On *your desk*?" She sat back like the object she had been leaning on was directly responsible for the death threat.

He chuckled, then took another long drink. "Yeah. That's the thing that is bothering me the most about the whole deal. I can handle the occasional threats, no biggie. Only the cleaning staff had access at night, but they have been through security checks and clearances."

"You don't think it was one of them, do you? Was anything else amiss?" Her mind whirled as she thought about her own chambers—she hadn't noticed anything out of place, but she hadn't been looking. Thankfully, there had been no picture on her desk and no obvious threat.

He shrugged, the action so foreign coming from this man that panic filled her. "Nothing appeared tampered with and my desk was locked when I came in this morning, but you and I both know that safety is nothing more than an illusion."

Actually, no…she hadn't felt that way, not until right

now. She knew criminals could find ways around the toughest security, but there was still a barrier.

How could this have happened? How could he be saying these things? Her anxiety intensified, but she tried to keep it in check by reminding herself that Hanes was a strong man. "I'm sure you will be okay, this will be okay," she said, her voice high and awkward as she lied.

To see him scared, terrified her.

He gave a sardonic laugh. "Here is hoping. But I've made a few calls to help me remain alive."

"What do you mean?"

There was a knock on the office door. Hanes smiled, the first time she had seen him do so since she came in the room. Getting up, he made his way to the door and as he did, she smelled the smoky aroma of scotch coming from him, making her wonder if he had been drinking before she had come to his office.

Hanes opened the door. Standing there, immaculate in his black suit, was the best-looking man she had ever seen in real life. He had short blond hair that edged the right way into red and a matching well-kempt beard. His sunglasses were perched on his head, and if she had to guess, he was some kind of agent. Had Hanes called in a joint task force?

Her body willed her toward him, but she resisted the urge. She didn't need anything that good-looking in her life. Nope. No way. Not today. Not ever. Good-looking men had a heck of a way of coming into her life and leaving her with nothing more than a bladder infection and a required date with her battery-operated best friend.

This was one man she would make sure to steer clear of; she didn't need antibiotics.

He walked into the office, smiling as he looked to her. Her cheeks warmed and she looked away from his green eyes.

She needed to get out more if this was going to be her reaction to handsome men in the same room with her.

"Good evening," Judge Hanes said, motioning for the man to take the chair next to her as if deliberately trying to make her squirm. "Thank you for coming on such short notice, Mr. Spade." He picked up a pen beside his computer and clicked it open and closed, a nervous tic she'd witnessed often.

"Please call me Evan." He gave the judge a nod in greeting, but extended his hand to her.

"Pleasure," she said, shaking his hand with as little contact as she could make happen without appearing to be a germaphobe. Even though their hands barely touched, she could still make out the distinct charge of attraction pulsing from her. Hopefully, he hadn't felt it, too.

"Evan is going to be working security for me," Judge Hanes said, his voice cracking. He cleared his throat and ran his hand over his mouth, looking physically uncomfortable. He cleared his throat again. "He is with STEALTH, a military contracting group out of Missoula here and he comes highly recommended." He coughed, taking another drink of his scotch. "Nice. Man," he croaked.

"I'm glad to see you hired some extra security," she said, trying to ignore the judge's discomfort. She looked over at Evan, heat once again rising in her as she caught his gaze.

The judge glanced at Evan, and as he did, she noticed his nose appeared to be taking on a strange purple hue. He moved to speak, but a strangled gurgling noise lurched from his throat, replacing his words.

"Are you okay?" she asked, jumping to her feet but two steps behind Evan, who was already standing beside the judge and had his hand on his back.

He collapsed toward the floor, but Evan caught him and laid him down gently.

"Do you smell that?" Evan asked, looking to her.

She shook her head.

"Mustard," he said. "Cover your mouth and get back."

She wanted to listen, she did, but instead she stood there in shock, watching.

After taking a black zippered kit out of his chest pocket, Evan opened it and pulled out a syringe. He plunged it deep into the judge's chest and pushed down the depressor before extracting the needle.

The judge coughed, harder and harder with each passing second. A bloody spittle dotted his lips and he glanced back up at her with wide, terrified eyes. His body went rigid and he started convulsing. Between his attacks, her honorary father whispered the words she had never known could strike so much fear into her heart, "It's…too late."

Chapter Two

The freshly dead had a distinct smell, usually that of body gases and drying blood. He hated it. To him, it was the odor of life's greatest fears. Most people avoided the sources of such things, and yet, he rarely had the luxury.

Dealing with death came with the territory of working in surveillance and military contracting for STEALTH, and it was one of his least favorite aspects of his job. If he smelled death at this range, either he had done something very right or very, very wrong—and damn if he hadn't caught a whiff.

In this case, if the judge died, his death would be on Evan's hands—he had failed to protect and he had failed at his mission.

Damn it all to hell.

He watched as the EMS workers put the judge into the back of their wagon and turned on their sirens to head toward the hospital. Hopefully, he had acted in time, injecting the pyridostigmine and atropine straight into the judge's heart. Though he wasn't the medic for his STEALTH team, they had all been trained in how to deal with chemical nerve agents that didn't immediately kill.

Thankfully, the police had yet to be called. When

Judge Hanes had hired him for protection, he had made it clear he was to keep everything private, and any sort of legal action would be taken by Hanes himself and none other. So far as the EMS had been told, the judge had come into contact with some sort of allergen and had had an anaphylactic response—thus the atropine. The doctors could figure out what had really happened with a little lab work.

In the meantime Evan needed to figure out who would have done this to the judge and why. And his first inclination was to look at the woman who had been sitting in the judge's office when he'd walked in. From what the judge had told him, there were only a small handful of people who were allowed into his private sanctum, and those were on an invitation-only basis.

"What is your name? We didn't seem to make it that far," he said, turning to face the blonde.

She didn't seem to want to meet his gaze, which only made the hairs on the backs of his arms tingle that much more. She was definitely acting guilty of something.

"My name is Natalie. Umm… Natalie DeSalvo. I'm a district court judge. Steven was my mentor."

Had she added those unnecessary details, details he hadn't requested, in order to passively tell him that she wasn't someone who would have been behind this attack on the judge? Something like that, preemptive information, was often a tell of guilt. And she had used past tense when talking about her *mentor*—odd for a person who didn't know if he was dead. But then again, nothing was ever simple when it came to his line of work in surveillance and security. Maybe she was as nervous as he was about what had taken place.

"Ah," he said with a slight nod. "Nice to meet you,

officially. I wish it had been under slightly different circumstances, but here we are." He gave a dry, dark laugh.

She didn't seem to appreciate his humor and her face puckered with distaste.

"I am sorry about your friend," he said, meaning it.

"Thank you." She stared in the direction the paramedics had been. "Do you think he's going to make it?"

Evan shrugged. "Depends. The meds I gave him should completely go into effect in about another fifteen minutes. Until then, he is in the EMS's hands."

"Yeah. By the way, what did you give him?"

Funny enough, he wanted to ask her the same question.

"Something to keep his heart pumping and neutralize whatever chemicals he had come into contact with—hopefully."

She scowled at him. "You think it was a chemical attack?"

For a woman who was topping his current suspect's list, she was either completely oblivious or playing oblivious rather well. Either way, he was going to have to keep her close until he had his answers.

"He presented with the correct symptoms. But we are going to have to dig into things."

Her frown disappeared. "We?"

"I need to know if you are in danger, as well, or if you were just at the wrong place at the wrong time." He smiled, as if trying to make her feel more comfortable. "I noticed you guys had glasses of something. Were you drinking together?"

She guppied for a moment, her mouth opening and closing, looking as if she had lost her words. "I…we… we were drinking scotch. I didn't drink much of mine.

Just a sip." She paused. "Am I…" The words fell like ashes from her fiery lips.

"If you didn't have a reaction yet, you should be fine. Are you feeling okay?" He watched her green eyes, a shade darker than his. She looked terrified.

And yet, he couldn't let himself believe she was innocent just because she was a beautiful damsel in distress—his weakness.

He took a step back as if being just a few inches farther from her physically could also distance him emotionally and mentally from the woman.

"I'm okay," she said, looking down at her body and running her hands over her curvy figure as if she was looking for a bullet hole.

He held back a smile at her reaction.

He took another step away.

"You look okay, but I think we should go back to the judge's office. Take a look around before anyone else gets a chance to go in there. Do you have access?"

She nodded, but her mouth was still opening and closing slowly like she was trying to recover the words that she had lost.

"You are okay. This will be okay," he said, equally concerned and on guard. "We just need to learn exactly what happened."

She nodded and started to walk back into the courthouse. He followed behind her, trying not to notice the way her pencil skirt hugged her hips.

Scanning her card, she keyed in the code through a series of doors until they were finally back into the judge's chambers. He watched carefully and was sure that, if push came to shove, he could get himself back into this area if the need arose. In fact, he couldn't help but feel like the security in this area and the court-house was woefully lacking. The place didn't even have metal detectors. Any geek off the street could walk in, strapped. It would only take a bailiff being slightly distracted and just about anyone could get killed here. Even something like a shooting—hard to pull off in a building like this—wasn't out of the question if the wrong person had the right incentive.

And as for the courtroom, he couldn't think of a more emotionally fraught environment. Here there was everything, good and bad, but copious amounts of the latter. Just look at himself—no one had blinked an eye when he strode through the building. Those who worked here had been acclimatized to the risk; that was perhaps what made danger even more of a possibility.

Complacency was death's knell, and today it sounded for Hanes.

The one thing he couldn't make clear sense of was the mechanism of death. There were many easy ways to kill a person, and yet, this attacker had chosen poison. Strange.

He had often heard that poison was the work of a woman, but having been in Iraq he could definitely say with 100 percent certainty that poisons and nerve agents were just as likely to come from a man in a war-torn country. Chemical nerve agents were one of the most effective and deadly weapons on the battlefield. A tiny bit of sarin released via unmanned aerial vehicles, and an entire town could be wiped out in a matter of hours.

And that was to say nothing about the fear that a little white phosphorous could drive into a soldier's heart. Weapons like those had often kept him up at night and were some of the reasons he was glad he was back working in the States—for now.

Yep, he liked his McDonalds and Americans' conversations about politics far more than just about anything that came with standing in the middle of a war zone. And yet, there was always one thing that drew him back into the fray—adventure.

There was nothing better than the feeling of being alive after a day spent just millimeters from death. That crap was addictive. It was like taking a straight shot of adrenaline each and every day. Being without it felt exactly like what he assumed drug addicts went through when they were trying to get clean.

This life, *his* life, was a drug, and damn if he couldn't ever get enough.

Natalie turned to face him as they entered the judge's office. "Here you go. What do you think we should be looking for? What are you thinking? How can I help?" In finding her words again, she seemed to want to say them all at the same time.

"Hard to say, but I'm sure I will know it when I see it." He didn't actually believe what he was trying to sell her, but he had to fake it until he made it.

One of the most common chemical nerve agents was sarin gas. But if their attacker had used that against the judge, how had he and Natalie not been affected?

He mulled over the thought as he walked around the spacious office, touching nothing. Everything seemed to have its place and was in immaculate order.

He kept his house and his apartment at the STEALTH compound just as clean. He was constantly picking up after his siblings' messes. A tiny smile took over his lips as he thought about his brothers and sisters and their dream team for STEALTH. Life had been amazing in bringing them all together and working for the same company. The past year had been fun, relying on one another and working as a well-oiled unit of people he knew without a doubt he could trust with anything— even things more valuable than his life.

Walking to the corner of the room, he noticed there was an open cabinet door beneath a number of shelves of books. Inside was a collection of what he recognized as expensive bottles of scotch. The judge had good taste. On the edge of the shelf was an opened bottle of water.

Sarin could be mixed effectively with any liquid. Was it possible that someone had drugged the water bottle, knowing how the judge took his scotch?

He didn't want to sniff the open container, but at the same time if there was any sarin in the water it was unlikely to give off much of an odor. He wafted his hand over the top, but all he detected was the mineral-rich scent of expensive bottled water.

Sarin, if in its impure form, could smell of either burned rubber or mustard. He'd caught a tinge of that when the judge had collapsed.

And yet, he reminded himself, he wasn't even sure if that was what they were dealing with here or not. There were a number of chemical nerve agents, many of which he probably hadn't even heard of yet.

Natalie tapped him on his shoulder.

"Hmm?" he asked, turning away from the side bar and glancing at her.

She looked afraid, her skin pale and a thin layer of sweat on her brow. "Steven had a tic." She pointed to the judge's desk.

"Okay," he said, the word coming out more like a question.

"When he was deep in thought, he always clicked his pen. Some days it drives me absolutely nuts." She pointed at a pen that rested beside his keyboard. "He clicked it when you walked in. Do you think someone could have delivered a nerve agent with that?"

Hell yes, they could have.

He nodded, trying to tamp down his excitement at a possible source. "Good idea." He pulled a Ziploc bag out of his back pocket and flipped it inside out over his hand. Moving to the desk, he picked up the pen and folded the bag around it, careful not to let the pen touch his fingers. As he zipped it closed, he caught the faint, distinct aroma of mustard again. He clicked the pen; at its tip was a ruptured rice-size capsule.

They had their suspect's weapon.

Chapter Three

He was watching her; Natalie could feel it. This security guard, this ridiculously good-looking man who probably had a variety pack of smoldering gazes at the ready, was staring at her. She hadn't blushed this much since she was in high school. What was wrong with her?

There were a million things she should have been concentrating on—making it to the end of the day would have been a great start—and instead here she was, twitterpated by Mr. Sexy Face.

She watched him carefully hold the bagged pen. He looked irritated. "Everything okay?" she asked.

"Huh? Yeah. Fine." His words rang false. "I think it would be best if we get out of here. If there has been a nerve agent deployed in here, we can still be in immediate danger."

"So you are now sure that was what happened? You don't think it could have been anything else?" she asked. She had been hoping against all hope that the attack had been something besides what he'd suggested.

He showed her the pen and its exploded tip. "This was definitely filled with sarin gas, or a close derivative of it. You are lucky to be alive." He took her by the arm and gently led her out of the office.

She felt the ache in her gut grow more intense. He had told her that she would have already been affected if she was to have been targeted by the attacker, but she didn't know this man from Adam. He could have been telling her anything just in an attempt to make her feel better.

If she didn't have anything to worry about, then why would he have been in a big rush to get her out of the office? Was he concealing critical information…or bad intentions?

At the realization, some of her insta-attraction diminished. Yes, more of that. She had to get this lust fest under control, and by thinking him a jerk, it would work like a charm. And she definitely didn't like that a man would just take her by the arm and lead her, but then again, he was trying to save her from being further exposed to a potentially lethal nerve agent. Yet, it still irked her.

Yes. She smiled at herself. More derision toward his behavior and she would be out of lust in no time.

"Is there anyone else working in this area right now?" he asked, looking around and then toward the ceiling as if he was searching for an overhead camera.

Yeah, right; we are closer to Flintstone tech than the Jetsons up in this place.

She glanced down at her watch. "The cleaning staff normally starts coming in an hour. They will be throughout the building for the rest of the night, but for now it is pretty quiet here."

"No cameras?" he asked.

This time his question made her wonder why he was so keen on knowing if there were potential witnesses nearby. "Why do you ask?" She stepped back from

him. "The sheriff's department headquarters is just one
floor up and we have deputies coming and going all the
time. There are plenty of people around who'd catch a
criminal in the act." It was as close to a threat as she
could muster.

"I thought you said this place was pretty well deserted for the next hour or so?" he said, giving her a
half-cocked smile that, if she hadn't been leery, would
have been what her best friend Kristin called a panty-
dropper.

She'd always loved Kristin, but in this moment she
could have kicked her butt for making her want to smile
when she was facing down a potentially dangerous man.

Actually, forget the *potentially*. Rather, he *was* dangerous—in so many ways.

"Look, I don't know if you're trying to freak me out
or if you are trying to impress me, but it isn't working," she lied.

His smile widened and he looked at her like he was
trying to figure her out. She liked it; in fact, she always
liked surprising the people she was around. There was
nothing worse than being predictable.

"You are a funny woman, you know that?" he said,
doing a quick up and down of her body. Not so much
to be crude, but enough to let her know that he was actively checking her out.

And there went her cheeks again. Before he could notice, she turned away and walked toward the employee
exit and the parking lot.

"Where are you going?" he called, and she could
hear his footfalls behind her as he rushed to catch up.
"I think it's best if we stick together."

She stopped and huffed. Sticking together was the

last thing she needed with this dude. "Look, you're not my boss. I've worked my whole life to get where I am and to no longer have to put up with men who think that they can push me around or tell me what to do," she seethed. "And strangely enough, the only man who remotely has any influence in my life is now lying on a gurney…after you were hired to protect him."

He went slack jawed. "What? Huh? Do you think… You are crazy if you think I had something to do with that attack."

"I didn't say you did, but you certainly jumped to your own defense. Something you wish to get off your chest?" She glared at him, looking for any signs of guilt.

"I… You…" He bristled, puffing up like some kind of porcupine.

"I'm not just some demure woman who you can lead around by the nose just because you know you're handsome…umm… I meant somewhat attractive." She felt stupid for letting her inside voice sneak past her filters and spill out of her lips.

He deflated, as if her backhanded compliment was the needle it took to bring him back down to normal size. He smiled that stupid, half-cocked smile she loved to hate. "You think I'm handsome?"

"Whoa there, Fabio, just because I said you were *somewhat attractive* doesn't mean that you can get off the hook for being a total—"

"Hunk?" he said, finishing her sentence with a laugh.

"Oh, heck no. I was going to go with pain in the ass," she said, throwing it back at him.

"And you're a ballbuster, so what a pair we could make."

"Wow, you didn't…" she said in forced outrage, but

secretly her mind raced toward the picture of the wedding dress she had taped up in her bathroom when she'd been in high school—lace with full sleeves. Beside it had been a picture of Ruth Bader Ginsburg. She didn't regret her decision to myopically focus on her goal of becoming a judge, but there had been many sacrifices in her personal relationships.

He gave her that sexy half grin again.

"Seriously, Fabio, cool your jets or you are going to be on your own." She gave him a side eye, waiting to see if he'd try using working together as an excuse to find a way to sneak into her bed.

"Not being Fabio, I swear. You are a beautiful woman, that goes without saying, but I don't need to *cool my jets* because they weren't fired up. I don't fantasize about having sex with every hot woman I meet. I just want you close because I think it's very possible you could unwittingly know who planted that pen in the judge's office. You showed me exactly how much access you have to him."

Now she felt like the porcupine—on one hand he thought she was hot and on the other he didn't want her, and then he also seemed to think she was bordering on inept. "I... I have known Steve since I was a child growing up in Missoula. I have worked with him since I first started as a clerk. He took me under his wing and helped me figure out the steps I needed to take to get where I am today. He has always been like a father figure to me. So yes, we know a lot of the same people, but like all judges, he has a million enemies."

He looked her over like he was searching for some kind of hole in her story and she hated it. Was there a part of him that thought she had something to do with

Hanes's poisoning? "It is the ones closest to us who can do us the most harm."

"If you think I had anything to do with this, you can stop right here and right now. I don't break laws. I enforce them." She could feel the burn of her words on her tongue; hopefully, he felt the heat, as well.

He nodded, but she could feel his gaze boring into her and it did nothing for her anger. "Good."

"In fact, as an officer of the court, I should be talking to law enforcement right now, not a man who was hired to provide security and failed and whose vocabulary probably doesn't include the word *justice.*"

He jerked as he looked up at her, hurt in his eyes. "I know you think you probably know me and know the people I work with, but you don't, Your Honor."

She had heard her title spoken by a thousand different people in as many times, but rarely had she heard it uttered with the level of derision in his voice.

Her anger oozed from her as she looked back up at his bearded face—no one dared to speak to her as he had.

There were gray flecks in his beard in and around his jawline that accentuated the lines around his mouth. She would bet his beard was soft, not the harsh, coarse kind that most men kept. For a split second, she imagined the texture against the tender skin of her inner thigh.

Look away, woman. She could almost hear her friend Kristin's voice talking to her.

She just needed to get laid, then whatever this craziness was that she was feeling could be stuffed back into the recesses of her stony heart and she could focus on the reality of the situation they were dealing with. Sexual tension never led to positive outcomes anywhere except for those brief moments of bliss between the sheets.

"Okay," she said, sighing as she looked at her car at the far end of the parking lot. "So we can both agree that neither of us would have done this to Steve even though we both *could* have?"

"Same page." Evan nodded. "And I apologize for losing my temper. I… You deserve a higher level of respect than how I just treated you. I'm sorry. As to talking to the law, let's keep in mind that the judge didn't want to go there, so if you can hold off on that, he'd probably appreciate it."

She considered his request and sighed. He was right. Justice Hanes had brought him in so he wouldn't have to get officers involved. She could honor that request, too, at least for a little while. She cocked a brow, shocked by his reversal and self-awareness. "Thank you. I've worked really hard to be where I am. There are always those around who wish to tear away at my foundation in order to build themselves up."

"I understand that," he said. "Which brings me to my next question—"

"No, I'm not single," she lied, teasing him.

He actually looked crestfallen for a moment. What kind of game were they playing?

She wished she could bring the words back. It was only her anger that had made her say them in the first place. In any other atmosphere and after any other day, she could have given this handsome, suit-clad man a run for his money in the bedroom department, but why did he have to saunter into her life today of all days?

"That's disappointing," he said. "But not exactly where I was going with my questioning. Rather, I was going to ask if you knew of anyone in particular who would have had a motive for wanting Judge Hanes dead."

"I'm sure he told you about the photo someone left on his desk? I would assume the attacker was behind the threat." She walked down the marble steps that led to the main floor of the courthouse; their footfalls echoed out and filled the empty halls.

"He did, but he only spoke to me briefly and at that time he didn't mention any possible suspects. Did he tell you who may have placed that in his office?"

"I told you everything I knew." She sounded just a touch surly and as she realized it, she noticed the heavy look on Evan's face. "Sorry," she said, hoping to make things slightly less tense between them. "I just mean that if he didn't tell you, then he sure as heck didn't tell me. Steve was a man who kept his thoughts and feelings pretty close to his chest about most things."

"So you can't think of anyone in particular? Someone who he had seen in the courtroom?" He opened the door leading out to the parking lot and held it for her until she passed by him. He smelled of expensive, fresh-scented cologne and she took it deep into her lungs.

She started to walk toward her car. "There are plenty of people who Judge Hanes had ruled against. Between those people and their families, I would say that would put about a quarter of the city's population on our possible suspects list."

It took a special breed to want to put themselves and their families at risk in order to cast judgments down in the name of justice, social mores and civil control. They all knew the risks that came with their calling. And it was partially this risk that kept her from seeking real relationships—she chose this life; she wouldn't impose it upon others.

"I was always proud of the rulings that Steve made," she continued. "There is none that I can think of that was unjustified. If anything, I think he was very careful to adhere to the letter of the law even when he was aware that the truth lay somewhere in the gray area. And he was good with the members of the public who served on his juries. He is a good man."

"If I had any lingering doubts about you trying to murder him, I think that little speech would have cleared you," Evan said with a laugh. "I bet he was glad to have you around if this is the kind of support you always gave him."

She laughed, waving him off. "Oh, we had our fair share of moments when we butted heads, but I knew my place, and he was like a father or brother to me, nothing more."

"And your husband?"

There was the heat again. "I was kidding about being with someone. No husband. No kids. No boyfriend. I don't even have a dog. So no, there is no one in my life who would have had anything against him."

Evan looked away from her, but as he did, she was pretty sure that she had finally spotted a bit of color moving into his cheeks. Yes, at least it wasn't her this time.

"As I'm sure the judge told you, his son Sven has had a lot of run-ins when it comes to the law."

Evan nodded. "He mentioned his son, and I'll look into him, but he made it sound like his son was at the bottom of our list. He seems to have gotten his life squared away. And he has no motive."

She clicked her car's key fob. As she hit the button there was a strange sound, a loud click instead of the slide she was accustomed to.

Before she could take another step, Evan had wrapped his arms around her and was pushing her to the ground. As he threw her down, there was a *whoomph*. The air of the shockwave pressed down on her. The heat of the blast scorched the skin of her back, and her polyester skirt was forming around, and melting into, the backs of her legs.

The bomb was deafening in the parking garage and her ears rang. There was the sensation of liquid in her ears. Blood, maybe?

There was the scent of burnt hair and it stung her nostrils.

Work. She had been at work. They had been walking. There was an explosion. Her car.

There was a side-view mirror burning on the ground to the left. Reaching up, she felt the stab of shards of glass across her cheek.

She struggled to get up, but there was a strange weight on her body. Her car. Had something landed on her? She couldn't make sense of exactly what was going on.

On top of her was Evan. He was staring at her and yelling something, but she couldn't hear him. Instead, she could only see his lips moving. All she could think about was the fact that someone, some stranger, wanted her dead.

Chapter Four

Thanks to all his working security, this was certainly not the first time he'd been asked to escort and guard a high-risk target, but it was the first time he had two attempted murders within such a close period. Not only that, but the methods were so innately different. It was one thing to be schooled in the art of chemical warfare and be proficient enough to sneak into a courthouse and into a judge's chambers without being noticed, but to have a suspect who was also more than capable in car bombs was unusual. In a terrible way, their perpetrator was incredibly skilled; that, or they weren't working alone.

This level of desire to kill was reminiscent of Evan's time in Beirut when it was at the height of civil unrest. If asked, he wouldn't even be sure that this wasn't worse. In Beirut he was constantly barraged by a variety of enemies—from Hezbollah to radical political leaders— but the one thing they all had in common was that when they attacked, they didn't hide who they were or why they were doing it. They wanted the world to see they were strong, and they wouldn't shy away from striking down anyone who stood in their way.

This perpetrator wanted to hide in the shadows and

fears created by their crimes. Whoever was trying to get her into their sights literally could have been standing behind them and they would have never known.

The one thing every country and culture had in common was that danger lurked everywhere.

Judge DeSalvo sat on the curb and looked at what had once been her Honda Accord. Its shell was still burning, and he could make out the shrieking wail of fire trucks and ambulances as they careened through the downtown streets toward them.

After assessing she was all right, he'd helped her up and away from the fiery vehicle, making sure her injuries were superficial, and she wasn't going into shock.

By now someone in dispatch had to be taking note about the many mishaps taking place at the courthouse. Next, snipers would be lining the roof and bearing down in a show of force that would hopefully prove to be unnecessary.

"Judge DeSalvo, are you okay?" he asked.

She simply nodded, staring out at her car, her gaze unwavering.

"Judge Hanes recommended we try to keep whatever happened under the radar. How do you think we should handle this?" He knew she would feel compelled to work with local authorities more than ever now.

Finally, she looked away from her car and up at him as he hovered over her. "I know he hired you for his protection, but he couldn't have possibly foreseen this level of violence. If he had, there's no way he would have asked you to keep this from law enforcement."

He nodded. There was only so much hiding and sweeping under the rug that could be done—especially when it came to such a public attack. "Whatever you

choose to do here, know that as long as you're in someone's crosshairs, I'm going to be here to protect you.
My team and I will do everything in our power to keep
you safe and neutralize your enemy."

She ran her hands over her face, leaving behind little
trails of fresh blood on her cheeks. "I've always prided
myself on standing against vigilante justice. There's
a reason we have laws and there's a reason that I am
the one the general assembly elected to enforce them."

He should have known that this would be her response. Justice could be sought in other places besides
the courtroom. Yet, he wasn't sure that now was the
time to argue the value of striking an enemy down without the law ever being involved. If he tried, she would
think that he was some kind of masochist, or sociopath.

Sometimes, his greatest ally was silence.

It was one of the things he loved the most about his
world and his teams. They didn't require anything beyond knowing what their objectives were and what it
would take to reach them. Once the mission was completed, they didn't expound upon their glories or celebrate the wins. The only time they even spoke about
past missions was to correct major flaws in their future procedures.

The sounds of the sirens grew nearer and as they
approached, the anxiety in his gut intensified. Many
former contractors with military-style organizations
became law enforcement officers, but that didn't mean
he would get an easy ride when the LEOs rolled up on
this scene.

Just because someone had the same mentality at one
point in their life didn't mean they presently had the
same goals. Law enforcement officers had to answer

to a hierarchy and public opinion, whereas contractors had more freedom—so long as they didn't take advantage of it.

Being in the limelight was for suckers.

He wasn't a sucker. "Judge DeSalvo, I know you want to do the right thing here, but I think we need to get you to a safe location." He wrapped his arm around her shoulders, and surprisingly, she didn't pull away. She seemed so strong, physically and emotionally, and yet, she leaned into him like she yearned for his support.

She nodded, weakly.

He held open his hand and she took it, allowing him to help her stand. She still gripped her briefcase as if it connected her to her life before the explosion. "You don't need to sit out in the open and wait to take a bullet all in the name of doing the honorable thing."

She spit out a laugh, the sound in direct contrast to the serious scene around them. He was relieved to hear it, and happy he had been able to give her the ability. He walked with her, leading her toward his truck—the only place he knew that she would be guaranteed safety. As he helped her into the passenger seat, the first set of ambulances arrived.

Her hair was disheveled, the blood was starting to dry on her cheeks and there was gravel on her chest from where she had lain upon the pavement, but aside from that she appeared outwardly unscathed—emotionally was another matter, but no ambulance or medical professional would be able to whisk away the trauma she had just endured.

Traumatic events had different effects on each individual. He had seen more than one man vomit after mortar rounds had exploded in the cars next to them, while others shrugged off similar events like they were nothing more than a Tuesday at the office. Admittedly, the latter were seasoned. How they had been affected by the death and mayhem when they had first encountered it was something they would likely never talk about.

In those moments in which a person was forced to see who they were at a noncognitive, purely instinctual level, few impressed themselves. People who experienced traumatic events had to confront themselves on a primal level and often were disappointed with what they found.

Ugh. He pulled on his beard as he made his way around to the driver's side of his truck. *Maybe I'm feeling too much. I need to shut that shit down. Feelings got people killed.*

Whatever was going on inside him was something he could think about later; right now he needed to focus on his job. Bury that stuff; deal with it later.

He rolled his shoulders and climbed inside, his game face on. "Are you in any physical pain?"

She looked up at him, a look of surprise on her face. Had she noticed that he wouldn't even use the word *feeling* in order to check on her? Or was it that she had picked up on the steel doors closing over his core?

"I'm fine."

"Let's grab one of the EMS workers and have them come over and check on you." Although she'd seemed to have only superficial injuries, he didn't want to take a chance.

She opened her mouth as if to speak, then clamped it shut and stared down toward the glovebox. They sat in silence for a long moment. He didn't press her. "I'm fine. Just… Let's go." She spoke slowly, like her words were fighting each other for air.

He hesitated, wondering if he should go against her, but he didn't say a word. Instead, he started the truck and pulled out of the parking lot. They passed by a fire-truck as they exited.

There was nowhere either of them had to be, nowhere that he could think of to go and nowhere he could think of taking her. Yes, there were the easy options: her place, his private house, his apartment at STEALTH HQ, or even a motel where neither of them would be recognized and where she could be safe. All of them were reasonable options, but none of them felt exactly right.

He hadn't been prepared for this outcome—he'd gone in for a meeting and come out with two attempted murders.

There was a right response to this situation; he just had to find it and put his dick back in his pants.

His truck's blinker clicked, the monotone sound barely audible over the road noise as he drove toward the interstate. He pretended to have a plan as he got on I-90 and started rolling east, toward Butte. Butte…there was an option. He could hole her up in some small B&B until this mess rolled over.

He glanced up at his rearview, looking for any possible tails. There was a white sedan three cars back, which had been behind them for at least three blocks before they had hit the on-ramp. He took the next exit, but when the white car didn't follow, he got back on the interstate. He half expected the judge to ask him what he was doing and why, as she didn't seem like the kind of woman to sit idle while in a time of turmoil, but she sat with her hands folded in her lap.

Would she continue to surprise him? People rarely did.

Most people were woefully predictable. In fact, there were a multitude of psychological studies that stated the brain of a listener normally could tell what a person speaking to them would say three words ahead of whatever was actually said. Remarkable science, but it only spoke to how unoriginal people could be. His thoughts moved to technology and big data. It was really no wonder that the internet and artificial intelligence had grown leaps and bounds, being one step ahead of the people actually using them. It was no secret that this accumulation of data, then mixed with the predictability of human nature, could be so dangerous.

STEALTH was deep into the world of black ops and tech warfare. So much so, that his boss, Zoey, was working on creating a new team just to handle the tech side of things. She had been doing a tremendous job, but unlike big data, she didn't have an automated system. She still required hands on a keyboard.

"Where are you right now?" the judge asked, pulling him from his thoughts as he drove down the highway.

He gave her a look of surprise. "What? What do you mean?"

"I mean, obviously you were thinking about something or someone right there. You going to tell me who she is?"

Oh, she is good.

She could try to elicit information from him all she wanted, but that didn't mean he would let her in. "You need to save your questions for the bench on that one, Your Honor."

She cocked an eyebrow, but she didn't continue her line of questioning.

After a long, quiet moment, he wished he had told her that she had been off the mark and that he hadn't been thinking about a woman—at least not a woman in the sense she assumed he was. There were no *women* in his life, not that way. He hadn't been with a *woman* in at least a year—not since his divorce.

Really, what did it matter what she knew or didn't know about his private life? All she needed to know was that he was there to help her and he would come between her and a bullet if needed. Anything beyond that was irrelevant. He was a damned professional, even if his heart wanted to make him become less than.

And yet, that gave him no right to be cold; he could be a decent human being to her and still have boundaries. "Sorry if I came off a little rude there. It's just, well, I'm not great with women. Or people, for that matter."

Some of the tension on her face diminished. "It's okay. I know how important it is to keep some secrets to oneself."

"Agreed, but I hope you accept my apology."

"Done. Now, are we going to go to the Canadian border?" she asked, laughing a tiny bit as she flipped down the visor and started to sweep away the crumbling dried blood on her face. "If we are, I probably need to run home and grab my passport."

He chuckled. "Are you telling me that you are good with just dropping everything and running away?"

"Well, given that no judge appears to be safe at the courthouse right now... I have to think I'd be better off just about anywhere other than there." She sent him a smile as she rubbed a smudge of dirt off her left cheek.

She must have been starting to feel better, as she had finally seemed to once again find her voice. Pulling her cell phone from her briefcase, she started to text someone.

"I'm sure I don't need to tell you this, but whoever is coming after you may very well be able to track that thing in your hands there." He motioned to her phone.

"I was just texting my secretary so he could take care of my upcoming trials and have them rescheduled or reassigned. He's also telling police I'll be in touch shortly since they obviously know of the car bomb, if not about Judge Hanes." She shot him a thin smile. "I'm putting myself at your mercy. You better be able to keep me safe. Can I assume I'm in good hands?"

Had she missed the part where he had been hired to protect Judge Hanes and yet Hanes had nearly died? If he was in her shoes, he would have told himself to get lost. He just had to fake it and make her feel like he was in complete control. A little "nothing to see here, folks," mixed with "I'll be back."

He chuckled at the thought.

"Are you laughing at me?" she asked, her smile growing.

"Hardly," he said. "I was just thinking about Arnold Schwarzenegger."

"Really? I ask if you can be trusted and you go full *Terminator* on me?" She shook her head, playfully. "You are such a dude. I should have guessed exactly what kind of moviegoer you were the moment you walked into Judge Hanes's office."

"Oh, hey now, what is that supposed to mean?" he countered. "Were you judging me?"

She laughed, the sound high and bright and in complete juxtaposition to the reality in which they had found themselves thrown. "That *is* my job."

She had a point. One that was completely inarguable. And yet, that didn't keep his curiosity at bay. "And what exactly did you think of me when you first saw me?"

She gave him a sidelong look, like she was trying to decide whether or not she would tell him the truth or pass off some kind of altered version of it. "I thought you looked competent."

Competent. He was really secretly hoping for something more like hot or devilishly handsome, but he would take competent.

"Fine compliment, coming from a woman like you. You are certainly *competent* yourself."

She smiled and her eyes brightened. The simple action made her look ten years younger and for a moment he wondered exactly how old she was. If he had to guess, she was probably about thirty, but he would never say it aloud. If anything, she looked younger than he was. And she was far more beautiful than any female judge he had seen before. Not that he'd been around too many judges; it wasn't in his nature to find himself in a position that required him giving testimony.

"It's funny that you should say that about me," she said, sounding contemplative. "There are many voters who think that it was a mistake to put me into the position that I'm in."

"Why do you say that?" he asked, careful not to assume anything.

"First, I'm a woman. This is Montana. We aren't

known for being especially progressive. Though, I like to think that is changing." She nodded, a look of pride in her eyes. "Second, I'm the youngest woman ever to be seated as a district court judge."

So she was likely around thirty. He didn't know a ton about the demographics of political and judicial positions, but he could guess at that one. "You must be incredibly proud of all that you have accomplished in such a short time. Seriously, you are an amazing woman."

"I told you, I wouldn't have been able to do it all without Judge Hanes's mentorship. He has been an incredible advocate." She sounded nearly reverent about the man, which made him wonder exactly how far their friendship went, but he didn't dare to ask.

He liked her and if she admitted that she had something with the older, fatherly type judge he wasn't sure how it would color his opinion of her. But what did that say about him? Who was he to have an opinion on who she slept with? It wasn't even his business, though technically in this circumstance it did border on his "needing to know."

"Is he married?"

Her brows furrowed. Of course, she would know what he was thinking even though he thought he had done a pretty decent job at hedging on the question of their past without actually asking.

"No, I haven't seen him naked. No, he is not married. And no, there is no romantic attachments between us," she said, nearly snarling. "You know, it is exactly that kind of thinking that has stood in the way of a woman being in a position like I'm in now. Everyone just assumes that for a woman to get ahead she had to sleep her way to the top. And I can tell you, with one hundred percent honesty, that I haven't opened my legs to get where I'm at nor where I'm going."

He nearly covered his head at the verbal beating she was giving him. He hadn't meant the question like that and he certainly hadn't intended on insulting her in any way.

Things had been going so well, and then…*kaboom*… he had to make a misstep.

He should have just stayed quiet. Why hadn't he listened to himself?

"I'm sorry, Judge DeSalvo. I certainly didn't mean to question your…" He paused, unsure of exactly the words he should say: *reputation, womanhood, respect, honor, integrity?* None of them felt exactly right. But what had?

Ugh.

"You're fine." She didn't let him find the word he had been looking for, but maybe that was for the best. He'd created a mess.

"No, really. I'm sorry." It was all he could think of to prove his sincerity. "The only reason I even approached that subject was out of necessity, not condescension. If there was any sort of romantic entanglement there, it means that there could also be some sort of third wheel complications that could happen."

"To be clear, you think that his wife would try to murder him and me?"

He pinched his lips together. Yes, that was exactly what it meant, but somehow it didn't seem like quite the right thing to say to her at the moment. Sometimes, when a person was at the bottom of a hole, it was best to stop digging.

"I'm just trying to narrow down the list of suspects.

Who would want you dead, and why. That kind of thing." He had to question her thoroughly on this, but he'd wanted to wait until she was safe and somewhat recovered from the explosion.

She ran her hands over her face one more time, getting the last remnants of blood from her skin. There were tiny lines on her face, thin scratches like little hyphens.

He'd always prided himself on policing a world and helping it to run in an orderly fashion. He reduced violence and provided safety, so civilians and high-ranking officials could go about their business and function appropriately. And the woman beside him provided justice. Together, they made the world a place worth living.

What am I, Shakespeare now? he wondered. *What is she doing to me? I'm a door kicker, not a philosopher. I need to keep my head in the game.*

"I have never really had this kind of run-in before," she said, thankfully unaware of the weirdness that was happening in his mind. "I knew that I could run into this kind of problem eventually, but it's only been about a year since I have been on the bench. I thought I would be safe a little while longer."

"It is the moment you think you're safe, that you are at your most vulnerable. Your guard was down. I get it. I see it all the time. It's funny when guys have been in country for a long time. In the sandbox, they become desensitized and what would've freaked out a grunt becomes commonplace for them. I knew a guy who stood up in a bunker to take a picture for Instagram and got his head blown off. Complacency has always been humankind's worst enemy."

She nodded. "Working in the judicial system, I have

to agree with you. Though I'm not sure if *complacency* is the right word. In my case, I think that narcissism is humankind's greatest enemy. People start to think that they can get away with anything if they are just smart enough."

He agreed with her there. The two parts often went hand in hand when it came to criminals. It was those who thought they were smarter than the rest of the world who grew bolder with time and lacked consequences for their terrible choices. Those choices grew darker, more nefarious, and they got what they wanted. Then they grew complacent and took things for granted. Sometimes they got caught, but not enough.

"Thinking about being complacent," he said, "you need to get rid of your cell phone. We can get you another one if you want, but for now you need to throw yours out on the interstate. Got it?"

Before he even finished speaking, the window was down and she was shoving the cell phone out.

"I wanted to do that with that stupid thing for years." She laughed, rolling up the window.

"I can only imagine."

"So where are you taking me? You had to have had some sort of plan for Judge Hanes in the event you guys had to bug out, right?" She paused. "Did I say that right, *bugging out*?"

"You can call it whatever you like, but in the end it all means getting the hell outta wherever you are. And no, I can't take you where I had planned on moving him to. Is there somewhere you think you would like to be taken? Somewhere you think it would be safe?"

She chewed her bottom lip, thinking. "There are always hotels?"

"Their databases are relatively easy to hack and if we use your credit card or my credit card, it would be pretty easy to track us down. We need something that won't leave a paper trail. How averse are you to spending a night out in the woods?"

She looked at him like he'd lost his mind. "You can't possibly think, for a single second, that I am camping." She motioned down to the clothes she was wearing. "This suit is a Dillard's finest—the best of the best in Montana. And if you think it is appropriate for sleeping outside, you are sorely mistaken. I'm more of a hotel girl. I need a hot shower and preferably a finger or two of vodka before I hit the sack."

Oh, I'd hit the sack with her, all right, he thought, then he realized what he had just let slip through the filter of his mind. *Shit. No. Job. Judge. Boundaries.*

His cheeks warmed. "You're right. No tents, no camping." No hitting of the sack…at least not together.

But if they couldn't go to a hotel and they couldn't camp, that left them with only a few options. They could go back to the STEALTH headquarters at the Widow Maker Ranch, but that would be the first place a hitman would look if they knew that Evan was involved.

"Up ahead, in just a few miles, is a little town," she said. "My pseudo-mom lives there and she would take us in. Her name is Judy."

"Would anyone think to look for you there?" he asked.

She shook her head. "Judy was my mother's best friend growing up, and when my mother died, she kind of filled her shoes. No one would know that but a select few. It is about the safest place I can think of."

"Tell me where to turn."

She nodded, and he could feel some of the tension slip away, momentarily. But as quickly as the pressure lifted, it was replaced with awkward silence.

But he could live in the silence.

Judge DeSalvo motioned at the next exit. "Turn here."

He followed her directions, but stayed quiet.

She clasped her hands together tightly in her lap; so tight that he could see that her fingernails were digging into the backs of her hands. There were any number of things that could have been bothering her, but he hated to assume or even talk about it. To talk about it and give it air would only make them grow closer. He couldn't want that.

"There is something about Judy," she said as she moved her neck like she was trying to remove some kind of invisible noose. "She is a worrier. If she hears about what has happened, it will be a whole *thing*. I don't think it best that we cause her any undue stress."

"So how do you want to handle showing up at her door? Won't she ask questions? I don't expect that you would normally just randomly show up at her door on a weekday."

She nodded. "We talk once a week and I only get to see her sporadically, when my schedule allows. Which, as of late, has been very infrequently. In fact, I don't think I've come to see her since I was elected. I've been horribly remiss in my duties as an honorary daughter." There was the hint of guilt in her tone. "But I'm hoping she won't ask too many questions on how we found ourselves on her doorstep."

In theory, he could understand why she would feel guilty, but since losing his own parents a few years ago he'd lost touch with what exactly she had to be going through. The closest thing he had to even an adoptive parent were his siblings. They had always gone out of their way to make sure they worked as a group, but the key word was *worked*. As members of the STEALTH team, they didn't mess around with the touchy-feely things about family. Emotional wounds were left untouched so they could knit naturally. None of them dared to pick at the scabs.

"Anyway," Judge DeSalvo continued, "I think it best if you just let me handle things with her. Okay?"

"I didn't intend on anything else." He smiled.

She gave an appreciative nod. "Perfect."

"It may surprise you, but I'm pretty good at just blending into the background." As he spoke, he couldn't shut up the little voice in his head that told him that the one place he wanted to be was at the forefront of her life.

The little voice was an idiot.

Chapter Five

Judy was going to be beside herself with excitement. Or, at least she usually was when they got the opportunity to chat. Her second mom was always upbeat and full of life, fiery and wild in a way that made Natalie feel guilty for not having the same zest.

After her parents had died, some of what little zest she had been born with had slipped away. But even before, she had gone at life more linearly and methodically than the woman who had stepped in to raise her.

The last time she had seen Judy, she had flowers stuffed in her hair and an apron she had crocheted for collecting eggs from her bevy of chickens. And though she was in her late sixties, she was often mistaken for being at least two decades younger. If Natalie had to guess why, it was because of the unshaded light in her mother's eyes and the glorious smile that always rested on her lips.

It was strange, though, as Judy had lived a life full of tragedies. She had lost a daughter at birth and a son when he was thirteen in a boating accident, which had also taken her husband. Maybe it was tragedy that drew the two orphans together; their nearly perfect lives had been pulled out from under their feet.

Judy didn't focus on the past, though. She felt it, spoke about it and lived it, but she had moved forward with her life and it had grown no less dim. She was the most resilient and courageous woman that Natalie had ever known. If only she could be half as strong, she would be satisfied.

As Natalie pointed to the last house on the left, Evan pulled into the gravel driveway. The home was a simple, aged, single-story ranch house with three bedrooms and two bathrooms—one of which was still 1950s pink. It didn't seem to fit the bigger-than-life, grandiose Judy.

Natalie nibbled on her lip as she picked up her briefcase and he stopped the car. Walking around, he opened her door. "Ready for this?" Evan asked.

"As I will ever be," she said, suddenly nervous about what could come. She didn't want Judy to get upset. Sure, Judy could handle the news, but it would get blown completely out of proportion if she told her the truth. And she didn't want to lie, but white lies were made to keep people from getting hurt.

As she carried her briefcase up the askew concrete-slab sidewalk, she was brought back to the day she had first come to this house to live. Instead of a briefcase, she had been carrying her Winnie-the-Pooh suitcase, complete with a Piglet-shaped handle, though she had been sixteen.

Those had been some rough years, the time in life when a girl was expected to act like a woman but still had the mind of a girl. But she had grown up fast. She had only gone on one date by the time she was a senior in high school. And yet, even without the complication of first love and first heartbreak, there were many growing pains that had come in the years she had lived in this little house.

How had she found herself feeling just as scared and lost as she had when she was sixteen and walking up this walkway with Piglet in hand? The only thing that had changed was the kind of bag she carried and the start of crow's feet at the corners of her eyes.

The front door opened and Judy flung herself in her direction before Natalie's foot had even hit the bottom step. "Natty! You didn't tell me you were coming! What are you doing here?" she squealed with delight as she threw her arms around Natalie's neck.

Natalie laughed into her mother's gray hair. No flowers today. But she did have a large red-tailed hawk feather poking out of her braid in the back. Knowing her, it was probably a feather she had found somewhere in the woods on her daily hike. Judy had always found beauty in nature and celebrated the littlest things.

And then there was Natalie, not even calling her before showing up on her doorstep. She was a terrible daughter. Here was the woman who had practically raised her after some of the hardest years of her life, a woman who could be satisfied with the littlest signs of appreciation and love, and she had brought her nothing.

"Hi, Mom, sorry. I should have called."

Judy gave her a kiss on the cheek and backed up, holding her by the shoulders and inspecting her. "You haven't been eating enough, and you look like you've been through the wringer. What happened?"

Natalie shot Evan a look before answering. "Nothing. Just took a tumble. I'm fine."

"Come in. I just made fresh fry bread. You and your friend here can pour some cinnamon and sugar on it and fatten yourselves up." She turned around and motioned them inside.

It shouldn't have surprised Natalie that Judy hadn't even batted an eyelash about her feeble explanation of her injuries or her bringing a stranger to her house—and not just any stranger, but an incredibly good-looking one. She had called him "her friend," which meant she must have assumed there was some kind of relationship between them, and in doing so she was clearly assuming that Natalie could bat in the same league that this man played in. She did not.

Evan opened the door and waited for them to enter. He gave her a confused look, like he wondered if it was just normal that a stranger would walk right into their house without so much as a simple introduction. *Oh, Judy.*

As Natalie walked by him, she made sure to take a quick glance at his ass. It was just as tight and muscular as the rest of him, and it solidly cinched the fact that he was too much of a man for her. If she had to bet on it, not that she was a betting woman, she would have put money on the probability that he dated model types. The last kind of woman he would be after would be one who was most comfortable in a beautiful black muumuu robe. The collar was nice, though. Maybe he had a collar fetish.

She chuckled at the thought as she stepped around him and went inside.

Though she couldn't turn around without being conspicuous, she was sure that she could feel his gaze trailing down her backside. She smiled at the thought. Maybe it was just wishful thinking.

She sucked in a breath, trying to collect herself.

If merely the disparity in looks wasn't a problem, there was also the fact that they lived and operated in entirely different worlds. He was the kind of man who came so close to breaking the law that he put cracks in it, while she was the one who was forced to come behind people like him and patch up the holes and repair the damage.

Yes, if they were friends at the end of this it would be a miracle. Actually, if he came out of this without her putting him in jail for breaking laws, she would be impressed. He had already skirted around procedures by sneaking her out of a crime scene before she could give a statement to law enforcement, something she needed to rectify.

She grumbled slightly as she thought about all the work she would have to do when she went back to Missoula. Things were going to be a mess, but at least she wouldn't have to worry about any trials for the rest of the week.

"Why the face?" Judy asked, looking at her as they made their way into the kitchen.

She forced a smile, even though she knew her second mom would see right through it. "Nothing. I was just thinking."

"Well, at some point I hope you do enough thinking to tell me how you got so beat-up looking. Must have been some fall you took." She gave Natalie a once-over. "I don't know how you do what you do, lady. So exhausting. And oh, the things you must see every day— I can't even imagine," she said, pulling a plate of fresh fry bread out of the oven and setting it on the island with a shaker of sugar and cinnamon. "I hope your friend here knows what a catch he has gotten in you. You are quite the woman."

Natalie could feel the fire rise in her cheeks. Judy

may not have been her mother by blood, but she didn't miss a beat in acting like she was—especially when it came to embarrassing her.

"Did you know that Natty graduated first in her class and was valedictorian in her high school? She is a smart cookie."

"Yes, ma'am," Evan said, finally piping up. "I didn't know she was valedictorian, but knew from the first moment I saw her that she was an incredible woman. I feel lucky to have her even grace me with her presence."

What in the hell was he playing at?

"Mom, Evan is—"

Judy waved her to a stop. "Shush now, Evan and I are discussing you. Just listen in and take the compliments."

She clenched her teeth, the muscles in her jaw protruding. Her mom knew exactly how much she hated being the center of attention, especially when accolades were being awarded. She would much rather have been getting yelled at by a defendant and telling them to stand down—at least there she could be in control.

"I hope your intentions are pure with our girl here," Judy continued.

Natalie sent Evan a look that said "get us out of here" in a thousand languages. Yet, he pitched his head back with a laugh. "I can tell you, ma'am, I'll be nothing if not a gentleman when it comes to your daughter."

Judy took him by the arm and led him to the plate. She nearly fed him herself after she fussed about a piece of bread and held it to him. He seemed to be soaking it all in with a level of aplomb that even Queen Elizabeth would have been proud of.

Judy whispered something to Evan she couldn't quite hear, but it made her even more uncomfortable. Knowing her, it could have been a threat against his life if he hurt her, or a promise of cookies and cakes if he was a good boy. Though Natalie was fine with her mother saying either, she wished she could at least hear so she could talk about it with Evan later and make sure he understood that whatever Judy said, it was coming from a place of love.

There was a reason Natalie had never brought a man here before. Not even when she had been dating had she wanted to bring them within a hundred yards of this house. Her mom was a wonderful woman, but she could get attached quickly. Attachment would lead to entanglements and when the relationship ended, which they always did, it would be even harder to disengage if Judy harbored feelings, as well.

Natalie glanced down at her watch. It was about an hour back to the city; if they left now, she could be back to her own bed at her regular time—death threats be damned.

"You know, Natty, looking at your watch when we have guests is rude."

And there she was, put right back into her sixteen-year-old shoes, being chastised by her favorite larger-than-life woman.

"Sorry, I was just—"

Again, she was waved off. "I know, I know." Judy sighed. "I will put together the back bedroom for you two. I assume you will be sleeping in the same room?"

Holy crap, way to cut right to the quick of things.

"Judy, Mom—"

"Ms. Judy," Evan jumped in, "for the respect of your house, if it is at all possible, I think it best if we slept in separate rooms. We wouldn't want any of your friends to think you were anything but a moral, upstanding woman."

Judy laughed, hard. "Oh my goodness. We don't live in Victorian times. And I couldn't give two figs about what any old biddies have to say. If they have a problem with how I live my life, they can take it up with me. Or not. My response will be the same."

He glanced over at her and Natalie shrugged. There were some things and some fights that Judy was never going to let others win, and she had a feeling that this was one of those spars.

"You go and grab your bags and I'll pull everything together." In true Judy fashion, she left them in a flurry of feathers and spice.

It was quiet for the first time since they had stepped on the property. The only sounds were of Judy talking to herself as she made her way down the hallway and to the linen closet.

Natalie let out a long exhale. "I should have warned you. She is a bit of a hurricane in person, but I swear she leaves things better than she found them."

"Then I would hardly call that a hurricane."

"Fire, then?"

He tilted his head back and forth like he was letting the idea roll around in his mind, and the effect was even more endearing than she could have imagined. "I'll allow it. And I can see her ripping through any forest and leaving only ashes and wildflowers behind her."

Natalie laughed. "I'm sorry that she seems to think we're dating. I'll make sure to set things straight with her. And I will get us separate bedrooms."

Just the thought of having to sleep next to this handsome, charming man made her no-no places clench. She had incredible restraint when it came to men and to falling to the needs of her body, but she wasn't sure that she would be as strong if she could hear his breath in the still of the night. And if he touched her, game over.

Yes, they definitely needed separate bedrooms. Better yet, they could go back to the city. Yes, the city.

"Ms. Judy seems to be soaking it all up. I think she likes the idea of us being together."

And I don't mind it, either. Her mind raced, but she checked it. *Don't be an idiot, woman. Slow your roll.*

"That doesn't mean we should allow her to keep assuming, incorrectly, that we are something we are not."

"But what does it hurt? In fact, it's a lot easier letting her believe you brought me here to meet her than telling her we had to run here after someone tried to murder you."

She paused. "You have a point."

But there had to be some kind of happy medium that didn't involve any kind of interrogations about relationships or loss of life. In truth, she didn't know which was worse when it came to having a conversation with her mom.

"If it makes you feel better, I will sleep on the floor and you can have the bed."

"Are you sure we shouldn't head back to Missoula?" she asked, biting the inside of her cheek as she envisioned him shirtless on the floor beside her. "Besides, we didn't even bring bags. You don't think my mom will notice?"

He looked at her and sent her a sexy half grin. "You forget—I'm damn near a Boy Scout den leader here. I'm always prepared. I got my go-bag in the truck." He went to retrieve it.

She found herself standing alone in the kitchen, staring down at the plate of warm carbs, as everyone around her was going out of their way to make sure she was comfortable and taken care of. Lucky; she was incredibly lucky.

But how had her life gone from sitting on the bench and making life and death decisions for others to standing in her mom's kitchen and making life and death decisions for herself?

She stuffed a piece of bread into her mouth, closing her eyes as the sugar melted on her tongue. What was the world trying to tell her in forcing her to do this, to be here?

Maybe it was a little too ethereal, and she should have been focusing on the danger that she faced, but what if the world or the fates had a plan for her? She didn't believe in coincidence. Everything a person did in their lives, every decision they made, led them to a place they were meant to be. But what had led her here?

Slipping on a coat Judy had hanging on a peg, she walked through the kitchen and stepped out the back door. The sun was starting to set and she sat down on the fence-rail swing in the center of the yard. She rocked as she ate the last of her bread and stared at the pinks and oranges glowing on the mountaintops that were covered with snow.

It felt wrong to relax, to be enjoying the beauty of nature and life when the world was threatening to burn down around her, but at the same time it felt right to just take time and breathe it all in. Maybe that was the purpose of this, to focus on living the moments that were granted to her—who knew how many she would have left? The thought made her heart lurch. What would it mean to be taken from this earth? And why? What reason would someone have to hate her enough to want to snuff out her life?

Every day she had to face herself in the mirror and answer for the choices and decisions she made when it came to people's lives. She always tried to do the right thing, to follow the laws, directives and choices that others before her had made. Life was built of injustices—most couldn't be made right. The vast majority of the tragedies in this life didn't happen due to random acts of nature, but choices. It could be as simple as making the decision to get in a car or to say yes when a person should say no. It was these simple moments that ruined lives and wrought injustice and mayhem.

It was the sands of mistakes that built up to create the speed bumps in life.

She sighed, soaking in the sunset as it billowed from yellows and pinks to purples and grays. Soon, the stars would come. Turning to her right, she could see Polaris shining in the distance. It was always there to guide her, no matter what was happening in her life. This wasn't a mistake. She was here for a reason.

She had once read a line in Philipp Meyer's *The Son*, which went something like: "May the stars shine so bright it is impossible to sleep." Tonight she felt those words' pull. The stars were bright.

It was odd how dancing the line between life and death could make a person feel more alive. There must have been something wrong with her that she found a modicum of joy and beauty in this moment.

There was the screech of the screen door as it opened and closed, but she didn't turn around. Whomever wanted her dead wouldn't find her here; only those who wished her alive.

Evan sat down next to her, touching her as they rocked in silence. He handed her a drink, and she took a sip. Iced tea. Her first of the year. Just another symbolic change in her life. Winter was heavy, but spring was taking root. Until now she had been in the winter of her life—living only to survive, but brought to a point today when survival was literal instead of just figurative. Was this her moment to spring? To revel in the stars and grow?

She had forgotten how beautiful life could be.

She couldn't recall the last time she had taken time to sit and watch the sunset turn into the stars.

Evan put his arm behind her on the bench. "Are you doing okay? I know something like this can take a toll on a person."

She nodded, careful to keep from touching him, as if it would bring them too close too fast; or maybe his touch would bring back the reality of her life and break the spell the natural world had placed upon her.

"Judy caught me inside. She said she was heading to bed, but she would see us in the morning." He smiled, his teeth sparkling in the thin light.

"What?" She had never known her mother to be an early-to-bed kind of woman.

"Yep," he said with a chuckle. "And she also said that she would make sure to have plenty of protein to 'rejuvenate' us in the morning."

"Oh. My. God. She didn't." Natalie nearly splashed her tea on her shirt as she moved to cover her face in embarrassment.

"Oh, she did." He laughed loud and long. "Your mom is freaking awesome."

There were any number of words she could think of to describe Judy right now—obtrusive, meddlesome—but the last that came to mind was *awesome*.

"I'm glad you brought us here. If anything it is making me laugh. Right now I appreciate a little lighthearted-edness. It's not something you often find hours after a murder attempt." His hand moved down and his fingers trailed on the top of her shoulder.

His gentle touch moved in time with the swing and as it did, it was like he was thrumming the strings of her soul.

"You know," he continued, "I am here if you need to talk about what happened back there. I know how hard it can be and all the things that can go through a person's mind when something like that happens."

She glanced over at him, staring at his green eyes. They were picking up the gray of the sky, making him look stormy.

"I appreciate your concern, but I really am doing okay. More than anything, I am just at a loss. I can't think of a concrete reason anyone would want me dead."

He thrummed harder. "Are you sure?"

She nodded, but all she was really thinking about was his fingers on her. "Wait… Do you have your phone?" she asked, holding out her hand, expectantly.

He scowled, the look making it clear that he wasn't the kind of person who would just willingly hand over his private information. And yet, he reached into his back pocket and pulled it out. He didn't hand it over. "What are you thinking?"

She wanted to just show him, but she honored his

privacy and dropped her hand. There wasn't a chance in hell she would have handed her phone over to a stranger without any sort of context, either. "Pull up Instagram and type in the judge's son's name."

"Why do you want to look him up?" Evan asked.

She shrugged. "It seems like the most obvious place to start looking. I know he and his son are close, but Sven has a history. And, if nothing else, at least we can cross him off our list." And she could think about something besides the way Evan's touch felt, even through her coat.

He moved closer and started clicking on the phone with the hand that was wrapped around her shoulders, and the action drew her closer into him. So close, in fact, that she could smell the cinnamon on his breath and the smoky residue of the car bomb on his skin. It was a strange combination, the spice and the danger, but it was an oddly heady mix. She closed her eyes as he clicked and she drew in a long breath of him.

The timing of this crush couldn't have been more off. She yearned to dance with this Devil, and yet a different manner of hell was threatening her world.

He typed in *Sven Hanes Missoula*.

"There," she said, pointing at his profile.

Evan opened it up; thankfully, it wasn't set on private. The last picture that Sven had posted was tagged at a restaurant in Kennewick, Washington. It was a simple photo, nothing more than a long-necked beer and a burger, but it put him hours from the crime scene when the attack had happened.

But just because a person tagged themselves at a place, didn't mean they were actually there. For all she knew, he could have been standing behind them now.

Social media wasn't known for its accurate representations of real life.

Sven could very well have posted something tagged in another state, just to throw anyone who thought he was behind the attacks off his scent.

"Hmm," she said, pinching her lips together.

"Have you had any cases that were out of the ordinary lately? Something that involved both you and Judge Hanes? We're going to have to go over this, but I wanted you to have some space first."

"Our caseloads don't usually overlap. He has his dockets and I have mine." She mulled over his question for a long moment. "But…on occasion we have lawyers and their clients who are all about playing games, and some who think one judge would be better suited for hearing their case than another. In fact, that happens quite a bit in complicated cases."

"Has it happened in the last few weeks?"

She nodded. "A few of those filings have floated over my desk, but I can think of one that surprised me… I don't have the details, but it was an odd case. It was marked assault libel and slander—not abnormal, except it was between two women. I thought I would be sitting on the bench. Any sort of cases involving women's rights are normally run by me. The local attorneys know that I am more of an advocate. However, this one they moved to Hanes."

"Did he hear the case, or did it end up being settled?"

"Strangely enough, he did—two days before the attacks."

His eyebrows rose. "What happened?"

"Like I said, I don't know the particulars, but I know Judge Hanes had a hard time with that ruling—he drank nearly a half bottle of scotch with me that evening. He mentioned that the defendant had to be taken away by the bailiff after finding herself in contempt of court. Apparently, she thought it was okay to try and climb up over the bench and attempt to punch Hanes." She let out a half chuckle. "At the time, we both shrugged it off. Most people don't come at the judge—they will yell at us, call us every name under the sun, but there is generally some sort of internal stop point before people try to physically assault us in the middle of the courtroom."

"I think you may well be on to something with this defendant—we need to look into her. You said she was found in contempt of court. Was she out of jail today?"

"She just had to pay a fine and she was released." Natalie shifted slightly and Evan sat back, releasing her from his hold. The cool night air swirled in and pulled the warmth away from where he had been touching her.

"Do you know anything about the case? Maybe the woman's name?"

"The case was Sanders vs. Rencher. When Hanes and I chatted afterward, he said it had to do with a custody agreement that had gone wrong. The two women had been married, but are getting divorced. They had shared custody of a child, but something happened and somehow the two women ended up in a fight. Sanders ended up threatening to kill the other, and it is my understanding that she nearly finished the job."

"Well, at least it wasn't a murder case."

"If the police hadn't interceded at the right time, I think it would have been." She understood rage, but had never understood how another person could murder someone they had once loved. "Regardless, if we are going down the list of who would be capable of taking us out, she would be one of the most recent suspects. There is nothing more dangerous than a pissed off mother."

Chapter Six

His boss, Zoey Martin, was not pleased when he called. He wasn't surprised. Zoey wasn't known for her softness, even after she'd gotten pregnant. If anything, she'd grown more cantankerous over the past few months. Even though she had grumbled and cussed when he had let her know all that had transpired, she had eventually validated his actions and agreed to send someone in to stand by Judge Hanes's hospital room and ensure his safety as well as try to get more info when he was responsive.

By the end of the conversation, she had even commended him for his quick action in treating the judge. Her praise was as rare as her smile, so he graciously accepted what she chose to give.

She'd also sent him all the records she could find on the case Natalie had mentioned as well as everything she could locate about both judges—including links to all their rulings—and even Hanes's marriage license. He chuckled as he thought about how little use he would see coming from that particular piece of paper. In his life, the ink used to print the document had been worth more than what it stood for.

He wasn't sure he would ever really like to get married again. Screw that. Love had only ever led to heartache and resentment. He preferred sitting in a Humvee in the middle of a war zone and taking rounds than having to navigate the minefield that was a relationship.

No doubt this Sanders woman likely had felt the same way. According to the court records, she and her wife had been in a tempestuous relationship with verbal and physical disagreements so bad that the police had been called out several times. Once, her partner had been slapped with an assault charge after Rencher had gone after Sanders with a knife. According to the police report of that incident, Rencher had said the incident with the knife had resulted from self-defense.

Sanders had brought the assault up in Hanes's courtroom, but in the end, Hanes had ruled against Sanders. That was odd. His ruling didn't make sense. Sanders was clearly the victim. And according to the documents in his hands, she should have won her case against Rencher for assault. Was there something here that he wasn't seeing? He had all of the records and the court reporter's full file, and no matter how many times he read through it, he couldn't understand Hanes's ruling.

He shook his head.

As he read deeper and deeper into the case, he wondered what Natalie would have made of it.

He glanced over at her as she slept peacefully in the bed. She wore pajamas she'd found in a dresser in the room. She'd been delighted to see there were things she could wear today. She must not have changed much since she'd lived here.

They'd talked briefly about her cases, and he planned on asking her more about other rulings, jogging her memory with the links Zoey had sent. Somewhere in her past was someone who'd been angry enough to lash out at her and Judge Hanes.

He had been more than happy to take the floor and keep the peace between the two women of the house. It made him laugh every time he thought about Natalie's matron. Judy was a hoot. Though he could tell that she embarrassed the hell out of Natalie.

That made him miss his own mom. She had died several years ago in a car accident, along with his father. He had never really gotten over their loss. There were so many things that they would never get to be a part of, so many things they wouldn't be able to enjoy—if only his mom could be teasing him the same way Judy teased them.

Judy would have made a great mother-in-law. Not that he was ever going to get back into a relationship.

He was tough, incredibly so, but when it came to being with a woman, he was too tenderhearted. Whenever he had fallen in love in the past it was like he had always chosen the one being who he knew he shouldn't have. His ex-wife had been completely different from Natalie. Maybe as strong but that was where the similarities ended. His ex had told him that all she ever really wanted was to be alone; he had run up against it and fought to earn a place in her life. For a while, it had worked.

They had loved each other. Or he had assumed they had loved one another, and then she didn't want him anymore.

He couldn't begrudge her for putting herself first, for fighting to be at peace with herself, but he couldn't stop himself from being hurt. He had offered her a part of himself, which he rarely gave to anyone, and it hadn't been enough.

She wasn't the one for him; logically, he realized that. But when the heart said something was right and the mind said "you're being stupid," it was crazy how often the heart won. From here on out, he was listening to his brain. It knew better, and perhaps it could save him from himself—if he was lucky and if he actually listened.

Then again, he had never been known for his emotional intelligence. Far from it.

Natalie sighed in her sleep and his heart flipped in his chest, like her subtle little noise had somehow jumpstarted the poor, wretched beast.

Down, boy.

This fight with the mind wasn't going to be as easy as he'd hoped. And really, how was this time with Natalie any different than before? Here he was, forced to be close to a woman he was protecting, a woman who was entirely off-limits. All he had to do was keep his distance.

It will get easier as soon as I'm out of this house.

Yep, that was it. It was just that they were too close. He leaned up against the bed, turning his back to her so he wouldn't be tempted to look up at the beautiful woman once again.

Maybe it was just harder than normal because they were pretending to be in a relationship that they couldn't really be in. In the past, when he'd been forced to go undercover, he'd adopted mannerisms and qualities of the characters he was playing, going so deep that he became them. Maybe that was exactly what was happening here. He was loving her because he was pretending to love her. Nothing more.

Yep, that had to be it.

Finally, a bit of relief drifted through him. If nothing else, he had a reason and an answer for the confusing feelings that were working through him.

Maybe he needed to take a page from his ex's playbook and just be alone.

He nodded to himself and as he did, Natalie's fingers touched him. He glanced back at her sleeping face. As he moved, she reached into his hair, stroking his head. She sighed as she ran her fingers through his locks. He moved into her touch like a soft, well-broken horse. Even if she was only pretending to be asleep, his longing to be touched like that outweighed the need to protect his heart and pull away.

When he woke up the next morning, his phone was on the floor next to his head, and at some point someone must have covered him with a pink rose-covered blanket. Though he was getting older with each passing day, when he sat up his body didn't hurt too badly even though he had been smooshed into the carpet fibers all night long. He rolled onto his back. Natalie's hand was hanging limply over the bed above him. Her nails were long and perfectly manicured. Did she pay to get them done, or did she sit at home once a week and do them herself?

He looked at his own nails. They were worn short and there was dirt and what he betted was spent gunpowder under their edges. The base of his thumb had a nice callus from his days spent on the gun range.

There were no calluses on her hands. No dirt. No

blisters from manual labor or backbreaking tasks. Her tasks only broke the soul.

He definitely didn't envy her work. But then, she probably would say the same thing about his.

They were never to be. They were too different.

He scratched at his nose, pulling off a piece of fuzz that had stuck to his face in the night.

There was a knock on the door. "Wake up, kids. Breakfast is ready," Judy said, calling in.

Natalie's hand disappeared. "All right. We will be out in a minute," she said, sounding sleepy.

Damn, only this woman could make mornings sexy. His body had its own mind and as he thought of her and of waking up alongside her, it rose to greet the day.

Or maybe he had just been lonely too long. Or maybe it was just morning. *Get it together, dumbass.*

He moved to his feet, careful to keep his back turned to her. The last thing he needed to have was for her to see where his mind was and for him to see her tussled hair and makeup-less face. She was probably even more beautiful in her natural state. Women never believed that, but he loved it when a woman was comfortable enough to show her true self to him.

And yet, she was probably sitting there all worried about what she looked like and feeling insecure. They had been pushed into this; there was nothing about it that had come naturally—except the pull he felt to be closer to her.

"You can turn around. I'm not naked," she said, half laughing.

He wasn't sure exactly what to say, so he went with the first thing that came to mind. "Sorry, your morning breath... Damn, woman, let me get you a toothbrush."

She punched him squarely in the right butt cheek, not hard enough to hurt but just enough to get his attention.

"Hey, now," he said, turning around. "Most women have to pay to touch that."

She laughed. "What are you, a stripper or something?"

"I swear I'm only putting myself through college," he teased, doing a little dance move that made it look like he was twirling a feather boa. He hummed a bawdy song as he tapped his foot.

She laughed, the sound bouncing off the walls. Her joy tore at his resolve, clawing its way through his self-built barricades.

She moved to the edge of the bed and sat up, her legs on each side of his. "Oh, yeah," she said, laughing as she pretended to flip money at him. "I'll make it rain."

He put his hands behind his head and did a hip shake in front of her.

"Oh la la," she said, but somehow as she put her hands up, he moved into her and her hand grazed against his morning's gift. "Oh. Hey. Um. I'm. Yeah..." Her cheeks turned crimson.

He stumbled on his feet as he fell backward, slamming against the wall behind him. "Crap," he said, trying to right himself and gain control over what his body had gotten him into. "I'm sorry. It's my fault. I didn't mean to—"

They both sat there staring at one another for a long moment. She couldn't have been as embarrassed as he was, and yet, from the color of her face, he was sure that she was.

"I...you..." she started, but stopped.

There was no getting out of this uncomfortable moment; it was best to just acknowledge it. "Yeah, now you are really going to have to lay down some money. That is like VIP room treatment right there." He laughed in an attempt to cover his unease. "Here, let's get you dressed. I need coffee before you use me for my body again."

Her eyes widened in surprise and she opened her mouth. He didn't know why he did it—maybe it was the laughter on her lips or the joy he felt when he looked into her eyes, but he leaned in and kissed her. She didn't move away, as he expected. Maybe she was just as surprised as he was; this wasn't something he had meant to do. It wasn't something he had even thought about doing, at least not in any real way, and yet, here he was…her tongue glazing over his bottom lip.

She ran her hands over his ass, pulling him into her. She ran her hands up his back, her action forceful, and he felt himself submitting to her will. It felt backward, like he should have been the one to take charge and lead the advance, but at the same time he liked this relinquishing of power. There was something so immeasurably sexy about a woman who took what she wanted and had the confidence to make her wishes known.

She leaned back, not breaking their kiss as she pulled him down on top of her in the bed.

He moved against her, her body answering in kind. His lips trailed down her neck and he unbuttoned her pajama top, revealing her naked breasts. Cupping them, he stared. Her nipples were the color of toffee and, as he popped one in his mouth, they tasted just as sweet. He licked at the nub then rubbed it over his lips like he was marking it as his, yes…forever his.

She arched her back and as she did, her nipple grazed

the stubble around his lips and she gasped. He ran his hand down her body, feeling the subtle curves of her stomach and the crests of her hip. Searching for her warmth, the heat drew him in until his fingers found what he yearned to find. He would taste that next.

Rubbing against her, his mouth found her nipple again and he sucked until her breath caught in her throat and he could feel the heat grow under his fingertips. Her wetness soaked through the thin cotton of her pajamas. He lowered his touch, dipping into her, and she lifted her hips to meet him. Trailing his kisses down her stomach, he found her navel. Stopping for a moment, he ran his finger around the indentation.

He'd never thought of a navel as sexy before, but there was no place on her body he didn't want to see and make his. His heart beat for her, and if she let him, it would beat for her forever.

"You're right," she said, touching his hands. "We should stop."

Holy shit, that had been the furthest thing from his mind. How had she gotten there? All he wanted to do was pull every piece of clothing from her body and make love to her until there was nothing left of him to give.

"Uh," he said, trying to compose himself.

She moved and he rolled off her. It physically pained him to move from between her legs. It was like he had finally found a place that he wanted to call home and it was being ripped from his grasp.

"I…"

"I know," she said, stealing his words. "Judy is holding breakfast for us. And I agree that this isn't a great idea—for a variety of reasons."

Damn. She wasn't wrong, but that didn't make his need for her dissipate.

What hadn't he done right that she wanted to pull away from his touch? Hell, that she *could* pull away from his touch? Should he have moved his fingers faster? Should he never have stopped to look at her? Should he have devoured her before she had a moment to collect herself?

He leaned back, adjusting himself. Nope. He respected her boundaries. Hell, maybe he needed to put his up with steel and stone.

Standing up, he moved away from her and smoothed his hair. He ran his hand over his normally well-groomed beard, like it was the reason she had pushed him away. Maybe he needed to shave it off. He nearly shook his head at the thought; he wasn't giving up his beard. He couldn't make her want him, but he could stop himself from giving up his facial security blanket.

Before he got any more stupid ideas, he walked to the door. "I'll meet you down there. Coffee? Cream and sugar?"

"Yes, please. Just black."

Yep, she was far stronger than he was, though he would never dare to admit that aloud to her. They had to have an equal position of respect if they were ever going to try these kinds of shenanigans again. Maybe that was why she had stopped the advance; maybe she had realized she was about nine miles outside his league. He wouldn't blame her if she had figured that one out, but until he was sure that she had, he had to try and keep himself in the game.

He made his way down the hall, giving himself a moment to let things settle before he saw Judy. He didn't need her noticing anything that would make her suspicions about their relationship, burgeoning or otherwise, rise to the surface.

As he approached the kitchen, he was met with the scents of hot coffee, pancakes and bacon.

How had Natalie ever wanted to leave this heaven?

If this was what he had every day, he would just curl up on the couch and never leave.

Okay, maybe that was a little extreme. He did love his job. There was little better than taking out a threat who put those whom he loved and cared about—or was paid to care about—in danger. He was the world's checks and balances in human form, and with that came an incredible sense of identity and self.

"Good morning, ma'am," he said, making his way around the corner and into the main room.

Judy was humming away as she did something in the sink and she turned at the sound of his voice. "Good morning. I bet you are hungry. Are you a bacon or sausage guy? What's your favorite?"

"My favorite is anything you are about to feed me. Seriously, I'm not picky. Just grateful."

Judy beamed. "Smart man."

"I wouldn't go so far as to say that, but I would say hungry," he said with a mischievous grin.

She dried her hands and came over and gave him a quick peck on the cheek. The simple action caught him off guard; there was something so European and old-worldly about it that it made him like this wonderful woman even more.

"Before my daughter gets down here, I want you to know something about her."

He wanted to know everything, but he was surprised

that she would want to help him. Not sure exactly what to say, he nodded.

She looked up at him, studying his eyes for a long moment before giving him a little nod. "I can tell you guys are new to each other. But there is something you need to know about her, if you want to keep her..." Judy looked over her shoulder as if she was checking to make sure that Natalie hadn't somehow snuck up from behind. "Natalie has been through some hard times. Incredibly hard. But her spirit gets her through. She is like wildfire... You either run with her or you will be consumed."

He didn't doubt that for a second.

"I think you need to know, we aren't—"

"Dating? Oh, I know. I could tell," Judy said with a wicked smile. "But that doesn't mean that there isn't something between you two. I can feel it. And I know you can feel it. It is my job, as a parent figure, to make sure that my daughter gets the best things in life." She grabbed the bacon plate and slid it toward him on the counter. "Now, you just eat up. Let me worry about the rest."

He took a piece of bacon and stuffed it into his mouth. No matter what he said or thought, he could see that he would be quickly outvoted by the spark plug of a woman. From what he could tell, the warning she had given him about Natalie could have easily been applied to herself—maybe Natalie had become like the woman who'd raised her.

Whatever had caused it, he was honored to be even a minimal part of their experiences in life.

That was all he had ever really wanted to be, decor in other people's lives. Most people wouldn't understand this desire, the want to never hold a key role. It was easier to be in on the sidelines, acting as the guard. It was so much easier than actually being forced to feel. To feel made a person real, exposed, raw. It was crazy that Natalie made him want to step into a real role again. Maybe it was just the pull of her lips that had drawn him to her. Maybe it had just been too long since he had been that close to a woman. But as quickly as that thought came to his mind, he brushed it away. She wasn't just any woman. She was something truly special—she was smart, strong and level-headed. She was everything he had ever wanted.

He couldn't put his finger on exactly what it was that made him want to be raw and exposed when it came to her. Until he could figure out what drew him in, he needed to stay emotionally away—or at least at arm's length. He wouldn't leave her alone in her moment of need, not when he had the ability to be exactly what she needed to stay safe.

Natalie walked into the kitchen, pulling a white sweater over her head and then patting down her hair, making sure every piece was solidly in place in her ponytail. As she strode over to the plate of bacon he was taken aback—how had he gotten so lucky to have tasted her and felt her warmth on his fingers? He couldn't help but feel like the luckiest, albeit most confused, man in the world.

She smothered her pancakes in so much warm maple syrup that he considered telling her to just grab a bowl of syrup and crumble some pancake on top, but then he followed her lead.

Judy walked to the refrigerator and took out a can of whipped cream and handed it to her, like this breakfast was some sort of routine the two ladies had been cho-reographing for years. It was their dance, elegant and smooth, just like the women it belonged to.

She reminded him of a swan. When they fell in love, they did a beautiful dance of head bobs and spins. Sud-denly, he wanted to take her in his arms and sweep her around the kitchen, dancing with her in a way that only they could. And yet, such a motion seemed out of place and gauche in their graceful world.

He would always be the door kicker in this world of ballerinas.

Judy was conspicuously quiet as they all sat around and ate; in fact, they barely said a word until each had drunk a full cup of coffee.

Maybe that, too, was part of their routine.

If it was, he loved them both more for it.

Finally, Natalie pushed her plate away and spoke up. "I don't know about you, Evan, but I need to get back to the city. Would you mind running me home so I can pick up a few things? Then we can come back here, if that's okay with you?" She looked at Judy.

The older woman sent him a look, but he didn't know exactly what to make of the question in her eyes.

"I would rather we stay here. I mean, what do you re-ally need that we can't find at a store?" He tried to send Natalie a look that said there was no freaking way that this would be a good idea—the last thing they should do is stick her head out of the safety of their tempo-rary den.,

He still needed to go through the list of past cases with her more thoroughly, especially the one that had landed in Hanes's courtroom.

She didn't look at him.

Did this sudden need to run away from this place have something to do with what had happened between them in her bedroom?

Damn it, he had been so stupid. What had he been thinking in going in for that kiss? Right, he hadn't been.

This was exactly the kind of nonsense that happened when a person went along with the needs of their body over the requirements of their lives. He had obligations, to his team, to his family and to her. He had compromised his objectives by acting as foolishly as he had.

Maybe if they went back to the city, he could call in one of his teammates and they could take over this security detail…for no money, and out of the goodness of their hearts. After all, it was Hanes who'd originally brought him in, and they were protecting the judge in his hospital room.

He gritted his teeth. Zoey had been behind his helping her; hopefully she could convince someone else from his team to help. A.J. had always been the philanthropist. He would probably step up if he was called.

He should have known that Natalie wasn't emotionally available, and maybe he wasn't, either.

Yeah, that was it. Emotionally unavailable. Wall up. Dick off. Life back to normal. He set his jaw.

"You guys are welcome to come and go as you please," Judy said, sending them each a smile, but her eyes lingered on Natalie. "I think you should stay here as long as your work allows, Natty. I think you need a bit of a break. You are looking a little overwhelmed this morning, even if you did clean up all those scratches I saw yesterday."

Natalie huffed into her coffee cup as she moved to take a sip. "It was a long night."

Judy laughed, making a blush rise in his cheeks he wished he could control. And yet, just like these two women, his body's response seemed to have a mind of its own. Damn if he didn't love them for it, but hate himself for it at the same time.

"Yeah, maybe it's best if we head back." He could sit here and argue why they shouldn't leave all morning, but the woman of fire was always going to get her way. It was better to have a plan in place for what she needed instead of trying to impose his will. Even if he was the type, it wouldn't have worked.

He downed his coffee and put the empty cup in the sink. "Thank you for having us, ma'am. I hope to see you again." He gave Judy a wink and she answered with a sad, reconciled smile. "Natalie, I will meet you outside."

It felt like he was running away, but he couldn't handle all the feelings that were whirling around in the kitchen. A moment later he grabbed his wallet and the truck keys from beside the bed, made a quick trip to the bathroom, and by the time he was walking outside he noted Natalie was already there, briefcase in hand.

Apparently, she was in a bigger rush to get out of here than he was.

Judy was nowhere to be seen.

He had no idea what to say, or how he should approach the judge. All he wanted to do was to apologize and tell her that lust had clouded his judgment and the pheromones had reared their ugly heads, but would be kept under better control.

"You and Judy make quite the pair," he said, making his way out toward her.

Yes, innocuous…it was his only play.

She looked at him and frowned. Had she expected him to just come out and talk about what had transpired between them, or had she been preparing for him to argue the point that they should have stayed at the little farm?

He went into instinct mode, viewing the area around his truck. His scan started at twenty feet out, then ten, and finally five. It was something he always did anytime he got in or out of a vehicle. It was an old habit he had picked up over the pond. Nothing appeared amiss at twenty feet or ten, but when he glanced at the ground near the driver's-side door, the dirt had been scuffed.

It could have been nothing, but given what had happened yesterday, and the car bomb in the parking lot, he wasn't going to take any chances.

Natalie leaned against the hood of his truck, waiting for him to open the doors.

"Step away from the truck," he said, trying not to sound too overly concerned, but serious enough that she would move.

She pushed off from the truck, looking back at it over her shoulder as she rushed to his side. "What is it? Is something wrong?" Her eyes were wide with fear.

He shrugged. "I'm sure it's nothing, but I just want to check things out. We don't want another bombing."

She visibly relaxed, her shoulders lowering from her ears. "No one knows we're here. We're good. You can relax," she said, waving him off.

"A person is at the most risk when and where they feel the most comfortable." He tried not to preach, but she needed to make sure she was as committed to her security as he was. "Look there," he said, pointing at the scuff mark on the ground. "You see that?"

She nodded.

"Overseas, that would be a key indicator that someone had been messing with our rigs."

"Thankfully, we are not overseas and, like I said, no one knows we are here. You know, you may want to talk to someone about PTSD. You've obviously been through a lot and one of the key identifiers in recognizing a person has it is that they begin to see threats in ordinary places."

He appreciated that she was worried about his mental health, seriously. There was no doubt in his mind that his life had been impacted by the things he had seen, but there was a thin line between being vigilant and safe, and complacent and dangerous. He would always choose to be aware of his surroundings because even when he was, things like what happened yesterday still had a way of coming around. And so far his vigilance had kept him alive and might help her stay that way, as well.

"Just go with me on this, please," he said, trying to keep his mixed emotions from leaking into his voice. "It's my job to worry about you, and to make sure you are safe."

The lines around her eyes softened and she smiled at him, then motioned toward the truck. "I suppose it doesn't hurt a thing to check and make sure that nothing is amiss." She paused and looked away. "And thank you. I really do want you to know how much I appreciate everything you're doing for me. I will make sure that your company gets paid for your services."

Though he heard everything she had said to him, all he could take from it was that she had relegated him to the level of the help. Had that been a way for her to keep her feelings at bay? Or had she finally just realized that she was too good for him? Either way, she wasn't wrong. He was here to labor for her, nothing more.

He hated that the woman of his dreams was standing at his fingertips, yet a world away.

"Don't worry about paying me. I'm here because I want to be here. This, taking care of people, is who I am." He put his hand to his heart.

And not because he thought she was beautiful. And not because right now, as he looked at her, all he could see was the sparkle of the morning sun in her eyes—and it made them appear even more green than when he had first looked upon her face in Judge Hanes's office.

He would keep her safe because that was what he had been born to do. And if this day was his last day because of this mission in life, at least he had led a life built on purpose and ended on a day in which he had felt her lips.

"I should have known you were the hero type." She smiled and touched his back, the first time she had touched him since they had been in the room alone together. "A girl could fall for that kind of thing, you know."

He half expected her to say, "But I'm a woman" and yet, she said nothing.

Did that mean that she was falling for him, or was that just wishful thinking?

And this, this mind game, this confusion, was what he hated the most about feelings and romantic attachments. It had a way of making a man feel crazy. Did she mean what she was saying or did it mean something else? Was she flirting with him or was he hoping to see something that wasn't really there?

It was so much easier just to stay in the friend zone.

"Let me go check on the truck." He hurried over to the driver's side and dropped down to the ground, hugging it like it was the lifeline that would keep him from falling into the trap that was his feelings.

He closed his eyes and took in a long, deep breath. The earth smelled of decay and dust and the heady aroma of burnt frost. Every place he had ever been in the world had smelled different, but the salty, mineral scent of dust was universal—it whispered of unanswered dreams, lost hopes, failed promises, false starts, spilled blood and the ashes of lives. And yet, behind those whispers were screams of the venerable and lives built on honor and joy. People had called him a hero in the past, but those who experienced the brief periods of time on the earth with love, honor and joy were the most heroic of all.

They had lived lives worth all the hell he put himself through in order to protect them. And he wished that Natalie would have all of those things, even if that future never crossed paths with his—and he gave every one of his days to the task of making her life one she, the hero, deserved.

Her secret protector. Forever.

He dabbed at the chill on the tip of his nose as he moved to inspect the undercarriage of the truck. The area right above his head had been wiped clean of dried mud and debris.

Odd.

There was no way that spot would have been clean given the number of miles they had racked up. Was his mind just playing tricks on him, and he was seeing things that weren't really there? He had been known to do such things—see threats where they weren't—in situations like this before. He stared at the clean spot on the undercarriage, wishing he knew slightly more about cars than what he did. Sure, he was competent, but being a full-blown mechanic wasn't in his wheelhouse.

Then he saw it. There, next to the crossmember, below his driver's seat, was a small black box. Unlike in the movies, there was no blinking red light or something to indicate that power was going to the IED. Instead, it was just a simple black box, and if he hadn't been looking for it or if he hadn't seen the scuff marks underneath the car, there was no chance he would have ever seen the object, even with a quick undercarriage inspection. That was what made these things so goddamn deadly.

He tried to control his breathing as he slipped out from underneath the truck.

Just like that, everything he had been thinking about and all the emotional turmoil he had been putting himself through, all came to a screeching halt. That box. It looked like nothing more than hard plastic put together with four little screws. Whoever had made the bomb must have used a screwdriver normally set aside for glasses and delicate work. Specialty screwdriver. Specialty chemicals. Specialty bomb maker.

At least he wouldn't have died at the hands of just some inept person who had gotten lucky.

And he had saved Natalie. He had trusted his gut, listened to the little voice screaming at him…the little voice he had wanted to ignore…and it had proven effective. To think he had almost let his mind grow clouded with things nonessential for survival. If he was going to protect her, he needed to focus.

He had to tell her what he had found, but he didn't want to alarm her. There were so many things that swept through his mind—how they had been found, who was behind it and what their possible next moves were. And yet, he couldn't find the air to make the words. It was as if the bomb had already gone off in his mind, sucking every syllable into its mushroom cloud and leaving him as nothing more than skin and bones.

"Are you okay?" Natalie asked, staring at him. "Is something wrong…something with your truck?"

He opened his mouth, then closed it, hoping the air would move back into his lungs and his tongue would work to sound out the words that had to be said. Instead, none came and he wrapped his arm around her shoulders. She didn't hesitate as he led her back to the house and walking inside, making sure to close and lock the front door behind them. Judy must have been in the kitchen. He heard the water running there.

He let go of her, hurrying around the living room and making sure all the curtains were closed. No one could see inside. He couldn't allow them to become even easier targets than they already were.

"What is going on, Evan?" Natalie asked, this time sounding more frantic than she had before.

"I don't want you to get upset." His words sounded out of place even to his own ears.

"I'm well past upset. What in the hell is going on?" Natalie sounded absolutely terrified—the one thing he had wanted to avoid.

"Don't worry. Everything will be fine." He knew she could hear the lies in his sound, regardless of the words he had chosen to try and assuage her terror.

She moved beside him and stepped to the window,

but he pushed her back. Her eyes and mouth opened wide, as though he had struck her instead of attempted to protect her.

"I'm sorry, I didn't mean—"

"What in the actual hell—"

"There is another bomb." He spit the words like they themselves were a ticking time bomb.

All the color in her face drained away. From her look, he could tell that the air had left her just as it had left him. He wanted to pull her into his arms and tell her that it would be okay. That this little setback was nothing. That they were safe. That they hadn't been found and that no matter what, nothing would happen to her while he was there.

But he couldn't lie to her.

She had every right to be frightened.

He didn't have to like it. And it made his bones ache in a way he had never thought possible just from looking at another person and empathizing with what they were going through, and yet, here he was.

Judy walked into the living room, drying her hands on an embroidered cheesecloth dish towel that reminded him of his grandmother. The embroidery was green and pink, a little girl in a bonnet and a daisy in her hair.

"I thought you guys were heading out. Did you change your minds? Forget something?" Judy smiled, but as she looked at Natalie, her smile disappeared.

The delicate towel slipped from her hands and fell to a heap on the floor. She ran to Natalie and wrapped her in her arms just as he had wanted to do. "It's going to be okay."

The steel and stone he had put around his heart started to crack ever so slightly.

"Someone planted a bomb underneath my car."

"When? Now? Last night?" Judy asked, taking over the questioning from Natalie like they were of one mind.

"Mom, it's okay," Natalie said, nodding as she wiggled from her arms. "You don't need to worry about anything. I'm sure it is just a training exercise or something. Isn't that right, Evan?" She gave him a look to play along.

He nodded, but he didn't like this. He'd had enough of the lies and the deceit. It hadn't gotten them anywhere but sleeping in a room alone together—and then falling into one another's arms and making the world more complicated.

"Judge DeSalvo, I think that, given the circumstances, we need to tell your mother the truth." He looked at Judy. Her shoulders fell and there was tiredness in her eyes that he had seen every time he'd ever watched a heart break.

Natalie sighed, giving up on their charade. "You're right, Mr. Spade."

She made his name sound like it was something less-than, but it could have been the resignation that marred her words.

"Mom," Natalie continued, "Mr. Spade was assigned to protect a fellow judge. There has been a series of attacks and we are concerned for my safety. As you can surmise, given the nature of this latest blow, we aren't completely out of the woods. Clearly, someone must still be targeting me."

"Do you know who it is?" Judy answered.

"Not yet, but we are working on tracking down leads."

He had to jump into action, to do something that

would make this all okay and ensure their safety. He took out his phone and dialed his team.

A.J. answered. "What the hell is going on?"

"Hey, tool bag, you guys doing okay?" Evan asked, making his way out of the living room and away from the two ladies. No doubt they would need a minute while Natalie filled Judy in on all the details.

"We are holed up on the homestead. All is good. You? Zoey said you had found yourself in a little action yesterday. Shit blow over yet?" A.J. asked.

"No, but that is why I'm calling. We got an IED. I need the team to come out, see what we can do to neutralize the threat." He tapped in the address and sent it to A.J. via text. "And I'm hoping you guys can get me some kind of information from it. Something to narrow down the list of suspects."

He could hear A.J. turn away from the phone and give whomever was in the office with him the order to get everyone pulled together.

A.J. had always gotten such a high from those moments, the rush of the call to action and the thrill of the unknown. It felt so good on that side of the ticket, and a whole hell of a lot better than it did when Evan was the one who had been forced to call in the team. Evan couldn't do this alone, but at the same time it made him feel weak that he had to turn to them. Yet, he didn't know why. This kind of thing, calling for assistance when he needed it, was just another day on the job.

Why did it bother him so much this time?

A.J. came back to the phone. "We will be there within a couple of hours. We'll put together an extraction plan, but for now you need to sit still. We don't want you getting into any type of confrontation with the enemy without your backup in place. Got it?"

His brother, always the man to spring into action. No emotions. No questions. Just see the hill, take the hill. No bullshit and zero room for anything more than survival.

Chapter Seven

Another bomb. Another freaking bomb. Before yesterday, Natalie had thought that car bombs were something that only really happened in war-torn nations and action movies. They certainly didn't happen in her mother's driveway in a tiny town in the middle of the woods in Montana. This just didn't make sense.

Until now she had really started to believe that the person behind it was Sanders or Rencher, after talking through that case with Evan last night. But she didn't recall that either of them had ever had this kind of know-how…or had been trained in the administration of nerve agents. Whoever was trying to kill her and Judge Hanes was a highly skilled mercenary…someone just like Evan.

She glanced in the direction of the driveway, where he was now standing with several other people who resembled him. The dark-haired man to his left looked almost identical to him, but was a few years older and had at least three inches on him. They had the same dark, brooding stare and as the man looked toward the house, she noticed that they had the same smoldering gaze when they were deep in thought.

Evan couldn't have been behind anything like this.

Her mind wandered. He had been present for the nerve agent attack, the bombing and the bombing attempt. In court, a lawyer would have argued that his being at all three events was nothing more than coincidence—circumstantial evidence—and there was nothing that directly linked him to the crimes. But what if whomever was coming after her and Judge Hanes was really targeting him?

She nearly laughed out loud at the thought. The idea was outlandish. He had been hired because Judge Hanes had received a threat; he hadn't brought trouble to them. She was just being crazy and trying to find fault where none lay.

Though she wasn't sure which of her actions had brought violence to her doorstep, she wasn't the kind of woman who would shirk accountability. If she had triggered this, then she was the one who needed to take responsibility for it, and then work to make sure it was peacefully resolved. As much as she didn't understand the why, she did understand her duty to herself and the people who had elected her a judge.

And maybe that was exactly what this was—someone's best attempt to keep her and Hanes from doing their job. She had been looking at the last few cases, but she had been foolish not to look ahead.

She wished she had her cell phone so she could pull up her caseload. Regardless, whether she located her enemies or not, they would continue to breathe down her neck. She was at their mercy until they chose to reveal themselves.

What kind of hellish reality had she found herself in?

She thrived on always listening to explanations, having some kind of answer at her beck and call, and then administering judgment with the strike of her gavel. Yet, here she was, stuck in the mire of anonymity and secrets. She could only hope that it wouldn't last much longer.

Whoever was gunning for her would have to step out of obscurity soon. She knew their game; it was a game she had played in a million different ways, and a game she could win.

"Are you okay, honey?" Judy asked, putting her hand on her shoulder and pulling her from her moodiness.

"Yes. You?" She forced a smile. "I feel like I need to apologize. I didn't intend on—"

"We are rarely allowed the ability to have our intentions reflect our reality. I know you did what you thought was best." Judy gave her a light kiss to the cheek, the same action she had used when she was younger and at odds with her soul. Even then, it had helped to calm the raging tempests. "And even if you had brought an entire army to my doorstep, I would still say let them come. You are more important to me than anything. If you need a safe haven, my doors are always open."

She touched Judy's cheek as they stood together watching the war outside her window. "You are far too kind to me. You always have been. I hope you know how grateful I am to have you in my life. Always."

"I could say the same thing to you, my dear." Judy patted her hand and gave it a squeeze. "My life was empty without you in it. You have given me purpose. My only regret is that I don't get to have more time with you. So really, if nothing else, this time together is a gift."

Only Judy could see a fight for life and death as a gift. It was this perspective that made her so special. She was one of those rare people who always saw the world through rose-colored glasses and looked for opportunities in the hardest of days.

"Why are you talking like this?" Judy's eyes darkened with concern. "What is going on? Is there something else you aren't telling me about what's happening here?"

"No," she said, feeling the weight of the word. "I'm sure this will all be taken care of shortly and we will all be safe."

Evan walked toward the door, his eyes even darker than Judy's as he looked in at them. Had he found something else? Some new threat?

She was strong, life had stripped any softness from her, but she wasn't sure how much more she could bear.

She had a gnawing feeling she had just told Judy a lie. Safety was a promise she shouldn't and couldn't make.

Evan made his way inside, and the curl of his shoulders and the heaviness in his steps made her want to tell him to sit down and rest. He wasn't the kind to stop, at least she didn't think so. But what did she really know about this man, this man whom her heart ached for? Maybe the ache was nothing more than some kind of hero worship or Stockholm Syndrome—though the only person who kept her prisoner was herself.

Until now she had prided herself on her independence and strength. However, looking deeper into herself, those qualities were also her weaknesses. They held her in place as much as they pushed her forward.

Would she ever be enough? Or was such a thing even possible?

There were days when *enough* seemed nearly doable, but then things like this happened and the world rained its anger down—not just on her, but everyone who wanted to do something good. Or was *good* also an illusion?

What was the point of all the anger, hate and pain that came with living if good, right and just were only illusions?

"I always hate when people tell me I look tired," Evan started, glancing over at her. "But if you are half as tired as you look—"

She waved him to a stop. "That's just a way of politely telling people that they look like crap, and you don't need to tell me. I feel it." She tried to smile, the simple action some kind of gesture of appeasement in order to help him understand that she wasn't upset with his assessment of her. "From the look on your face, it's clear you have something you don't want to tell me. What is it?"

He glanced down at his hands and then back up at her.

Judy cleared her throat. "I will go put a kettle on for tea. If anyone wants to warm up, you know." She excused herself.

Evan strode over to the couch and sat down on the edge, steepling his fingers between his knees as he attempted to collect himself before speaking. She wanted to tell him to just start talking, to tell her everything that was on his mind and what he had found out, but terror rattled through her. Whatever he was about to tell her was going to be the kind of ugliness that tore a soul apart.

Finally, his gaze found hers. "Did you ever hear about the Unabomber?"

She nodded, her throat tightening with his every syllable.

"Did you ever hear about his bombs, his signature? You know the way the FBI was finally able to tie him to several of his devices?"

She shook her head.

"In every one of his bombs, there was a metal plate—usually in the end of the pipes. He would stamp initials into them—FC. And even though many of these plates were destroyed in the explosion, the FBI's teams were able to reconstruct them."

She didn't know what the Unabomber, Ted Kaczynski, had to do with what she was going through. He was in prison, and definitely not responsible for these bombs.

"The FBI found a metal plate, similar to what the Unabomber used."

"What?" she asked. "Have you been working with the FBI?"

"My team is working with Agent Hart from the Missoula office. He was nice enough to send us a copy of the bomb's parts to see if we could make sense of it." He swallowed hard, making her wonder what else he held back.

No doubt he had more contacts in the Bureau and every other alphabet soup acronym agency from a variety of governments. And here she had assumed, up until now, that she was the one with all the political pull. He could probably work over her head, if he needed to.

Hopefully, she would never have to find out if she was right or not.

"Anyhow," he continued, "have you ever heard of Rockwood?"

She did a quick inventory, but couldn't think of anything offhand and she shook her head.

"They are a manufacturing company, one with a desire to be involved in helping to develop weapons for the government. They have been known to do some questionable things in order to try and get their hands on manufacturing contracts, including but not limited to murder and blackmailing international diplomats."

"And you think they have something to do with the bombing?" she asked, confused how a company she had never heard of would have anything to do with her attempted murder.

Attempted murder. The words made a chill run down her spine.

"We aren't sure if it's just a coincidence or indication of a larger issue, but there has been a recurring issue with Rockwood in and around Missoula County and a variety of businesses that work in that sector. Which leads me to my next question, and while I think I know the answer, I have to ask." He searched her face, but she had no idea what he was talking about.

"What?" she asked, hoping to quell some of the thrashing in her chest.

"Have you had anything to do with any *other* kinds of work, aside from the normal comings and goings of your position as judge?" He didn't blink.

"Are you asking if I have another job…with a *separate* acronym-laden government agency? No." She shook her head vehemently. Working in the CIA or similar agencies would have been a conflict of interest, but she found it a bit of an ego boost that he would think her capable of that.

His lips tightened and he let out a metered breath. "That's not quite what I meant."

And then it hit her. He was asking if she was on the take, crooked in her dealings. "Evan. You wouldn't." She sat down on the ledge in front of the fireplace at the center of the room. The fire was crackling behind her, but she didn't feel its heat—only the raging fire that swept up from her core at his accusation.

He remained silent. She had expected him to recant, to see what his words had done to her and work to retract them before they had a chance to really burn through her, but he didn't. He simply stood there, watching her. He really was a shadow team man; only those like him could ignore the tension and weight in a room in order to get the answers that they needed. She had thought she'd had the same strength, but she could feel herself charring under his gaze.

"I haven't been a judge for long," she started, but her voice cracked with unwelcome hurt and it forced her to clear her throat. "Even if I had been a judge for decades, I wouldn't act in a way that was less than honorable. I pride myself on my integrity. I wouldn't compromise myself for money."

He nodded, but the power in his eyes remained the same. "Money isn't always the greatest motivator. Many things can make a person act against their character and better judgment if a person is given the right opportunity and motivation."

That was an element of crime she knew all about. And she hated that he thought he could interrogate her like she was on the stand. She could feel the growl forming in her throat, primal and deep. Wolfish.

Silence. Stealth could be one of the greatest assets in a predator's arsenal. This was one of those times in which she needed to bare her teeth, but only when the moment was right.

But it felt wrong that she would look at him this way. He wasn't her prey. He was a fellow predator; an alpha wolf just like her. He had stood at her side and helped her get out of danger, and oh, the way he kissed her lips. If anything, they were the leaders of the pack. They were to stand tall together, not fight amongst themselves.

But he was wrong if he thought he could attack her credibility in any way and not get bit.

"Judge DeSalvo, Natalie." He said her name like it was a whisper on his lips and it made her anger dissipate. "I'm not saying that you have done anything. Know that. All I'm asking is that if you have any *dealings* that I don't know about that could have caused this, it is best if you tell me now. I'm a safe place for you, but I can't help you if I don't know everything."

"You know everything," she said, nearly snarling. "I am not that kind of judge. If you don't believe me, then you can leave right now."

His eyes opened wide. "I'm not leaving you."

"But you don't believe me?"

"Your reaction, that tells me everything I needed to know. Thank you," he said, sounding apologetic but resigned to his method.

"You wanted to make me upset? To get me to a point where I could visualize punching you directly in the nose?"

"Your indignation—it comes from innocence, not fraud," he said, sending her a soft look.

Now she wasn't sure what she was more upset with—him for how he had made her feel or herself for allowing him to emotionally hijack her in this way.

In one of her many classes in college, she had a professor who had spoken on the psychology of crime. She had told the class that to treat feelings as if they were not one of the primary senses—with the same driving needs as hunger or sex—was a mistake. Feelings, in many ways, were often even more of a critical sense than any of the others. They controlled everything, and could be used to control and manipulate a person if they weren't aware.

It wasn't like she didn't face her feelings every day when she was sitting in the courtroom. She wouldn't be human if she didn't feel hate and disgust when shown many of the things she was required to see. Most of the time she could restrain herself, set her jaw and listen while allowing the time and the lawyers to move forward. She rarely lost her cool, but Evan had broken her down in just a matter of minutes.

What did that mean—was it good that he could make her *feel* when so many others tried and failed, or was it bad for the very same reason?

She sucked in a long breath and exhaled, forcing the questions from her mind. Right now her emotions didn't matter. They had to go back into the little vault at the bottom of her soul where they would remain in perpetuity.

"Now that we have established that I can be trusted, and I hope you can be trusted, what else did you find?"

She adjusted the knees of her pants like they were her robe and she was back in her domain.

He furrowed his brows. "In addition to the initials, the FBI sent us the results of their analysis of the chemicals and chemical signatures from the bomb at the courthouse. They want to talk to you, obviously, but we've told them you're in a safe house for now, and you'll be sending a statement."

"Okay, good. I'm glad. Anything of note in the bomb analysis?" Was he going to ask her if she manufactured chemicals and distributed them now, as well? "Did they come from Rockwood's facilities?"

He shook his head. "No, but the chemicals used were odd."

"How so?" She straightened her back.

"I'm sure you are aware, but there are several different classes of fires. Yes?"

She had sat on the bench for a few arson fires, but they had been few and far between and even then, her knowledge of firefighting practices was sparse. "Okay," she said, not sounding overly convincing.

"There are a variety of classes, A, B, C, D and K—all depending on the combustion sources and the requirements needed to combat each type of fire."

She nodded.

"The bomb that this person, or group, placed under your vehicle was created with Class D combustible materials. Meaning they used metals, alkalis to be precise, to create a hot fire that would engulf your entire car."

"So whoever did this not only wanted me dead, but they wanted to destroy my body, as well?"

His face pinched. "I don't want to jump to that."

Whether he wanted to jump to that or not, it meant

something. Someone who perpetuated this level of attack was enraged. They had been pushed to the brink in order to rise to this level of violence and harm. They hated her.

Which meant their attacker either had some sort of mental illness that caused psychosis, or it was likely a person who knew her—and knew her well.

Her chills returned.

"The compounds that they chose to use to create a Class D fire is what got my attention. According to the chemical analysis, the fire was created by using zinc phosphide."

Now he was officially speaking Greek to her. He must have known, based on the look on her face, that she didn't understand.

"It's okay. I had to do a little digging and make a few phone calls to understand, too. Zinc phosphide is used as a rodent killer. Farmers and ranchers kill pests in their fields with it, but few know about its use as a fire catalyst."

She was thankful she had decided to shove her emotions away. She wasn't sure that she could handle all the ramifications that would come with picking apart all the facets of the attack.

"What about the new bomb? Was it made the same way?"

He shrugged. "We are trying to neutralize the bomb, and then my team is going to take it to the Missoula crime lab. I'm not sure if they are going to try and detonate and then analyze or try and work with the bomb as it is. As this attack is the third on a judge, I think they may try to keep the bomb intact."

"I don't want anyone to put themselves in harm's way

over this. If we get the choice, I would prefer whoever is working with this does this in the least dangerous way. Can you let them know?"

"I'm sure that they will be safe," he said, walking over to her and putting his hand on her shoulder. "I think it really says something amazing about you that you put the safety of others ahead of the needs of yourself."

She didn't want to blush, but she could feel her cheeks warm. "It just doesn't make sense. We will get this perpetrator one way or another."

His fingers pressed against her, and she wanted to move her body closer to his and lean on him, but she stopped herself.

The windows rattled and she felt the blast against her skin. She fell to the ground, not sure if it was him pushing her or her pushing him, but they moved together and pressed their bodies low.

She turned her head, looking in the direction of the blast, expecting the windows to be spider webbed with fracture lines, but they were standing as they had been only moments before.

Through the ringing in her ears, there was the din and rise of a man's wail—it sounded almost like a howl. She looked to Evan. Over his right eye was a long, bloody gash. His lips were open and she realized he was the one, the wounded animal, whose call pierced her soul.

Chapter Eight

He sat up, trying to figure out what exactly had happened to him. Evan ran his fingers over his forehead and drew them back; they were covered in blood. He tapped his fingertips together feeling the stickiness, like he hadn't felt it a thousand times before. What had happened to him?

All he could remember was there was a loud blast and then nothing but darkness. And yet, somehow, he had found himself sitting alone in a hospital room, only God knew where.

He pressed the little button at the side of his bed. The bed was hard, unforgiving, as he rolled to his side and he was almost positive he smelled moth balls and mildew, but he wasn't entirely sure. He pressed the call button again, but nothing—no static or ward secretary answered his buzz. But he could see a thin light casting an orange shadow over his door from out in the hall.

He took in a deep breath. Over the scent of his moldy bed, the odor of cleaning products and decay wafted to him. The 1970s orange-and-brown curtains strung up around the bed would have been a dead giveaway that he was in some kind of throwback facility. It kind of reminded him of hospitals in nonindustrialized, poor countries. In fact, quite often third-world countries' hospitals were far better than this; at least there he had been able to watch the flurry of nurses and doctors rushing between rooms.

"Hello?" The eerie silence made him wonder if he wasn't stuck in some sort of purgatory-like dream. He called out again, but there was still no answer.

Was this death?

It wouldn't have surprised him. This would be the type of place he would have been sent to upon dying. He had always expected to die all alone, and find himself sequestered in the one place he hated more than anywhere else.

He swung his feet around to the side of the bed, but as he sat upright his head swam and his vision blurred. Nope, he definitely wasn't dead. If he was, he wouldn't have felt this crappy.

The light stopped flashing in the hall, and a woman stepped into his room. Saying she looked like Nurse Ratched would have been a compliment. The woman standing in front of him was in her late sixties and her lips were creased with the folds of a lifelong smoker. When she saw him, her mouth curled up with disgust and he noticed a scar on the side of her nose, like she had long ago lost in a bar fight.

"What the hell do you think you're doing?" She rushed toward him. "You shouldn't be sitting up. You need to be resting. I thought I told you this before."

The way she talked to him made him wonder if he had woken up once before, but didn't remember it. Was there something very wrong with him? Did he have some sort of short-term memory loss going on, or was it something worse?

"Where am I?" He glanced down at his bloody fingers, and they swirled in and out of focus.

She frowned as she basically pushed him back down onto his bed and fluffed the pillow around his head. "You are at the Marcus Memorial Hospital just outside Silver Mountain. Your friends brought you here after a particularly nasty fall."

He tried to relax into the bed, but as he moved a spring rose up from the mattress, poking him in the back. Really, what kind of hospital was this? If they were trying to legitimize their services and reassure their patients that they were getting the highest-level care possible, they were failing—hard.

"Wipe that look off your face. You are lucky that you have a bed. It's not every day a veterinary hospital finds themselves caring for a two-legged creature. If this hadn't been a hospital decades ago, you wouldn't even have this kind of luxury."

"Wait… I'm in a damned *veterinary* hospital?" He couldn't help the little laugh that escaped his lips at the thought of the situation in which he found himself.

"Yes. And to be clear, I like dogs far better than humans." She walked out of the room, but a second later she looked back in from the hall. "But if you are a good boy, I might have your girlfriend bring you in a dog treat."

"Natalie is here?" he asked, but as he did, he realized she had been the first person he had thought of when the woman said *girlfriend*, even though there were many women friends in his life.

He had promised himself that he wouldn't think of her like that, and yet, after a near-death experience, his instincts had acted and shown him exactly who and what he wanted. Maybe it was just his loneliness rearing its ugly head.

Yep, he was buttoning that crap up.

"She is out in the waiting room." The nurse didn't say anything and ducked back out of the room.

Was she going to tell Natalie he was awake? Send her in? Who else was there?

He opened his mouth to yell after the woman, who he realized now wasn't actually a nurse but likely a vet tech who had been tasked with babysitting him. No wonder she had been so annoyed. He should have told her he preferred the company of animals, too; maybe it would have softened her up a bit.

He touched his head again, this time letting his fingers rest on the edge of his cut where the blood had started to dry. He couldn't have been here too long if his wound was still weeping. That was something. And his cut mustn't have been too bad if they hadn't treated it while he was unconscious. Maybe it was nothing more than a bad scrape; faces tended to gush. And there was just enough redhead in him that he was more of a bleeder than most people he knew. It was probably his Irish blood.

He tried to catch a glimpse of himself in the window to the left, but all he could see were the snowcapped mountains that were just outside his touch. The mountains were craggy, granite beasts like rock trolls from worlds past who had collapsed in battle and broke apart under the weight of the sky.

A profound sadness filled him, but he didn't know if it was because he felt like one of those trolls himself or if it was just the melancholic grayness of the frozen world. Or maybe what was bothering him was that in his pain, he was alone.

There was the patter of footsteps and he looked in the direction of the sound. Natalie poked her head into the room. "You decent?" She sent him a dazzling smile.

"If you mean dressed, yes." He ran his hand over the leg of his black pants, not caring about the bloody mark it would leave behind.

She walked in carrying the blue-and-white cups that seemed to be in every medical facility in every part of the globe. For a brief moment he wondered why that was. Maybe they were a requirement to be certified for treatment. Or maybe they came free with every order of medical supplies. *Here are your ten boxes of nitrile gloves, and with it one thousand crappy cups. Free!* His thoughts came in a voice reserved for late-night infomercial actors. It made him chuckle.

Maybe the blow to the head had caused more damage than he had initially realized.

She handed him a cup of coffee. It was swirling with cream, and his heart warmed ever so slightly. "You look like I would expect after you took a lamp to the head," she said, grimacing as she stepped closer and looked over his forehead. "I told them to leave the gash alone. They wanted to stitch it up, but stitches leave scars and I didn't know if you were the kind of guy who would be averse to such a thing."

"You think I care about my looks?"

She reached over and gave his beard a little tug. "I don't think that you are indifferent, Grizzly Adams."

"Oh, popping out the old-school movie references today, I see." He touched her hand as she drew away from his beard. "I like it."

It struck him that in this moment, it wasn't the things that were being spoken aloud that were being said. Rather, the real conversation was happening in the ways her eyes looked pained when she gazed at his wound and the tenderness with which her fingers had touched his hair.

She didn't love him, he didn't see that in her, but he could see an affinity.

Here he had been thinking he was all alone, when in fact, he had a friend who was only a few footsteps away and waiting to touch him just like that. She didn't have to love him; that was fine. But he was certainly beginning to have an affinity for her, as well.

As long as they were working together, he would be more than happy to communicate in this unspoken language of touches and looks. If a kiss happened again, he would suffer through it, as well. He smirked. Yes, the only word for kissing her was *suffering*; for to kiss her would be to open his heart, and to open his heart was to open himself up for the pain that came with love. And to love, that was the worst kind of pain of all.

Here was hoping she could keep her emotions in check when she was around him and keep them to only a low-grade crush. She probably had the emotional fortitude of a saint. At least, he'd wish.

He took a sip of the coffee and though she had tried to fix it up for him, it still carried the ashy flavor of cheap grounds. This place really had been a hospital in the last century, and apparently, the coffee was from those days, too.

But he wasn't about to complain; it was still better than the coppery flavor of blood that had settled into the cracks of his lips. He let the cream soak into his tongue.

"Your phone has been buzzing nonstop," she said, handing it over to him. "I haven't looked at anything, but I think you have a lot of people who want to know you are okay. Don't worry. I got in touch with the FBI and let them know what was happening."

"My team here, too? Did anyone else get hurt?" he asked, looking behind her like they were about to walk in, as well. He clicked on the screen. Natalie was right: twenty missed calls and thirty-six text messages were waiting for him. He clicked off the screen. He'd focus on them when he could muster more brainpower.

She shook her head. "Everyone else walked away unscathed. They are still on the farm. Your brother felt terrible about what happened. He hasn't stopped apologizing and I bet that at least half of the messages on your phone are from him." She gave him a slight smile.

"He should feel bad. Did a lamp actually fall on my head? Is that what hit me?" he asked. "And by the way, thanks for no stitches. I will take some skin glue, though."

She reached into her pocket and drew out a brown antique-looking bottle. She opened it, and with it came the scent of pain. He lost count of the number of times he used that particular crap on his skin. Would he ever get used to that sensation, the burning and ache of the antiseptic glue as it touched the newest scar on his soul?

"Here, I've got it for you," she said. "It's going to hurt."

All that he knew. As a brush touched his forehead he tried not to grimace.

"You're taking this like a champ." She brushed on a second coat of the glue as she pressed the edges of the wound together. The pinching almost hurt worse than the glue.

"What can I say? I'm a tough guy," he said, a touch of ego flecking his voice.

She chuckled, but he could tell she was trying to bite it back.

"Trying to work here," she said.

"Thanks for doing this. I appreciate you not letting the vet do the heavy lifting here."

She nodded. "Your brother wasn't sure how bad your injuries were, so they did run a series of X-rays on you. Wanted to make sure there was no major internal bleeding. From everything they could find, it seemed like the only injury was to your head. So no major damage." She laughed.

"Oh, I see how it is. As long as my body is okay and ready to function, you're not worried about me," he teased. "I should've known you only liked me for my body and not my brain."

"I said no such thing," she said, smiling wide. "But yeah, I admit it. I'm only after you for your body." She let go of his forehead and he could feel the pull of the dried glue. She slapped his arm as she turned away and slipped the skin glue back into her pocket. "Actually, I was worried about your brain. But until you were awake, there wasn't a whole lot we could do here. There was talk about sending you back to Missoula for more testing, but given the circumstances, I didn't think that was the best idea."

And just like that, he was back to reality. He needed to get back to work. He was the one who was supposed to be protecting her, and yet, she was the one gluing him up and standing over him in his time of need. This was not how it was supposed to go.

"Is your mom okay? Did my team get her out?"

She nodded. "They didn't tell me where they were taking her, but I think it was better that way. If my enemies can't get their hands on me, I don't think that they would go after her, but I don't want to take the risk." She sighed. "My mom's already been through so much and this is all very stressful for her."

"I'm so sorry this happened. I thought I'd cleared our escape of any tails, but it's pretty hard to shrug anybody off in Montana when there's only one main interstate. They must've had people spread out on a few exits and used a team to follow us. It's what I would've done if I was in their shoes. From our perspective, everything would look all right. I put your mom in danger." He realized he was explaining this mostly for his benefit. Maybe it was his attempt to assuage some of the guilt he was feeling over bringing her enemies directly to her most sacred location.

She shrugged. "My mom has always been a fighter. She would be happy to take up arms against whoever is doing this—she already told me. She's a tough cookie, but she's the only family I have left and I don't want to put her in danger. So I'm glad you called in your people."

He nodded, only wishing he had gone to them sooner. "What about you? Are you doing all right?" He looked at her.

"I'd be lying if I said I was fine, but I know we will get through this."

His phone buzzed in his hand and he looked at the screen. A.J. was calling.

"Answer him," she said. "I know he's worried and I haven't had a chance to call him and let him know that you're awake."

He nodded, clicking on the call. "Hello?"

"Holy balls, it's alive!" A.J. sounded positively enthusiastic. "Dude, of all the ways I thought you would go out, a lamp to the head—unless wielded by a woman—was the last thing I thought would happen."

"Wielded by a woman? No, man, that's something that would happen to you."

A.J. laughed. "Well, I'm glad you're feeling better. Asshat. You had us all real worried for you."

"You know, you wouldn't have had to be worried about me if you would have all just handled the explosives with slightly more care. What the hell were you doing, playing football with the car bomb?"

A.J. laughed, but this time the sound was more clipped, anxious and guilty, no doubt. "Hey, you should be thanking me. At least I pulled it off your truck before it detonated."

"I'm surprised. You've been after me to get a truck for a long time. If you blew it up, it would have forced my hand to buy a new one." He laughed. "Was anyone else hurt?"

"You were the only one whose blood was spilled. Truth be told, we think that it may have been on some kind of timer. It was sitting over by the firewood when it went off."

"Good to know that at least our bomber wasn't sitting up in some tree. I was worried it was a remote detonator."

"Thankfully, it wasn't, or who knows how many of us would have gotten hurt. We got lucky, man." A.J.

paused, like he was letting the words soak in, though he hardly needed to. "Speaking of getting lucky, we also managed to pull a bit more information about the bomb's materials while we were waiting for you, Sleeping Beauty, to wake up."

"I'll Sleeping Beauty you square in the ass if you don't watch yourself," he grumbled.

A.J. scoffed. "Oh, big talk for a dude who got knocked out cold by a lampshade."

"You are asking for an ass kicking."

"Please just change out of whatever little hospital gown they got you all wrapped up in. I don't want you coming after me with your ass hanging out any more than it already is."

He laughed at the mental image. "Ass."

"Jerk."

Goodness, he loved having brothers sometimes. No, make that all *the time.*

"So you got lucky?" Evan asked.

"Yeah, according to the analyst who ran the chemicals, the compound that was used as the bomb's catalyst was a specific kind of rodent bait. It's only sold at three locations in this state and all of them are for industrial uses only. As such, most are sold in bulk and only to professional organizations and industries. Zoey ran through their sales records for the last year. I'll email you what she found. Maybe you can make sense of it."

"Great. And did you get any leads on the pen? The sarin?"

A.J. sighed. "Nothing there, but that is a chemical that can't be easily made. I'm thinking you got a chemist on your hands—or somebody pretty well trained in chemicals."

"Huh. Damn." He sighed. "Thanks, bro."

"Let me know what you come up with, if anything. Later." A.J. hung up.

A few seconds later his phone pinged with an email of the findings. He opened it up. He scanned down the list of buyers. Many were exterminators and large corporations, but near the middle he found a name that popped. Rencher, and she was listing a textile company in Missoula as the business. A company that worked with a variety of chemicals—and Rencher, working there, must have been well versed in what they could be used for.

But before he could jump to conclusions, he had to make sure of a few things. "Where does Rencher work?" he asked, looking to Natalie.

She shrugged. "All I know was that she owned a textile company in the city. It was one of the main sources of contention in her divorce with Sanders, aside from her kids."

He pushed his legs over the side of the bed. His head was still swimming, but he felt slightly better. Even if he wasn't, there was no sense in staying put. They needed to question their lead suspect.

Chapter Nine

There was no way she was going to let him drive and, though he seemed to understand, he'd been sulking ever since. He had done nothing but stare blankly out the window since they left. Actually, he'd been acting off ever since they'd kissed.

That had been stupid.

It was always a mistake to take any relationship past the point of respectful acquaintances. Beyond that, and she opened herself up to all the reciprocal allowances and allocations required in relationships. It was best to keep the circle small when it came to friends and lovers.

But there was no putting that cat back in the bag. She had given up the truth, that she was attracted to him and wanted him for more than just the protection he provided.

They sat in silence until they were entering the canyon that opened up into the valley and the city at its heart. His eyes darkened as they approached the traffic.

"I hope you don't really mind that I'm driving. If you do, then I think we may need to renegotiate the nature of our relationship. I don't want a man in my life who is going to be upset when a woman takes the lead." She tried to check herself before she snarled. Even as she spoke, though, she realized that she wasn't really mad at him or mad at all. If anything, she could feel herself grasping at anything that could be used to push him away.

"Huh? What?" He gave her the most confused dude look ever. "What are you talking about? You think I'm mad I'm not driving?"

She huffed. "You've been pouting ever since you got in the car."

He frowned. "One, I'm not pouting. Two, I wouldn't want to drive—you had to help me to the truck. We should definitely not let the dude with a probable concussion drive."

"Then what is wrong with you? Why aren't you talking to me?"

He looked at her and sent her a gentle smile, then reached over and opened his hand and motioned for her to take it. "Natalie."

She stared at his fingers for a long moment. It would feel so good to touch him again, to feel the strength of his fingers against the back of her hand. But was that the smartest thing? She was doing well, or at least she had *thought* she was doing well, in pushing him away.

Reaching over, she took hold of his hand and he wrapped her hand in his. "I didn't even realize I was being quiet. I'm sorry." He lifted her hand and pressed the back of it against his cheek. He was so warm, almost abnormally hot. Why did men always run warmer than women?

"What were you thinking about?" she asked.

He put their entwined hands back down on the console between them. "To be honest, I was thinking how annoying it is to be in an area where my internet doesn't work. It would be nice to be a little more prepared walking into our interrogation."

She nodded. "Do you even think she will be somewhere we can find her?"

He shrugged. "Whoever planted the bomb didn't stick around, at least so far as we could tell. It was more of a drop and trot kind of thing. If she's smart, she will be at work. It would give her a credible alibi."

At least it would be an alibi for today and this morning. But it wasn't that far of a drive to and from the farm and she could have easily made it back and forth in time to get to work.

"Did you look into her phone records yet?"

He shook his head. "My team is supposed to be doing it, but again, no network." He lifted his phone from where he'd had it perched on his thigh.

They drove out of the canyon and the city was abuzz with midday traffic. The on-ramps were backed up and she pulled behind the long line of cars just as Evan's phone beeped.

"Yes! And we are back online." He tapped away on his device. He rattled off the textile company's address and something about what they did—laundry for local businesses and a few other things—but she was only paying half attention as she drove. "Anyhow," he continued, "it looks like—according to the cell phone tower records—her phone has been in the valley all week and she hasn't gotten any phone calls aside from political spammers in the past sixteen hours."

"That doesn't mean she didn't leave the city limits. It just means she was smart enough to leave her phone at home." It was always the most prolific criminals who knew how to avoid being detected and thus, from being prosecuted.

There was nothing like looking down from the bench, knowing in her gut that the person in front of her was guilty of not only the crimes they were arrested for but also likely a medley of others, and not being able to do a damned thing about it. Instead of saying, "You are free to go," she often wanted to scream.

"As this is our primary suspect, I don't think it's a good idea that you go inside. She may respond better if I questioned her alone."

Natalie bristled. He wasn't wrong, but she didn't want to be left out of the action. "You know, if she is the person we're after, she is going to know exactly who I am, and I'm sure she will make her feelings known. And, if she doesn't recognize me, well…that can be a helpful sign, too."

He sighed. "I should have known you would balk at the idea of not being involved." He gave her hand a reassuring squeeze. "I get it, though. I would be the same way if someone was trying to kill me. Plus, I think it's best if we stick close to one another until we have our suspect in custody."

And there she had been thinking she was going to have to make a stronger argument for not being left in the truck.

"Agreed." She pulled the vehicle to a stop just across the street from the downtown headquarters for the textile company.

The company's front bay doors opened and a large white delivery van made its way out on to the main road. The place was busy as men and women, workers mostly, came and went from the main entrance.

As she watched, she realized she didn't even know the face of the woman they were going to go and talk to. It was dumbfounding. How could this woman want to kill her when she herself didn't even know her face from a million others?

She understood hate; she had felt it countless times just in the past year. And she had long ago realized she could empathize to the best of her abilities and sometimes still not understand what drove a person to do the things they did. In fact, the more time she spent around the public, the less she understood about human nature. There were core needs that never wavered, but how people acquired, kept and maintained those needs were all up for grabs.

"I would say that it may be best for me to lead the questioning when we get in there, but you are pretty unique. You may have more practice in eliciting information than myself. So I guess we will play it by ear. Okay?"

She gave a stiff nod. "And what if this comes to nothing?"

He shrugged. "We will cross that bridge when we get there. Let's just hope that this is our perpetrator and we can get you back to your normal life as quickly and safely as possible."

Did that mean he wanted her gone? No doubt it would be easier for him without her in his life. He could go back to whatever his normal life looked like—a life she had no idea about. The realization made her ache. She couldn't make him open up to her any more than he naturally did, but that didn't mean she didn't want him to.

He gave the back of her hand a quick kiss before letting go and getting out of the truck. He walked around to her side and opened the door for her. The simple act of chivalry surprised her in all the right ways. It had been a long time since a man had gone out of his way to do anything for her, unless it was in the courtroom—where everyone was always trying to buy her favor.

He helped her out. His walk was steady; he must have been feeling better. She wanted to ask him if he was feeling okay and if he was really up for doing this, but even if he wasn't, she was positive he would lie to her in order to get the job done…and get her out of his life, maybe.

Then again, he had been so kind to her and held her hand.

He opened the door for her and followed her inside; meanwhile, she reminded herself that just because a man was kind didn't mean that he was flirting with her.

The man at the front counter looked up from his phone and barely masked his disgust at having been disturbed. "Help ya?" he asked, his words truncated, like it took too much effort to say a complete sentence.

She disliked him already.

"We are here to see Ms. Rencher or Ms. Sanders, if one of them is available." As Evan spoke, the man smirked like he knew a secret they weren't privy to…a secret he was dying to tell.

"Ms. Rencher is in the back. She doesn't like being disturbed these days." The man looked back and forth between them, seeming to hint at the divorce to see what they knew.

She made sure to keep her expression as neutral as possible. This young, disgruntled man couldn't know she was one step from running away, that a lump had formed in her throat that threatened to strangle her from the inside out, or that the last thing she wanted to do was look her potential murderer right in the eyes.

She could only imagine how it would feel to see such unbridled hate directed solely at her. What if the woman was carrying a gun? She could draw and fire before Natalie even knew she was under threat. Sure, they were in public, but that likely wouldn't stop this killer.

Her hands started to sweat.

Until now she hadn't thought about the feelings that were enveloping her and threatening to unleash a panic attack.

At least she wasn't facing this alone. Or, worse, having to sit idly by while others handled the entire situation. At least by taking an active role in bringing down her assailant, she held control over her own welfare.

The man picked up the phone, said a few quick words and turned back to them. "She said she'll be right out. Good luck."

Her heart raced, and she tried to take back control of herself by counting her breaths. One. Two. Three.

The door leading to the back opened, and a brunette woman stepped into the lobby. Her hair was loose, cascading down her shoulders, and she was far younger than Natalie had assumed she would be. If she had to guess, she was somewhere in her midthirties. When the woman saw her, she sent her a big smile.

Was it fake? Was she pretending she didn't know her?

"Hi, how can I help you guys?" Ms. Rencher asked, her voice high and chipper.

The man who had greeted them in the lobby had warned that she was not one to be trifled with, and yet, this woman was nothing like she had expected. It had to be a show.

"If you wouldn't mind excusing us," Evan said to the other man, who was now standing and watching them with a bemused look on his face.

The man dipped his head in acknowledgment before making his way out. She couldn't help but notice that he looked over his shoulder one more time before letting the door slip closed with a click.

The woman frowned. "What is going on here?"

Evan smiled, but even someone who didn't know him would have known that the action was false. "We are here thanks to an investigation in a case of attempted murder." He paused.

The woman cocked her head to the side, looking confused. "I don't know how I could possibly be able to assist you with anything to do with murder."

The woman's gaze never moved to Natalie as she'd have assumed it would have, had Rencher known what Evan was actually talking about. It was strange how the body would give away so many clues, if a person just knew how to watch for them. And Natalie desperately wanted to see something that would prove this woman was responsible for what had happened to her, but right now she wasn't sure if she was actually the person they were looking for.

"I'm certain that is probably the case," Evan said. "However, we just need to make sure we cover all of our bases and talk to anybody that would potentially know anything about the case we're trying to solve."

"Did my ex send you here?" Ms. Rencher's lips puckered and her expression soured. "If she did, you need to know that she is just a vindictive brat. There is nothing she wouldn't do just to screw with me. I can't believe it. And people wonder why I hate her. It's not that I want to hate her. It's just that she keeps doing this kind of crap." She let out a long, tired sigh.

Evan slipped Natalie a look, like he was beginning to think perhaps this woman wasn't who they were after.

"Can you tell us a little bit more about your relationship with your ex?" Natalie asked.

The woman crossed her arms over her chest like she was protecting her core. "We are going through a pretty nasty divorce. Things are getting really heated. And we share a daughter. She is contesting the parenting plan and pretty much everything else. It wouldn't surprise me if she did something like this, and somehow got me involved in a legal battle with potential felonies in order to take away my daughter."

The way she spoke made Natalie wonder exactly what had befallen the woman before they had arrived. Though she had looked through some of her case file, there had been no reference to any crimes beyond the so-called knife fight. Was it possible that the other woman, Ms. Sanders, was responsible for the attacks and was trying to pin it on her ex?

"Do you mind telling me where you were last night?" Evan asked.

The woman shrugged, seemingly unconcerned. "I was here until midnight or so, then I went home."

"Is there anyone who can vouch for your whereabouts for the past twenty-four hours?" Evan asked.

"There was no one here when I left last night, but there are cameras everywhere. And you can definitely take a peek if you'd like. And there's also the camera on my front porch that would show me coming and going last night and this morning."

Evan nodded. He reached into his pocket and withdrew a business card. He handed it over to her. After taking it, she slipped it into her back pocket.

"If you wouldn't mind sending me a digital copy of those videos, I'd appreciate it." Evan smiled. "And hey, if you hear anything that you think would be helpful, don't be afraid to call."

"I just have one more question," Natalie said, interrupting. "Have you ordered any rodent killer for the business lately?"

The woman pursed her lips, thinking. "We don't have a rodent problem here, so long as I know about. And I definitely haven't ordered anything to mitigate it. Why?"

"Would your ex have access to any of your ordering or business affairs?" Evan asked.

"Unfortunately, yes. I have been trying to remove her from my business accounts, but it is impossible until the final divorce decree is granted. For now she is on most things—even my car insurance," Ms. Rencher said.

"I know just how hard going through a divorce can be," Evan said, ever the kind man she had come to know. "I'm so sorry you are going through this."

The woman looked down at her hands and she could tell that she was struggling in her attempt not to cry.

"I just don't understand why it has to be so hard. What's worse is that we still really do love each other."

Love and hate were sometimes only millimeters apart, and damn if this wasn't one of those times. The poor woman.

"I know this is hard, but we really do appreciate your

help." Evan took his phone out of his pocket and pulled up the information his team had sent. "Here is a copy of the rodent killer company's orders for the past few months. Do any of them look familiar?" He pointed at the screen.

The woman squinted like she was having a hard time seeing the type, even though she was relatively young. Oh, had she actually thought *relatively*? Natalie grimaced. The woman was maybe a few years older than she was. Though Natalie felt like a grown adult, big job and all, she wasn't ready to check the box for middle-aged. Not yet anyway.

"Yeah, I didn't make an order, but I can see how you would assume I had. If you like, I'd be happy to show you around the entire facility so you can see that there's nothing like that currently in our possession." The woman seemed genuinely open to their searching the building.

Yeah, this wasn't their person. However, she had a sinking feeling that somehow, she was connected.

The woman squinted harder, pulling the phone closer. "I have to say, though, this guy here, VanBuren, I'm surprised he would make this kind of order." The woman tapped on the screen.

"Why is that?" Evan asked.

"VanBuren is the training officer for the city fire department. He seems like the last person who would order something from this kind of company. He doesn't do any kind of maintenance work for the city, so I can't see why he would need rodent killer." The woman frowned.

The knot in Natalie's stomach tightened. It was odd that a firefighter would need something like this. That was, unless they were going to use it for some kind of training—or he had some kind of vendetta against the district court judges. A city employee, one who worked around criminals and arsonists, could probably name at least one time when they didn't agree with something a judge did. Or maybe the training officer just didn't like them on principle.

Until now the training officer hadn't even crossed their suspects list. However, he did have the knowledge and the access to the chemicals it would have taken to perpetrate the attacks—he may have even had the access to their chambers and to police scanners and informational systems. He could totally be their guy, or not.

If nothing else, they would need to talk to the training officer. Even if he wasn't their perpetrator, he would likely have a wealth of information about who would have access to the knowledge to create the devices that they had found.

Sometimes, in moments like these, where they stumbled onto names and ideas, she was reminded that it was better to be lucky than it was to be good.

Chapter Ten

He was sure that if they went over to Ms. Sanders's that they would run into the same nonanswers that they got from Ms. Rencher. Handling questioning was not one of his favorite exercises. Elicitation had always been Mike's stronger suit. His brother could get answers from just about anyone about anything and his ability to read people was on point. As hard as Evan tried, he had not come by those skills naturally.

Maybe he should call him and have him step in on this investigation. The last he had heard, Troy and Mike were taking turns sitting with Judge Hanes in the ICU.

Thinking about the judge, he took out his cell phone when he got to the truck and typed out a text message to Elle, asking about the judge's status. A few seconds later his phone pinged. Apparently, Judge Hanes was still unconscious, but the doctors were saying he would likely survive.

He asked if they had found evidence of sarin gas.

The lab tests had been inconclusive.

Such a thing wasn't a huge surprise. In the middle of Montana the last thing the doctors would be looking for would be chemical nerve agents. But not knowing what had poisoned Hanes meant lots of dead ends awaited them.

"You okay?" Natalie asked.

He nodded, slipping his phone into his pocket. "Yeah, I'm good. Your friend, the judge, is still alive."

She sucked in a long breath and her hands balled into tight fists.

"I don't have much more information than that. But at least it's something. I'm so sorry, Natalie."

"You've nothing to apologize for. If it wasn't for you, he wouldn't even be alive right now. As it was, he was lucky." Her eyes softened as she looked at him.

"Do you want to see him?" he asked.

She shook her head. "I wouldn't want him to see me like that, so I can't imagine he would want me to see him in that state, either."

He didn't bother to argue. When a powerhouse was taken out at their knees, they often didn't wish to be seen. The judge likely had enough people coming and going that he wasn't alone.

"The best thing we can do for him," Natalie said, "is to find whoever did this."

He nodded.

"Are you still thinking that whoever poisoned him is likely the same person that planted these bombs? I'm having such a hard time believing that one person could be behind all of this. Poisoning and bombing are so different."

"Are they? If someone is good with chemicals, it really isn't that big of a leap." Evan watched as she started the truck. "Now, we can't be one hundred percent sure this is the same perpetrator, but given the proximity of the events and their rapid succession, if it wasn't the same person, it was at least the same team."

"Do you think it could be one of the divorcées?"

"I think they have a thin motive, but right now they are definitely still on our list. However, I'm not about to stop looking into our other leads."

"I agree. Let's keep this simple." She chuckled. "Let's just keep checking things off and working down our list. Next up, I think we need to hit up the ex, Ms. Sanders."

He nodded, glad to be working instead of stuck in the heaviness of confusing feelings that had been resting between them.

"Also, about what happened at Judy's..." she started, stripping away any relaxation he was feeling.

"We don't have to talk about that. Let's just call it a lapse in judgment," he said, though he could sense the falseness of his words square in his chest.

From the tired look on her face, she could hear it, as well. "No. We are both adults. We don't get to just sweep what happened under the rug. That's not how it works."

In his experience, that was exactly how it had worked. Then, his previous relationships had been with a different caliber of women. He wasn't used to a woman who pushed for more. If anything, he seemed to attract a certain type of woman, the kind who was looking for danger, a one-night stand that they could tell their friends about, but then never have to worry about calling him again.

He wasn't the kind of man women went to in order to pour their emotions or feelings out, and they certainly didn't expect it of him. The few who had attempted to have a real relationship with him, even his ex-wife, always ended up resenting him for his lack of emotional depth—a problem he really wasn't having with Natalie, which was what confused him the most.

There was something wrong with him; he was aware. Until meeting Natalie, he thought he wasn't like most people in the sense that he didn't want to talk about what he was feeling. He'd never wanted to delve into the deep emotions that came with the relationship or even a real friendship. It was hard enough working with his family. The only thing that kept them strong was the fact that they all had a similar mentality of live and let live.

"So…" she started. "Do you want to treat it like it was a lapse in judgment? Or should we be completely honest with one another? Truth be told, I think you are as lonely as I am."

He was shocked by her candor. He wanted to have some romantic, sweet comeback, but he didn't know what to say. Yes, he was lonely, but that wasn't his driving force for falling for her. But more than anything, he wasn't used to a woman being so open about this kind of thing. It was shockingly refreshing.

He opened his mouth and closed it a few times, hoping that the right words would just come to him. They didn't.

"I'm going to take that as a no." She rounded a corner with the truck. "I know a woman doesn't normally admit that, but I'm not going to play games. And I'm not looking for a one-and-done kind of thing. If I only wanted sex, I would go get sex. It's not hard for a woman to find a lover. That's not what I want. And I know that with everything happening, and with my life hanging in the balance, it isn't the right time for you and me. I do. We need to be focused. But I can't help the way I feel about you. I want more."

To say he was overwhelmed by her openness was an understatement. In many ways, in fact, in all the ways, she was exactly the woman he wanted in his life. But— there was always a but—it *was* the wrong time.

"Do you believe in destiny?" As he asked, he felt ridiculous. "I don't mean like stars in the astrology woo-woo way. I just mean do you think that we are put in place where we are meant to be at certain times?"

As she drove, she nibbled the side of her cheek. "The girl in me says yes, but the judge in me... Well, I just can't say I agree. So many things happen to good people, just because they're in the wrong place at the wrong time. And then they find themselves in front of me. Half the people don't deserve it, or at least they don't seem like they deserve to have been beaten down by life in the ways that they are. If there's something pulling the strings, or call it destiny, or whatever, it's a fickle beast. It's easier to just believe that the world is a random conglomeration of chaos. Sometimes things work out, and sometimes they don't."

"Nihilism from a judge. I should've expected." He sent her his best half grin. "Regardless, I agree with you. It's hard to know exactly what life is really about. However, when it comes to relationships and love, I think that if they're meant to be, they should come to you easily." He shrugged, knowing that what he said was not quite exactly what he meant, but he just couldn't find the right words. Eloquence and discussing emotional matters, well, they weren't his strong suit.

"You think love is easy? That relationships are?" She scoffed. "I thought you said you had been divorced. Regardless, I'd venture to guess that you haven't had many serious relationships. For me, relationships and love are the hardest things not only to find, but also to keep."

Though her words could have been embittered, they weren't. Rather, they sat flat in the air, a simple statement of how he and Natalie differed.

"I suppose you're not wrong. And yeah, I'm not much of a relationship guy. In my line of work, one thing does not lead to the other."

"What do you mean by that?" she asked.

"I just mean that relationships don't lead to happy endings. And working in military contracting doesn't often lead to love—"

"It only leads to death," she interrupted.

At first, her response made him indignant, but then he realized he couldn't really argue. She was right. More, his work led to resentment and hate. And once a person hated something with every fiber of their being, it was hard to even believe that love existed.

Yet, as he looked at her, he couldn't deny love's existence. He would give up his life for her. He would give up everything for her. But he would never ask the same of her; she was far too good for him. If she gave him her heart, it would only break her.

He would be left to live with the weight of the ghost of her love for the rest of his life. Each day he would have to look himself in the mirror and know that he had done a major disservice to a wonderful woman. It was better to call it off now. To stop her from getting any more feelings. If anything, it was the merciful thing to do. It was wrong to make her suffer because of his failings.

"Turn left up here," he said, leading them toward

Ms. Sanders's house, according to his records. If she really lived there or didn't, well, they would find out. More than likely, even if she did reside there, she wasn't going to be home in the middle of the day. He should have asked Ms. Rencher more questions.

Though Ms. Rencher had been forthcoming with information, he had learned long ago that the right answers weren't always the most truthful ones.

Natalie followed his directions and the midday sun was high overhead when they finally arrived at a large colonial-style house. Although the paint on its black shutters and white siding had started to crack and peel, it was still beautiful.

After pulling into the driveway, she stopped the truck and they got out. "What if we are too late?" Natalie asked.

"I don't think you can ever be on time when it comes to this type of thing. Chaos, remember?" He sent her a rakish smile.

She laughed, the bright sound breaking through the odd silence that seemed to surround the house and ooze into the neighborhood. She clamped her hands over her mouth, as if she knew how out of place her mirth was.

"Let's just see what we can make of this. What shall be, shall be," he continued.

She reached toward him like she wanted to take his hand, as if they were ascending the walk that led to a weekend dinner party instead of an interrogation. He chuckled as he realized that the difference between the two events was minimal; both were terribly uncomfortable and filled with awkward, deafening silences.

Come to think of it, he preferred interrogation.

Yep, he was definitely some kind of broken.

He knocked on the door, looking around for cameras and surveillance equipment, but finding none. If this was their lead suspect, he had a sinking feeling that they were chasing a dead lead.

He could hear a series of footsteps approaching the door and the slide and click as someone opened a peephole and must have looked out at them. Instead of the door swinging open as he would have expected, the person on the other side stood still as if they were all playing some kind of game of chicken—who would be the first to admit that they all knew what was truly happening?

He was more than happy to take the loss. "Will you please open the door?" He used his deepest baritone, the one he reserved only for moments when he meant business—he called it his "cop voice."

A woman cleared her throat. If he had to guess, she was smoothing herself and trying to shake off any anxiety she was feeling. She'd probably answer the door with a plastic smile.

The door cracked open and a raven-haired woman with deep-set eyes looked out at them. She smiled, but the action was limited to her lips alone. "I'm sorry, I'm not interested." She moved to close the door again, but he pushed his foot into the jamb, blocking her.

"Ma'am, we are here looking for Ms. Sanders. Is she home?" Natalie asked, sounding abnormally breezy and alight with joy.

What were they doing here, playing good cop-bad cop?

He checked himself before he smirked. At least this was better than chicken.

The woman frowned. "She doesn't live here. Actually, she rented this place to me for the next year. She's me and my boyfriend's landlord."

He felt himself relax. "Do you know where we could find her?"

She let the door swing farther open and she turned around like she was going to get something. "Hold on. Let me just see what I have as far as her address. I just send her a check once a month. In fact, we've only lived here about two months." The woman waved behind her like what she was saying was of no consequence.

And maybe to her it wasn't, but to them it could mean a great deal.

"Where you from?" Evan asked.

"Small town on the east side of the state. I just moved over here to be closer to my boyfriend. He needed my help with a few things. Plus, my sister is here in town. Family, ya know?"

Evan nodded. That was nice, but it was a big step for a woman to move for a man. She must have really loved the guy.

"To be honest, I'm not even sure that she's getting these checks," the woman continued. "She hasn't cashed last month's and I sent it two weeks ago." The woman walked back, carrying her cell phone. "I called her to make sure she had received it. I'm a huge fan of direct deposit, but she didn't want to set things up that way. When I called her about the check, she didn't answer. She hasn't gotten back to me."

"Is that normal for her, to be unresponsive?" Natalie asked.

The door opened fully as the woman leaned against the doorjamb and skimmed through her phone. "Like I said, we haven't known each other that long, so I don't really know if that's normal for her. But when I called about renting the place, I got a return call within twenty-four hours. And I was in by the end of the week. She is going through a divorce and it's not going particularly well. I don't know all the details, and I don't press."

He wouldn't press anyone for divorce details, either; to do so was to open a whole floodgate of things he didn't want to talk about. That was one part of life he never wanted to revisit, and if he could have bottled it up and thrown it all away, he would've.

"Here it is," the woman said, lifting her phone so she could show them the contact card for Sophia Sanders. He took a quick photo of it and stuffed his phone back into his pocket.

"Thank you. That will be very helpful. He reached in his chest pocket and pulled out a business card and handed it to the woman. If you hear from Ms. Sanders or you manage to make contact with her in any way, would you please give me a call?" His business card had nothing but his name and phone number, no identifying details. It was so much easier that way.

The lady looked him up and down, staring at the cut on his head for a long moment before letting her gaze move lower and rest on his official-looking suit. "You mind me asking what this is all about?"

Once again, he almost found himself laughing. The regular public could give up so much information about their life without even realizing it. It struck him right now how easy it would be to be a criminal. All a person had to do was appear normal and they could get all the information they needed from a trusting person. He wished he could be as obliviously happy and like the general public instead of always looking around the corner for the next possible threat.

"We're just here with her book group." Natalie smiled, and he was impressed with how quickly she had come up with a lie. "We've just been worried about her. She hasn't been attending any of our meetings lately."

"Oh, okay." The woman nodded, seeming to buy in to the explanation. "I'm a little surprised, though. She didn't seem like the bookworm type of person."

Natalie's smile widened. "Our doors are open to anyone who is seeking guidance through great literature."

Evan took hold of Natalie's hand. "If you're ever interested," he said, tipping his head in the direction of the business card in the woman's grip, "you know where to find us. Have a good day now."

"You, as well," the woman said. "I'll give you a call, if need requires."

With a backward wave, they retreated. As soon as they reached the car and got inside, he sighed. "You know, Natalie, you wouldn't make a bad spy."

Chapter Eleven

Natalie was starving. After grabbing a cup of coffee and a muffin to go, they found themselves back on the road. Moving as much as they did, and concentrating on the investigation, she found that she wasn't looking over her shoulder quite as much as she had been when they had been sitting still. People may have been following them, but at least they weren't going to give them enough time to plant another bomb. If they wanted her dead, they would have to physically pull the trigger.

The thought reminded her that maybe she wasn't the most normal person after all. Few people had a preferred method to go in case they were murdered. Given the circumstances, this was the best way she could think of to deal with the pressures around her. She could bury her head in the sand and pretend like her life was filled with roses, but that was so far from the truth. It was better to face things head-on, face the reality presented to her, and deal with it. She'd never be passive.

Perhaps her strength lay in that inability to address life in a laissez-faire fashion. It was remarkably hard to swallow the bitter morsels life shoved down a person's throat; many would've closed their mouths and clenched their jaws tight, then hid away from reality. But not her.

"You feeling better?" She looked at Evan and the puckered, glued gash over his eye. The edges had taken on a dark red color, and a bruise had settled in.

"Huh?" he asked, clearly not following her train of thought. "I'm fine, why?"

"I'm talking about your head. How are you feeling?"

He ran his fingers over the lump on his forehead, stopping at a point that must have been sensitive. "Oh, yeah. I forgot about it. I guess that's a good sign."

"I don't know," she teased. "I think if you start forgetting things, that's actually a bad sign." She smiled.

"I don't know about that. Always found when I start forgetting things, I start feeling better. Maybe it's a bad sign, but it makes for an easier life."

She mulled over his statement. It sat in the air between them for a long moment. She couldn't argue with him. He did have a point. If only she could forget more of the things that happened to her. And once they were through this, she looked forward to being somewhere in the future where she would be able to put this behind her, as well. She'd be fine if it was left to the recesses of her mind, only popping up on occasion, and just as quickly shoved back.

Except that would also mean she would forget about him. That, she didn't want. He had made it clear he wasn't interested in a relationship with her, but he cited time, not the absence of feelings.

If anything, she should've probably been thanking him.

One of them needed to be the reasonable one. They really hadn't known each other that long. And for all she knew he was terribly broken. Men in his line of work typically were. They'd been through so much and seen so much that either they valued love in such an incredible way that they were the greatest of spouses or lovers, or they were the kind that only truly lived for themselves.

From what she could make of it, she assumed it was because they had learned to trust only themselves. And she could understand that. In life and death, people always promised to protect the people they loved and cared about: their spouse, their lovers, their teammates, their children. But when faced with such realities, those people normally ended up standing alone and completely vulnerable. It was better not to have a connection—he would never let anyone down.

"Do I dare ask what that look on your face is about?" he asked.

Of course, he would be reading her right now, when she had thought she had a good poker face, but he had her rethinking that assessment.

For a moment she considered what she should say in response. To tell him the truth would open up a whole line of conversation that she wasn't certain she wanted to have. Especially given how poorly she assumed it would go—if she brought up the fact that she cared for him, and that she had feelings toward him, no doubt he would once again try to push her away.

But clearly, he could read her face. She was at an impasse. And she sat in silence for a moment too long.

"I retract my question," he said.

She laughed. "Thank you, Counselor."

He shook his head in acknowledgment and gave her a big, toothy grin. In the center of his front teeth was a poppy seed from his muffin. It was exactly what she needed to see in him, some kind of flaw and silly thing to remind her how human and beautifully imperfect he was.

"You have something, right here," she said, pointing to the gap in her front teeth.

"Oh, son of a… And there I was, trying to be cool and stuff," he said, pulling down the visor and opening the mirror behind it. He sucked his teeth before flipping out the debris.

And stuff? Did that mean he was trying to be cute? Did he want her to keep being attracted to him? That he was just as much at odds with his feelings as she was?

Ugh. She couldn't go there. Not now.

"Well, why don't you be cool and tell me how to get to Ms. Sanders's place?"

He quirked an eyebrow, as if he was a bit surprised that she wouldn't fall for his boyish charms. Closing the visor, he opened his phone and rattled off the directions. It wasn't too far from where they found themselves, yet, nothing in the city was more than thirty minutes away on good traffic days.

Today wasn't one of those days. She tried not to lose her patience as she stared out at the jammed mess of cars that sat virtually parked on the road in front of them. For a moderately small city, she would never understand why they had the traffic issues they did. Far larger cities, with less available public transit systems, had them by leaps and bounds when it came to safety and transit times.

She ground her teeth, feeling the muscles in her jaw tense.

"Don't worry," he said, giving her that same smile once more. "Again, manageable chaos. That's all we can hope for in all of this."

"I should have mentioned that in my world, I don't thrive on chaos. I like everything well-ordered and scheduled in advance, at least as much as possible." She tapped her fingers on the wheel. "You should see my house. Everything has its place."

"Ah, you're one of those." He sounded blasé.

"Don't be dismissive of my system. It works for me. Has worked for years now." She smiled, trying to pull him back from judging her too harshly for her near-compulsion. "Don't judge."

"I know…that's your job," he joked. "But tell me, how do you keep your towels?"

"Which ones? Hand, kitchen or bath towels?"

He laughed. "The fact you have to ask me that question tells me most of what I need to know about you."

"What is that? That I'm not a dude who uses one towel for all of his needs?" She smirked. "Remind me to never take a shower at your place—I don't want to get pregnant when I go to dry off."

His mouth opened into an o-shape then he started to give a deep belly laugh. "Of all the things I thought you would say, that was the last thing I imagined coming out of your mouth," he said between bouts of laughs. "But I have to admit. I kind of like all the places your mind went right there. Most of all, you thinking about taking a shower at my place."

She wasn't sure that he really meant that; most men would've gone the other direction with where her thoughts had gone.

"By all means, if you want to go to my place and check it out and take a shower or whatever, feel free," he said.

She reached over and gave him a light cuff to the

shoulder. The action was juvenile, and she recognized that, but she couldn't help herself. She didn't know how else to respond.

"Thanks for the warm invitation, but if anybody is staying anywhere between the two of us, you're going my way, not the other way around. If you only have one towel, I hate to think about your sheets situation."

He wiggled his eyebrows and his smile widened. "Yeah, you keep thinking about my sheets."

He was cute. Yet, she wasn't going to fall for any of that kind of nonsense.

She wanted to point out that he had been clear in his plans for a relationship. And she wasn't about to start anything sexual with a man who didn't want a relationship. But what was the harm in a little no-commitment flirting?

"Do you like that?" she asked, sounding coy.

She could see him tense, and his hands moved to his knees like he was trying to ground himself. She loved that she could have that effect on him. There was nothing like leaving a man speechless.

"I wonder if they are made of cotton, satin, or hmm…maybe flannel. I can see you being a flannel sheet kind of guy," she teased.

He let out a slight chuckle. "This time of year, it's flannel all the way. In fact, if I could have them on all year, I would."

"I don't find it hard to believe."

The car in front of her moved a few inches. It wasn't even worth taking her foot off the brake. At least they had stopped to eat something before they got stuck in traffic. He took out his phone and clicked on some buttons, making her wonder if he was just as annoyed with the traffic jam as she was.

"Is this normally how you go about your surveillance?"

He looked over at her and shook his head. "Nothing about the situation has been what I would consider normal. Yet, like Muhammad Ali said, 'we all have a plan, until we get hit in the face.' Seems like no matter what the objective, and the best laid plans by my team, everything goes as it needs to. Rather than the way I would like."

"So this is abnormally normal?" She tried to make herself feel better about what an uproar she had caused in his life.

"Hardly." He paused. "Normally, I'm not the guy they send in to do this kind of surveillance. I'm more of a security guy. The trigger puller, ya know?"

That surprised her, but at the same time it didn't. He didn't seem comfortable in the role that he was playing right now, but she was glad they could be in this together. "Don't take this the wrong way, but if you're not the surveillance guy, then why didn't you ask your team to send in someone else to help?"

He looked at her like he was studying her. "Is that what you want? Someone else besides me working with you?"

His offer gave her pause. She hadn't expected his answer. What would she do without him? Without them working together to chase down their leads? They could go back to her house and she could show him her *towel* collection, but that would be far more uncomfortable than being in the crosshairs of a murderer's sights.

"Would you be more comfortable away from me?"

she asked, silently praying he wouldn't say anything to hurt her.

"Never. Once I take a job, I finish it." He lifted his phone to his ear and motioned that he was making a call. "Hello, Elle?"

She could hear a woman's voice on the other end of the line.

He nodded a couple of times. "Yeah, we're stuck in traffic. I'm going to send you an address. Can you guys look into it for me and see if anyone is currently in the house? Either way, can you please set up a UAV on the target to keep an eye on her?"

Did he and his team really have the kind of resources that with a single phone call drones could be released and put on targets? The thought equally terrified and thrilled her. She had power, but she certainly didn't have weapons on speed dial.

"Yeah," he said. "I'll text you everything you need. No biggie. Great. Thanks." He hung up and glanced over at her. "They will let us know about Ms. Sanders." He texted something.

"Who is Elle?" She hadn't meant to sound jealous. She was merely wondering what role the woman he'd spoken to played in his life, but her tone was all wrong.

Based on the look on his face, he had heard her unintentional slip, as well. "Elle is my sister. My team is a small one from within the larger STEALTH group. We are part of their Shadow Team."

"Your sister?"

"Yes, my entire team is made up of my siblings. There are six of us. Like I said, small team."

"I bet it's great working with your family." She wasn't sure of what else to say.

"Some days are better than others, but all in all I can't complain. I'm a lucky man. I have a job and a team I love. I'm like a big kid most of the time."

"Did you watch a lot of *Rambo* when you were a kid or something? Was that how you got into this?"

"Ha. Yeah, something like that," he said. "Actually, it was the family business. My parents worked in this field, so it was a natural progression. After they died, it was a way for all of us to continue their legacy."

"How did they die?"

"Car accident. Well, we thought it was a car accident, but it looks like we have had people gunning for our family for a while now—Rockwood. We have reason to believe they were somehow involved with my parents' accident. But it's hard to prove. It happened a few years ago. But dollars to donuts, they killed my parents."

"I'm so sorry." She held her breath, like breathing would fill his tragedy with air again if she did.

He merely shrugged. His face hardened, like he hated talking about it as much as she hated what had happened to him and his family, but she was also grateful that he was finally beginning to really open up to her.

"Is that the company whose name was on the bombs' plates?"

"One and the same. They are corrupt and stop at nothing so long as the ends justify the means." He sighed. "Did you hear about the shooting downtown last year? The one with the sniper?"

She nodded. "That was a rough day for me. The courthouse was placed under complete lockdown and I was forced to go into the basement and seek shelter with all the other judges and officials. I had to sit with the district attorney for two solid hours. It was...*fun*."

"I can only imagine." He snorted. "Did you learn anything worthwhile from her?"

She huffed. "I had only just started as a judge. But she said a few things that raised my hackles."

"Anything about Rockwood?" he asked, the question making her wonder what she didn't know about them.

"No. I hadn't even heard mention of them until you."

How did the company have so many enemies? What if she and Judge Hanes hadn't been the real targets? He had to have had those thoughts already, but he hadn't admitted them to her. Was that why he had stuck around? Was he worried that perhaps Rockwood was coming for him and she had just stepped into the crossfire?

No. She reminded herself that they hadn't known the company was even tangentially involved until after the bombs had gone off and they had gotten the results back. Besides, if this company was going after the Spade family, there were a million other ways they could go about it without pulling in judges and teams from the FBI.

If this company was as bad and as ruthless as Evan had alluded to, there was no way they would have done anything that would have drawn scrutiny and investigations from federal organizations. At least not on purpose.

"What did the DA say that bothered you?" he asked, forcing her from her thoughts.

"She seemed to have some kind of sense that because we were both women in a predominantly male field, that we would have some kind of quid-pro-quo deal. I had to set her straight."

"Had you met her before?" he asked.

"Not at that point, but she had a case coming up on

my docket." She cleared her throat. "I don't think that she is corrupt or crooked, but I think she thought she could find more favorable treatment."

"Are you absolutely sure that was what was going on? What exactly did she say?"

She shrugged. "I don't remember what she said verbatim, but it was something to the effect of she 'hoped we could come to an arrangement' on one of her upcoming trials."

"Don't you think it is a little odd that she would say something like that?" He opened up his phone and she could see that he was looking up information about the DA.

Finally, traffic started moving again. As it did, his phone rang. "What's up?" he answered, seeming to know the caller. After a few yups and uh-huhs, he hung up.

"All okay?"

"Elle said they have signs that there is someone inside the house with the address we sent them. From the heat signature, they don't know who it is, but they think we could safely head over there."

"That is one hell of a team to have right on hand. I can't even imagine all of the capabilities you guys must have in tech and surveillance when it comes to getting things done." She paused. "I just hope you are judicious with your applications."

He chuckled. "Oh, don't worry, Judge DeSalvo. We run a little close to the line between legal and illegal, but we are always ethical."

"Unlike Rockwood?" she countered as she drove down the streets leading to Ms. Sanders's apartment.

"Exactly. I promise we are the good guys."

She believed him, but she couldn't help herself. "You know, on the bench, the bad guys are always trying to convince me that they are good guys, too."

"I'm sure that by now, even with only a year under your belt, you have learned to read people almost as well as I can."

"You do know who a murderer looks like, don't you?" she asked, a wicked half grin on her lips.

"Yeah, they look like everyone else." He snorted in what she thought was disapproval. "Are you saying that you think I'm not on your side?"

Did she think he wasn't? Did being on her side make him a good guy?

"No," she said. "I didn't mean for the conversation to go here. I know you are doing what you think in your heart is right. I appreciate you putting your neck out for me. Truly. But I have to admit that I'm a little surprised that this Rockwood company would be sniffing around me when it seems to be very focused on you."

"I'm not sure what has happened to you has anything to do with them. If anything, I'm thinking that whoever planted those bombs…maybe they knew the Shadow Team and STEALTH would be called in. Maybe it was a message to us."

"Do you think my attacker is threatening you in order to make you stand down?"

"That's exactly what I'm beginning to think now that you and I are talking about all of this." He nodded and looked down at his phone, staring at a picture of the district attorney. She wasn't bad-looking. "When we approach Sanders's place, don't park too close. We don't want to give ourselves away."

He resumed tapping away on his phone until she pulled to a stop a block ahead of their next suspect's house.

She could see how he was drawn to this kind of work; it was thrilling to be this close to danger all the time. Though she couldn't say she loved being the one who was coming under attack. However, if she was like him and given the option to protect a civilian, she would have jumped at the chance, as well. There was power and a sense of glory in what they were doing…tracking down bad guys before they could hurt anyone again.

"This okay?" she asked.

He looked up and he appeared a bit surprised at the fact they were already there. "Yeah, this will do. I'll take point on this."

"Like last time," she said with a nod.

"May it go so smoothly."

Though she had never thought of herself as superstitious, the moment the words fell from his lips it was like she could sense a curse falling over them, shrouding them in danger.

Maybe she was just imagining things, but there was no doubt in her mind that things were about to go fifty shades of full-blown wrong.

Chapter Twelve

The door swung open before they even hit the threshold. Evan reached for his sidearm, careful to keep his draw out of view as Sophia Sanders stepped out and sneered at them. "What in the hell are you doing here?"

Natalie stopped walking and he carefully stepped around her, shielding her with his body.

"I heard you were asking around about me." Sanders was red-faced and the color seemed more vivid against the backdrop of her jet-black hair. "I don't know why you think you need to show up on my effing doorstep like I'm some kind of criminal."

"Ma'am, I don't know who you believe we are, but I can assure you that we have no intention of causing you harm." If anything, it was more that he wanted to make sure that she wouldn't hurt the woman he had come to care about. "We would just like to speak to you a little bit, ask a few questions."

"You take your lies somewhere else. I have no interest in talking. You need to leave my property, now." She pointed in the direction of their truck, like she had been sitting there watching them the whole time. It was almost as if she knew they were coming.

As he watched the woman, he noticed she barely

glanced in Natalie's direction. Either she didn't want to give her bad intentions away, or she really didn't know who Natalie was. He hoped for the latter. Yet, this was their primary suspect and if she was as smart as he thought she was, she would go out of her way to keep her secrets and her crimes from being brought out into the light. For this woman, her daughter and her future were on the line. She had all the motivation in the world to act innocent.

"Did you hear me?" the woman asked. "You're not welcome here. I don't care who you are or what you think you're doing. I have nothing further to say to you, unless you show up here with a warrant or a set of handcuffs."

Maybe she wasn't so good at acting after all. She was guilty of something.

There was the rev of an engine as a Dodge Charger careened around the corner of the road and then came to a skidding, tire-screeching halt in front of the house. Ms. Rencher, Mary, stepped out and hurried toward the house. "Damn it, Sophia, I told you not to make a scene."

Sophia let out a choking laugh and pushed past him, knocking against his elbow as he let his hand fall from his gun. Something about this didn't feel like his life was in danger, but somebody's ass was definitely going to get chewed.

"You have no business being here. I told you that you weren't to set a foot on this property ever again. You made your choices, Mary." Sophia's hands were balled into tight fists as she glared at her ex.

"Whoa," Natalie said, trying to get the women's attention. "Let's not let things get out of hand here. We were just hoping to come and—"

"Ask a few questions," Sophia said, finishing her sentence for her. "Mary told me all about you showing up at our headquarters."

"It's not *our* headquarters anymore, Sophia," Mary countered. "And, to be clear, the only reason I called you was to ask you about the order. If you have been using my accounts without my permission, you know I could have my lawyers on your ass so quick that it could make your head spin."

Evan was at a bit of a loss as to how to handle the fighting women. He wasn't sure if he should put up ropes and just let them go full MMA or intercede in what was clearly a long-standing fight.

"If you wanted to bring in the lawyers, you know you already would have. Which means you're being cheap, you are afraid of what I am going to tell these people, or you wanted to see me." Sophia sneered. "Which is it?"

Mary strode up to Sophia, stepping so close that their noses almost touched. "We both know that if we never saw one another again, it would still be too soon."

Evan moved toward the women. "You guys are welcome to continue this fight when we leave, but I need to ask you both a few more questions."

"What?" Sophia jerked her head in his direction. "I can't believe you brought law enforcement to my house. Again. I would think you would want to protect our daughter, but it's like you thrive on this kind of drama. When are you going to grow up?"

Natalie moved by his side and gave him a look. They needed to separate the women if they were going to get any of their questions answered. He gave her a nod and moved his chin in Sophia's direction.

Natalie touched Mary's arm, and as she did Mary jerked. "What?" Anger soaked through her voice.

"I think it's best if you and Ms. Sanders took a few steps back." She gently but firmly pushed the woman back.

"Now," Evan started, "all we really need to know is who ordered those chemicals."

The women pointed at one another. Finally, Sophia spoke. "This woman wants to get me into all kinds of trouble. And the last thing I want is to have anything to do with her. I wouldn't order chemicals. Even if I had access to these accounts, I wouldn't do anything. It wouldn't even surprise me if she had done this herself and pinned it on me in hopes that I would get into trouble. I don't know if you've heard, but we are in quite a contentious divorce."

"If I had done it, why would I call you and warn you that these people were going to show up and ask you questions about it?" Mary countered. "If anything, I wanted you to be prepared. I didn't want you to get into trouble. Little Bean needs both of us. We don't have to be married anymore, but you're still her mother. We signed up for this together. Now we are in this together, forever."

Was that what this all was—some weird interfamilial drama playing out in front of them?

Sophia took a deep breath. She closed her eyes and ran her hands over her face like she was trying to dispel some of her rage. "Look, I'm sorry." She glanced at him and then at Natalie. "I didn't mean to jump down your throats when you showed up here. I just… Anytime I have to deal with her—" she pointed at her ex "—it sets my teeth on edge."

Evan nodded. "I understand how infuriating an ex can be. Relationships, especially those involving children and divorces, can be quite acrimonious."

Sophia's eyebrows rose like she was somehow impressed with his word of the day. Or maybe it was his empathy; he wasn't sure. "Obviously, things between her and me haven't been going well."

"Obviously." Mary crossed her arms over her chest and gave Sophia a sour look, one full of pain.

"There is a lot of bad blood between the two of you," Natalie said. "In my line of work, I see this kind of thing all the time, but I hope you both know that you need to be civil, especially when it comes to your child."

Sophia looked over at Natalie, finally seeming to actually notice her. "You're a cop, too?"

Is that who these women thought they were, police officers? Or was this woman just putting them on? Ignorance, in this situation, could be a great defensive move.

Though she did look unsure of them and Natalie. If he had walked into this cold and unprepared in any way, he would have believed the woman. She didn't have any indicators that she was lying, only that she was defensive—likely due to the fact her ex was standing in her front yard and they were asking her questions. But she wasn't shuffling her feet, cocking her head, or itching—all simple body language cues people exhibited when they were lying.

"Do you mind showing me the order for the chemicals you guys have been talking about?" Sophia asked, motioning toward him.

"Of course," he said, realizing that they hadn't actually given her any information about their being there.

He was glad he hadn't wasted time trying to figure out a plan when it had come to talking to this woman. Once again, they were getting punched in the face, but he had learned to take the hits and keep on fighting.

He took out his phone and opened the information. Holding up his phone, he moved closer so she could take a look at what had brought them to her doorstep in the first place.

She stared at the image for a long time. "Do you mind?" she asked, motioning to scroll the page.

"What do you need?" he asked.

"What company did we place the order with?" she asked.

He scrolled up. "It looks like it is a place called GenChem. You know them?"

A smile broke through the woman's tight features. "Ha. I know what this is." She did a small hop from one foot to the other, like an excited kid. "The company has a long-standing order with them. One on a yearly order cycle."

That made sense, but he still didn't understand why, if they didn't have a rodent problem, they were continuously using such a chemical.

"Our maintenance teams use it mostly in the alleyway and around the doors to the business. I don't know if you realize this, but there is a complete underground city beneath the streets. There, it's like the New York City sewage system with rats and vermin. If you don't stay on top of the problem, it can get bad quickly. Well, according to our company's teams…"

Sophia's face soured. "I mean *your* company..." She shot Mary a hurt look.

Mary gave a stiff, acknowledging nod.

There was a long, painful pause. He had always hated this kind of breakup thing when it had been happening in his life, but it was almost as agonizing when it played out in front of him. He wished he could just talk to them both, free of emotions and pain, and see what had really come between them and see if it was fixable. But this wasn't his place. These were his suspects.

He couldn't be this tenderhearted.

For all he knew, they were in on it together and were playing him and Natalie like fools.

"I'm glad that we have all that sorted out," he said, turning off the screen on his phone. "However, given the nature of your relationship, Mary, may I ask why you warned Sophia of our coming here? And why you weren't forthcoming with the information about her current whereabouts?"

Mary looked down at the toes of her work boots.

"You know," Natalie said, jumping in, "when people hide things, it makes a person look exceedingly guilty."

He clicked his phone on and scrolled through his emails. "Mary, that is also to say nothing about the fact that you didn't send me the videos you promised me— the ones which proved you were home alone last night."

Mary's chin moved impossibly closer to her chest until there was a tiny roll of skin pinched there, under her chin.

"Are you really that embarrassed of what happened?" Sophia asked. "Just tell them. It doesn't matter. They seem like they will understand. Besides, what happened isn't worth getting in trouble over."

Mary finally looked up. "Have either of you ever gone through a messed-up, confusing-as-hell divorce?"

"Sure have, why?" he asked.

Natalie looked at him with a bit of surprise. No doubt she would have questions for him later.

"Loneliness can lead to questionable decisions." Mary held her hands together in front of her. "Not that I don't like how things went last night, Sophia…" She looked up and the two women's eyes locked.

For the first time since they had arrived, there was a degree of softness and congenial familiarity between them.

"I would hope not," Sophia said, the sound somewhat breathless.

He knew that tone. They were lost in their dance with each other. It sounded stupid, his likening their relationship to such a thing, but that was exactly what relationships were—a dance. They could be fun, inspiring, heartwarming and filled with love and laughter… and yet, if one in the pair lost their footing or got behind, it could all come to a screeching halt or a stumbling mess of disasters. They were definitely navigating the disasters, and it was all made harder by the love that still resided between the couple.

"So you guys were together last night?" Natalie asked, but he could see the twitch of a smile at the corner of her lips. Had she been rooting for the offbeat couple just like he was?

Maybe they were equally as tenderhearted as the other. That could definitely make the feelings he was having toward Natalie that much harder to dance—and he wanted the ballet.

"If you guys knew what all we have been through,

you would understand why I didn't want to admit that we were together," Mary said, "but we were. And sometimes, no matter how badly someone hurts you or how badly you have hurt them, there is still just a pure, aching love between you." She smiled at Sophia. "And I don't know if we will make it or not, but I want you to know that I love you. I will always love you."

Sophia stepped over to Mary and took her hand. "I love you, too. And I'm so, so sorry. I don't think we can ever go back to what we were. There is too much water under the bridge, but maybe we could take things slow and be a team again at least for Little Bean. She needs us to be a cohesive unit."

Mary leaned into her, putting her head on Sophia's shoulder. "You got it."

From the look in the two women's eyes, this wasn't some farce.

This messy and confusing moment was real. This was love and life all wrapped into one duct-taped, wired together, big ball of the best everyone could do. It may not have been pretty, but then again maybe it was this ethereal, emotive chaos that made everything worth it.

These imperfect moments, with all their jagged edges—were what made living beautiful.

Chapter Thirteen

"That was...*raw*," Natalie said as they got back into the truck and she started driving, though she didn't even know where she should go.

"Very real," he said, looking out the window. Was he afraid that if he looked at her, what was happening between them would become real, too? "There are a lot of bombs going off there, but I don't think they were involved in any in your life."

She shook her head. "No. They aren't the kind to go after me. They are too focused on what is going on in their lives to branch out and start striking at those around them."

"Yeah, but it also means that you are still in danger. And, we're back to square one."

Her stomach sank. He was right. They could keep grasping at straws, and fighting to find who wished her harm, but the thought exhausted her. They were chasing their tails. "All I want to do is go home and get into my bed and not move for a while."

"I get it," he said, glancing over at her. "I'm exhausted by this, too. Running on high emotions all the time can be so draining. If you need rest, let's go get some rest. We are no good if we're not thinking straight."

"I'm so glad you said that. I have really been missing my pillow." Natalie ran her hand over the back of her neck.

"Yeah, about that…" he started. "There's no way you can go back to your place. We could go to my apartment, but my family's there, and trust me, you don't want that kind of baloney. But I've got a line on a private house, if you'd like. And I know for a fact that it has great towels—a whole selection of them." He laughed.

Her entire body tightened. She had known on a certain level that the night would come again and they would be staying together, but she hadn't expected to feel this pull toward him. Could she be that close to him and keep her distance—for both of their sakes?

She had just witnessed how wrong things could go, complete with lawyers and children…houses and businesses. Did she really want to get into a relationship? A friendship with this man was far safer and smarter in the long run.

Men and women could be friends, right?

She sighed at the thought.

"No? You don't want to be alone with me?" he asked, looking over at her.

"No, that's not it," she said, waving him off. "A house would be great. Definitely smarter. I guess I can always go buy a good pillow if push comes to shove."

"We could go to a hotel, too, but I have a feeling that you would definitely need to buy a pillow in that case," he said, winking at her.

What did he mean by that? Was he thinking about them naked?

Her thoughts went to him behind her, her face pressed into a down pillow.

Stop.

Those kinds of thoughts weren't going to help her keep her hands off him.

Oddly enough, she wasn't feeling quite as tired as she had been before.

"Yeah, a house is good. Separate bedrooms." She sounded clipped.

"Yes," he said.

His quick agreement bit at her. He hadn't even had to think about it. Did he not want her, at all? She should have never let him kiss her. When would she learn? As soon as a man got a taste, it was like they no longer had any need to pursue. And if they'd had sex he probably would have left her in the middle of the night—regardless of his proclamations and promises to keep her safe.

Men.

He clicked away on his phone, making her miss hers all that much more. How nice it would be to pick it up and escape for a while. Though that was what she had loved best about giving it up in the first place.

She thought about all the work waiting for her as soon as she came back online—no doubt she would have to answer more questions about Judge Hanes and she'd probably have to take over some of his cases if he didn't get back on his feet soon. Being here, with Evan, was simpler in all the ways that didn't involve her heart.

"I just got word that your friend, the judge, has woken up."

She smiled. "Thank goodness. I'm so glad. How is he doing?"

"They said he is not making a whole lot of sense yet, but he is gaining ground each passing hour." He paused. "But they are worried about him being a fall risk. Apparently, he keeps talking about getting up and walking out. He is pretty out of it."

"I'm just glad he's alive. Do you think he will make a full recovery?"

"Nerve agents can have some long-lasting effects. And none of them are good. If he ends up being able to even go back home within the next few months that would be a real positive."

She knew he was right, and yet she hated it. "Are you sure there isn't any way we can find out about the sarin?"

"I talked to Agent Hart. He's looking into that from his side. But I haven't heard anything on that line yet." Evan shrugged.

She hated how little progress they had made and if they went to go see the judge, she wanted to give him some kind of good news—that they were no longer going to have to worry about their personal safety. Instead, the next time she saw him, she would only be the bearer of bad news.

It was terrible, but she was somewhat glad Steve Hanes wouldn't be able to understand. She could at least save him some of the anguish of knowing that whoever attacked him was still on the loose.

The only comfort she could find in any of this was that if the attackers still wanted Judge Hanes to be dead, at least he was being watched over by the other Spade family members. If Evan's siblings were anything like him, there was no way Hanes was going to be left alone. They couldn't always stop the bad things from happening—that was outside anyone's ability as long as the perpetrator was on the loose—but at least they would do everything in their power to keep Steve safe, and to get information from him when he was capable of speaking coherently.

Until she saw him, though, at least she could rest.

The house where Evan took her was high up on a mountain, overlooking the city nestled into the valley floor. She hadn't grown up in the city; rather, her familial home had been about fifty miles down in the Bitterroot Valley near Hamilton, Montana. Both were tucked into the mountains where they were protected from the extreme cold and heat that much of the eastern side of the state would encounter. She'd always loved those mountains. They were the backbone of the United States, and if she was to pick the heart it would have been the city whose lights were reflecting off the clouds above them.

As they pulled up to the house, she was surprised. She had expected a rental that was like some little dingy pillbox house near the university campus, where they would bump against each other while passing in the hall. And yet, the house that stood before her was a grand log home. Inside, someone had left the light on, and through the living room window, she could see an antler chandelier and a buffalo blanket adorning the far wall. It looked far more like a hunting lodge than a city dwelling.

Whoever their interior designer was, she needed to hire them. This place was the epitome of Montana living. Many out-of-staters yearned to move here after seeing homes just like this one. There was just something about being perched on the top of the mountain overlooking the quaint city on one side and the wild on the other. It was like a metaphor for life.

Evan got out and opened her door for her. She pulled

her jacket tight, blocking the wind as they walked up the stone walkway into the house. Snow had drifted into the corners of the entryway and she found it a bit soothing—nature was gently battling with mankind's intrusions. She loved this home, but nature's subtle war reminded her of her own. Over time, eventually she would go back to nature just like this place. In the meantime, she could let the weaker souls wear away while she stood strong. She only had so many days left on this planet, and she'd make the most of every single one of them.

"I hope you like the place. We even have a bottle of wine ready, if you're interested." He pressed a series of numbers on the door lock, and it clicked open.

She'd be more than happy to have a glass of wine and just relax. It wasn't maybe the smartest thing to do given the circumstances, but she didn't care. Sometimes enjoying life meant knowing when to relax. They had been going nonstop all day and had started the morning off with yet another threat. She needed a little time. Maybe it would help her to make sense of things, and maybe she could unpack some of the feeling she had been trying to stuff away. At times like these, it was impossible to deal with everything right in the moment.

"Do you think there's a chance of the perpetrator finding us again?" she asked.

He shrugged. "I know you said you thought no one would find you at your mom's place, but if someone had really done their research into you, I think it would've been easy enough for them to track us down. So for tonight I think you can relax."

"Didn't you say that when you're at your most comfortable, that is also when you are in the most danger?" she asked, a playful grin on her face.

"How dare you use my words against me?" he teased. "But yes, you're right and I didn't say that I would be relaxed. I just think you could."

He opened the door, and the hinges didn't even make a sound. As they walked inside, the place smelled like cinnamon sticks and apples. Though they had eaten not that long ago, it made her mouth water.

Her first impression of the log home paled in comparison to the charming entryway. It had at least a twenty-foot cathedral ceiling, complete with slate floors, which led into a variety of rooms. In the living room, there was a crackling fire in the river-rock fireplace. It was an open floor plan; the only thing dividing the living room from the kitchen was a large quartz countertop. Even from this far away, she could make out glittering flecks of gold in its surface. The cabinetry in the kitchen was built of natural wood, with curls and knots in their surfaces. Though they were a shade lighter than the surrounding log walls, they were perfectly offset.

The place was breathtaking.

At the center of the counter in the kitchen was a large bouquet of red roses and white lilies. The arrangement had always been her favorite and it made her wonder if someone had known, or if it was just one of those odd coincidences that happened in life.

As he closed the door behind them, she walked to the flowers and gently ran her finger along the silky edge of the lily. Was this all some kind of message, a sign? Did she even believe in signs? Some days she thought such things were complete drivel; if a person looked for something hard enough, they would always find it...

good or bad. This time, though, she had a surge deep in her belly that made her wonder if she had just been forced by the universe to face the fact she had been brought to this place, this time with this man all for a reason. It felt almost as though she was meant for this. What exactly *this* was, however, was still up in the air.

He had made it clear he didn't want a relationship, and she had made some of the same arguments, but the heart wanted what the heart wanted. There were few words that could make two souls, who wanted to love one another, stop from loving. But just because her soul called to his, it didn't guarantee that his did for her.

He had seemed attracted to her, but maybe he had rebuffed a relationship with her out of some misguided kindness to cover his change of heart. If he wasn't attracted to her, it would have been so much easier for her if he just came out with it—or, maybe not. His saying "I'm not attracted to you" would hurt, too.

He walked past her and washed his hands in the sink. After drying them, he went to the stainless-steel fridge and opened the door. Inside was a bottle of chardonnay and a plate with a bow atop. Taking them out, he then placed the bottle and the plate next to the flowers. Unwrapping the cellophane revealed a circle of soft cheese, smoked salmon and an array of crackers.

"Whoever your friends are that own this place, I am going to need to meet them." She took a cracker and added a bit of cheese and fish to the top and popped it into her mouth.

"The owner is pretty cool," he said. "And keeps the place well stocked."

She could tell he was holding back something, but she didn't mind that he wanted to keep his relationship with them quiet. Her life was forced to be treated in much the same way. Thanks to her variety of roles in the legal system over the years, she had learned more secrets about people than she had ever thought possible, secrets she would never share.

Yet, that didn't stop her from being slightly curious if the person who owned this home was another contractor like Evan, or if they were a client. If she had to guess, she would say client. No contractor would live this…this *boldly*.

"Is your apartment anything like this?" she asked as he opened a drawer and pulled out a corkscrew.

"Ha. No." He shook his head. "There, I live with my family and my team. But it is nice to have a private place to crash when I need a break, so I keep an apartment on the side."

His *family*; the word echoed in the high-peaked room.

"Have you ever thought about having a family? You know, kids with your ex or anything?" she said, bringing up the subject with tiptoeing words.

"We talked about it, but we had gotten married so young and we both agreed that we didn't want kids. We just wanted a life full of adventures and travel." He paused. "In the end, she changed her mind. Adventure begins to lose its allure after a while. Even travel does. At a certain point, what you yearn for the most is to be home with the people you love."

"But if you don't mind me saying, wasn't she the person you loved—your family?" She cocked her head to the side and ended up hoping he would hear the question for what it was and not perceive it as some kind of needling.

He rolled his lips together like he was trying to keep from saying something, or possibly he was just thinking. "I believe that ideally your spouse should be. And I think that for most people that would be true. But she and I... We should have never gotten married. We're still friends, though. But even as friends, going through divorce is tough. I'm not one who likes to fail."

"Just because you got divorced, it doesn't mean you failed." She scowled at such a ridiculous idea. "There are a million reasons couples don't make it. I've heard most of them. Choosing to walk away from one another is far harder than staying in a relationship you know isn't working. In fact, I think that you call your divorce a success. You're still friends. That's admirable. It means that you chose, as two respectful adults, to accept that your relationship wasn't a good fit. It's astounding to me the number of people who try to force a marriage to work and then end up hating each other."

He nodded but she could see that he still struggled with feeling like a failure.

"Besides," she continued, "if you had stayed, can you imagine how different your life would be?"

He stuffed a bite of cracker into his mouth. He popped open the wine bottle, grabbed two glasses from the cupboard and poured them each a healthy glass. He handed hers over. "What about you? Any successes or failures? You know, in relationships or whatever?"

"I..." She didn't know how much she wanted to tell him. If she opened up to him and let him know exactly how mundane her life had been, would he lose interest—this man of adventure? "I haven't had a lot of serious relationships. Never been married. I have been asked, but I have always been so focused on my work and my goals that I failed in my relationships."

He huffed out a laugh. "I can respect that."

She smooshed her lips, dispelling some of the tension from the air. "Yeah, I'm a crappy girlfriend and I knew I'd make a crappy wife."

"Why would you say that?" He looked at her with genuine interest, like he couldn't possibly understand why she would have said something like that about herself.

She shrugged, even though she knew the innumerable reasons and arguments that she could put forth in order to validate her assessment. "Like I said, I've never been very good at putting my partner first."

"That's crazy."

She scowled. "What is crazy about it? It's in every relationship how-to book and every episode of midday television…you have to put your loved ones first in order for your love for one another to survive."

He seemed to once again scoff at the idea. "Don't get me wrong…" he started. "I love Dr. Phil-isms as much as the next person, but who says we have to conform our love and our lives to what society deems as 'perfect' or 'ideal'? You and I are cut from a different cloth. What if we were going to be together? I would never expect you to put me before your job. Ever."

She didn't know what to say.

"Seriously. What you are doing with your life…you are making a difference in the world. Who would dare to ask you to stop putting yourself and your work first in order to affirm your love for them? You love them or you don't. You don't seem like the kind of woman who would mince words or waste time."

She couldn't possibly have been hearing him right. Men, especially alpha types, were rarely this progressive when it came to relationships. In fact, the few men she had dated—mostly cops—had been more of the caveman type. She was lucky not to have been clubbed when they had tried to take her back to their caves for the night. What had made those dates even more frustrating was the fact that they knew exactly who she was, what she wanted in her future and where her priorities lay and yet, it was like they didn't know those things when they were finally over their initial phases of lust. Then both men had wanted her to settle down, to conform.

They were left wanting.

"Are you screwing with me right now? Telling me what you think I want to hear?" she said, taking a sip of the wine.

"No. Because I feel the same way. I mean what I say. I can change my mind about many things, but once I tell someone I love them, I love them forever."

She wasn't sure how she felt about the thought of him still loving his ex-wife—most women would have been jealous, and maybe she was a touch, but mostly she found it endearingly sweet. Throughout a person's life, they loved many people—lovers, family and even friends. To think that he would give it forever, no matter what happened between them, that was incredible. She cherished the thought that a person whose love was so pure and unending was in her life. Not that he loved her. But to think he was capable...

She needed more wine.

She took a long drink, emptying her generously filled glass. He poured her another as soon as she sat

the glass back down. She was glad she didn't have to
go through the questions of "do you want another" and
then feel like she had to pretend to be in favor of tem-
perance. It was like he knew what she wanted without
her speaking. She could get used to this.

"About work before love," he said, taking a drink
from his glass and setting the bottle down. "We need
to go over the other people who've ordered the chemical. And I should check in with the FBI. They might
have more info by now."

She nodded, and then had to stifle a yawn. Despite
her pleasure at being in this home with him, the day
was taking its toll.

He must have noticed.

"We're tired, and won't be at our best. It can wait
till the morning."

"Okay," she said. "But go on—about work and love
and priorities."

"I didn't want to give the impression I think either
of us should not value the other more than their job. I'm
just saying that it's okay for your priorities to be on suc-
ceeding in life. Happiness in one area of your life tends
to lead to happiness in all the others."

Did he say us?

She smiled at him, her chest threatening to explode
with joy. "I never realized what a philosopher you were.
I like it."

Though it was probably the endorphins or dopamine
hitting her brain and making her feel a rush, as his gaze
settled on her and his lips pulled into that sexy smile,
she didn't care what the physiological reason was for
her yearning to touch him. All she wanted to do was
reach out, pull him between her thighs and kiss his lips

until they were both unable to do anything but bask in the flavor of the other.

"I'm no philosopher, but I definitely have seen enough of life to know my way around it. Though I'm more than aware others may have different perspectives than myself." He looked down at his wineglass.

Was he worried that she felt differently than he did? How could she? Everything he had said so far made complete sense to her. If anything, it was almost as if he could read her mind. Or was telling her what she wanted to hear, like she assumed before.

"I think an indicator of a good relationship is one that brings out the best in both people."

He nodded but had a contemplative look on his face. "I agree, but I think it's impossible for two people to expect perfection from each other. While you can bring out the best in each other, in a relationship I think you can also expect to bring out the worst. It's how you deal with those moments of weakness that separates you from who makes it and who doesn't."

"What do you think is your greatest weakness?" she asked.

As soon as she asked the question, she wondered if that was the most prudent thing she could have done. Oftentimes, the best thing a person could do was remain silent. But if they were really going to seek a relationship with one another, like she hoped they would, she needed to know the weaknesses in his case along with the strengths.

He took another long drink of his wine and then refilled his glass. "Do you want an indexed list, or would you prefer the top ten?" He chuckled.

"Hit me with your best shot," she teased, quoting one of her favorite '80s songs.

"Okay, Pat Benatar." He laughed, throwing his head back.

As he moved, she caught sight of a few silvery hairs in the dark underbelly of his beard. Damn. He was so damned sexy.

"I guess if I had to pick my worst fault… I would say that I can be super hard on myself. I mean, look at this situation. I feel *terrible* that I haven't been able to keep you completely out of harm's way. When we get through this, and I know we will, I am going to go over every turn of events at least a thousand times in my head. I will pick it apart and overthink—all so I don't make the same mistakes."

"Like kissing me?" she asked, looking down at the flecks of gold in the countertop and running her finger along the stem of her wineglass.

"That is one thing I will definitely be replaying in my mind for the rest of time, but not because it was a mistake. Rather, I will wonder how I got to be so lucky."

Heat rose in her face and she was embarrassed by such an adolescent response as her blush deepened. What a vicious cycle.

"If anyone is lucky here, it is me in meeting you. You may not see it this way, but if you hadn't walked into Hanes's office when you did, it's very likely that I would have died—possibly either way—by now. You saved my life."

He looked away, humbled. "That's not true. If I would have shown up a few minutes earlier, maybe neither of you would have fallen into harm's way."

"It's unfortunate about the judge, but even if you had

been there earlier…he still would have fallen under attack." Emboldened by the wine or maybe his words, she reached over and put her hand on his. "You couldn't have seen that coming. It was an innocuous thing. No one would be wary of a pen. None of this is your fault."

"It happened on my watch."

"That doesn't matter. A lot of things happen independently of us. We just have to deal with the consequences. I would like to say it's indicative of our jobs, but I think everybody has exactly the same problem. Everyone in the world is just doing the best they can after what some other person has done to them."

He twisted his hand so he could take hold of her fingers. "At least there has been something good to come of all of this." Leaning forward, he kissed her knuckles, his hair brushing against her skin and making goose bumps rise on her arms.

Her mind went straight to all the other places she would love to feel his beard scrape against her.

He looked up, his mouth still on her skin, and his cheek lifted with his smile. His eyes were devilish. Even if she hadn't secretly loved him before, that look and she would have been done for. She was his.

"Do you even know where the bedrooms are in this place?" she asked, not bothering to beat around the proverbial bush.

He nodded, taking her hand and motioning for her to grab her glass of wine.

She walked behind him as he led her upstairs and to the large bedroom at the end of the hall. "Wait." She stopped, trying to fight the buzz of the wine to bring forward some amount of lucid thought.

She couldn't jump into bed with him just because

she wanted to…and he wanted to. There was no real rush if they wanted to be together.

"I know we talked about this before, and I know it's going to be a major mood killer, but if we do this… I don't want it to be a one-night thing."

He smiled back at her, the same look in his eyes as when he had kissed her downstairs. "Me neither."

"So if this happens…we…you and I are going to *do* this whole *relationship* thing?" she asked, suddenly more nervous than when she had been thinking about having sex with him.

He stopped abruptly and turned to face her. He put his arms around her waist and she followed suit. They stared into each other's eyes. "I hate that you have to look at the world like that. I mean, I understand why. I get that sex has turned into an item of convenience. But it hasn't for me. I don't just have sex with anyone. If we're going to do this it means that I care for you, and you care for me. And I want a relationship."

Though it was the last thing she wanted to do, she could feel tears forming in her eyes. Thankfully, he didn't seem to notice.

"Now, do I think the relationship is a great idea? No. But like you said, love isn't convenient. Relationships aren't always convenient. But I think that in this world, where two people who meet and actually have the same feelings toward one another is completely unusual, I would like to give it a try. What do you think?"

She wanted to jump in with both feet. She wanted to press her lips against his and shut him up right then and there. She wanted him to promise her forever. And yet, the realist in her—the one who had seen the most heinous crimes and terrible pain—kept her from doing so. The cynic in her reminded her what a bad idea all relationships were, even with the man of her dreams.

There was no such thing as a perfect person. And right now she was so enraptured by this man that she had to have been blind. He told her his greatest fault was that he was too hard on himself. So how would that affect their relationship? Would he always be the whipping boy? Would he be able to bring equal power in the relationship? What if she was more controlling than he was, or he was more controlling than she was? She couldn't be with somebody who wasn't her equal.

He moved closer, brushing his lips against the side of her cheek. "Don't overthink this. I know that face. I make that face. And when it comes to things like this, matters of the heart, sometimes you just have to go with your feeling. And right now all I want to do is make love to you."

He scooped her up into his arms and carried her to the master bedroom.

Even if she had been tempted to continue questioning what was happening, she could do so no longer.

"How do you know your way around this house so well? Do you bring a lot of women to this place?" she teased, giggling.

"This house is actually mine. It's the only secret I have. No one knows about this place. I bought it a year ago and I hide away here when I can't be around my family for another second. A lot of times they think I'm working, but really, I'm up here watching television and vegging out. I love them, but they can be a lot."

"Wait…" She put her hand on his chest. "You *own* this place? Are you messing with me? This is my *dream house*."

He answered with a huge smile. "Mine, too. And you are the one and only person I have ever had here. I haven't even let a delivery man in this place."

She wasn't sure how such a thing would be possible, but she believed him. "I'm honored."

"I just hope you like my bedroom. It's a bit of a man cave. I never intended on having a woman up here. Well, to be more accurate, I had no plans to bring anyone here, not just a woman."

Now he was the one blushing.

She sat up slightly in his arms and kissed his lips as he carried her over the threshold of his bedroom. She closed her eyes, savoring the juxtaposition between his soft lips and his coarse beard. She'd never dated anyone with facial hair before. This was something totally new. Reaching up, she ran her fingers through it. "I love this." She gripped his hair, giving it a gentle tug.

He grumbled.

Holding her with one arm, he reached up and pulled her hair, exposing her neck to his kiss. He starting kissing at the base of her ear and moved down her neck, making an electric charge move through her body. Her core clenched as the wetness grew.

How had *she* gotten so lucky?

She was in the house of her dreams with a man so hot she wasn't certain she could have even imagined him or described him to her friends. And yet, here he held her and he was kissing her neck.

All clear thoughts left the building. The only thing she could think of was the feeling of his tongue as it flicked her earlobe and mixed with the heat of his breath in her ear. She wanted to make love to him right in this second, but at the same time she ached to hold out...

to make him kiss every part of her before she let him take her.

She wanted to make him earn her and to want her so badly that the moment he slipped inside he would beg for release—and she would make him wait.

Yeah, maybe she was a bit of a control freak in and out of the bedroom, but she loved every damned second of it.

He moved to the bed and set her down. She was enveloped by the thick down comforter, complete with little red reindeer. His bed looked like something out of Santa's mansion, complete with big, fur-covered and red-quilted pillows. She ate it up.

Laying her down, he moved to her pants and carefully undid the top button. "I'm afraid I don't have anything for you to wear." He passed her an impish grin. "I hope you are okay with that."

She was dripping. "I…" She struggled to find words as his hands worked her zipper down and slipped her pants free of her legs. "I…won't…"

"Hmm?" he asked, cocking his head to one side. "Having a hard time finding your words?" he teased, tiptoeing his fingers up the insides of her thighs and tracing them back down toward her knees.

He had to see the wetness soaking through her panties by now.

Had she shaved her legs?

Crap. She couldn't remember. Hopefully, he wouldn't care.

And… Whatever. This wasn't only about his satisfaction.

Her entire life, when it came to sex, all she had ever cared about was pleasing her partner. But why? It wasn't hard to make men happy. Why couldn't she seek her own satisfaction in this moment? Undoubtedly, if she found the ending she wanted, he would, too. And better, he would get to know that he had made her feel something so beautiful.

As he opened up the buttons of her shirt and kissed her naked skin, she thought about all the pain and hate in the world. They had both seen so much evil. It was moments like this, where two souls connected and shared in this special secret, that brought goodness to life.

Yes, she was going to live this moment up. If it was to be the first time of many or the last time she was to feel his lips on her skin, she was here. This was love.

Could love live in a single moment? Or was this something else? Was it only lust?

He had said he wanted a relationship, but if this was only to be tonight, she would have to tell herself it had only been lust. But right now all she felt was love.

His tongue found her center, over her panties. She gasped. He pushed them to the side and his tongue flicked against her nub. She nearly quivered with excitement. Oh, it had been so long.

He pressed his tongue inside her and then moved up, circling her with the tip of his tongue before flicking her, hard. She jumped, loving every second of it. She relaxed back into the bed, letting him explore her body. This was for him, too.

But what if he didn't like her?

What if she tasted bad?

She put her arm over her head. Why? Why did she have to have these thoughts when all she wanted to do was to let herself savor the moment? All she had to do was feel and yet, all she could do was think.

What in the hell was wrong with her?

Stop. She had to stop this crazy spiral of thoughts. *Be present.*

She sighed as she ran her fingers through his blond hair. He pressed his mouth down on her.

Flick.

Roll.

Dip.

She gasped. Yes. That. She loved *that*. Whatever *that* was that he was doing to her.

He pulled her into his mouth and sucked. And just when she thought it couldn't feel better, he flicked.

If she died in this moment, she would have been satisfied with her life.

How. Yes. Oh. Yes.

"I…" she started, but she was stopped as he sucked and flicked again.

Seriously, she had no idea what he was actually doing to her body, but it felt better than anything she had ever felt in her entire life.

"You…"

"Yes?" he asked, finally releasing her.

"You. Are. The. Best," she said between ragged, wanting breaths.

"And so are you." He dove down, back between her legs.

Her legs shook as he pulled her into his mouth and pushed his fingers inside her. She lifted her hips, letting him push deeper into her.

More. She needed more.

Reaching down, she let him know what she wanted. She rolled on her side and guided him into her. He eased into her gently though she was more than ready to take every bit of what he graciously offered. She took hold of his muscular ass and pressed him into her, throwing her head back as he took control of her and made her gasp.

After a moment he rolled on top of her. He looked into her eyes as he slowed, letting her feel every sensation…the feel of him between her legs, the heat of his breath, the dampness of their skin as they pressed against one another.

He picked up his speed and she pressed her face into his neck, kissing him and nibbling as if she could taste the ecstasy as it edged close. His breathing quickened and she could feel him grow harder within her.

"Not yet," she begged.

"Yes. This. Is. For you." He stopped, collecting himself.

He moved to sitting and lifted her legs so they rested over the tops of his shoulders. He moved slow, controlled. Using the tip, he ran it over her, playing. He eased into her again.

Putting her hands on the cold wooden headboard, she pressed herself down on him. Now it was her turn to take control.

Rocking her hips, she used one hand to help herself, making him watch.

"Yes," he begged. "Please." His words sounded ragged and heavy as he waited for her. "Let's do this together, baby. Please."

A low primal sound escaped her throat as she let go.

This. Him. Now. All of this. She wanted him. All of him. And not just now; she wanted him, always. As it seemed, he was more than happy to give it all.

Chapter Fourteen

Evan could think of no moments better than those he and Natalie had shared. They had barely slept and when they weren't making love, they were lying in bed next to each other, talking and laughing. If he could have, he would have stayed in that moment forever. In those hours, nothing else but her mattered.

And damn if he didn't love her. Hard.

He'd wanted to tell her last night, but he'd stopped himself several times. In the sheets was hardly the right time to tell someone you loved them for the first time. It should be *real*, not expressed when a person was so filled with happy hormones that they could love a toaster and mean it. Natalie was far too special to just blurt it out.

Thinking of special, he hoped he had made her feel that she was special to him last night. He had pulled out all the stops in satisfying her and he had given it a solid college try to kiss every inch of her entire body. Though he had no doubts she had enjoyed herself—he would need to throw the sheets in the wash later—he hoped she knew that he had never had a night like they had shared ever before. And he doubted that he would ever have a night as good as it again. This was the best first, and hopefully the last.

He sat out a cup of coffee and a plate of biscuits and gravy for her on the kitchen island and when she finally appeared, freshly showered, she smiled and gobbled it down. She barely took a breath and he was glad that she appreciated his cooking.

"Want any more?" he asked.

She shook her head as she took a long pull from her coffee mug.

"Are you sure? I know I worked you over pretty hard last night," he teased, his thoughts moving to how good she had looked on top of him with her hair falling down over her shoulders.

His body was tired, but apparently, not too tired.

"I'm fine. I was just hoping we could hit the ground running today. Oddly enough, I'm feeling reinvigorated," she said, sending him a cute grin over the lip of her coffee mug.

"Glad to hear it. I'd hate to have to help you find a renewal of energy again sometime. Or, I can ask Judy for one of her special breakfasts."

They laughed. "Oh, she is going to love our being together."

"Definitely. You want to go check on her soon?" He made sure to stand well covered behind the counter.

"Not until we find my attacker. I was hoping we could maybe look into the rest of the list of chemical buyers today."

"Great minds," he said, leaning slightly to adjust himself. He walked around the counter and gave her a kiss to the head. "Let's hit it."

It didn't take them long to get to the main fire station downtown and be buzzed in. The place was awash with the sounds of men talking and a blaring television. The place smelled like old smoke and a chemical he couldn't quite put his finger on, but something oily. The door from the main lobby to the garage was open and from where he stood, he could make out the sounds of a basketball bouncing and the clink and rattle as someone made a basket.

The place reminded him of a military base with men making dark but damn funny jokes. The only thing missing was the sounds of rounds being pinged off in the distance. A woman walked around the corner and gave them an acknowledging tip of the head. "Can I point you in some kind of direction?" she asked.

"Actually," he started, "we were hoping to talk to Mr. VanBuren. He working today?"

"Hmm…yeah. He is not normally here on the weekends, but I think I saw him poking around in his office earlier. I think he was filling in for our battalion chief. Follow me." She led them down a white-tiled hallway and deeper into the building until they came to a row of glass-walled offices and a large classroom at the end.

To their left, sitting in his office and leaning back in his chair while he chatted on the phone, was a man with VanBuren on the nameplate affixed to his white uniform shirt. He looked up as they stopped. He frowned, looking a bit put out that he was being bothered. The woman motioned they were there to see him. He lifted his finger, said something to the person he was talking to on the phone, then hung up and waved them in.

"Have a good one," the firefighter said as she turned and went back to the main area.

"Thanks again," Natalie said.

"No prob," the woman called behind her.

VanBuren opened his office door and poked his head out. His hair was almost completely gray, but there was a smattering of brown through it. His eyes were red, like he hadn't had a great deal of sleep. "What can I do for you?" He looked over at Natalie and stared for a moment, almost as if he was trying to place her. "Judge DeSalvo? What are you doing down here?"

She gave the man a warm smile, but her face was tight like she didn't really know him. "Actually, I don't know if you heard, but my car was bombed a couple of days back."

"Oh yeah," VanBuren said, walking out into the hall. "Bad business. Has the FBI made any progress on tracking down the individual responsible?"

She shook her head. "Not yet, but they are working on it."

"Glad to hear you were safe. You have any ideas who would have done something like that? I got word that Hanes got hurt that day, as well. Any word on his condition?" the man asked.

"He's going to survive," Evan said, looking the man in the eyes.

"Glad to hear." VanBuren looked away and Evan tried not to read too much into it.

This man was on their short list of suspects, but it didn't mean much and it was normal for people to avoid eye contact, especially when one or both were feeling at all uncomfortable. And, no doubt, standing in front of the district court judge would make anyone working under the umbrella of the city a little bit nervous. Evan wondered if VanBuren had ever had to sit in or testify in her court. Even if he hadn't, it was probably only a matter of time until he did.

"I know your station was the one that took the call for the bombing," Natalie said. "Did you hear anything about what had happened or about the bomb itself?"

The man shrugged. "Not a whole lot. Our investigator worked with the FBI in pulling together what he could, but I haven't talked to him. Why?"

Evan tried to disarm him by leaning against the wall and letting out a long yawn before speaking. "Well, one of the chemicals in the bomb was something you are on record as ordering."

"Huh. What?"

"Zinc phosphide," Natalie answered.

"Ah, yeah. I use it in my training." The man looked slightly relieved, like he was afraid they were going to ask him straight out if he had helped to make the device. "We were working on Class D fires a few weeks ago with a few of the rookies and younger guys."

Evan had once heard that most firefighters were arsonists at heart. To battle fire, a person had to love it. It was right in line with cops being one different choice away from being criminals. He believed it, but according to that logic he would have been one step away from being a murderer; that was a hard pill to swallow.

"How did the training go?" Natalie asked, seeming genuinely interested. "What did you do?"

"Just the normal thing. I created a fire in our tower. Made them establish what kind of fire it was and how best to battle it. The different teams did well, but they still need a little more work before I'll be satisfied." VanBuren shrugged. "Why?"

Natalie looked like she was going to answer, so Evan

stopped her by saying, "How many did you have in your teams?"

"Well, let's see..." The man stared into space and said a few names aloud. "Oh, and there was Lewis and Barber. Oh...and Hanes."

"Hanes? Sven Hanes?" Evan asked.

The man nodded, but there was a flicker of annoyance on his face and he ran his hand over his mouth. "The one and only."

What was that supposed to mean? Did the man dislike the judge's son? He wanted to press him and ask him about his feelings directly, but he knew that the man's loyalty—regardless of his personal feelings—would always be with his fellow firefighters and not some stranger off the street.

Natalie nodded, seeming to have noticed the man's body language, as well. "I've heard mixed reviews on that kid. How is it going with him?"

The man looked directly at Evan before peering back at the judge. "Meh. Hard to say. He's only been with us about a year and I don't work with him a whole lot, other than on the training stage. We will see his stuff when he hits the big leagues."

Evan wasn't sure exactly what the man meant by that. He would have assumed that all firefighting was dangerous and *big league*, but he didn't bother to ask.

"He's smart, though?" Natalie continued. "Quick to learn?"

The man shrugged. "He's been having some personal problems that are getting in the way of his reaching his full potential, if you ask me. But when he gets his ducks in line, there will be hope for him. Maybe."

"What kind of personal problems?" he asked.

The man lifted his hand as he shrugged. "Relationship things according to the gossip I've picked up, but there is talk of more. How much validity there is in the rumor mill, well…you know."

He could tell, based on the indifference on the man's face, that either he didn't know much more about Sven or wasn't about to divulge what he did know.

"Do you mind showing us the zinc phosphide?" Natalie asked, sounding endearingly curious.

The guy looked at her like she was crazed, but he shrugged. "Not much to see, really."

"I sure would appreciate it," she said, touching his shoulder like he was a lock and her fingers were the key.

It was great watching her in action. She was smooth when it came to her getting what she wanted without the other person realizing. Had she used the same moves on him? He almost shook his head. It was impossible. He had come into her life and wanted things and he couldn't think of her asking him for anything…well, other than in bed last night.

He smiled at the thought. There she could make him do anything she liked.

VanBuren led them out of the hall of offices, talking to Natalie quietly as he followed behind. They walked through the garage where the crew was still playing basketball and didn't even seem to notice intruders in their midst. The officer opened up a large door, which led to a concrete room filled with a variety of canisters and boxes stacked on a series of steel shelves that lined the walls. In the back corner of the long, thin room, was a white five-gallon bucket on the floor.

"I used most of it, but left enough for one more burn."

VanBuren went over and pointed at the bucket, seeming to think that it was the bucket they wished to see.

"Do you mind opening it for me? I am just curious to see what it looks like." Natalie smiled.

He could see the man lose brain cells at the smile. He'd always known that women had a magical power to make a man lose his mind, but it had been a while since he had seen it on display.

VanBuren pulled out a pocketknife and made quick work of unlatching the thick plastic lid. "Huh."

"What is it?" Natalie asked.

"I would say about half of what I left is missing." The man looked at them like they knew something he didn't, and he didn't appreciate it. "How did you guys know I was going to find it like this?"

"To be honest, we were grasping at straws here. Just running down a list, you know. In fact, we thought we'd find nothing with you or the department." Evan sighed.

"About Hanes..." The man looked down at the bucket. He shook the contents as if doing so would magically make more appear. "If you think he's got something to do with what's been going on around town here, I can't say...but what I can say is that he works with lots of chemicals. He and I have done a heck of a lot of training exercises and...well, if he has gone off the rails, he could be a real dangerous man."

Chapter Fifteen

They sat on the steps of the Federal building, waiting for the FBI agent who was supposed to be meeting them soon. The Bureau had been amenable to their help, thanking them for the assistance with the case, but she had a feeling the agent she had spoken to on the phone had been rolling his eyes while she had been talking.

She was happy to wait out in the cool air, if it meant she didn't have to get pulled into some flurry of politics. Evan, on the other hand, kept looking around, and she knew he was scoping out the area for trouble. He'd wanted to wait inside.

She would much rather lean against Evan, relax into him like she had last night.

Stepping out of his magnificent house this morning had been a slap back to reality. It had been so nice to escape with him. He had nearly worn her out, not that she would have ever admitted that she was anything less than a sexual dynamo who was capable of demigod stamina and insatiability—at least not to him.

The thought made her smile. Yes. Demigod, that was what she was. Albeit one who feared losing control. Though, thinking of it, wasn't that what most Greek figures had struggled with, as well?

"What are you smiling about?" he asked, nudging her knee with his.

She looked at him. "I was just nerding out for a minute."

"How nerdy did you go?" he asked.

"I was dipping into thoughts of Phobos."

He cocked a brow as he looked to her. "As in the god of fear?"

"And there I was, wondering if you were just a door kicker." She touched the side of his leg with the back of her hand. "You are always surprising me."

"Oh, honey, you ain't seen nothing yet."

The front door of the Federal building opened up and the secretary who had met them when they first arrived looked out. "Hey, guys," he said, looking apologetic. "I hate to tell you this but Agent Hart can't get away from his desk right now. I'm sorry. He requested you guys go pick up some late breakfast and he will catch up with you at his earliest convenience."

She gave a stiff nod. "Fine." She stood up and brushed the bits of snow off the back of her pants. She was angry, but she wasn't about to lose her patience on the messenger.

"Tell him lives hang in the balance," Evan said, annoyed. "We will be waiting for him."

The man nodded and disappeared behind the doors.

"So what are we going to do?" she asked.

"On a positive note, if the agent assigned to our case is this busy, then I think it's fair to say he is giving your case the attention it requires. I hope."

She wasn't a federal court judge, so she didn't usually work directly with the FBI, but she found it hard to believe they wouldn't come to her aid with the same level of professionalism and professional courtesy as if she was one. There had to have been something else going on.

"I hope you're right about that," she said, waving him off. "From what I know about those who work behind those doors, they are a good crew."

He ran his hands over his face. "I know…one of my brothers is married to one of their former agents."

She gaped at him. "What?"

"Yeah, Kate Scot is Troy's wife."

"How have you not told me your sister-in-law was an agent?"

"Actually, she still is one, but she's working out of Kirtland in New Mexico. I think she probably still has some pull here, but what can she have them do that they aren't already?"

She sighed, resigned to the fact that even though all she wanted to do was act fast and strike down her enemies, all she could do was wait.

Or could she?

"Hanes wasn't working today, right?"

"VanBuren didn't mention whether he was or wasn't. He could have been at any one of the other stations, on shift."

"Text him." She reached behind him and pulled his phone out of his back pocket.

He tapped away as they walked out toward the road where they had parked. His phone pinged. "VanBuren said he is working at Station Three today. It's over on Thirty-Ninth and Russell." He looked at her. "His social media had him somewhere else at the time of the attack on his father, but it's easy to manipulate those time stamps."

"Let's go." She smiled. "And text Agent Hart and tell him to meet us there."

"Wait," he said, coming to a full stop as he neared his truck. "This isn't a good idea. First, they have to buzz us in, just like at headquarters. What do you think he is going to do if he sees us and he is the guy who is responsible for the bombs—and attack on his father?"

She scrunched her lips as her thoughts drifted through a variety of scenarios, some less bloody than others. "First, we don't know if he is responsible or not. I mean, I know he and his father have had some problems in the past, but why would he attack now? Out of the blue? And just because some chemicals are missing, chemicals he had access to and trained with... That wouldn't prove his guilt if you were standing in front of me and arguing this case."

"You know as well as I do that if this is the guy, he already wants you dead. If we back him into a corner and he gets wind that we have added him to our list of suspects, he will strike. Hard. Fast."

"And if he isn't, then we will be able to keep looking for who wants me dead." She could hear the exasperation in her tone, but it wasn't a frustration with him, just the entire situation. "I have been at risk since the moment I decided I wanted to work in the criminal justice sector. I regularly work with people who most would deem unstable. I knew that I would face danger every day with my job. Sure, this week has been a little hairier than most, but I'll make it through. I always do."

"Are you serious, Natalie?" He chuckled. "You know I can stand behind a dangerous job. I mean, look at me." He put his hand on his chest. "But that doesn't mean you put yourself in unnecessary danger just because you can. When you're in a foxhole, you don't stick your head up unless you want it to get shot off."

"Then I guess it's lucky we aren't in a foxhole." She smiled and got into the truck. He flopped in beside her and slammed the door behind him. "And, thankfully, I've got you at my side." She put her hand on his leg as she started the truck and slammed it into Reverse.

She was definitely being impetuous and playing with fire, but she was done being careful and hiding away. Besides, if things went as they had been, going to see this guy was just going to be another wild goose chase.

As she made her way out of downtown, Evan took out his gun and pulled back the slide.

"I'm telling you, I don't think anything bad is going to happen here." She shook her head at his extreme overreaction.

"You said you were ready for all the danger that comes with your job, but if you aren't a little bit nervous about what we are about to do, then you aren't as ready as you think." He slipped the gun back into the holster concealed in the waistband of his pants.

"If you are really worried about me," she said, pointing at her purse that was sitting between them on the truck's floorboard, "would you please put one in for me? I never carry with a chambered round."

He lifted his brow. "You have been carrying this whole time and you never told me?"

"The whole point of concealed carry is for it to be concealed." She winked at him. "Besides, you never asked."

"I should have known you wouldn't mess around," he said, reaching into her purse and unzipping the side compartment where she carried her Glock 42.

"I love that little gun," she said, looking at it fondly. "Fits into my running fanny pack perfectly and I can wear it under my robe without anyone being the wiser."

"Hey, you aren't supposed to carry in the court-house." He laughed.

"Yeah, and I wouldn't if I thought all people were law-abiding citizens." She scoffed. "My bailiff can do a lot to keep me safe, but at the end of the day, my life rests in my hands."

"Not when I'm around."

She wasn't sure that she had ever heard anything more romantic. How had she gotten to have him in her life? He was such a complex mix—sweet and sexy, strong and capable, and best of all he was vulnerable and surprisingly open.

There had to be something about him that she didn't like…that she could use to keep from loving him, at least so soon. He supported her, wasn't even mildly sexist and he wanted the best for her. And yet, he was still the alpha male she had always been drawn to.

Yeah, she was so done for when it came to loving him.

He slipped her gun back into her purse after charging it for her. "Don't forget it's loaded. I can remind you when—"

There was the deafening roar of a diesel engine and the shattering of glass.

The world spun around her. Flipping and turning.

There was glass. Glass everywhere. The windshield crackled like when she was a child and had walked on too-thin ice. But under this ice, instead of the inky black of freezing cold water, there was the powdery explosion of snow and the whirling gray of the truck's hood flying up as they rolled.

The seat belt cut into her shoulder and across her stomach, holding her back. But there was something hard pressing against her chest and she looked down. Evan's hand was pressing into her sternum, like in this small action he could hold her back and keep her from being hurt.

Her head slammed against the airbag as it exploded from the side of the truck and the other exploded from the steering wheel. It hit her in the nose so hard that she could feel it start to bleed, but she couldn't tell if it was from inside or the outer bridge of her nose.

There was no pain.

Why was there no pain? There should have been pain by now—in her nose or maybe her shoulder.

She looked back down. Where had Evan's hand gone? Was he still touching her?

Yes. There was his hand. She closed her eyes and looked over at where her hand was also on him and sandwiched between him and his airbag.

They had both tried to protect each other.

The truck skidded to a stop, jerking her hard against the side. It took her a minute to get her bearings. Somehow, the truck had come to rest back on its tires, or what was left of them, but it listed to the right and the air was filled with the acrid scent of antifreeze and smoke.

"What…what happened?" she asked, though not to anyone more than herself. "Evan. Evan, are you okay?"

His face was pressed into the steadily deflating airbag and his eyes were closed. If she hadn't known better, she would have thought he was just catching a catnap.

"Evan?" she said again, her voice strangled.

He didn't move.

There were the sounds of voices around her, men yelling something she couldn't quite understand. All she could think about was Evan and the thin bead of blood that was starting to flow from somewhere above his eye and in his hairline. If his blood was flowing, that had to mean he was still alive. Right?

She pressed her hand harder against his chest and touched his hand resting on hers with her other. Focusing, she could feel a heartbeat but she wasn't completely sure if it was his or if it was hers. The fabric of his shirt was thick, the kind that pilled with too many washes.

"It's going to be okay, honey. I'm going to get you out of this." She didn't think he could hear her, but it didn't matter; she had to say the words.

Here he had been promising her that he would do everything in his power to protect her, and life had come out of nowhere and stripped them both of the one thing they wanted—to stay safe.

If she didn't do something quickly, it would take his life, too.

She moved to undo her seat belt, but her fingers fumbled with the latch. It was like her fingertips were heavy, weighted down with the adrenaline and the fear that was coursing through her. As she moved to release the belt, she looked up at a flurry of motion outside his window. A firetruck was careening toward them.

It was coming too fast.

It was coming straight at them.

It was going to hit Evan's side.

She pressed the gas pedal down as hard as she could, not sure if the truck was even running or not. The engine sputtered but the truck lurched forward a few feet.

The firetruck struck, hitting the bed of the mangled truck and spinning them around like a top. Her head hit the deflating airbag to her left, but she didn't feel pain. Only shock.

A firetruck. Hit. Them. They had been attacked using a machine usually driven by heroes, men and women who had been called down to save them. This driver, this plastic hero, wanted them *dead*.

She fumbled for her purse, thinking about the gun inside, but her seat belt held her back. Evan had a gun, but it was too far away and out of reach.

She took a breath, trying to click her brain into gear. She had to move. Sitting still only meant death.

There had to be a way.

She pressed on the gas pedal with her left foot, not caring where the truck edged to as long as they moved. The engine sputtered again, clicking as smoke started to fill the cab. With her right foot she swept the floor until she found her purse. She wiggled the toe of her boot into the purse's strap and lifted it until she could grab hold. Reaching in, she pulled out her gun, stripping it from its holster.

The truck shuddered and died. They were sitting ducks.

She lifted her gun to a low, ready position. Evan's head was pressed against the side of the door, and the blood was flowing steady and hard from the gash that had reopened over his eye. Blood streamed down the back of his neck and was staining the cloth headrest behind him.

As she stared at him, she could smell his clean, fresh cologne mix through the acrid smoke.

Her side window was gone even though she didn't

remember hearing it break. As she realized it, she felt the shards and crumbles of glass that were piercing into her hands as she held the gun low in her lap.

Screams. There were the sounds of screams.

She looked out the broken windshield. The firetruck was sitting askew on the road in front of her, head-on. The driver's seat was empty and the door was open. So was the passenger's door.

Had there been two people in the firetruck?

What was going on?

A woman appeared a few feet from her window. Her raven hair glistened like a freshly sharpened blade in the wintry sun.

It was the renter, the woman whom they had spoken to. The woman who had been staying at Ms. Rencher's old place. But why…why would she be here?

"I bet you thought you wouldn't see me again." The woman sent her a wicked smile, giving her the appearance of a crazed beast.

"What in the hell are you doing?" Natalie asked.

"I'm getting you out of our way, Ms. Goody Two-shoes."

There was something hilariously outdated in the woman's jibe and strangely, Natalie felt the urge to laugh at the craziness of it all. Had she hit the hysteria level of shock?

"Getting me out of the way of what?" she asked, careful to slide her gun under the edge of her shirt and out of sight of the approaching woman.

There was the crunch of glass on pavement and she turned to see Sven Hanes standing outside Evan's door. He reached down and tried to open the door, but it was jammed. Thankfully, the window on that side was still intact, though she couldn't imagine how.

"Kill her, Becky." Sven pointed at his neck.

"Why? Why do you want me dead?" she asked again, struggling to make sense of everything.

"Shut up. Just shut up." Becky snarled at him. "Your screwups have already gotten us into enough trouble."

So not all was well in love land.

"Becky, it's not too late," she started, hoping she could have a chance at talking the woman down.

The woman chuckled as she pulled a syringe out of her pocket.

"You don't have to do this. I'm a judge and if you stop right now, I can make sure that you are treated fairly when you are arrested. Just don't do anything you're going to regret." Natalie put the palm of her free hand up, surrendering. The last thing she wanted to do was to draw down on this woman and pull the trigger. "I don't know how you got yourself into this situation with Sven, but it's not too late to do the right thing. Make the right choice. I know how hard this kind of thing can be and how hard it can be to get out of it."

"I know exactly who you are. And if you would have just gone along with my sister, we wouldn't have to be in this mess." The woman glowered down at her. "You are the one who screwed everything up. You put everyone at risk."

"Your sister?" she asked, now totally confused.

"The district attorney. She asked you to play along. All you had to do was say yes. Steve and Sven had a great thing going and they made a lot of money working with the DA to get things done. But you had to eff it all up. This…all of this, is on your head."

She had known the district attorney had made a gesture to see how amenable Natalie was to being bought, but she had no idea that it was because she already had a thing going on with Judge Hanes—Natalie's friend. The judge who had brought her into the fold. The judge who had trained her. Who had basically gotten her a seat on the bench.

He had set her up. He had used her to grow his crooked dealings.

But why? Why had his son and Becky tried to hurt him?

She wanted to tell the woman she sounded crazy and that there were a million other ways around the situation that they were in, but Becky wasn't going to listen. She was frenzied…backed into the corner like a snarling dog and now it was fight or die.

"Whatever it is that you think I screwed up, don't you think we could *fix* it?" she asked, playing her deadly game.

"Don't you think it's a little too late for that?" Becky sneered. "*Our* plan is going along just fine. All that's left is for you and your crappy little guard over there to get a dirt bath."

A dirt bath?

"You haven't done this kind of thing before, have you?" she asked.

Out of the corner of her eye, she saw Sven walking around the front end of the truck. He stopped as a bystander started to come over to help. Sven put up his hands, but she was forced to look back at the most immediate threat—Becky.

Becky moved toward her, the needle mostly concealed by her hand; only the tip was sticking out.

Natalie jerked, putting up her left arm in self-defense. The woman laughed, the sound sour and angry as their arms connected. Becky grabbed her hand and pressed her arm down and into the broken glass that was smattered on the windowsill. The glass cut into her arm and she gripped the gun in her hand, hard.

All she had to do was pull the trigger.

Becky lunged, the needle moved toward her and she watched it happen in slow motion as something in her lizard brain clicked into place. Kill or be killed.

She was a fighter. But if she pulled the trigger, she would have to spend every night after this thinking about all the other things she could have done to get out of this situation. There had to be another way.

There was a loud boom, and the air around her reverberated with the gunshot.

Had she pulled the trigger? She looked down, confused as she pulled the gun from beneath the edge of her bloodied shirt. Her finger wasn't even on the trigger.

Evan said something, but she only heard the muffle of his voice and couldn't make out the edges of his words in the ringing deafness left by the gunshot.

His hand moved off her chest and he took hold of her shoulder. In his right hand, the trigger still pinned, was the gun. He shook her as he looked at her. His mouth moved and she could tell he was asking her if she was okay, but she didn't know how to respond.

She moved her hand up to her neck, feeling for Becky's needle. There was nothing. Nothing protruding out of her neck, only the slivers and grit of exploded glass.

Her gaze moved over toward the window. Becky was no longer standing beside her, but her hand was still on her arm, pressing it into the glass. She lifted up her arm and pulled it out of the woman's limp grip.

Dead or alive, she didn't care.

Sven turned, he reached down like he was going for a gun, but before he could clear and pull, she already had her gun pointed at him. When had she drawn?

She moved her finger to the trigger, pressing down the safety and easing it back.

"No!" Evan yelled.

Releasing her grip, the trigger slipped forward and back on safe.

The bystander who had been coming toward them grabbed Sven from behind, throwing him to the ground.

As the man moved, she saw a flash of a badge and a set of silver handcuffs come out from behind the stranger's back. He slapped them on Sven's wrists.

"Are you okay?" Evan's hand tightened on her shoulder.

She nodded.

"Give me your gun," Evan said, extending his hand.

As she moved to hand it over, the gun shook violently. If she'd been forced to pull the trigger, she had no idea what she would have hit, but she doubted it would have been Becky.

He took the gun and slipped the mag out and emptied the chamber. The round dropped into his lap and he picked it up and put it back into the mag. "I will give this back to you later. I'm sure that the police will want to hear all about what has happened here."

"Thank you..." she said, suddenly aware of everything that was going to come next—the hospital, the police, the lawyers, the courtrooms. They would be cleared, without a doubt, given everything that had happened and the scene Becky and Sven had created in their attempt to kill them.

Evan smirked, his lip was starting to grow puffy and there was a split on the bottom. "No need to thank me, ma'am."

"I'll take it that you are okay?" she asked, staring at the cut that was starting to bleed on his lip.

He put his fingers up to the reopened cut on his forehead. "I think I'll be fine with a fresh dab of skin glue, a couple Tylenol and an ice pack."

She pointed down at his legs where the door had been crushed inward. "Your legs?"

"Good." He wiggled his feet and lifted his knees. He glanced out at the smoking firetruck and the police cars that were skidding to a halt on the icy intersection around them. "As for the city, I think we've done a number on it."

She laughed, but then felt ridiculous for doing so.

He let go of her shoulder and took her shaking hand in his. Lifting their hands, he gave her knuckles a kiss. "We are going to be okay. We're in this together."

They sat there for a long moment, collecting themselves.

A police officer rushed over to the truck and squatted down beside Becky and she assumed he was taking her pulse. He stood back up and peered in at them, assessing the situation. "You okay?"

They both nodded.

"Just don't move. We will be with you in just a minute." The officer turned his head toward his handset and started talking to the dispatcher on the other end of the radio.

Evan squeezed her hand. "Babe?"

"Yeah?" she asked, looking over at him in all of his bruised glory.

"I need you to promise me something." He smiled, but winced as the split in his lip opened and his smile faded from view.

"Hmm?" She looked out at the melee of action around them.

"When we get through this... I want us to be together. Like you move into my place. Okay?"

She slowly turned her head to face him. "What?"

"I want to take you out, into public, for a real date. Spaghetti, wine, dancing...the whole thing. And if that doesn't sell you, I must add that I can dance."

"Spaghetti and a dance? Is that the best you've got?" she teased.

"Hey, don't bash spaghetti. What has it ever done to you?"

"Okay, I'll move in and you can take me to have spaghetti and go dancing...but only if you promise me something in return."

"Whatever you want." He squeezed.

She smiled at him. "I want to keep you, forever. I clearly can't go anywhere without my protector—and the man I love." She leaned over and their lips met.

"I love you, too, baby." He nodded. "And clearly, I can't go anywhere without mine. We are in this together."

Epilogue

Three months later everything had started to quiet back down in the little city. The cuts, bruises and her sprained ankle had healed and she was finally starting to feel almost back to her normal self once again. It was odd, but the hardest part of going through a gauntlet of death threats was not the initial action, but the echoing silence that came afterward.

She was always looking over her shoulder, wondering who would be following her and ready to draw a gun. And when having to drive somewhere, she never got in before hitting her key fob at least twice and actively looking under her car.

Yes, Sven and Becky had been caught, and the direct threats to her life had ended, but the fear they had created within her had failed to subside. Maybe one day she could get into a car without being afraid it would blow up, but here was hoping.

Evan opened the restaurant door for her and motioned for her to step inside. She glanced over her shoulder one more time.

"Don't worry, honey," he said, but not before she saw him do the exact same thing.

He would never admit that he was still on high alert;

he would only tell her that this was his normal level of awareness, nothing more. She found it draining, but it also brought her a strange sense of comfort.

The hostess at the Italian restaurant greeted them and led them to a table in the back. "Will this do?" she asked.

"Yep, thank you very much." Evan pulled back Natalie's chair and helped her get settled and then he took his seat with his back to the wall.

The hostess retreated, leaving them to listen to the little string band that was playing "My Way." It was strangely sad but it fit the day. Evan reached over and took her hand in his. "I'm glad we finally found time to have a date, honey. I'm just sorry that you and I have to do it after such a ridiculous week."

It was just the break she needed after the flurry of cases she had been allotted after Hanes had been dismissed as a judge, pending investigation of any deals he'd made in the past. Even if he hadn't been fired, he would never have been able to come back. The nerve agent had done significant cognitive and pulmonary damage.

"Steve was moved back into the ICU today. Apparently, he fell and hit his head on his hospital bed." She ran her thumb over the back of Evan's hand.

"I know you're struggling with this, honey, but you couldn't have changed a damned thing. Steve made some bad choices. His son made bad choices."

"I know you and I talked about the fates, but can you imagine how different everything would have turned out if Steve's wife hadn't been killed by a drunk driver?" She paused. "Sven wouldn't have had half the problems he had. He wouldn't have forced his father into unethical positions to save him. One choice, a seemingly independent decision made by a stranger…one who I will never know, ended up almost costing you and me our lives, as well."

"You know these things… It's life. It is chaos. Plain and simple." He squeezed her hand.

"I'm just glad I was able to help set things right for all the people whose cases and lives were screwed up because of Judge Hanes, his son, the crooked district attorney and her sister." She couldn't stand the thought of how one simple conversation with the district attorney could have sent her on a completely different trajectory.

"Do you think Sven and Becky knew what they were doing when they used the Rockwood plates in their bombs?"

Evan shook his head. "According to his lawyers, Sven didn't know about any ties my family has to the group. But I still have a feeling that there is something more there. Regardless, I think Sven is going to play the insanity card as his defense in court."

"I have a feeling a judge will see right through that. Sven is going to have a nice long stay in a federal prison." She couldn't help the smile that flit across her lips. "And so far, the court of appeals has overturned several of Judge Hanes's rulings and many innocent people have been released from prison."

"I can only imagine how many guilty people are walking free because of them," Evan said, shaking his head in disgust.

The waiter came over and took their orders—two heaping plates of spaghetti and a bottle of Chianti.

Evan smiled as the man walked away. "Regardless of what has brought us together, I want you to know that

I'm grateful. You are all I can think of, morning, noon and night. You are always on my mind. I don't think that will ever change. It's like, in meeting you, I found my soul's other half."

She put her hand on her heart like it could control her swoon. "Honey, I love you, too."

The band started their next Sinatra song, "I've Got the World on a String."

She smiled as he stood up and extended his hand. She slipped her fingers in his.

"Can I have this dance?" he asked, straightening his suit jacket as she stood.

Her dress pulled around her legs, forcing her to take small steps to the center of the room. It felt like all eyes were on them. He led her in a graceful dance, and his subtle control made her feel more beautiful than she had in her entire life. She felt like a swan, gliding around the room like her feet didn't even touch the floor.

"I had no idea you were such a good dancer," she said, whispering into his ear and then returning to gaze into his beautiful green eyes.

They were alight with joy as he looked at her. "My mother made sure I took dance lessons as a kid. I hate to admit it, but I was an All-State Ballroom dancer when I was a senior in high school."

"Your mother was a smart woman. This is one time-less and elegant way to make a woman fall madly in love."

His smile widened. "I thought you were already madly in love with me."

"I love you more every day." She gave him a light kiss to the cheek as he pulled her into his arms before he spun her out of his grip.

She giggled as he moved her. It felt oddly invigorating to be at the mercy of such an incredible dancer. She was dancing out of her league, but she didn't care.

He pulled her back against him, hard. Apparently, he was having a good time, as well.

"I can think of nothing better than being in your arms like this," she said, nearly breathless. "I know we've waited a long time to have a night completely for us, but this is beyond any expectations."

"Most of the time, I would agree with you," he said, leading her around the dance floor. "Yet, there is something I can think of that would make our long-awaited date just that much better."

She giggled. "What is that?"

"If you would wear this," he said, dropping to his knee and opening up a box she hadn't seen him take out of his pocket.

At the heart of the box was a princess-cut diamond and set beside it was a set of sapphires. It was beautiful.

"Baby, yes…" she said, putting her hands over her mouth and then extending her left one.

He slipped the ring on her finger and stood up. Taking her lips with his, they needed no words. In that moment she had everything she would ever need or want and she could share it all with a man who was her equal.

No matter what the future held, or the chaos they would face, they would face it standing beside one another. They would be one another's shields from the ravages of the world—and they would do it all empowered by the strength and ferocity of their love.

* * * * *

COLTON 911:
SECRET DEFENDER

MARIE FERRARELLA

To
My Baby Brothers,
Michael Vincent Rydzynski, The Musician,
And
Mark Adam Rydzynski, The Actor,
Who Have, Over The Years,
Grown Into Good, Decent Men—
And Also Are Now Older
Than I Am.
Thanks, Guys.

Prologue

If it wasn't for the excruciating pain shooting up and down her leg to the point that her eyes were filling with tears, Nicole Colton would have been utterly furious with herself.

Of all the stupid things she had done in her life—and there had been a number of them over the last fifty-eight years—this definitely took the cake.

She felt like the pathetic embodiment of that awful commercial she had always felt was created for no other reason than to embarrass and humiliate older people—she steadfastly refused to use the term "senior citizen"—and make them feel clumsy and utterly inept. The fact that she was here, sprawled out on the floor after inadvertently taking a slip because of a wet spot, was exceedingly aggravating.

Especially since she found that she was unable to pop right back up the way she usually did. The pain was just too agonizing.

The cutting words "I've fallen and can't get up" kept echoing through Nicole's head even as she literally *dragged* herself across the living room floor until she could grasp the side of the sofa. She tried to pull herself up but failed. All but completely drenched in sweat from her effort, Nicole paused, panting hard and trying to regroup as she desperately searched for a second wave of strength.

"Okay, Nic, you can do this," she said through clenched teeth, urging herself on even as another sharp wave of pain sliced right through her. "You raised three boys on your own, started your own business. You can certainly get up off the floor on your own."

It wasn't easy.

Several pain-filled minutes later, Nicole finally managed to get herself up to her knees at the sofa cushion. But rather than stand up, she could only get herself into a half-lying position and then roll painfully over, all the while biting her lip to keep the cries from emerging and echoing throughout her large house.

Breathing hard, Nicole finally managed to get into a sitting position. When she did, she was all but panting from the exertion.

"Okay, I lied," she said, her face dripping with perspiration. "I *can't* do this."

Instead of going away, the pain multiplied by leaps and bounds, bordering on unbearable. Although she hated the thought, she had to admit that she had definitely broken something. Moreover, she resigned herself to the fact that she was going to have to call someone and ask for help. Something that went against absolutely every fiber of her being.

But there was no way around it.

Nicole was sweating profusely now. Admitting to weakness was just not in her makeup. She was the one who went out of her way to hold everything together, the one who worked nonstop and still had time to cheer on her sons—her biological son, Aaron, and Aaron's two half brothers, whom she had taken in when they were barely seven and eight—in their endeavors.

They were her ex-husband's sons she had opted to care for when their mother died and her ex decided they were dragging him down. She treated them like her own and made certain that these "endeavors" they undertook were of their choosing and not hers.

Her catering business was a success. Things were finally going so well—and now this, she thought as a new wave of disgust washed over her.

Her head began to spin. The pain got much worse.

Okay, time to get someone here to help her, as much as she hated the idea. Thank heavens she usually kept her cell phone with her. That had more to do with her catering business than anything else, but right now, Nicole was truly grateful that she had slipped her phone into her pocket this morning.

Taking a breath to steady herself and to keep the pain at bay long enough to make the call, she pressed the keys that would connect her to Aaron's phone.

She definitely wasn't looking forward to this conversation.

Her oldest son ran a gym and she quite honestly didn't expect him to even hear his phone, much less answer it. But to her surprise, Aaron picked up after the fifth ring.

Just by chance, Aaron Colton was about to make a call when he felt the phone vibrate in his hand. When he saw the name on the screen, he had a really bad feeling about what he was about to hear.

His mother *never* called him when she knew he was working.

Turning away from the boxing ring, Aaron blocked out all the other noises in the gym as he answered the call.

"Mom? What's wrong?"

More than anything in the world, Nicole Colton hated admitting to weakness. But the pain was making it really difficult to even breathe now.

Still, she protested, "What…makes…you…think… anything…is…wrong?"

If he hadn't thought there was anything wrong before, he did now. The pain he heard in his mother's voice unnerved him.

He signaled to his assistant to take over as he quickly made his way to the door. "Tell me where you are, Mom. I'm coming to get you," he promised.

Chapter One

Damon Colton, the youngest of the three Colton brothers, burst into the waiting room of the hospital's surgery. Accustomed to sizing up, at lightning speed, any area he walked into, he was able to spot Aaron and Nash within seconds. He made a beeline for his brothers.

"How is she?" he asked breathlessly before he had even had a chance to reach them.

"Ornery as ever," Aaron answered.

Feeling stiff, Aaron shifted in his seat. He and Nash had been sitting here on the orange plastic sofa, keeping vigil ever since the ambulance had brought Nicole to the hospital. Although things seemed to be going well, neither brother wanted to step away—just in case.

"I think he's asking about her hip, not the ongoing argument we were having with her about her going to a rehab center once this is all finally behind us," Nash told Aaron.

"Rehab center?" Damon echoed. He hadn't even thought that far ahead. He was just worried about her immediate condition. "Just how bad is Mom?" he asked, looking from one brother to the other. He had gotten no details.

"Not as bad as Aaron is making it sound," Nash told Damon.

It was obvious to them that their undercover DEA agent brother had come here straight from his assignment, without bothering to take the time to change out of what he was wearing. Because of his attire and his rather shaggy, longish hair, Damon was getting suspicious looks from the security guard. The latter had made it a point to slowly circle the area. For his part, Damon gave the impression of a man on the move who appeared to be less than trustworthy. That was his main intent when he was on the job.

It was all part of the role he was playing.

But role or no role, Damon, like Nash and Aaron, dearly loved the woman who had been mothering and caring for all of them equally all these years, whether or not they had actually come from her womb.

Aaron took over the narrative. "The short version is that Mom was in a hurry—as she always is—and she slipped on a wet spot on the floor. According to her, she went down hard, and much to her everlasting annoyance, wound up breaking her hip," he told Damon, repeating verbatim what he had already told Nash when his architect brother had shown up at the hospital shortly after he and his mother had arrived.

Damon, who faced down dangerous drug dealers without batting an eye, physically winced when Aaron was done speaking.

"Wow, that must have really hurt. Is she going to be all right?" he asked, looking from one brother to the other for reassurance.

Aaron nodded. "The hip replacement went without

a hitch. No complications," he said. The relief was all but palpable in his voice.

Damon had been holding his breath the entire way here, not knowing what to think. He'd never been summoned to the hospital because of his mother before. He breathed a sigh of relief now. "Is she awake? Can I see her?"

Aaron had just waylaid a nurse moments before Damon arrived and gotten an update from her. "The nurse said that she was still in recovery. We can see her when they finally transfer her to her room."

Damon nodded. And then he remembered what his brother had said when he first inquired about their mother's condition.

"You said something about her being ornery. What did you mean by that?"

"When I first got to the house and found her after her fall, it kind of got to me," Aaron admitted. "I guess I lost it and told her she needed to move into a smaller house, not one that was sprawled out on three levels." He flushed. It wasn't his finest hour. "Needless to say, that didn't make her very happy."

"Oh, hell, Aaron, you should have known better." Damon sighed. "You know how independent Mom is. She has more energy and acts younger than women who are half her age. Saying something like that to her is like rubbing salt into her wounds."

Nash nodded in agreement. "Yeah, you definitely said the wrong thing, brother," he told Aaron, then softened his words. "For all the right reasons," he granted. "But it was still the wrong thing."

"I know, I know." Aaron exhaled. "But be that as it

may, when Mom finally gets to go home, we are going to have to make some changes—whether she likes them or not." Aaron had always been the decisive one in the family and now was no different than before. "She's going to need a nurse or some live-in help. Maybe both," he added, looking from one brother to another to see if they concurred.

For once, they were all in agreement.

"No argument," Nash told Aaron. "Whatever the cost, we can take care of it."

"You can count me in," Damon said, adding his vote to the others'.

"Cost isn't the issue here," Aaron told his brothers. "Whatever it is, it is. The problem, we all know, is getting Mom to agree. You *know* she's going to see this as a restriction."

As if on cue, all three brothers nodded their heads. Their mother was a fighter from the get-go, and knowing her, it was going to be a very steep, uphill battle to get Nicole Colton to loosen her grip on the reins of her life and actually listen to her sons. Even if she knew that their only concern was her safety.

Easier said than done, Aaron thought as he saw the operating room nurse head straight in their direction.

All three brothers rose to their feet in unison as if they were all joined at the hip.

And all three had their fingers crossed as they went to meet the nurse partway.

A single thought was going through their heads. Nicole Colton *had* to be all right. Anything less was just *not* acceptable to the brothers.

"No, no, no," Nicole told her oldest son in no uncertain terms.

It was five weeks since the accident, five weeks since the emergency hip replacement surgery had taken place. Rather than the standard surgical procedure, she had gotten the more superior "anterior-posterior repair" version, which allowed her to heal faster. But not even her surgeon had expected her to make this much progress, certainly not so quickly, even though she was exceedingly fit, especially for someone her age.

She'd had the surgery on Wednesday. On Friday she'd gone home and, over all three sons' rather loud objections, Nicole had actually walked up the stairs to her room. She had totally ignored the boys' complaints about her doing too much too soon.

As she crossed the threshold to her bedroom, Nicole felt as if she had just reclaimed a little of her life back. She was *not* about to give that up, not even to placate her sons.

The chorus of "nos" she had just uttered was in response to yet another attempt by Aaron to talk her into having a nurse come and live with her until such time as *they* felt she had recovered.

"Aaron, I don't need a nurse. You saw me walk up the stairs. If I can do it on the first day I came back, I can do it on the second. And the third," she emphasized proudly. "That means I can take care of myself the way I always have. I don't need someone keeping tabs on me."

Aaron tried again. "Mom, getting someone to stay here with you isn't an admission of weakness. And it doesn't have to be a nurse," he relented, although he really didn't want to. He felt like a man who was struggling to win at least a portion of the battle before the war was declared officially over. "It can even be a competent, paid companion." Although he really would have preferred that person to be a nurse. "Think of her as being just a warm, intelligent body who can step in to help you out if the need should come up."

By the expression on his mother's face, he could see he wasn't getting anywhere with her, and after spending basically two weeks away from the gyms he ran, Aaron really felt that he needed to get back to work. "Look, Mom, if you refuse to do it for yourself—"

She smiled at that. "Now you get it," Nicole told him happily.

But Aaron wasn't about to be detoured. "Do it for me," he concluded.

Nicole stared at her son in disbelief. "You're not serious."

"Oh, I'm very serious," Aaron assured her. He was accustomed to being listened to without any argument from his employees at the gym as well as the boxers he trained. This, however, was going to take diplomacy, a gift he hadn't quite developed. He gave it another shot. "Look, Mom, you are very precious to me. To all of us," he stressed. "Granted, we didn't lose you, but we could have, if the circumstances had been different.

"Think of this as putting our minds at rest," he continued. "Nash has a job to do, I have a business to run, and Damon, well, if Damon doesn't keep his mind clear and focused on his work, it could very well end up costing him his life."

Unwavering, Aaron went in for the kill. "You don't want that to happen, do you?"

"Of course not," Nicole cried with feeling. "But I also don't want to become an invalid by just surrendering my independence to set everyone's mind at rest, either. We need a compromise."

Aaron sighed. He gave it one last try. "Okay, the way I see it, Mom, hiring someone to help you is a compromise."

Nicole met her son's eyes head-on. "Not hiring anyone would be an even better way to go."

"Mom." There was a warning note in his voice. He was reaching the end of his patience. "This is as far as I'm willing to give in. Now, until the doctor gives you the all clear, you are going to need someone to be here with you when I can't be, and you are going to *have* someone. The way I see it, you can either pick out that someone yourself, or I will do it for you," Aaron said. "Your choice."

Nicole frowned. "I don't really *feel* like I have a choice."

"Trust me, you do," Aaron told her. "Because if you don't make a choice here, I will." Standing over her like this, he knew he was being intimidating—but apparently she needed that. This, he told himself, was for her own good—not to mention his own peace of mind. "So what's it going to be?"

Nicole thought of the young woman she had met and talked with during her first physical therapy sessions at the rehab facility after her surgery healed. She had taken an instant liking to Felicia Wagner, a perky, friendly and fresh-faced young woman who was working at the facility part-time.

Nicole smiled as she raised her eyes to her son's. "I think I know someone who would be willing to take on the job. It's a woman I met at rehab."

"Ah, finally. Progress," Aaron declared with a sigh. "Why don't you give this lady a call? Whatever she wants to be paid—within reason," he stipulated, not wanting to be taken advantage of, "just say yes. And don't concern yourself with the cost. I'll take care of it."

Nicole shook her head. "You're a good son, Aaron, but I can take care of my own bills."

He dearly loved this woman, but there were times when she could be exasperatingly pigheaded. "Mom, everything doesn't have to turn into a tug-of-war. I'm making the request and I'm paying for it. End of discussion," he told her. And then, looking at her face, he added, "Okay?"

A gracious smile rose to his mother's lips as she obligingly nodded her head. In her opinion, she had won. "Okay."

Relieved that this argument had finally been put to bed, Aaron bent over and kissed his mother's forehead. "That's my girl," he said with genuine relief.

He knew how much it had to cost his mother to give in this way. She had always been the last word in independence and for her to agree to have someone come in and stay in the home she considered to be her domain was a huge deal.

He had to admit that part of him hadn't expected to win this confrontation so easily. Obviously, playing the "do it for me" card seemed to have worked wonders, he thought, congratulating himself.

But he wasn't going to overanalyze it. That kind of thing was for working with the fighters who came to him for guidance and training. His analysis kept them alive and moving up the championship ladder. But this was about his mother and he knew better than to be anything but really, really grateful she had stopped fighting him on this and had agreed to do as he had suggested.

Right now, it was time to get his mind back on running his gyms. The boxers who sought out his particular gym weren't there because of the showers and the state-of-the-art weight equipment he had stocked at the gym. They were there to gain insight into his specific training methods as well as the host of other insights that he could offer them.

"Do you want me to put in that call for you?" he asked his mother.

Apparently making plans in her mind already, Nicole seemed confused at his question. "To whom, dear?"

He began to wonder if she had been putting him on after all. "To this person you said you would be willing to have come stay with you until you're ready to be on your own," Aaron explained to his mother, enunciating every word.

Because she loved him, Nicole smiled indulgently. "I still know how to make a phone call, Aaron."

"Then you have her number," he assumed. He knew he was treating his mother like a child and she was going to resent it even if she didn't show it, but he needed to have all this spelled out so he was sure that she was going to do as he asked and not find some way to wriggle out of it.

"Yes, dear, I have her number," she answered patiently. She didn't roll her eyes, but it was there in her voice.

"Good. I can make the arrangements," Aaron offered again.

This time, his mother did roll her eyes. "Aaron, I said I would take care of it. There may come a day when you will have to take care of me, but—much as I appreciate the thought—that day is *not* today."

"Okay, I get that," he allowed, looking at the situation from her point of view. "But I still want to meet this 'caretaker,'" he stressed.

"And you will, dear—once she accepts the job and has gotten accustomed to staying in this 'barn of a house' as you referred to it in the hospital. But for now, just let me handle this my way."

He wasn't about to back away from this totally. "Will I be meeting her soon?" he asked.

Maybe it was the spill she had taken and the hip fracture that had resulted, but Nicole found that her patience seemed to be in shorter supply than it normally was.

Still, she managed a civil reply. "Yes, you will be meeting her soon. Felicia is a very sweet, accommodating young woman, so I'm sure she would be willing to put up with your scrutiny."

Aaron nodded. "'Felicia,'" he repeated, rolling her name over on his tongue. "Pretty name."

"If her name was Maude, would that disqualify her from the position?" Nicole asked, amused.

"No, I just—" Aaron paused, realizing what his mother was doing. "You're yanking my chain, aren't you?"

"With both hands, dear," she answered, flashing a wide smile. "Now, don't you have a life to get back to?" she asked him. "A life you've been away from for much too long?"

"Nothing is more important than you, Mom," he answered honestly.

"I appreciate that, dear," she said. "But I have taken you away from that gym you worked so hard to get up and running long enough, not to mention the other gyms you're overseeing. Remember, guilt is not helpful for my recovery."

"Point taken." There was that independence of hers, rearing its head again. "But I still don't want to leave you alone in the house."

She looked at him, knowing exactly what was going on in his head. "I'm not going to fall again."

"I wasn't worried about that," he answered a bit too quickly.

He was lying, she thought. "Yes, you were. You have a tell, Aaron," Nicole said, leaning forward. "When you're not being completely truthful, you get this little furrow in your brow." She flittered her fingertips across his forehead. "Now, you don't have to stay here and hover over me. If it makes you feel any better, Vita is coming over."

Vita Yates was her former sister-in-law. The two women were very much alike, both having weathered divorces from their respective Colton husbands and survived the dealings of a viperlike mother-in-law who could have very easily run a school for unemployed witches in her spare time. The two women had bonded early on and their relationship had only grown stronger as the years went by. They also acted as each other's support group, providing encouragement when needed most.

"Aunt Vita?" Aaron asked, surprised. His mother should have told him this to begin with. "You're sure?" He wanted to be certain his mother wasn't just trying to get rid of him.

"Aaron, I broke my hip. I didn't hit my head and get a brain injury. Yes, I am sure, now go before I show you what a needy, clinging mother can *really* be like."

He made no move to leave. "When is Aunt Vita coming?" he asked.

The doorbell rang just then. "Now," Nicole answered with a smile.

"Okay, you win this one, Mom," he said as he went to answer the door.

"I win them all, dear," Nicole called after her son with a smile.

Aaron sighed. He knew she was right.

Chapter Two

Felicia Wagner pressed the red button on her cell phone, terminating the call she had just received, and smiled.

Really smiled.

She couldn't believe her luck. Something was finally, *finally* going her way. That lovely woman she had met at the rehab facility where she was working part-time as a physical therapist had just offered her a job. An actual live-in position at her home! And from where she stood, the job was an *absolute godsend*.

For the last two years Felicia had been piecing together a meager living, accepting odd jobs that were strictly off the books. She did that because she didn't want to leave any sort of a paper trail that could ultimately be used to trace her. She was terrified that if she did leave any sort of paper trail, it could be used to pinpoint her current location.

There was no way in the world that she could afford to take that chance. Doing so, she had no doubt, meant that all hell could very well break loose when she least expected it.

Felicia had been there before.

There was a time when she wouldn't have thought

that way, but at this point, after everything that had happened to her in the last few years, Felicia was convinced that Greg, the man she was still trying so desperately to elude, was the type who was capable of anything.

Better to be floating around anonymously, moving from place to place like a nomad, than to take the chance of him finding her.

That was why, after the last frightening incident had taken place almost two years ago, Felicia had packed up only her essential belongings, changed her name and moved to Chicago. She did her damnedest to blend in with the crowd.

And it seemed to be working, at least so far. But she knew better than to let her guard down. Greg Harper was not a man she could afford to underestimate.

Ever.

Felicia was convinced that the next time their paths crossed could very well be her last time—permanently. Which was why when she had hesitantly answered her cell phone—a burner phone—and heard Nicole's sweet, motherly voice on the other end, asking her if she was interested in coming to live with her as her physical therapist/assistant, Felicia thought she had died and gone to heaven. She was close to tears when she accepted the offer.

"I'm not browbeating you into this, am I?" Nicole had asked after asking her if she would do it. "It's just that my sons insisted that I don't stay home alone while I'm 'convalescing' with this annoying hip replacement. It seems that all three of the boys are obviously afraid that history might just repeat itself," Nicole had complained.

Felicia knew all about history repeating itself. Each time Greg had abused her, he had sworn passionately that it was the very last time. That he was a changed man.

And she, pathetic, lonely soul that she was, had believed him. Time and again. She was that desperate for her happily-ever-after ending—until she finally had to admit to herself that, at least in her case, the happily-ever-after was never going to happen. Not with Greg, no matter how good-looking and intelligent he was.

Out loud, though, Felicia had compassionately told the woman, "You really can't blame your sons for worrying about you, Nicole."

"Oh, yes, I can," Nicole had countered with feeling. "They know me. They know that I'm not one of those frail, delicate women who break if you so much as blow on them," she had protested.

"Oh, I know that," Felicia had said, and not just to placate Nicole. She meant what she said, especially when she added, "But you have no idea how lucky you are to have a family, and one that genuinely cares and worries about you. It's not something to take for granted."

She had sounded so sad that for a moment, the woman on the other end of the call had been at a loss for words. It had convinced Nicole more than ever that this was the right move on her part, offering this position to Felicia. Bringing her into her home, Nicole felt, could help them both do each other some good.

"Maybe so," Nicole had agreed. "So you'll take the

job?" she'd asked, quickly adding, "You'll have your own bedroom and bath," to sweeten the deal.

Felicia had laughed then. "You don't have to sell me on it, Nicole. You had me at, 'Would you be interested in coming to work for me?'"

"Good! All right, do you have a paper and pen handy?"

Everything within the tiny motel room where Felicia was staying—again, temporarily—was within reach. "Yes."

"Here's my address." Nicole had quickly rattled it off. "How soon do you think you can get here?"

"How soon do you want me?" Felicia had countered with a smile forming on her lips. She no longer believed in things that were too good to be true, but in this case, she made an exception.

The job she currently had at the rehab facility was temporary at best, like all her other positions in the last couple of years. And maybe it was just wishful thinking on her part, but she had a good feeling about coming to work for Nicole. Equally as good was the fact that the job came with a place to stay.

One less thing she had to deal with, Felicia had thought, relieved.

Nicole had laughed at her response. "How long will it take for you to get here?"

That was when Felicia had thought of a possible problem. "Won't your sons want to meet me first?" She had gotten very good at anticipating complications.

"Damon and Nash just want someone here with me. As for Aaron, my oldest, he has put himself in charge of my life, but don't worry about him. At bottom, he wants me happy, and having you living here instead of some fussy, bossy nurse watching my every move would definitely make me happy—so he's not going to give me an argument about choosing you."

Nicole Colton was one of a kind, Felicia had thought with a smile, once again glad that she had met her. "Okay, if you say so."

"Oh, I definitely say so," Nicole had assured her with feeling.

Once again Felicia thought that this was almost too good to be true, afraid to allow herself to believe this was really happening.

"And you really want me there as soon as I can manage it?" Felicia had asked, wanting to make sure that she wasn't just allowing wishful thinking to govern her actions.

"Sooner if possible," Nicole had replied. "Now, stop talking and start packing, girl, because the sooner you get over here, the sooner Aaron is going to have to stop threatening me with bringing in squadrons of nurses and housekeepers."

"I don't think I've ever heard it put quite that way before," Felicia had said with a laugh.

"That's because you've never met anyone like my oldest boy," Nicole told her. "Actually, he's not a boy— he keeps reminding me of that," Nicole had confessed. "But I'll let you in on a little secret. No matter how old your kids get, they will *always* be your kids. Even when Aaron became this big, brawny professional boxer, I couldn't get myself to stop worrying that he was going to wind up getting seriously hurt in the ring."

Nicole's description had given her pause. "Your son's a professional boxer?"

"He was," Nicole had answered. "Before he got injured. Luckily, it wasn't anything overly serious—just enough to keep him out of the ring, thank heavens. Now he runs a gym. Actually," she had amended, "he runs several gyms. That makes me feel a whole lot better about his chosen profession. People who own gyms don't get hurt, at least not like the way a professional boxer can. Anyway," Nicole had said abruptly, "I've talked much too much. We can continue this conversation—if you're interested, of course—when you get here."

Actually, Felicia had thought, she was interested in continuing the conversation. Having no family of her own, she was hungry for any kind of details when it came to someone else's.

"It's a deal," Felicia had told her just before she terminated the call.

Felicia paused just long enough after the call ended to pinch herself.

And smiled. Broadly.

Then she went to pull the meager wardrobe she had escaped with out of her closet.

That was the only way she could describe what she had done. Escaped. Because even though she hadn't been married to Greg all that long, when he showed up on her doorstep that last time and threatened to end her life, she knew that she wouldn't be able to "quietly walk away" anymore. She had truly felt as if her life was in serious danger.

Moreover, she had found, much to her disappointment, that there was no help—or hope—forthcoming from the police in her case. When Greg had appeared on her doorstep, drunk and blaming her for absolutely *everything* that had gone wrong in his life, she had somehow managed to get away and call the police. The police had come quickly enough, but after questioning Greg, they didn't make an arrest. The way they saw it, they explained, it was only her word against her ex-husband's.

They did escort Greg from her apartment, but that didn't do her any good, since they ultimately did let him go free.

That in essence left Greg free to do to her anything he wanted to.

Felicia had no idea what happened after that, because she had taken off that very night. Truly terrified of what Greg could do to her now that he felt so reassured that he was "untouchable," she had fled to Chicago. There was nothing to connect her to the city.

And in doing that, she had given up any hope of having anything like a normal life.

Until just now.

Thank heavens she had taken courses in physical therapy so that she had a vocation to fall back on. The ironic thing was that was where she had first met Greg. They were both working toward a degree in physical therapy.

Looking back now, she was aware that dreams died hard. For the most part, until just now when Nicole had offered her a job, Felicia had gotten by with stitching together various part-time jobs and praying for the day that she felt secure enough to attempt to get back to a normal way of life.

She sighed. Even with Nicole in her life—temporarily, she reminded herself—it didn't feel as if "normal" was going to happen any time soon.

"Knock it off, Fee. This is getting you nowhere," she told herself as she laid open her battered suitcase on the sagging bed. "Pack, don't talk," she ordered. "You've finally got a decent position. Make the most of it."

Packing didn't take long. When she had put away all her worldly possessions into the suitcase, it struck her that there wasn't much to show for twenty-eight years of living.

But then, she couldn't allow herself to look at it that way. She had to look at the positive side of the situation. She was alive—for a while, the alternative had been a highly likely possibility. And according to what Jeanne, the woman who had helped her initially escape from her soul-sucking marriage, had said, "Where there's life, there's always hope."

Yes, it was a trite saying, but nonetheless, it didn't make it any the less true. And she intended to make everything she could out of this unexpected opportunity that had come her way.

After that, who knew?

Checking the closet one last time to make sure she hadn't left anything behind, Felicia snapped the locks shut. She was ready to go.

Felicia was all paid up to the end of the week, and even though money at this point was very precious, not to mention scarce, she was not about to attempt to get a refund for the three days that she wasn't going to be using. The last thing she wanted to do was call any extra attention to herself than she had to.

Telling the clerk at the front desk that she was leaving early would be doing just that. Everything she did these days was done with her being mindful that Greg might just track her down and use the information to his advantage.

Felicia left everything just the way she had found it when she checked into the small room. Tidier actually, she thought, giving it one last look around. But then that was just her nature. She didn't like leaving things in disarray.

The suitcase on the floor, ready to go, she looked out the window. She wanted to assure herself that there was no one out in the courtyard who could bear witness to her exodus. At the very least, she wanted to be sure that no one saw her carrying her suitcase to her car. She had actually considered putting all her belongings into two shopping bags and carrying her clothes out that way.

But the thought of doing that was just too depressing to bear. It would have meant that Greg had beaten her down to a new low. She had no place that she could actually call, or even think of, as home.

Someday, she promised herself. Someday this would all be behind her and she would be able to forge a new life for herself, but until that day came, she had to make the most out of any opportunity that came her way, and this was definitely an opportunity.

She had taken an instant liking to Nicole Colton when she was working with her at the rehab facility. In an odd way, the feisty woman reminded her of herself, Felicia thought. She could only hope that when she was Nicole's age, she would have half the woman's spirit, half her fighting attitude.

She glanced out the window again. There was still no one in the courtyard. The path appeared to be clear. Taking nothing for granted, Felicia opened the front door to her motel room just a crack. Her eyes swept over the immediate area, then looked a little farther, until eventually, she had taken in as much as she could. It was still clear, but who knew how long that would be the case? She had to leave now.

Slipping out of the room, she eased the door closed behind her. She made her way forward, not slowly, not quickly, but at a normal, unhurried pace. She had purposely gotten a room on the second floor so that she could hear someone coming. The floor directly in front of her door creaked if anyone passed by.

Fortunately for her nerves, that didn't happen very often.

Satisfied she was alone, Felicia made her way down the stairs to the first floor and then into the parking lot where she had parked her small, beige vehicle.

She didn't relax until she finally made it to her car and then into it.

Sliding behind the wheel, Felicia was quick to lock her door even before she buckled up.

Only then did she release the breath she was holding.

Key clutched in her hand, she inserted it into the ignition and started up the vehicle as quietly as possible. Now wasn't the time to rev up her motor, even by accident. She wanted to be as unobtrusive as possible.

Holding her breath again, she slowly drove out of the spot and then away from the motel. She was more than ready to begin a new phase of her life.

Again.

Chapter Three

Nicole Colton's home was located in the Chicago suburb of Bartlett. As Felicia drove up to the impressive old Victorian-style, three-storied redbrick house, she was so awestruck by the edifice that it all but took her breath away.

So much so that for a moment, she wasn't sure if she even had any business attempting to work for anyone who lived in a house as fine as this.

The building made her think of old families coming from old wealth, while she, at best, was an interloper just trying to make her way through life and not get noticed.

But she had given her word to the woman that she was coming, and Nicole Colton was expecting her, so rather than give in to her mounting insecurity and turn around, Felicia pulled up in front of the house and parked.

She took a deep breath, trying to gather her courage together and focus on putting one foot in front of the other.

She left her suitcase in her car for the time being,

got out of the vehicle and went up the steps leading to the front door.

Pressing the doorbell, Felicia heard a series of chimes ringing softly and melodiously. But when the front door opened less than a couple of minutes later, she found herself looking into the soft brown eyes of someone who was definitely not Nicole.

"I'm sorry, I must have made a mistake," she apologized. Her hand on the banister, she was ready to go back down the steps and to her vehicle.

"No, no mistake, dear," the slender, attractive woman with the short, dark-haired bob told her. "That is, if you *are* Felicia Wagner. Are you?" she asked, doing a quick assessment of the young woman in front of her.

"Yes," Felicia replied. This was someone new and unknown to her. She was *not* at ease with new people. They represented the unknown and thus a possible danger to her very existence. The smile never left her face, but her heart had begun hammering.

"Felicia, this is my sister-in-law, Vita Yates," Nicole called out to the young woman as she came into the foyer to join them. "Or rather, my former sister-in-law. She had to be tough in order to survive her marriage to my ex-husband's brother. But sometimes she forgets that she no longer needs to come across that way. Don't let Vita intimidate you. Please," she said, waving the young woman into the house, "come in, come in."

Nicole, looking amazingly fit considering that her operation had been a little more than five weeks ago, came to greet Felicia. The first thing she noticed was that Felicia had brought nothing with her.

"Where's your suitcase, Felicia?" Nicole asked.

Felicia nodded behind her toward the door. "It's in my car."

"Well, it's not going to do you any good there," Nicole told her new physical therapist. She turned toward her former sister-in-law and eternal confidante. "Vita, would you mind going to get Felicia's suitcase?" she requested.

"No problem," the other woman replied obligingly as she started to go out the front door.

"No, please, I can get my own suitcase. I just wanted to be sure I had the right place before I brought out my baggage," Felicia said as she doubled back down the front steps. Within a few moments, she had retrieved her suitcase and returned.

Nicole looked at the suitcase, amused. "That's not baggage, dear. That's hardly enough to qualify as a backpack. I take it you're not sure about staying?" she asked pleasantly as she linked her arm through the one that Felicia wasn't using to carry her suitcase.

"No, these are all my belongings." Seeing the skeptical look on Nicole's face, Felicia added, "I like to travel light."

Nicole rolled her eyes. "Oh, darling, the first thing I'm going to do once you've established a routine for me is take you clothes shopping."

"Don't mind her," Vita told Felicia, as if sharing a secret. "Nicole likes to mother *everyone*, whether they feel they need it or not."

Rather than comment on Vita's assessment, Felicia spoke to the woman she hoped was still going to be her new employer. "I'm here to help you with your physical therapy, Nicole, not to acquire a wardrobe."

Vita nodded, pleased by the comment. "I like her, Nicole. I think you picked a good one."

"I told you I had good instincts," Nicole said to Vita with a wide, satisfied smile.

Vita turned toward Felicia. "I know that Nicole would like to take you on a tour of the entire house, but given the fact that she is technically still recovering from her surgery, albeit faster than anyone thought she would, that task falls to me. Unless, of course, you'd like to eat something first. Are you hungry?" She waited for a response.

Felicia shook her head, not in refusal, but in sheer wonder. "You two do go a hundred miles an hour, don't you?" she marveled.

Vita laughed, clearly taking the remark to mean Nicole, not her. "You should see her when she's built up a full head of steam." Her eyes smiled as she told Felicia, "That's when everyone makes sure to get out of Nicole's way."

"Which is why I found Aaron's hovering over me like a mother hen insulting," Nicole said, putting in her two cents. "I'm afraid that it got me angrier than it should have."

"But it did get results," Vita pointed out, gesturing toward Felicia. "So, what do you say, Nic? Shall I take her up to her room first?"

"Sure. Go find a home for your suitcase, Fee, and then come on back down so that we can visit some more," Nicole said as she accompanied Felicia and her sister-in-law to the staircase and then called up after them, "Over lunch."

"You know, you've made her very happy by accepting her offer," Vita told Felicia once they had reached the second-floor landing. "Nicole is a very independent lady and her boys weren't going to give her any peace until she agreed to having someone stay here with her. She likes having a say in matters."

"Well, it's a two-way street," Felicia replied. "She's made me very happy, as well."

Vita studied the young woman for a moment. "I get that, but you're not just smiling because of that, are you?"

These were two very sharp ladies who didn't stand on ceremony, Felicia thought. She was definitely going to be on her toes, working here, but she also felt that she was going to enjoy the experience.

"You're right. I have to admit that I'm getting a kick out of both you and Nicole referring to what I assume are grown men as 'boys.'"

"Honey, when you get to be Nicole's and my age, anyone who is ten years younger gets placed into a younger realm. Besides, we knew these grown 'men' when they were in diapers. It's hard to think of them as full-grown adults, even though admittedly they are."

"It's also hard," Vita confided, "to put up with the idea that people you once diapered suddenly think that they can take over your life. I understand exactly where Nicole is coming from."

"So do I," Felicia admitted.

"You?" Vita marveled. "You're a baby."

"That's just it. I'm not," Felicia said, thinking of everything she had been through. "The way I see it, this is a tug-of-war between kids who have grown up and parents who don't welcome the idea of their children taking over their lives. If they've somehow managed to earn it, everyone has the right to be independent."

"That sounds like a hard-won lesson," Vita observed, studying her.

Felicia flushed. She had said too much. "I didn't mean to sound as if I'd gotten on my soapbox," she murmured.

"No need to apologize, dear. If you ever need anyone to talk to, I drop by Nicole's on a regular basis," Vita said. "Even before she broke anything, I used to help out with her catering business. I still will," she amended, knowing that Nicole had no intentions of backing off from the business she had worked so hard to build and get off the ground.

"Thank you, I'll keep that in mind," Felicia said, even though she had no intentions of confiding in the older woman. Except for one instance, she had always kept her own counsel and she intended to continue doing so.

Feeling as if the door had just closed on this subject, at least for the time being, Vita turned to the business at hand. "So, let me show you the spare bedrooms and you can decide which one suits you."

Mindful of the fact that they had left Nicole by herself downstairs, Felicia wanted to get back to the woman as soon as possible.

"This isn't about the room," she told Vita. "I'm sure that they're all equally very nice." Certainly nicer than the motel room she had just left in her wake. "I'll just take this first one," she proclaimed, stepping into the room just far enough to leave her suitcase inside the door.

Vita laughed. "I could have really used you when my kids were growing up. They were a picky pair," she recalled with a wistful note in her voice, her eyes getting a faraway look in them as she thought of her son and daughter. "And I'd do it all over again," she told Felicia with a wink.

"That makes you a good mother." Felicia smiled. "Shall we go down?"

"You sure you don't want to look at the other three bedrooms?" Vita asked. "You might find you like one of them better."

"No, this room is just fine," Felicia assured the woman. "Besides, it's not about the room. It's about my working with Nicole and helping her get back to her old self. As long as the room isn't a tiny, dark shoebox, I'm fine."

"I *definitely* could have used you when my kids were growing up," Vita told Felicia. "All right, let's go downstairs and let Nicole know that you've picked out your room and are currently in the process of settling in," she said, thereby leaving the door open for Felicia to change her mind if it came to that.

When they went back downstairs, Nicole was not where they had left her.

Vita frowned. "Nicole?" She looked around the immediate area. "Where are you?"

"I'm in the kitchen." The other woman's voice drifted out to them from what sounded like a distance.

"I should have known," Vita said with a patient sigh.

She glanced in Felicia's direction. "If it doesn't have to do with her sons, the woman lives and breathes her catering business. She's either filling an order, or barring that, puttering around and creating new recipes." Vita shook her head. "Personally, I don't think the woman even knows *how* to sit still and do nothing," she confided to Felicia in a deliberate stage whisper so that her voice would carry as she brought Nicole's new physical therapist into the kitchen.

The outside of the house might have presented itself as an old-fashioned Victorian-style home, but the kitchen, at its center, was nothing less than state-of-the-art. It was large and functional, with all the very latest, not to mention large, appliances.

Scanning her surroundings, Felicia felt not unlike Alice in Wonderland right after Alice had fallen down the rabbit hole.

As she looked around the large, bright and exceedingly sunlit area, the first word that came out of her mouth was "Wow."

"You like it?" Nicole asked needlessly.

"Like it?" Felicia echoed in wonder. "I think I'm in love with it. If this kitchen was a person, right now I'd be asking it to marry me," she confided before she could think to censor herself.

It was definitely the right thing to say. Nicole beamed in response. She had put a great deal of effort into remodeling the kitchen and was very proud of the results. It was while she had been busy remodeling the kitchen that her husband, Erik, had decided to walk out of their marriage.

"You should have seen it before I got to work on remodeling it." She looked around the room as if seeing it for the first time. "This house was all I asked for when Aaron's father decided he wanted to get a divorce," she stated matter-of-factly.

"Asked for?" Vita echoed her friend's phrase, amused. "The woman fought for this house like her very soul depended on it," she told Felicia. "I have to admit that Nicole surprised all of us. Up until that point, she had always been a mild-mannered person. She was the kind of woman who never argued over anything but just went along with whatever was asked of her for the sake of peace." Vita looked at her sister-in-law with unabashed admiration and pride.

Nicole frowned. "You're making me sound like I was a pushover. I was *not* a pushover," the woman underscored with emphasis.

Vita inclined her head. "No, you were definitely not a pushover," she agreed, and turned toward Felicia. "Now you can see why we were all so very protective of Nicole. Underneath it all, she was always our standard-bearer. More than anything, we all wanted to make sure that nothing but the right things was done by her."

"Well, I will do my very best to make sure not to disappoint her—or you," Felicia promised.

"I know you will," Nicole responded before her sister-in-law could comment on the assurance. "Now let's stop all this talking and speculation and just sit down and have a very nice lunch." She led both women over to the functional kitchen table and gestured toward it. "I wasn't sure what you were in the mood for," she told her physical therapist, "so I made a potpourri lunch.

There's a little bit of everything here—individual pizzas, sandwiches, soup and, to top it all off, a wide selection of desserts to choose from."

Felicia looked at the impressive selection in awe. "You did all this *after* you called to offer me the job?" she asked in wonder.

Nicole laughed, amused by the young woman's wonder. "I'm fast, dear, but I'm not *that* fast," she assured Felicia. "What you see here is the new menu that I was working on when I put in a call to you." Her eyes crinkled in amusement. "Let's just say that the idea of hiring you inspired me to do a little creating."

While Felicia appreciated Nicole's creative bent, she was concerned about the woman's health. In her estimation, Nicole was spending much too much time on her feet.

"Aren't you pushing yourself a little too much?" she asked.

It was Vita who answered her. "You'll get used to this after a while," she promised. "This is just Nicole being Nicole."

Suddenly all this was pushed into the background as they all heard a deep, masculine voice calling out from the front of the house.

"Hey, Mom, where are you?"

"And that," Nicole announced, glancing at Felicia, "is Aaron about to be Aaron. Brace yourself, Fee," she warned just before she responded, "I'm in the kitchen, dear!"

Felicia had no idea why, but hearing the deep voice, her heart began to beat just a little harder.

Chapter Four

As he drove up to his childhood home, Aaron Colton had told himself that he had no intentions of interfering with his mother's choice of a nurse, or whatever this person she wanted to hire chose to ultimately call herself. Whoever his mother decided on hiring was fine with him.

But by the same token, Aaron felt he needed to know that the woman was qualified to care for his mother. He was not about to allow just anyone to come waltzing into his mother's home and try to hoodwink her.

Not that his mother was a fool, but she did possess an exceedingly kind heart and that at times caused her to turn a blind eye to certain flaws a person might have. Otherwise, how could he have explained his mother marrying his father?

He just wanted to check out this person whom his mother was entrusting with her care, and after he was satisfied, he would be on his way.

But he did need to be satisfied. After all, Nicole Colton was his mother and he wanted to ensure that she was well taken care of. Since she absolutely refused to allow him to check her into a rehab facility, which, in his opinion, was the better way to go, he had to be content with his mother getting professional care.

And since his mother had to be satisfied that he wasn't going to attempt to push her into accepting his decision, he had agreed to back off.

However, that only went so far. In this case, it involved his final approval of his mother's choice of a caregiver.

In that light Nicole Colton might have been able to intimidate his two half brothers and get them to go along with whatever her choice was, but he was not them. He took a stand. Not an unreasonable one, he liked to think, but a definite stand nonetheless.

Walking into the house, Aaron looked around for his mother and the woman he had come to meet.

However prepared Aaron Colton might have thought he was to meet his mother's new physical therapist, he was wrong.

Dead wrong.

For one thing, the woman, whose name he had been told was Felicia Wagner, wasn't some middle-aged nurse type in thick-soled, sensible shoes. Instead she was a young woman who looked as if she would have been far more at home on the cover of a fashion magazine touting the future stars of tomorrow.

Maybe he had made a mistake, Aaron thought. Maybe she was just a friend his mother had made at the rehab facility. Youthful in spirit, his mother had the ability to attract young and old alike.

"Hello," he said, stepping forward and putting his hand out to the young woman. "I'm Aaron Colton, Nicole's son."

Belatedly, Felicia took his hand and shook it. "Yes, I know. Your mother talked about you a great deal, as well as about your brothers," she added, thinking it was safer mentioning all of them in the same breath.

She had to admit that Nicole's oldest son was far more distractingly good-looking than she had first imagined he would be, given what Nicole had said about him. She had to concentrate in order to keep her mind on the subject at hand.

"You have me at a disadvantage," Aaron confessed, feeling just the slightest bit awkward. He certainly wasn't prepared to be this taken with the woman his mother had hired. With her long, light blond hair and brilliant blue eyes the woman was flat-out gorgeous. That made him doubtful about her capabilities. "Mother didn't exactly mention a lot about you. Mother?" he asked, glancing in Nicole's direction to have his mother fill him in on the details.

"I mentioned her all right. You just don't listen," she told her son. "All right, let's make this formal," Nicole declared. "Aaron, I'd like you to meet Felicia Wagner. Felicia is the young woman you practically hounded me into hiring—no offense, dear," she added as an aside to Felicia.

Aaron looked a little perplexed. "I didn't tell you to hire her," he protested, still thinking his mother was hiring someone who looked like a sensible nurse.

"Yes, you did. You told me you wanted me to hire someone I liked having around. Someone who would be helpful and could work with me when it came to physical therapy. Well, this is her," Nicole announced, gesturing toward Felicia.

Aaron was having trouble reconciling the idea that a woman *this* beautiful could have a useful skill. She was just too damn attractive in his eyes for that sort of thing.

"Her?" he asked his mother dubiously.

"Yes, dear, *her*," Nicole said with finality. She looked at Felicia. "He usually has better manners than this, although in his defense, he did sustain more blows to the head in the ring than I was happy about. Thank heavens he quit when he did, because I shudder to think what might have happened if he had decided to continue that dangerous boxing career," she told her new confidante with a sigh.

"We're not talking about me, Mom," Aaron told his mother pointedly, uncomfortable with the personal reference. "We're talking about your exceedingly young-looking physical therapist here and her qualifications. You do have qualifications, don't you?" he asked, focusing his attention on Felicia.

"Aaron," his mother said sharply, appalled by his probing tone.

She had been subjected to worse, Felicia thought. Much worse. "That's all right, Nicole. He's your son and he's concerned. He has every right to ask about my qualifications." Felicia turned to Aaron. "I received my education from the Austin School of Physical Therapy. I graduated with a certificate in the field."

It was all well and good to claim that she had certification from a school, but he needed more than just her word for it. He knew this was going to sound hard-nosed, but this was his mother and he was not about to be careless about this.

"You don't mind if I ask to see it, do you?" Aaron inquired.

There was a problem with that, Felicia thought. The documentation wasn't in her name. Not the one she was currently using at any rate. And her real name had become a secret she needed to guard. "Unfortunately, it was lost in the move I made from Texas to Chicago."

Much as he would have wanted to believe her, Aaron found her story highly suspect. "How convenient," he commented.

Nicole instantly felt her back going up. She had had just about enough of her son's behavior. "Aaron, I didn't raise you to browbeat a young woman I have chosen to work with me and help me." Her eyebrows drew together in a deep V as she frowned at her oldest son. "Maybe I should hire someone to teach you manners, since I didn't seem to have done a good enough job of that myself.

"Now, this might have escaped you," Nicole continued, "but I am still your mother and I am still capable of making my own decisions. I have decided to hire Felicia as my physical therapist.

"And if you are finished giving this poor young woman the third degree when her only sin was to agree to come live here and help me attempt to become as flexible as I was before I took that dreadful flier across the floor," she crisply informed her son, "you can join us for lunch."

Aaron was nowhere near done asking questions, but

he knew his mother and that tone. She was not about to stand for what she obviously viewed as his interrogation of this cover model. He could only hope that this either worked out for the best or that his mother became disenchanted with the young woman on her own.

A third alternative was for him to track down Felicia Wagner's PT certification, which he still might attempt to do, he thought, debating that course of action.

As for lunch, he was going to have to take a pass. "Sorry, Mom. Maybe some other time." Aaron leaned over and kissed his mother's temple. "Nash and I are meeting with Dad to find out why he's pursuing this lawsuit against the newly discovered branch of the family." At least, he thought, new to him and his brothers and two cousins.

The lawsuit was something new and he wanted to look into it. Both he and Nash had a feeling that this undertaking was *not* Erik Colton's idea, although he knew that there was no love lost between their father and the newly unearthed other half of the Colton family.

Still, it wasn't like his father to instigate this kind of legal action on his own. There had to be something or someone behind it.

Aaron nodded at the table with its tempting layout. "I'm going to have to take a rain check," he told his mother. Turning toward Felicia, he nodded politely. "Nice meeting you." *To be continued*, he added silently.

Felicia had her doubts about the sincerity of Aaron's statement, but saying as much right now was definitely not the way to go—unless she wanted to lose this position. While she felt that her new friend genuinely liked her, Felicia knew that if the woman were put in the position where she had to choose between her physical therapist and her son, she would no doubt side with the latter.

Going along with things was definitely the safer way to go.

So Felicia mustered the best smile that she was able to manage and told him, "Same here."

For the briefest of moments, their eyes met, and without thinking Aaron found himself smiling at the woman he had just challenged.

"You know, I almost believe you," he told her. And then he issued what could have been seen as a warning of sorts. "Take good care of her, Ms. Wagner. She's the best mother in town."

Vita, who had tactfully kept out of the exchange between her nephew and the young woman her sister-in-law had just hired, finally spoke up in an attempt to lighten the mood.

"I think I've just been hurt, Aaron," she told her nephew.

Aaron turned toward Vita and kissed his aunt's cheek. "You know I think you're great, Aunt Vita. But Mom expects me to lay it on thick when I talk about her," he said with a wink. "I'll see you both very soon," he told the two women, then spared a final glance toward the young woman who had just been ushered into this dynamic. "And you, too, Ms. Wagner—if you decide to stay," he deliberately added.

Nicole sighed and shook her head. "I do apologize for my son," she told Felicia even before her son had left the house.

"No need," Felicia assured the older woman with

genuine feeling. "He's your son and he has every right in the world to worry about your care. He doesn't know me from Adam."

A whimsical smile curved Nicole's lips. "If that were the case, I'd be far more worried about him than I am now," she told Felicia with a laugh. And then she looked at the two women who were at her side. "All right, I am only going to say this one last time—let's eat, ladies."

"Well, you don't have to twist my arm," Vita proclaimed, slipping into a seat at the kitchen table. She smiled whimsically. "The only reason I hang around here is because of the food."

Felicia took a seat opposite Vita. Nicole sat between them at the head of the table. Felicia looked at the woman who had hired her. "You mentioned you had a catering business," she said, changing the subject.

"Not just a catering business," Vita proudly interjected. "Possibly the best catering business this side of Chicago."

"She's only saying that because when she's not running her nursery with her husband, Rick," Nicole told Felicia, "she's trying to tell me how to run my business."

"I'm just trying to give you helpful suggestions, dear. Just giving you helpful suggestions," Vita emphasized cheerfully.

"Ha!" Nicole pretended to dismiss Vita's claim with a laugh. "She's ordering me around like she's some kind of decommissioned general. You'll find that on occasion, Vita entertains delusions of grandeur," Nicole confided, leaning in toward Felicia.

Felicia made no comment; she merely sat back and enjoyed the semiplayful exchange between the two women. She had never managed to find anyone in her own life whom she trusted or liked enough to be able to indulge in this sort of banter. But then, she had been too consumed with attempting to hide out of the way and avoid any sort of detection. One wrong move and it would be all over for her.

Nicole and, by association, Vita were as close to women she was able to trust as she had ever come. Even so, she still kept her guard up because one never knew where and when Greg was liable to turn up. Whatever else his shortcomings might be, her ex had always been very good at charming information out of women.

There was a time a little more than five years ago, when she was still very trusting, that Greg was able to get her to admit to things that he was able to use against her, innocent though they were.

She eventually became afraid to talk because Greg was able to twist almost anything she said.

Now that she had moved here, she would have given anything to be able to relax, to take things at face value and not be constantly on her guard. But those days were gone and she knew it.

All she could do at the moment was enjoy the fact that at least she had a job and that for a little while, she was able to contribute to someone else's well-being.

But she wasn't fooling herself. This wasn't going to last.

"I hope Aaron didn't wind up spoiling your appetite," Nicole was saying as she gave Felicia another serving of soup. "He means well, but sometimes he gets a little too heavy-handed."

"You don't need to apologize," Felicia assured her. "I already told you, you're lucky to have someone who cares about you that much. Actually, from what I gather, you have several 'someones.' A lot of people would give anything to be in your shoes."

Nicole exchanged glances with her sister-in-law. It was clear to Vita that Nicole thought Felicia was among those who found themselves wishing they were in that position.

Nicole resolved to find out what Felicia's story was and just what was behind those very sad, dark blue eyes of hers.

"I've decided that while you're working to get me more fit, I am going to do my damnedest to fatten you up a little, dear," she informed Felicia.

"I don't think you can," Felicia said. "I've always been on the thin side."

"Much too thin if you ask me," Nicole said with a smile.

"Leave the girl alone, Nic. She has a right to be thin. The rest of us only wish we were," Vita told Felicia, leaning forward and putting her hand warmly over the young woman's. She gave it a quick, affectionate squeeze.

"I just don't want her getting sick," Nicole protested. "How would that look? I take her into my home so she can help me get back to my former active self, and as a reward, I get her ill?"

"Among other things," Vita told Felicia in an aside, "you might have noticed that Nicole is a worrier."

"Speaking of worrying," Nicole interjected, thinking of her son's reason for not staying for lunch, "what do you think Erik is up to?"

Vita shook her head. "Thinking about that will only ruin your digestion," she warned. "Nothing that our former husbands do would bear up to any sort of close scrutiny."

"Most likely, it has something to do with Carin," she guessed.

"Carin?" Felicia couldn't help asking, looking from one woman to the other for an explanation.

"Our former mother-in-law, otherwise known as the Wicked Witch of the West," Nicole said.

"As well as of the East and every other direction to boot," Vita added. "Forget about her," she told Nicole, waving her hand. She raised her glass of fruit juice high in a mock toast. "Here's to your more than full recovery," she declared.

Felicia followed suit, raising her own glass and more than willing to join in. "I will definitely drink to that."

Chapter Five

Aaron was not looking forward to being in the same room with his father, much less confronting him. However, he felt that he needed to get to the bottom of what was currently going on purportedly in the name of his family. He didn't understand why his father was suing the recently discovered other half of the family—the one that had been fathered by his grandfather Dean's legitimate twin sons. He was painfully aware that his father and his uncle, another set of twins as it turned out, were not viewed as being in the same category.

Strange though it seemed, the family had recently found out that Aaron's father, Erik, and his twin brother, Axel, were his grandfather's illegitimate sons. It was a fact that his grandmother Carin never failed to use to her advantage. In plain terms, Carin, a very unlikely grandmother, was not above blackmailing his grandfather whenever she could.

Everything had come to light when the legitimate set of twins were recently found murdered.

Aaron had thought that after the turmoil died down, the tensions in the family would finally be eased. But apparently, he had thought wrong. Trouble was stirred up again when an old will surfaced. Aaron had a feeling that his grandmother, the exceedingly coldhearted Carin, was behind this new discord.

It stood to reason. Carin Pedersen had never remotely been the typical grandmother, not in any manner, shape or form. When she caused unrest, it wasn't with an eye to benefiting her children or grandchildren's future. She only did it to make Dean's family suffer any way she possibly could.

If Aaron hadn't met his grandmother, he wouldn't have thought that pure evil could actually assume a human form.

But there she was, Carin Pedersen, the personification of evil.

Aaron had never considered himself the last word in morality, but he did feel that it was up to him to stop Carin if he could. If he didn't, he would be condoning whatever evil the woman was up to.

Right now, stopping Carin involved finding out if she had instigated this lawsuit his father and uncle had put their names to. Neither one of the men struck him as intelligent enough to do something like this on their own.

So today, he was confronting his father.

"Thanks for coming with me," Aaron said as he stopped by Nash's house to pick up his half brother.

When he heard what Aaron intended to do, Nash had cleared his morning schedule and volunteered to go with his big brother.

"Don't mention it. I'm as curious as you are to get to the bottom of this," Nash told him. "It's not exactly as if our dad's a good man—no offense."

"None taken, trust me," Aaron assured his brother.

"The man tends to live beyond his means," Nash pointed out, "and is always on the lookout for easy money. But he's a talker, not exactly a doer." He shook his head as he looked out the front windshield. "This whole thing smacks of intricate planning and that's just not something our dad's capable of. That's more up Carin's alley."

Like Aaron, Nash had never been able to refer to his father's mother by a term as benign as "grandmother." There was nothing grandmotherly about her. "I guess I'm as curious as you are to find out just what that devious woman is up to," Nash admitted.

Aaron nodded. "You realize that in all likelihood, she couldn't have told Dad the truth. Knowing Carin, she probably made it sound like if he didn't sue the real heirs, he was letting that branch put something over on ours. Maybe she even has him thinking that 'our' inheritance is being stolen."

Nash was in total agreement with his older brother's theory. "You're probably right."

"I know I am." Now that he had said it out loud, Aaron was more inclined to believe it himself. "Still, thanks for coming. I could use the backup."

It wasn't that he was afraid of the man. At five foot eleven, Erik Colton had once been a well-built, broad-shouldered man, but time had made his frame sag, grayed his dark brown hair and taken away the twinkle from his green eyes. At this point, his father had aged far more than his twin brother had.

The real reason Aaron was bringing Nash with him

was that he was afraid of losing his temper with his father. Nash was there in order to ground him.

"Hey, don't mention it," Nash said, brushing off Aaron's thanks. "If your mother hadn't volunteered to take Damon and me in after our mother died and good old Dad had decided to split not long after that, who knows where he and I would have wound up? I owe a debt to her I could never begin to repay, but being there for you is at least a very small start."

Like everyone else who knew her, Aaron was aware of what a good heart his mother had. But being effusive about the matter was just not his way. So he said, "Well, still, thanks."

Nash knew enough to drop the subject and turn to one that was less personal. "Hey, did you get to meet that nurse Mom insisted on hiring?"

"You mean the physical therapist," Aaron corrected. He thought of the very attractive young woman he had attempted to question. "Yes. I met her."

"Okay, physical therapist," Nash echoed. "What's she like? Probably all austere and sensible shoes, am I right?" he guessed.

Aaron laughed dryly at the inaccurate description. "More like the cover girl of a fashion magazine a teenage boy would hide under his bed," he answered as he turned down the block where his father's condo was located.

Erik Colton spent most of his time living in his mother's house because it was bigger and more luxurious, but there were times when he wanted his privacy. There was usually a woman involved during those times.

"You're going to have to explain that one, Aaron," Nash said, slightly confused.

Aaron was not happy about the physical therapist his mother had hired, but he had to trust in his mother's common sense. Besides, this Felicia person seemed to be able to make her happy. That didn't mean that he wasn't going to have her investigated the first chance he got, he promised himself.

"I could be wrong, but Felicia looks like she's barely out of high school," he told Nash.

"Felicia, is it?" Nash echoed, his interest captured. "Maybe I *should* have gone with you to check her out." He had opted out of going with Aaron earlier so his mother could get her rest. After what the woman had been through, he and Damon felt that heavy doses of peace and quiet were in order. "I still might," Nash added with a wide grin.

Aaron felt he needed to warn Nash, just in case. "I'd be careful if I were you. It seems that Mom's very protective of her."

"That's because you come on like a bear—and not the soft, cuddly teddy bear type," Nash said, his grin widening.

Aaron didn't bother denying it. Nash knew him all too well. "All I was doing was just asking her questions about her background and where she got her certification."

Nash laughed, envisioning the scene. "Yeah, I know how you ask questions. Like a prize-winning boxer going after the win in his title match. It's a wonder you didn't scare the poor girl to death."

"I was just being thorough," Aaron protested. "Or

trying to be. Anyway, Mom told me to back off, so I kind of had to." But that wasn't going to stop him from having that background check done first chance he got. Or rather, have Damon do it, since he had the resources for that.

"If she makes Mom happy, that's all that counts," Nash told him. "Just think if Mom was like one of those women who just curled themselves up in a ball at the first sign of pain." He had no doubt that fall had to have been excruciatingly painful even though his mother had said nothing. "Then what would we do with her?"

They were lucky that way, Aaron thought. "Yeah, I guess you're right," he conceded.

"Well, the odds are that sometimes I have to be." Nash grinned whimsically.

"Don't let it go to your head." Aaron parked his car in front of the condo and got out. "Okay, here goes nothing," he said.

"Emphasis on 'nothing,'" Nash agreed, thinking of their father as he got out of the vehicle on the passenger side.

Not waiting for Nash, Aaron had already walked up to the front door of the condo and rung the doorbell. When no one answered after a couple of minutes, he rang the bell again.

"Maybe he's over at Carin's," Nash suggested. "After all, that's where he usually stays."

Aaron shook his head. "His car is over there," he said, pointing to the fancy vehicle their father liked to refer to as his "babe magnet."

"I guess I let wishful thinking get the better of me," Nash quipped philosophically.

Aaron was about to press the doorbell a third time when the door suddenly swung open. The wide smile on Erik Colton's sun-lined face instantly faded when the man saw who was at the door. It was obvious that he was not expecting to be looking at two of his sons. He must have been waiting for someone else.

"What do you two want?" he demanded.

"And hello to you, too, Dad," Aaron said wryly. And then, because he didn't want to spend any more time with his father than was absolutely necessary, he got down to business. "What's this about you bringing a suit to court saying that half the money behind Colton Connections actually belongs to you and Uncle Axel?"

"Well, it does," his father declared defensively, standing in the doorway like a slightly aged roadblock. "We found a will that says so, so why shouldn't we get the money?"

Aaron and Nash had their doubts that there were any such terms in the will. This all sounded highly suspect.

"Why would you even think that?" Nash asked.

Before he could think better of it, Erik blurted out, "Because your grandmother found an old copy of the will that those two dead guys left behind."

"By 'two dead guys' you mean Ernest and Albert, Grandpa's sons with his *real* wife?" Aaron asked his father, emphasizing the fact that Ernest and Albert were Dean's legitimate sons.

"Who else would I mean?" his father snapped. "Now, if you're finished satisfying that annoying curiosity of yours, do me a favor and get lost," he said harshly, looking beyond Aaron's shoulder. "Both of you. I'm expecting company."

Aaron made no effort to hide his disgust. "Don't you ever give it a rest, Dad?"

Erik clearly resented the comment. "Why should I? I'm not dead yet, and there's still a lot of life left in me."

Aaron looked at Nash. "That's all we need," he murmured under his breath. "Another sibling to join the group."

"Hey, mind your tongue. Just because you're this washed-up fighter doesn't give you the right to talk like that to your father," Erik yelled at Aaron. "Better yet, just get the hell out of here, 'big shot.' Now."

Having gotten the confirmation they had come for, Aaron and Nash turned around and made their way back to the car.

"Well, we found out one thing," Aaron said as they got into his car. "The Wicked Witch of the West is behind this."

"You think that Dad knows that Carin is using him and Uncle Axel to attempt to steal our newfound cousins' money?" Nash asked as they drove away from their father's condo.

"Well, I'd like to think not," Aaron said honestly. "Not because he's a decent soul—because he was never that—but because that would take a lot more brains than Dad was blessed with. This has Carin written all over it."

Nash thought about the reason they had left so abruptly. "You know, at this point in his life, you would think that Dad would just stop tomcatting around like that." There was disappointment in his voice as he shook his head.

"That would take growing up, and Dad never managed to do that. He'll probably be chasing after women until they plant him in the ground," Aaron speculated. He pressed down on the accelerator, picking up speed. "Well, I've got gyms to manage and I've taken you away from your work long enough, as well."

"Yeah, I do have to get back," Nash agreed, then volunteered, "I'll fill Damon in on what's going on with this so-called suit the first chance I get."

Nash paused for a moment, looking at his brother's profile and thinking. "What are we going to do about Carin?"

Aaron spared his brother a glance. "Why?"

"Oh, come on, Aaron," Nash said. "I know you. You're not just going to drop the matter, especially without saying something to Carin. For one thing, you're too honorable."

Aaron sighed. "Not that it would do any good, but yes, I do intend to call her," he confirmed. "If for no other reason than to let the woman know that we're on to her and that she can't just coast through life ruining people's lives the way she's been doing. I don't like being dragged into Carin's unsavory plots like this. I hate guilt by association and I know that you feel the same way."

"At least we don't have to endure seeing her anymore," Nash said, genuinely grateful for that. "Remember when we were younger and Mom felt obliged to go through this charade because she thought we could feel 'normal' having a grandmother in our lives. Boy, that was certainly the wrong call. I've never known Mom to be so wrong."

"Everyone's entitled to being wrong once, and Mom

has a pretty damn good track record otherwise. The point is that we have all tried very hard to distance ourselves not just from our father's and uncle's get-rich schemes and plots but from the cold-blooded machinations that Carin was always engineering."

"Did you ever wonder what it would be like to have a normal grandmother in the family, one that liked to bake cookies at Christmas?" Nash asked, extending the fantasy a little further.

The minute the question was out of his brother's mouth, Aaron began to really laugh at the imagery that created.

"What's so funny?" Nash asked.

"Can you just picture her?" Aaron asked. "Carin Pedersen, standing over a hot stove, baking chocolate chip cookies?"

"Cookies with cyanide, maybe," Nash said. "But chocolate chip? Not likely. Are you planning on going over to her place to see her?"

"No, I think a phone call is about all I can handle after that visit with Dad," Aaron told his brother. "I'll drop you off at your place and then head back to the main gym. That way, after I talk to Carin, I can take out some of my aggression in the ring, or at least on a punching bag."

Nash laughed. "Sounds like a plan." He knew how aggravating any face-to-face meeting with their father's mother could be. "Give me a call and let me know how it went and if you learned anything, once you lose the urge to stop cursing," he added knowingly.

Aaron smiled. "You got it."

DESPITE THE FACT that he knew what he was up against, once he dropped Nash off and drove to his main gym, it took a little bit of psyching up on his part before Aaron could get himself to call Carin.

Like his brothers, he really hadn't been able to think of the woman as "grandmother" in over three decades. That title was reserved for someone for whom there was at least a drop of affection or, barring that, some sort of respect. When it came to Carin, there had never been either.

Closing the door to his office, Aaron sat down and dialed her number.

She had never been one to pick up quickly and now was no exception. She waited until the fifth ring before she lifted the receiver.

Because she had caller ID and because he wasn't trying to hide his number, Carin knew who was calling, although she had no idea why.

And because she did pick up, Aaron knew Carin was curious rather than just her usual dismissive self.

Clearing her throat, Carin spoke in measured tones. "Aaron, to what do I owe this…pleasure?"

The question tickled him, so he decided to have a little fun with the woman who had no concept of fun. "Do I have to have a reason?"

"You do up until now," she answered. "Don't play coy, Aaron. It doesn't suit you. Now, why are you calling?"

He decided to get to the point. Hanging up was beginning to sound very appealing to him.

"The word is out that you're suing Grandpa's other family. I just wanted to ask why."

As soon as she began speaking, Aaron knew he had rattled her cage.

"What I do or don't do is none of your business, Aaron, and I'll thank you not to stick your nose into it. Now, if you don't mind, I have better things to do than pretend to be accountable to a washed-up fighter who undoubtedly sustained more than his share of blows to the head in the ring and is obviously unable to think straight."

Rather than get angry—he knew that was the reaction Carin was going for—he only took one thing away from her response.

"So you won't answer my questions?"

"Maybe you're not as addle-brained as I thought," Carin declared coldly, her tone all but giving Aaron frostbite.

The next moment, the line went dead. Carin had terminated the call.

Chapter Six

Carin Pedersen scowled at the cell phone in her hand. Her forehead, however, never moved, thanks to the newest wave of Botox injections she had just gotten.

Eighty-one last spring, the thin, five-foot-four woman didn't look a day over sixty-four, thanks to a little nip and tuck at the very first sign of sagging or wrinkling anywhere on her body. Carin also made sure she was impeccably dressed at all times.

At this moment, with fury in her green eyes, the woman came very close to throwing her cell phone across the room.

How dare he? How dare her son Erik's young *whelp* have the nerve to question what she was doing? Did he think that after all these years, she should turn into some docile grandmother, sitting in a rocking chair and knitting, while Dean's "other" family hoarded all that money he had left behind? Well, he had another think coming. She had as much of a right to it as they did.

Actually, *more* of a right, because she had given Dean a family before that *other* woman, his mousy wife, did. Granted it was only by a few weeks, but first was first and that was all that mattered.

No way in hell was she going to drop this suit. She was going to get what she felt she deserved, no matter what it cost the rest of the family emotionally. Dead or not, Dean owed it to her, and she intended to collect, whatever it took. And she wasn't about to leave this up to Erik and Axel to handle, because they wouldn't. She loved her boys as much as she was capable of loving anyone, but she knew that there wasn't a viable brain between the two of them.

No, this was up to her—the way everything had always been, she thought, her lips curving in a malevolent smile. And she intended to do whatever was necessary to see this through and get what was coming to her, the other Coltons be damned.

BECAUSE HE HAD neglected his main establishment, Southpaw Gym, Aaron wasn't able to come by and check on his mother for a couple of days. Southpaw Gym, located on the outskirts of the North Loop, was where he trained boxers who were actually looking to make their way up the ladder. His other three gyms, which were scattered throughout the Chicago suburbs, needed to be managed, too, but they were geared toward the millennials who regarded boxing as a form of exercise.

The gyms were his pride and joy, especially the first one, which he had purchased with the prize money he'd won from the bouts. Because of the injuries he had sustained, and to spare his mother her mounting concern that he would sustain a life-altering injury, he had quit boxing.

But because he loved the sport—he always had—

Aaron had turned his attention to training professional fighters instead of being one.

Not long after opening his main gym, he had begun working with at-risk teens. He wanted to show them how to properly channel their aggression in positive ways, and thereby save them from wrong choices.

Aaron was very proud of all of his work, training fighters *and* working with those teens. He would have been content living at the gym, not just above it. But at the present moment, he needed to come by and check on his mother's progress.

He still wasn't 100 percent sure that he had not made a mistake in allowing his mother to hire this Felicia woman. Because he had so much to catch up on at the gyms, he had yet to check out the woman's qualifications, or get in contact with Damon to ask him to do that.

Because his mother was so set on Felicia, he had admittedly taken the easy way out and gone along with her choice.

Aaron sincerely hoped he hadn't made a mistake doing that.

Pulling up in front of the house, he got out and walked up to the old, imposing building's front door. He had a key to his mother's house, as did his brothers. Since they had all grown up here, Nicole had insisted on it. But given the circumstances, he didn't want to just walk in unless he really had to.

He felt that if he did use his key, it might give Felicia the impression that he was trying to spy on her. That, in turn, might create an uncomfortable situation for his mother, which was the last thing he wanted to do.

No, if this Felicia woman was not right for the job, he felt pretty certain that he would pick up on that fact fast enough.

Ringing the doorbell, he found himself standing there longer than he had anticipated or was happy about.

Where is everyone? he wondered. Aaron had just slipped his hand into his pocket to fish out the house key when the door suddenly opened.

He was about to comment on the amount of time he'd had to wait, but the words died in his throat. His jaw went slack and his mouth dropped open at the sight he saw, which he was totally unprepared for.

Felicia was indeed in the doorway, but a completely different Felicia than the woman he had met. She was dressed in a workout halter top and very trim black shorts. For just a moment, as he took in her slim figure and the legs that looked as if they could go on forever, Aaron found himself utterly tongue-tied.

The sound of his mother's laughter in the background snapped him out of his momentary reverie. Knowing he had to say something to cover up staring so hard, he said the first thing that came to his mind.

"Um, are you going to the gym?"

His question, coming out of the blue, caught Felicia off guard. "What?" The next second, she realized that he had to be referring to what she was wearing. "Oh, no. I was just helping your mother with her physical therapy."

That conjured up all sorts of images that he had to fight back. In addition, he was doing his best not to stare at Felicia, but it certainly was not easy. Clearing his throat, he murmured, "I guess you really get into your work."

"Actually, she does," Nicole told her son, coming into the room to join them. She was wearing workout clothes, as well, although hers fit into the sweatpants-and-sweatshirt category. She flashed a smile at her new friend. "And she thinks nothing of making me work up a sweat."

Felicia laughed as she took the towel she had slung over her shoulder and handed it to the older woman. "You think that's hard?" she teased, with a fleeting sparkle in her eyes. "You ain't seen nothin' yet."

Nicole looked at her son, feigning concern. "Maybe I was wrong in hiring this tyrant."

Felicia took the comment with a grain of salt. "The next time you go dancing and can kick up your heels, I want you to remember this conversation," she told her patient.

Coming closer, Nicole impulsively hugged the young woman as she looked at her son. "Didn't I tell you she was great?"

Aaron's eyes met Felicia's. For a moment, it felt as if there was some sort of private communication taking place between them.

"Not in so many words," Aaron allowed, tearing his eyes away from Felicia. "But you did manage to get the idea across," he told his mother.

Seeing his mother happy and almost back to her old self was extremely gratifying as far as he was concerned. He had to admit that he was glad she had overridden his initial doubts.

In this case, "mother really did know best," he

thought. But then, she had always been a sharp woman. He had only to reflect on his own earlier life to know that. She had stood by him even when he had given her nothing but grief over taking in his semiorphaned half brothers when their mother died and his father carelessly went back to his old life. It was a life that didn't include two little boys dragging him down, his father had loudly insisted.

At the time, Aaron had felt cheated and put-upon. It was his mother's kindness and patience that finally made him take in the bigger picture and see that what she was doing was decent and kind.

Looking back, Aaron realized that probably the only misjudgment his mother had ever been guilty of was marrying his father in the first place. But she had been young and in love and he knew he really couldn't fault her.

Because Aaron knew that his mother was still waiting for him to say something about the current situation, he looked at Felicia and forced himself to say, "I'm glad I didn't scare you off and you took the job. I can see that you're very good for my mother." And he meant that.

Felicia felt that Aaron Colton wasn't the type to just toss around empty flattery. She felt heat rising to her cheeks, coloring them.

"Thank you." Gesturing toward Nicole, she told Aaron, "Your mother's made a good deal of progress in the last couple of days. She's pushed herself more than I would have."

"Can't make any progress if I don't push," Nicole said simply.

"We all know that, Nic," Vita said, walking into the room and joining them.

Aaron looked at his aunt in surprise. "Aunt Vita, you're still here?" he asked, pausing to kiss the woman's cheek.

"Of course I'm still here," she answered as if there had been no other choice. "Someone has to rein in this woman if she gets out of control. I don't want her running right over Felicia. Besides, Rick can take care of the nursery for a few days," she said, referring to her husband and the plant nursery they owned and oversaw.

Built directly in front of their own home, Yates Yards housed six acres of plants, flowers and a variety of trees. The nursery offered just about everything anyone could have wanted for the home garden, as well as landscaping services. Over the years the Yateses had cultivated an extremely loyal clientele thanks to their excellent work ethic.

"And before you start to feel sorry for my husband, he's not going to be overworked," Vita told her nephew. "We have really great people working for us."

"Well, so do I," Nicole said as she smiled at Felicia.

"I know," Vita responded. "And for the record, I wasn't worried about you. I was worried about Felicia here." She nodded at the physical therapist. "You have to admit that you do have a habit of going full steam ahead when you want something, and heaven help the person who might get in your way."

Felicia looked at her employer. "I believe that was how all of this happened in the first place," she said drolly, referring to the fall Nicole had taken that had brought them to this juncture.

Witnessing this three-way exchange, Aaron couldn't help smiling. "I don't think I have anything to worry about—from either side."

Aaron still intended to check out Felicia's credentials, but it was no longer as pressing a matter as he had initially felt it to be. Since, like his mother, he considered himself a pretty good judge of character, and to his way of thinking, Felicia seemed like a decent, capable sort. Moreover, he could see that she and his mother genuinely liked one another and that sort of rapport, he felt, could not be faked.

Since he dealt with all sorts of people, he was confident that he could spot a phony or a con artist. Certainly he could pick up on someone out to bilk his mother. Not that his mother was rich by any stretch of imagination, except when it came to the people who loved her. But in his experience, con artists were just out to take what they could get and never mind how impoverished that left their mark when it was all over.

But Felicia didn't have any of those signs about her. As a matter of fact, the more he observed her, the more Aaron felt that she inspired the same sort of protective instincts in him that his mother always had.

Maybe that came from dealing with men almost exclusively. On the rare occasions that he did interact with women, more likely than not he found himself leaning toward feeling protective. Even his aunt Vita inspired that and Vita, he had always felt, was tough as nails. But nails could break under the right circumstances and that was what he was concerned about.

"Well, now that you're here," his mother was saying to him, "maybe you'd like to watch your ol' mom in action. That way you can see for yourself what kind of hoops Felicia has me jumping through."

Aaron took exception to her phrasing. "You're not old, Mom," he protested, partially because he knew that was what she wanted to hear and partially because he honestly felt that his mother was someone who would be able to go on forever.

While it was true that he wasn't able to come by as often as he—or his mother—would have liked, the idea of a world without his mother in it wasn't a world he wanted to know—not for a very, very long time.

Nicole seemed pleased by her son's response. "And don't you forget it," she told him with a playful wink. "Now, enough talking. Come on up to my gym."

He looked at her, surprised by this new turn of events. "You have a gym?" he questioned. "When did all this happen?"

"It's not a real gym," his mother was forced to admit. "Felicia told me about this place that rents equipment for physical therapy, so we had them ship a few things here so I could get started."

"I've got equipment, Mom," he pointed out. "You should have told me what you needed," he said, turning to address Felicia. "I could have brought it over."

"I have no need for a punching bag, dear," his mother told him, patting his cheek.

"I do have other things in my gyms," Aaron pointed out.

"I know, but this way turned out to be simpler," his mother informed Aaron as she began to head toward the staircase.

He hadn't expected her to just walk away in the middle of the discussion. "Hey, where are you going?"

"Why, to the gym," she repeated. "We converted one of the spare bedrooms into a temporary gym. Keep up with the conversation, dear," his mother teased.

Aaron quickly moved right in front of his mother, blocking her way. "Upstairs?" he questioned uneasily. "Are you sure you should be using the stairs?"

"Well, that's where the gym is located, dear," his mother answered patiently.

"But you just had a hip replacement," he protested. He glanced over his shoulder at Felicia for some backup.

But it was his mother who deflected his protest.

"I know that, dear. And in case it has escaped your attention, I am doing beautifully. Aren't I, Felicia?" she asked, turning toward the young woman.

"Your mother is an incredible woman," Felicia told Aaron.

"I know that, but—" Obviously, Felicia was pushing the matter, and he wasn't happy about that.

"No buts, dear," Nicole told her son. "Now, do you want to watch Felicia put me through my paces, or do you want to stand here and argue about it like some old fuddy-duddy?"

Vita leaned in and pretended to whisper to her nephew, "I'd go with choice one if I were you."

Out of the corner of his eye he saw Felicia's broad smile as she stood to the side, taking this all in. It was the first time he had seen his mother's aide relax. It was a nice look on her, he couldn't help thinking.

Rather than answer either one of his relatives, he

decided to ask Felicia for her opinion. "What do you think? Is my mother pushing herself too hard?"

"She's doing fine," she told him. "Really."

Maybe he was being overprotective, he thought. He supposed it was possible. He decided to back off for now. "All right, then let's go and watch my mother sweat."

Nicole sniffed. "I don't sweat, dear. I perspire. You above all people should know that."

Aaron inclined his head, a smile playing on his lips—a smile that was not lost on Felicia, although she tried to look unaffected. "I stand corrected," he said. "Let's go and watch you perspire."

"That's better, dear," Nicole said just before she took the stairs, deliberately moving up the steps at a good clip.

Chapter Seven

Aaron had to admit that he was impressed.

He had expected Felicia to just have his mother go through a few random, light exercises and then declare that the therapy session was concluded. He had *not* expected to see anything this extensive or thorough. But observing her, he could see that Felicia had put together a whole collection of exercises, none of them lasting longer than several minutes each. But they were all-inclusive.

They ranged from what appeared to be simple exercises to slightly more challenging ones.

Felicia had made certain that none of them put any undue strain on his mother. Nicole didn't complain, and for the most part, went along with all of them.

However, she did express dissatisfaction with one of the exercises, which involved standing up and raising and lowering her legs as if she was marching.

"I really feel silly doing this one," she told Felicia as she went through the exercises.

Felicia was marching right alongside of Nicole, setting the pace. "Don't. It's to strengthen your leg and thigh muscles. Remember, everything starts out small and you build on that. Before you know it, you'll be ready to go hiking."

"I don't care about hiking. All I want to do is be able to get back to my catering business full-time," Nicole said.

Aaron told himself he would stay out of it. However, physical therapy was partially in his field of expertise. Besides, he did worry that his mother, in her zeal to get back to her life, might wind up overdoing things.

"Mom, don't push it," Aaron warned from the sidelines. "You're already doing more than Mrs. Abernathy did at this stage—or even further down the line, now that I think about it. So just take it slow, all right?"

"Mrs. Abernathy?" Felicia asked, glancing between Nicole and Aaron. The name meant nothing to her.

"Mrs. Abernathy was an old neighbor. She fell off a ladder and broke her hip when we were kids. It took the poor woman *forever* to heal. Even when she did finally get better," he continued, "she wound up with a permanent limp."

"Well, that's not going to be your mother's problem," Felicia told him. "She's progressing very well. In addition, I've found that it's good to have goals to shoot for. Your mother is the definition of a perfect patient. She's eager to get better and she listens to instructions." She recalled several other cases she had handled. "I've worked with patients who moan and complain about each and every exercise. With any luck, your mother won't even need me in a couple of weeks, which will be good for her," she told Aaron. "But bad for me."

Now that he was more than satisfied with her efforts, Aaron hadn't even thought about her leaving. In light of the way his mother was responding to Felicia, he considered what the young woman had just said.

"Oh, I'd rather have you work with my mother a while longer," Aaron told her.

His mother smiled at him, pleased by the comment. This was definitely a nice change, inasmuch as he had initially grilled Felicia and seemed almost bent on catching her in a contradiction.

"Well, I'd be very happy to stay on," Felicia told him. "As long as you feel that I'm doing some good."

Much as she liked being here, working with Nicole, she didn't want to feel as if she was taking advantage of the situation. That said, she found that this present position was perfect for her, as was the woman she was working with, not to mention her living conditions. Felicia had gone through so much in the last six years that part of her fully expected to wake up and discover that this had all been a wonderful dream and she was back, trapped in an extremely cruel existence.

"Well, Nicole, I think we're done for the day," she announced. "Good job."

Felicia was about to hand the older woman a towel when the sound of a door being slammed somewhere on the premises echoed through the area. Startled, she gasped and looked as if she was about to jump out of her skin. Embarrassed, she avoided making eye contact with Aaron as she picked up the towel she had dropped.

"Sorry, I guess I'm a little skittish today," she murmured, although there really wasn't a reason for that. Today was no different than any other day.

Aaron was about to comment that he'd had days like that himself, in an effort to gloss over the incident, when, quite by accident, he caught a glimpse of several deep scars on Felicia's back. She had moved a certain way, and the scars were visible with the halter top she was wearing.

It took him totally by surprise. Aaron put that together with the uneasy look on her face. Now that he thought about it, while he had been observing her during the session, he realized that Felicia kept looking over her shoulder. It was as if she was expecting someone to pop out of the shadows.

But why?

And who?

Aaron had dealt with enough runaway teens in his time to spot the behavior of someone who was afraid of something or someone. Felicia's skittishness, along with the scars he had seen on her back, suggested that she might have been abused, and not all that long ago in his estimation.

He also knew that asking Felicia about it directly would only spook her, or worse, even make her clam up totally and leave. And that would be a bad thing. He wanted her to feel safe here.

In the blink of an eye, Felicia had gone from someone he wanted to question to someone he wanted to help.

His gyms had programs that were meant to help at-risk teens raise their self-esteem and also learn a few self-defense moves so that if they needed to, they could protect themselves. That went a long way in building up their confidence, not to mention keeping them safe.

There was no reason these same programs couldn't

be used for other people, as well. Because he had challenged her to begin with, Aaron felt he needed to build up Felicia's trust if he was going to be able to reach her.

"You know, that was really impressive," he commented as they all walked out of the makeshift gym and went back downstairs.

"What, my nearly jumping out of my skin?" Felicia asked with what she hoped was a convincing, lighthearted laugh.

She was afraid he was going to start asking her uncomfortable questions and she definitely didn't want to explain her behavior or tell him anything about her ex-husband. She was ashamed that she had let that situation go on for so long. Looking back, she knew she should have walked out on Greg when his behavior had started changing toward her, not lingered around with the hope that he would go back to being the man she had first fallen in love with.

The fact that she hadn't left, that she had allowed herself to become a victim, bothered her down to the very bottom of her soul.

Aaron felt his best course of action was to just wave away the incident. When she grew to trust him, they could revisit the reason why she'd seemed so afraid. Right now, he focused on making her feel more secure.

"No, I'm talking about what you've managed to accomplish with my mother." It helped that he meant what he was saying. "It's great that you have her going through her paces so well."

Felicia was relieved to talk about his mother and her progress. "Like I said, your mother is really willing to work and I've learned that that is really more than half the battle right there." Her eyes crinkled as she smiled at Nicole.

Aaron nodded. He was searching for a subtle way to offer to teach Felicia some self-defense moves. He was certain that it would do a lot to help her stop being as edgy and nervous as she was.

It occurred to him that the simplest way was probably the best one.

"Say, why don't I take you over to my gym?" he suggested. "The big one," he clarified. "I can show you around and that way, you can judge for yourself if there's anything there that you might be able to incorporate into my mother's treatment routine. How about it?"

He saw his mother looking at him, and from the expression on her face, he could see that she knew exactly what he was doing. There was no putting anything over on his mother, he thought with a smile. The sharp woman must have noticed Felicia's nervous reaction to the sudden noise and put two and two together.

For her part, Felicia was surprised by Aaron's suggestion, but she could immediately see the merit in it. In addition, she was gratified, not to mention extremely pleased, that Nicole's handsome son had apparently done an about-face and now seemed to approve of her. She would have loved to relax, but she knew better than to do that. She had learned that the hard way.

Greg had kept her on an emotional roller coaster perpetually. One moment he would be attentive and loving, then suddenly, just one wrong word and he would become furious and abusive. Felicia never knew what to expect, except that she would end up paying for every sweet moment in her life with a dozen moments of pure anguish, if not hell.

Before she was finally able to make good her escape, she'd come to realize that she couldn't attempt to cling to the good because it would always, *always* be followed by the bad.

Still, wary though she was, Felicia felt she couldn't just turn Aaron down. But old habits had her making sure that she would be safe.

"Will there be anyone else at the gym?" she asked, trying to sound casual. It wasn't that she was suspicious of him, but until she felt assured that she wasn't making a mistake by being too trusting, it was better to ask questions.

Her question made him smile. "Well, with any luck, yes. I do run my gym for profit," Aaron reminded her. "So there should be people there."

"Yes, of course. Sorry, I didn't mean to imply that your gym was empty." Damn it, she was tripping over her own tongue. Right about now, she really wished that the earth could just open up and swallow her whole.

"No apology necessary," he told her good-naturedly. "There was a time when I first opened that I was actually afraid no one would come," he admitted.

Nicole laughed at the image he was presenting. "You were a champion boxer who had more than three dozen wins under his belt. Would-be prizefighters wanted to rub shoulders with you just for luck," she reminded him. "Don't let his modesty act fool you, Fee. He knew they would be knocking down his door the moment he opened his gym."

Felicia didn't follow sports in general, but she knew that you didn't quit when you were at the top of your game. "Why did you quit professional boxing?" she asked, curious.

"I'll tell you why," Nicole answered. "He did it for me." She looked at her son, nothing short of gratitude in her eyes. "He knew that every time he entered the ring, I died a little bit, terrified that this time, he wouldn't be able to walk out on his own. That this time he would sustain a blow to his head that would render that wonderful brain of his incapable of carrying out a single thought—or worse."

Cupping Aaron's cheek affectionately, she smiled at her oldest son. "If anything ever happened to Aaron, I know that I wouldn't be able to survive the terrible ordeal."

Aaron winked at Felicia. "My mother tends to be a little melodramatic."

"But nonetheless right," Nicole told Felicia. "Everyone is always focused on the fighters who emerge as champions," she pointed out. "No one ever keeps any real record of the fighters who wind up severely impaired because of a fight that went wrong."

"Don't mind her," he advised Felicia. "She does tend to exaggerate."

"Be that as it may," Nicole continued, "Aaron humored me and gave up the ring. I know what that had to cost him. He did leave the arena as an undefeated champion and, like I said, for that I will be forever grateful."

Realizing that she had gone on and on without meaning to, Nicole apologized to Felicia. "Sorry, I just wanted Aaron to know how very thankful I am that he did that for me. I have no doubt that any other son would have just told me to let him live his life the way he saw fit and be done with it."

"Ha," Aaron interjected. "I'd have never heard the end of it if I had done that—or if I had gotten really hurt in the ring. I figured that stepping away from the professional ring was a small price to pay for peace and quiet," he told Felicia.

She found herself believing him. And, in the short span of time that she had spent being filled in on Aaron Colton's background, she'd started admiring the man.

From all indications, Aaron Colton seemed to have been on the fast track toward a world championship. He had given it up because continuing would have placed his mother in perpetual agony.

"So you gave it all up for your mother," Felicia said out loud. There was no mistaking the respect in her voice.

Aaron shrugged. Outside the ring, he wasn't comfortable with having attention focused on him. "Something like that."

"He's being modest again," Nicole told her. "It was *exactly* like that, and no matter what else comes to pass, I can't forget that my oldest-born found it in his heart to turn his back on the potential pot of gold at the end of the rainbow and humor his nervous mother's wishes."

Nicole could see by the way the young woman smiled at her son that Felicia saw it that way, as well. She found herself entertaining thoughts about Felicia that had nothing to do with a physical therapy program.

Nicole turned her attention momentarily toward her

son. From his body language, she could tell that he was getting ready to leave. "Are you sure I can't fix you something to eat?"

"I'm sure, Mom." He glanced at his watch. It was a gift he'd given himself when he won his very first match. "It looks like I'm overdue at the gym." He dropped a quick kiss on his mother's temple. "I'm really glad you're doing as well as you are."

And then he looked at Felicia. "And if you don't mind, I'll give you a call to arrange a tour of my main gym."

Felicia felt herself responding to Aaron's smile and warned herself to keep things in perspective. At the very most, he was just being courteous. As for the least, well, she knew where the least led.

Inclining her head, she told him, "I'll be looking forward to it. As long as it doesn't put you out."

She was grateful for the job and for the fact that he had decided not to challenge her the way she had initially believed he was going to. But she didn't want him feeling obligated to do anything more than that. She was content just doing her job and staying out of everyone else's way. Not for the first time she thought of this job as a dream come true.

"See you around," he said to his mother and Felicia. "And tell Aunt Vita I said goodbye."

The moment the front door closed, Nicole turned toward Felicia. "He seems to be quite taken with you."

"It's not me," Felicia denied. "He just wants to make sure that I take good care of his mother."

"I know, but you have to understand, Aaron is a very skeptical young man. He doesn't just give his seal of approval lightly. And, heaven help me, he *is* very protective of his mother—to the point that there are times when he acts as if he believes I'm incapable of making the right decisions for myself."

It was obvious she would have been annoyed if that same set of circumstances didn't point to the fact that her son was fiercely protective of her.

"Oh, I'm sure he knows how capable you are," Felicia assured her.

Nicole laughed. "You'd think so, wouldn't you?" she asked, amused. "But he does worry about me a bit too much. And it's not just because I took an unscheduled fall on the floor. I think ever since his father walked out on us and then turned out to be so much less than an honorable man, Aaron has been leery about all the things that could go wrong in life.

"Maybe having you here might help him to calm down a bit, perhaps even convince him that things are really far more in sync than he initially believed."

Nicole stole a glance at Felicia to see if she was buying any of this. She wasn't able to tell, but that just meant that she was going to have to work harder to get things moving.

Because, in her mind, Nicole had already decided that her physical therapist needed to get together with her firstborn.

For both their sakes.

Chapter Eight

Because he was training a boxer for his second professional match, Aaron wasn't able to make good on his promise to bring Felicia to his gym for several days.

But the first opportunity he got, he called her to make arrangements for her visit. However, first he needed to synchronize their schedules, something that took more of an effort than he had initially thought it would.

"Don't wear her out," his mother warned him when he finally came to pick Felicia up. "I need her. On second thought," she said as she walked out with the pair, "wear her out. That way maybe she won't work me so hard."

"Don't let her fool you," Felicia said fondly as she walked toward Aaron's car with him. "Your mother's hip is getting really strong. A lot faster than her doctor even anticipated."

"I don't think there's any danger of my wearing Felicia out, Mom. I'm just showing her around the gym for now." He saw the smile playing on his mother's lips and wasn't really sure what to make of it. But rather than ask what she was up to, for now, he decided that it was best to let the whole matter go.

"It's not far from here," Aaron said when he finally started up his vehicle and began to drive away from his mother's house. "It's located in the North Loop of town," he added.

Felicia was just beginning to familiarize herself with the different areas in Chicago. "What made you pick that location?" she asked, curious.

That was easy. "Convenience," he told her. "It was the only gym in the area that had a loft above it. I converted that into my living space. That way I can be at the gym ten minutes after I get up."

"You live above the gym?" Felicia asked. This new piece of information made her feel vulnerable, not to mention uneasy, even though she told herself it shouldn't. After all the man had been a perfect gentleman up until now. Right?

Aaron didn't notice the look on her face. He was focused on the exchange between them and what he had just told her. "Yeah. Like I said, it makes getting to work really easy." And then he laughed to himself, explaining, "I'm not exactly what you call a morning person."

The man lived above the gym.

The words replayed themselves in her head. She wouldn't have agreed to come see it if she had known he had living quarters above the gym. He seemed like a nice guy and she didn't really expect him to try to take advantage of her...but then, she hadn't expected Greg to turn into a monster, either. When they had first met in class six years ago, he had been so sweet and thoughtful. They were both taking physical therapy classes together, and Greg had been funny, charming and just everything she thought she could have ever wanted.

It wasn't until after she had married him and he began drinking that she found herself blindsided by his darker side.

Really darker.

Sitting in Aaron's car beside him, Felicia could feel herself growing progressively anxious. She tried her very best not to let him see the change, but she had a feeling that he did anyway. That he saw through her became really obvious when she suddenly heard Aaron's question.

"Are you all right?" He had pulled up in front of his gym and turned the engine off.

Felicia heard the concern in his voice and almost felt guilty.

Almost.

"Yes, I'm fine," she answered defensively. Then, getting herself under control, she asked casually, "Why?"

Aaron couldn't help wondering if the close proximity between them was making her nervous. There didn't seem to be any other explanation for the shift in behavior.

Well, there was only one way to find out, he decided, although he doubted that she would give him an honest answer.

"You just seem a bit jumpy," he told her. "So I thought I'd ask."

She felt guilty lying, but she fell back on a standard

answer and hoped that would satisfy him. "It's just that I have a lot on my mind."

Maybe there was a problem he could help her with, Aaron thought. It was worth a try. "Mind if I ask what?"

So much for her being able to fluff off the questioning, Felicia thought. She got out of Aaron's vehicle and closed the door behind her.

She was stalling now and she knew that *he* knew it. But there was no way she was going to tell him what was actually bothering her: that on two separate occasions, she could have sworn that she saw Greg following her.

She knew exactly what that would have sounded like to Aaron—like the delusional rantings of a paranoid woman.

Added to that, every time she had turned around to look, Greg wasn't there. It was just a case of her imagination running away with her. Felicia *knew* she was stressing out. Logically, there was no way Greg would have known that she had moved to Chicago, much less been able to follow her here. If nothing else, Chicago was a big city. There was no way he could have located her. She was just making herself crazy, imagining things.

What she needed to do, Felicia told herself, was to just relax.

She took in a deep breath and then slowly released it. "Nothing important," she told him, responding to his question as to what she had on her mind. Switching subjects, she said to him as cheerfully as she could, "So, impress me. Let's go in and see this gym of yours." She flashed him a broad smile and added, "The one that turns boys into men."

"I never put it that way," Aaron corrected her. "What I said was that it gives them the tools to be able to *act* like men."

"By punching each other?" she asked, humor curving her mouth.

"By employing strategy. Boxing really isn't about getting in the first punch," Aaron explained. "It's about using your opponent's own body against them." Opening the gym's entrance, he held the door for her. Then, as nonchalantly as possible, he offered, "While we're here, I could show you a few self-defense moves." He slanted a look at her, hoping she didn't see through what he was attempting to do.

But the next moment, he knew his attempt had failed, because he could tell that her antennae had gone up.

"Why would you think I would need that?" she asked.

Aaron shrugged a little too casually and he knew it. It would have been so much easier to be honest and straightforward about this, but he knew that would just serve to scare her away from the topic. He was convinced that the woman needed some sort of help and he intended to give it to her.

"Everyone needs to know a few self-defense moves. You never know when it might come in handy. In case you haven't noticed, we're really not all at the point where we're holding hands and singing campfire songs.

"Sadly, there are some really nasty people out there and I'm guessing that we would all feel a little more prepared to face them with a few good moves under our belts." Then, in case she thought he was trying to pressure her, Aaron said, "But those are just my thoughts on the matter."

Maybe it *was* just a random remark on his part, Felicia thought. She really had to stop viewing everything as if it was intended as a warning signal.

Felicia tried to redeem herself. "And they're good thoughts," she told him. "I was actually just thinking about taking some classes in self-defense earlier." She hadn't been, but now that Aaron had mentioned it, it did seem like a pretty good idea. After all, it couldn't hurt to be prepared. "I guess that you just caught me off guard with your dead-on suggestion." She flashed what she hoped was a disarming smile at him. "It's as if you were a mind reader."

Aaron wasn't about to get caught up in that notion. "Not even close," he told her. "If anything, that was just a lucky guess on my part. Besides, I'm partially in the business of teaching people self-defense."

For the time being, he changed the subject. "Okay, let me show you around here, and then, if you like, we can turn our attention to a couple of basic moves you can use if the occasion ever arises," he told her.

Felicia looked down at her clothes. "I didn't come dressed for that," she pointed out.

"If someone comes up behind you, intending on doing you harm, you're not going to be able to call a time-out because you're not dressed for it, are you?" Aaron asked her.

She flushed. When he put it that way, her excuse sounded really silly. "No."

"All right, then, you're dressed for it. Come with me."

Beckoning her forward, he took her up to the main ring. There were two fighters confronting one another. As Aaron approached, the two men in the center of the ring dropped their arms and stopped what they were doing. Aaron addressed them.

"Jake Quartermain and Peter Sullivan, I'd like you to meet Felicia Wagner. Felicia is my mother's physical therapist."

"How's your mom doing?" Jake asked his mentor, concerned.

"Fine, thanks," Aaron answered.

Felicia could see that the men all had a relaxed attitude toward each other.

Peter Sullivan, the taller of the two men, asked her, "Are you here to show us how to take care of our bruised bodies?"

"That's easy," Jake answered, speaking up. "Don't get into fights you can't win."

Aaron laughed. "Sound advice. Except that I'm here to teach you how you can always win."

"Unless you're fighting an eight-foot giant," Jake quipped, nodding at his opponent.

"Especially then," Aaron countered. When Jake looked at him, mystified, Aaron answered, "Just use the man's weight against him." He turned toward Felicia. "That's what I intend to teach you today. Just a few basic tricks in how to use your opponent's own body weight against him—or her. It works every time."

She thought about Greg. Her ex-husband was nearly as strong and strapping-looking as Aaron was. The very sight of him frightened her and put her at a disadvantage. Still, she didn't feel as if she could contradict Aaron, since he was putting such an effort into making her feel safe. "If you say so," she replied uncertainly.

Aaron wasn't fooled by her tone. He could see that she would need extra reassurance. "I've been doing this for a while now," he told Felicia. "And I say so. Why don't you come with me to one of the side rings so we'll be out of the way? I figure you don't want to hold an exhibition out in the open for everyone to see."

She shrugged a bit self-consciously. "No, not really."

He knew this went without saying—but he said it anyway.

"And don't worry, I'm not going to hurt you. The point of undertaking this whole exercise is for you *not* to get hurt." But he could see the wariness in her eyes. "Do you trust me, Felicia?"

She had to be honest with him, which meant that she couldn't just answer automatically. So she paused, and then said, "I guess so."

He took her hands in his and looked into her eyes. He was the soul of sincerity as he told her, "The last thing I would want to do is bruise my mother's physical therapist. Trust me, I *know* that she would never let me hear the end of it." His mouth curved.

Unable to help herself, she smiled, too. Pleased, Aaron nodded in response. "That's better," he said with approval. "Now, I just want to go over a few basics with you and you can go home and practice them—just make sure it's not on my mother," Aaron added with a wink she found incredibly sexy.

"I wouldn't dream of doing that. Especially not after all the work I put in getting her *back* to shape."

He realized that she had to have misunderstood his meaning. "Oh, I didn't mean I thought you'd hurt my mother. I taught her a few tricks to use, and purely out of reflex, she could turn around and wind up using them on you," Aaron told her.

Felicia had no idea if he was kidding or not, but the exchange did serve to lighten her mood.

"Okay," she said, preparing herself. "Why don't you show me a few of those moves you were talking about?"

"I'd be very happy to," Aaron told her. "Okay, right off the top, the most basic thing to remember is to avoid alleys and stay in well-lit areas. But if you find that you have to walk in one of these areas, remember to always carry your keys in your hand."

"So I can get into my car quickly?" Felicia guessed. That way she wouldn't be wasting any time digging for those keys.

"Yes," he agreed, "but you can also use your keys on your would-be attacker." Holding his keys in his hand, he went through the actions to show her what he meant. "You use your keys and push them into his eye." He saw the look on her face and immediately knew what she was thinking. "You can't be squeamish, Felicia. Remember, it's you or him and I'd much rather it was you who came out ahead than some reprehensible attacker."

Thinking that was enough on the subject, he turned to another move.

"The next most basic move is one that every woman should instinctively know. Use your knee to kick him in the groin," he told her. "Trust me, no matter how big the

guy is, this move will definitely stop him in his tracks
if you make direct contact. One really well-placed knee
will have a cavalcade of stars descending on him, not
to mention totally stealing away his ability to breathe.

"What you have to remember," Aaron continued, "is
that every part of your body can be used as a weapon.
The heel of your palm, your elbow against his ribs,
just everything." He could see that she needed further
convincing. "Tell you what, let's try this," he proposed,
moving so that he was directly behind her. "Let's say
someone grabs you from behind and in essence has
you in a bear hug. Okay, what do you do?"

She could feel his breath on the back of her cheek
and for a second, she felt a warm shiver shimmying up
her spine. Divorcing herself from the sensation, Felicia
tried to pull away. But the movement turned out to be
completely ineffective.

"All right," Felicia declared, surrendering. "I give
up. What am I supposed to do?"

"Instead of pulling away, draw your arms into yourself and go down as if you're fainting. Your assailant won't expect you to just slide down. The sudden
move allows you to wriggle out of his grasp. Then you
turn around and kick," he advised. "Okay, let's practice that," Aaron instructed.

"Now?" she asked uncertainly.

"You have a better time?" he asked.

"No," she answered.

"Okay, I'm coming up behind you and wrapping
my arms around you," he told her, narrating his every
move.

There was only one problem with that. Once he put

his arms around her from behind, Felicia found herself immobilized.

Not because he was holding her so hard, but because she was reacting to the feel of his arms wrapped around her. Her heart began to pound rapidly, like a drumroll. And then her breath caught in her throat. Instead of drawing her arms in and dropping down, she turned around to face him.

In that moment, her face was very close to his.

Her breathing became more rapid as she looked up at him.

"I think I got confused," she admitted in a soft whisper. She could feel a wave of desire stirring within her chest. She wanted to connect so badly with him that she could hardly speak.

"Yeah, me, too," he admitted. He could all but taste her lips and very nearly gave in to the overwhelming temptation to kiss her.

In that one moment in time, there were only the two of them in that small room.

And then the spell was broken as one of the men in the ring called his name.

"Hey, Aaron, where are you? That kid you promised to take on is here to talk to you. You got a minute?"

Aaron looked at Felicia, mourning the opportunity that had just slipped away.

"Yeah, I'll be right there," he called back. "Just hold your horses." His eyes met Felicia's. "I'll be right back," he told her.

"I'll be here," she said, her mouth suddenly incred-

ibly dry as she did her best to look away and pretend
that she hadn't come so close to kissing Aaron.

But there was no getting away from the fact that
she almost had.

Chapter Nine

Steve Holloway, the kid who had come looking for Aaron just now, was one of the at-risk teens he had taken on when he had first come up with the idea of helping them. Since Steve was part of the first group, Aaron was more familiar with the young man's story than he was with the backgrounds of some of the others.

Even though he was in a hurry to get back to Felicia, Aaron didn't want to cut Steve off too quickly, either. The kid had been through enough as it was, and despite all that, Steve had made huge progress in the right direction.

So, exercising patience, Aaron heard him out. When Steve seemed to finally be finished, Aaron was able to excuse himself.

He hurried back to the auxiliary gym. He found Felicia acquainting herself with various pieces of equipment as if she was actually trying to figure out their usage.

"Sorry," Aaron apologized. "I didn't mean to keep you waiting so long. I had no idea that it was going to take me as long as it did."

She turned around to face him and waved away his words. "That's all right. When you come right down to it, I'm the one taking you away from your work. If you need to go back to finish up…" Felicia's voice faded away as she left the decision up to Aaron.

"No. As it turned out, Steve just required a little hand-holding at this point."

"Steve?" she questioned. He hadn't told her the person's name previously.

"Holloway," Aaron interjected, completing the teenager's name. "I've been helping to train him for his second big bout." There was a fond, satisfied smile on his lips. "Until just recently, he really wasn't ready. It's not even a matter of technique. It's just a matter of his having enough confidence in himself," Aaron explained. "So what I did was put together a tape of Steve's training sessions so he could actually *see* himself in action." Aaron smiled to himself at the outcome. "That helped do the trick.

"You know it's funny," he continued. "A lot of the people I come in contact with have egos that all but suck the oxygen out of the room, egos that are definitely not warranted. Steve, on the other hand, for some reason doesn't seem to think enough of himself. I guess it comes from being so small when he was younger." Steve had shot up over the course of the last two years, stunning everyone. "Now he's this big, powerful guy and he still can't shake the self-image he has of himself," Aaron told Felicia. "Sometimes we can be our own worst enemy."

She got the feeling he was actually directing his

words at her. She couldn't help wondering just what Aaron thought he had detected in her makeup.

Just when she had started to relax.

"This Steve is lucky to have found you," she said.

Aaron shrugged. "I wouldn't make a big deal out of it. If it hadn't been me, it would have been someone else. That tape I made for Steve wasn't exactly a phenomenal breakthrough. Just something he needed to see."

"Still," she pointed out, "you took the time to make the tape." Stepping back, she looked around the secondary gym with its various pieces of equipment, some of which appeared to be the latest models. Either Aaron was on the receiving end of some sizable donations, or he was putting a great deal of his own hard-earned winnings into these gyms he owned in order to help these at-risk teens, as well as training hopeful fighters.

Aaron Colton was definitely a good man, Felicia couldn't help thinking.

Careful, Fee. Don't get carried away, she warned herself. She knew exactly what could happen if she dropped those barriers she had carefully constructed around herself. Heaven knew that she had once viewed Greg in the same favorable light, and she was still paying dearly for that mistake, right up to the present day.

Deliberately divorcing herself from thoughts of the past, she turned her attention toward the various pieces of equipment that looked as if they were just begging to have someone put them to good use.

There was no doubt in her mind that Aaron was making a real difference in the lives of the boys he was mentoring, giving them hope where previously there had been none.

She could feel herself wavering again in her wariness toward him.

Changing the topic, Felicia said, "You know, you have a very impressive place here."

Aaron believed that she was being sincere and wasn't just saying empty words that she felt he wanted to hear.

"Thanks. Ethan, one of the kids who trains at the gym, told me that he really looks forward to coming here. He said that even though this is a gym, it's a lot cleaner than the home where he grew up." A sad smile played on his lips as Aaron thought about the interaction with the teen. "It took a lot to get him to open up, but when he did, he confided that his mother took off when he was five and his father lost his last three jobs because he drank too much. Ethan finally dropped out of school because he couldn't put up with the ridicule. He kept getting into fights.

"That's when he decided that maybe he should give boxing a try. I took him aside and started coaching him. Damned if he wasn't right," Aaron told her. "Nobody was more pleased than Ethan when he discovered that he had an actual talent for pugilism."

Felicia couldn't help smiling at the term that Aaron used. "Did Ethan even know what that word meant?"

"Not at the time. But he does now." He flashed her a smile. "It's all part of the learning process."

"Like I said," Felicia repeated, "these boys are lucky to have you in their lives." Without Aaron, she had no doubt that more than one of these kids would have wound up behind bars.

"It works both ways," he told Felicia. "I learn a lot from them. Not to mention the fact that I realized just how good I had it growing up. I always felt as if I had been deprived because my dad took off when I was a kid. But hell, I have a great mother I'm very proud of and even those half brothers that I initially felt saddled with turned out to be a real asset in my life, so I have no complaints."

"Looks like you've got everything together."

"Yeah, I think so." He paused for a moment, weighing whether or not to ask her what he wanted to ask her. And then he decided that nothing ventured, nothing gained, so he pushed ahead. "So, what about you?"

"What about me what?" Felicia asked warily.

She was getting defensive again, he thought. But he wasn't going to learn anything about her if he didn't push forward at least just a little bit.

"What's your story?"

"No big mystery," she answered. "I like helping people, which is why I got a degree in physical therapy. And here I am."

He had given her an opening and she hadn't taken it. He wasn't about to push the matter, but he did think that he could do with just a little insight into the woman. The simplest thing was to ask her if she had any family to speak of.

"Yes, here you are," he agreed good-naturedly, then asked as nonchalantly as possible, "Do you have any family?"

The question took her by surprise. "No," she replied

flatly. Even as she said the word, she felt an aching repercussion in her chest.

"No brothers or sisters or second cousins, twice removed?" Aaron asked, thinking of his own family dynamics.

"That's what *no* means," Felicia replied, then flushed. "Sorry, that was flippant and you don't deserve that. The fact that I'm alone is kind of a sore spot for me."

He believed her. Part of him felt guilty about making her aware of that sore spot. "Well, you're not alone anymore. I've got enough cousins to lend you some of mine," he said with a smile. "Not to mention that my mother and Aunt Vita can't stop singing your praises, so you can just feel that you're part of this family."

A warmth filled her as her eyes met his. "You're serious."

Aaron couldn't judge if she believed him or not. "Why wouldn't I be?"

The reason was easy. Greg had lied to her so many times she had never known when to believe him and when to be skeptical. Since he represented her very first experience with a man, she just assumed that they were all like that: given to lying and being abusive, while equipped with a mercurial temper.

Maybe she was being foolish—or desperate, she thought—but she found herself believing Aaron. Still, she knew she had to answer his question honestly. "Because I found that men lie."

"*Some* men lie," Aaron corrected. "But definitely not all. Not by a long shot." Felicia had been hurt, he could see that. The only question was, was the man responsible for that just passing through her life, or was he someone she had been seriously involved with?

He had a feeling it was probably the latter, because she seemed so leery when it came to certain subjects.

Aaron supposed that he could ask Damon to look into her background for him. That way he could get some actual insight into the woman he found himself attracted to. Still, he felt that he would be better served if she trusted him enough to actually tell him the truth on her own.

He decided to let the matter go for a little while and give her the opportunity just to talk to him on her own for now.

"For instance," he said, continuing on the subject he had started, "*I* don't lie."

She would have expected that from a man. Greg had professed not to lie on several occasions. "Oh, so you're a saint?" she asked, a touch of dry humor curving her mouth.

"No," he told her honestly. "I just have a poor memory."

She stared at him, not seeing the connection. "How's that again?" Felicia asked.

"To lie effectively requires being able to keep track of all the details that you've come up with in fabricating your story," he told her. "Quite honestly, I always found that the truth is hard enough to keep track of. If you're lying to begin with, that can get extremely confusing to remember, so I don't. It's as simple as that."

Felicia looked up into his eyes again. It occurred to her that that old saying was really true. Eyes truly were the windows to the soul.

At least his were.

And she found herself mesmerized.

Felicia realized that she believed him. Maybe she was being foolish, but then again, maybe not.

It was extremely comforting to feel that the person she was talking to was being honest with her and that he wouldn't somehow just turn everything she had said around against her.

"You know, I really wish that there were more people like you," she told him in all sincerity.

He looked at her for a long moment, then asked, "What was his name?"

And just like that, her mouth went dry and a wave of insecurity took a huge bite out of her.

"Excuse me?"

He knew he was pushing it, but he really wanted to know. "The man who hurt you."

She should have just backed away, she thought, upbraiding herself. "What makes you think there was someone who hurt me?" she asked defensively. She should have terminated the conversation before it had gotten to this point.

That was easy enough to answer, he thought.

"I've dealt with enough troubled teens to know the signs."

She stiffened. "In case you haven't noticed, I'm not a troubled teen," she informed him, hoping he would just back off.

"No," he granted, "but the signs are still the same. I found that sharing helps lessen the impact and the pain of whatever it is that you're carrying around. Look, I'm not going to push. But I just want you to know that I'm here for you," he said, "in case you do want to talk about it."

He watched intently.

Felicia looked away, unable to meet his gaze. "I'll keep that in mind."

He really wanted her to open up to him, but he knew he couldn't force her to do it. That had to come entirely from her.

"You do that," he encouraged, nodding his head.

She needed an excuse to get away from him, or else she knew she was going to break down and tell him about Greg. She didn't want to involve Aaron. Neither did she want to be on the receiving end of his pity. That would just ruin everything.

"But for now," she told him, preparing to head toward the door, "I think I should be getting back to your mother's house." When she saw him raise a quizzical eyebrow in response, she explained, "Nicole has another set of exercises to do."

"Another set?" he asked, curious. "I just assumed that you were done for the day."

She could see why that might have confused him. "Normally, that would be true, but I found that breaking up her workout and doing part of it in the morning, part later on in the day is more beneficial for her. Everybody's different. That way your mother gets more therapy in and she doesn't wind up being exhausted by it," she told him. "It's also a way to build up her endurance. And, like I told you previously, your mother is doing really well. So, for now, we're going to keep up two sessions a day."

Aaron nodded. "I owe you an apology."

She wasn't sure she understood why he was saying that. "Why?" she asked, once again wary.

"Well, if you remember, when my mother first wanted to hire you strictly on the strength of the fact that she liked you, I was against her doing it. And when I finally got the chance to come by to see for myself how you were doing, I have to admit that I thought you were too young and too attractive to really know what you were doing."

Felicia caught herself being amused by his statement. "You're telling me that you think only people who wind up stopping clocks as they walk by are equal to doing a good job?" Despite the serious nature of the conversation, there was laughter in her eyes.

He knew how nonsensical his assessment had to have sounded to her.

"Not exactly, but I felt that you had to at least have some 'miles' on you instead of being so damn attractive," he told her honestly.

"I'm actually ninety-seven," she deadpanned.

He pretended to nod his head at that. "Great makeup," he said, commending her.

Felicia didn't miss a beat. "I think so. You don't have to be old to be good," she told him seriously. It was just one of the things she firmly believed. "You just have to be really dedicated."

He nodded, seeing the error in his thinking. She had certainly turned out to be really good. "You're right."

She thought of something to further illustrate her point and really bring it home. "For instance, someone could say that you're just too good-looking to be a decent boxer. You should have a bunch of scars and at the very least a broken nose to look as if you're a serious fighter."

Aaron laughed. "Point taken."

"You know," she went on, "I wouldn't have believed that you bought into something so stereotypical," she told him.

Aaron smiled at her, tickled. She could stand up for herself if need be, he thought.

"I guess that you were a revelation," he admitted. "All I know is that I'm glad my mother stuck to her guns when it came to you, because even though she is a very stubborn woman, she couldn't have made so much progress in such a short amount of time if it hadn't been for you."

"Well, let's not overlook the fact that most of the credit belongs to your mother," Felicia pointed out with sincerity.

"I know," Aaron agreed, "but it's because you know just how to get her to adhere to the program. According to Aunt Vita, my mother lights up whenever she's doing those exercises with you."

The remark pleased Felicia. "It works both ways," she told him. "Now get me back to my patient."

The corners of Aaron's eyes crinkled as he smiled at her.

"Yes, ma'am. Your wish is my command." And with that, Aaron lightly took hold of Felicia's elbow and escorted her out of his gym.

Chapter Ten

"So, what did you think of Aaron's gym?" Nicole asked Felicia once Aaron had dropped her off at the house and then left.

True to her word, Felicia had gotten Nicole started on her second round of physical therapy exercises for the day. Within five minutes of arriving back at the house, she'd had to corner Nicole in the kitchen and drag her away from the dinner she was preparing for the next day's catering event. Nicole was doing her best to pick up her life from where it had been before her accident.

Refusing to listen to excuses, Felicia had insisted that she get started as soon as possible. She might have been mistaken, but she got the impression that the woman liked being bullied a little. Nicole respected someone who stood up to her.

"Well, I have to say that Aaron certainly keeps the gym a lot cleaner than I'd thought it would be," Felicia said as they got started. The only gym she had been to recently could have used a deep power cleaning.

Nicole smiled. She loved hearing good things about her firstborn. "That's because I raised him right and made a point of having him pick up after himself. Considering the rough patch I had with him when I first took in Nash and Damon—there was a time when Aaron's hostility could have taken him in a whole different direction—I am very proud of the way that boy turned out." And then Nicole flushed, and it had nothing to do with the energy she was exerting. "Although he's hardly a boy," she added.

"No, he's clearly not," Felicia agreed, then realized how that had to have sounded to Nicole. "Let's focus on these exercises, shall we?" she asked, gesturing toward the equipment that had been set up for the second half of the therapy sessions.

At this point Felicia was having Nicole do fifteen different exercises. Initially she had started out with five and had slowly been adding to the total each day. To keep Nicole interested and motivated, Felicia had been doing the same exercises alongside her. It was as much to set an example for Nicole as it was to give the woman a pace to keep up with. The fact that it also helped to keep her limber was an added bonus as far as Felicia was concerned.

Nicole frowned as she watched the young woman go through her paces. "Show-off," she murmured accusingly, although her smile gave her away.

"I just wanted you to have someone to gauge your progress against," Felicia explained. "You know, if you keep this pace up, you're not going to need me for much longer."

A look of dismay creased Nicole's forehead. "Oh, don't say that. I'm not feeling nearly as strong as I think I should be," Nicole told her.

Felicia raised an eyebrow. "Now you're just making things up." She knew a fabrication when she heard one. "I bet that if I left you a list of exercises for you to follow, you could do them all perfectly well without having me hovering over you."

But Nicole shook her head. "Oh, I think without you around, I'd just wind up slacking off." Her eyes crinkled as she looked at the younger woman. "You make all of this fun, Felicia."

She sounded sincere. Felicia felt her heart warming. "Well, I'm not going anywhere yet," she told Nicole. She really did like living here, and working with Nicole was a total pleasure. She couldn't remember the last time she was anywhere near this happy.

"Good," Nicole declared. "Because I think you're good for me. And for Aaron."

A warm shiver suddenly danced through her body. Felicia did her best to ignore it and push forward. She couldn't allow herself to dwell on Nicole's words and get distracted. "Why? I'm not having him do any exercises," Fee said with a laugh.

"Maybe not," Nicole said, moving onto the next set of exercises, "but he looks more relaxed than I've seen him in a long, long while now. Until you came along, he was so caught up with that teen-at-risk program he was running, not to mention the fighters he's always training, that he was always on the go without stopping to even breathe." Nicole smiled. "You've provided a very nice break for Aaron just by being here."

Felicia grinned. She was obviously not going to change Nicole's mind, so she just went along with what the woman was saying. For a moment, she even pretended that it was true.

Taking out what looked like a cycle meant to exercise Nicole's calves and ankles, Felicia placed it right in front of the woman.

"Sit down," she coaxed, moving a chair so that it was directly behind Nicole. "Five minutes." Taking out the egg timer, she set it for the allotted time and placed it close by so that Nicole could shut it when it went off.

Nicole glanced at the timer. "You know, I'm beginning to hear that thing going off in my sleep."

The younger woman laughed. "You're not the only one," she confided. When she had first gotten started giving the physical therapy sessions, it seemed as if the sound of the timer was going off and echoing in her head all the time.

Nicole nodded at the timer. "Not to mention that I use that when I'm preparing meals for my business. It's getting to the point that I don't know if I'm coming or going," she said with a grin.

"Don't look at it that way," Felicia advised. "I prefer thinking of it as keeping you on your toes."

"Oh, it's more than that now," Nicole told her. She blew out a breath as she finished up a set of exercises. "I don't think I'm ever going to be able to hear the timer go off without thinking of you."

"I don't know if you're flattering me or if I should take that as a complaint."

"Let's just go with the former," Nicole said with a wink.

In the midst of all this camaraderie, Felicia felt a sudden pang. She was going to miss working with this woman when her job was finally over. Nicole was like the mother she fervently wished that she'd had but never did.

Well, you're not gone yet, so instead of missing the woman, just enjoy this experience while you're still able, Felicia told herself as the timer went off, signaling the end of yet another round of exercises.

"Okay, on to the next exercise," she said.

Nicole groaned. "How many more are there?"

"I'll let you know when you're close to the end," Felicia promised.

"And?" Nicole asked quizzically.

"Not close yet. Now stop wasting time," Felicia directed, suppressing her grin.

MYLES COLTON WALKED into his older cousin's gym like a man with the weight of the world on his shoulders. At times he thought of the place as his own personal haven. This was one of those times.

"Hey, Aaron, are you around?" he called out. Stopping the first gym employee he came across, he asked him, "Is your boss around here somewhere?"

Rather than verbally answer him, the man pointed to an area located right in front of the locker room.

"Thanks," Myles murmured. Spotting his cousin, he strode over toward him.

At this point, aware that he was the object of his cousin's search, Aaron remained where he was. "Give me a minute," he told the fighter he was training. Turning his attention to Myles, Aaron could feel a wave of sympathy and concern washing over him.

Myles, five years younger than Aaron, was a successful lawyer with more business than he could currently handle, and married to Faith, a schoolteacher. They had a little boy and appeared to be the perfect couple. A love match straight out of the storybooks.

However, recently the pair had suddenly separated, surprising and distressing everyone who knew them. To a person everyone reacted the same way: If Myles and Faith could grow apart, then what hope did any of the rest of them have of making their relationships work?

Trying to keep a positive outlook for Myles's sake, Aaron smiled at his cousin. "To what do I owe this unexpected pleasure?"

"Who said anything about pleasure? I'm here because if I don't blow off some steam soon, I'm just liable to explode, if not self-destruct altogether. You did say it was okay to come by anytime, right?" Myles asked him.

"Yes, and I meant it," Aaron assured his cousin. Glancing back at the fighter he had been working with when Myles walked in, he held up his hand, spreading out all five fingers, asking for an indulgence of five minutes.

Nodding, the fighter went back to working out with a punching bag.

Aaron turned back to his cousin. "So what has you so steamed?" he asked. "Is your senior partner piling on the work and making you jump through hoops?"

Myles waved his hand at Aaron's question. "I can handle that. It's what I've been working toward this last year." He sighed. "Hell, I can handle just about anything—except not seeing Jackson." He was referring to the apple of his eye, his four-year-old son, whom he adored and who was currently with his estranged wife.

"Not being able to see that little face every day is just killing me," he confessed sadly. "You know, I was so certain when I married Faith that we were perfect together."

"Everyone else thought so, too," Aaron told him in all honesty.

"Yeah, well, everyone was wrong." Myles huffed irritably. "It's like the more successful I became, the worse things got at home. It's almost as if she doesn't *want* me to succeed."

"Have you tried talking to her about it?" Aaron asked.

Myles threw up his hands. "Who can talk to her about anything?" There was sheer pain in his eyes. "Aaron, I haven't even seen my kid in a week and it's just *killing* me!" he declared louder than he had intended.

Several pairs of eyes turned in his direction, but Aaron could tell that his cousin didn't notice. The younger man was locked away in his own personal world of misery.

"I'm on the verge of making partner," he confided. "This is supposed to be a really exciting time for me, and I've never been so miserable in my whole life." He shook his head. "I told Faith I wanted to try to have a second baby, and her answer was to pack up, take Jackson out of the house and move in with her mother. Why would she *do* something like that?" he cried, looking at Aaron.

"Damn it, Aaron, we've been together since high

school. We didn't even date anyone else in college. The minute we graduated, we got married. I figured we'd be together forever, and now...now I just don't know anymore." He looked like he was desperate to understand why this was happening in his life. "Why is she doing this to me?"

"I wish I knew, Myles," Aaron told him honestly. "I really don't know what to tell you. Do you want me to talk to her?" he offered, although the idea didn't make him feel all that comfortable. He liked both Myles and Faith, but he didn't believe in butting in to people's private lives.

Myles shook his head. "No, she'd probably tell you that everything is just fine."

"But you said that she moved back in with her mother," Aaron pointed out. "That doesn't exactly point to things being 'fine.'"

Myles dragged his hand through his hair, sighing. "I know. But her excuse is that I haven't been home all that much lately. The job took me out of town a lot," he confided.

Aaron couldn't help wondering if perhaps his cousin being gone so much was part of the problem. He considered bringing it up with Myles, then decided not to, at least for now. This came across like a sticky problem and heaven knew that right now he had more than his share of far more pressing things on his mind. Since Myles hadn't specifically come out and *asked* him for his help or advice, and was here for just the use of his gym, Aaron decided to keep out of it for now.

"Look, I've got to get back to working with Joey. He still has a lot of rough edges that need to be addressed," Aaron told his cousin. He patted Myles on his back. "But feel free to stay here and work out your anger for as long as you need to," he said just before he began to go back to Joey.

Myles didn't reply. Instead, he strode over to the nearest punching bag and began swinging at it aggressively.

Aaron stopped walking away just for a moment to observe him. For a man his size, Aaron thought, his cousin's punches didn't exactly pack all that much of a wallop. Most likely, he was out of shape because of all the extra work he was putting in at the firm. If he was working with Myles, he would have had to seriously address that problem. He had a feeling it could be easily resolved.

But, all things considered, Myles wasn't going for some championship. He just needed and wanted to knock off some steam, and as far as that went, what Myles was doing was good enough.

"Okay, Joey. Your time-out is officially over," Aaron told the young man he was training. "Let's get back to turning you into a champ."

Joey looked positively eager as he abandoned the punching bag and got back to the ring.

"Is it my imagination, or are these workouts getting longer and longer?" Nicole asked.

Finally finished, she lay down and stretched out on the workout table. Felicia placed a cold pack on Nicole's hip. Wrapping it into place, she set the timer for ten minutes.

"It's not your imagination," she assured the older

woman. "Are you acquainted with the saying, 'No pain, no gain'?"

Nicole laughed softly under her breath. "I'm aware of it, yes."

"Well, it's a little known fact that it has its roots in physical therapy," Felicia said with a wink. "And I have to say that you have been progressing a great deal faster than my usual patients. I've even had to step up the whole program to keep up with you, so that's probably why it might seem as if we're just racing along," she told the woman with a warm smile.

"To be honest, I really wouldn't know," Nicole said. "This is the first time since I was in high school that I've done any sort of regular exercise. I've always been too busy making a living as well as a life for my boys to spend any regular time on myself."

"Haven't you heard, exercise keeps you young."

That was exactly what Nicole was talking about. "Exercise was always something I would get to when I had the time," she confided.

"Well, guess what?" Felicia gave her a wide smile. "You just got the time."

"You know, I do have to get that dinner prepared."

"But you also said it was tomorrow," Felicia reminded Nicole.

"Yes, but I don't like putting things off to the last minute."

"But you're not," Felicia countered. "What you are doing is taking care of your body—pampering it so that it's ready to use when you need it."

"You're beginning to sound like a drill sergeant—but a kindly one," Nicole remarked.

Felicia considered that for a moment, then nodded. "As long as I get you to listen to me, I'm willing to sound like anything I need to."

Nicole allowed the compress to do its magic and got comfortable. "Felicia?"

"Yes?" she asked as she readjusted the compress.

"How long have you been doing this?"

The question caught Felicia off guard. "Why? Do you feel like I'm neglecting something with your hip you need addressed?"

"No, no, that's not what I'm saying at all," Nicole assured the young woman she was beginning to look upon as a daughter. "I'm just curious about you. You really don't talk much, do you? I'm just trying to get to know you."

"Not much to know. I got a degree in physical therapy and immediately started working in the field. That's been the last four years." The timer went off much to her relief. *Saved by the bell.* "Okay," she announced. "You're free to get back to your catering." She unwrapped the compress. "And I have to get back to making notes," she said, walking out of the room quickly.

Leaving Nicole sitting up and watching her go, perplexed.

Chapter Eleven

Felicia sat on her bed, willing herself to calm down. She took in a long, deep breath, then held it before slowly exhaling.

She really needed to calm down, she told herself again.

Wrapping her arms around her knees, she rocked a little, doing her best to comfort herself. She had been warned about this. Abby, one of the women she had met at the shelter when she finally got enough nerve to leave Greg for good, had told her this might happen. PTSD. It wasn't just soldiers who were afflicted with the disorder. Women in abusive relationships had been known to suffer from it, too.

At the time, she had just thought it was an exaggeration, or maybe even a myth. Yet here she was, convinced that someone was following her. It had happened today, when she went to the store to pick up a few things.

Believing someone was there, she had turned around repeatedly to look, and she'd found no one each time. If that wasn't PTSD, she didn't know what was. It had got to the point that she felt as if her mind was bent on torturing her.

The last time had been just as she was about to get into her car. Her heart had started hammering like a kettledrum. She was positive that she'd caught a glimpse of a telltale shadow.

But again, when she really scanned the area, there had been no one there.

Felicia felt as if she was losing her mind.

She needed to come to grips with this, she thought fiercely. It was a "damned if you do, damned if you don't" situation. No one was going to want to have her around if there *was* someone stalking her. Because if there was, it meant that she represented some sort of danger that could materialize at any moment.

Nice as he seemed, Aaron Colton would quickly send her packing if he thought that having her on the premises might endanger his mother. And she certainly couldn't expect anyone to take up her cause. She had no proof that the person who seemed to be stalking her was Greg.

At the very least, Aaron would think she was crazy. Best-case scenario was that she was telling the truth. But that just meant, as she'd already thought, she'd be endangering his mother, and that was definitely a reason to terminate the verbal contract with her and send her packing.

And if there *wasn't* anyone stalking her, it meant she was losing her mind, and why would he want to employ her, then?

Felicia sighed.

No, this was something she needed to ride out.

She just had to pray she was imagining things—even though something deep down in her soul told her that she wasn't. That this was all too real.

Playing it cautiously and wanting to be prepared, Felicia kept her things packed up in her suitcase—just in case she needed to leave quickly. She felt that she couldn't afford the luxury of being complacent and relaxed.

The threat felt too immediate.

Even though she had left the last place she lived in the dead of night and was fairly certain that Greg had no idea what her final destination was, she had learned the hard way not to underestimate her ex-husband. To do that would be tantamount to swimming next to a shark wearing a necklace made out of chum. The results could very easily be deadly.

Okay, she told herself, she just needed to remain calm—and be ready to take off at a moment's notice.

With that, she went to find Nicole. It was time for their second physical therapy session for the day.

AARON ARRANGED HIS schedule so that he wound up having the afternoon to himself. That way, he could check on his mother's progress—and coincidentally, also have an excuse to see Felicia. After leaving his assistant in charge at his main gym, Aaron drove over to the house where he had grown up.

When he rang the bell, he was only slightly surprised to find that it was his aunt Vita who came to answer the door.

Vita's face broke out in a wreath of smiles as she greeted her nephew with a huge hug.

"Well, hello, handsome. Looks like we both had the same idea. And, before you ask—" she knew how his mind worked "—no, nothing's wrong. I'm just here to check on your mother's progress—and to help out with that catering delivery she has for later today," she said.

He knew that his aunt wouldn't lie to him.

He also trusted Vita's assessment of the situation. She didn't sugarcoat things.

"So, how is my mother doing?" he asked as he closed the door behind him and flipped the lock. Luckily this was still a nice neighborhood, but it never hurt to be extra careful.

"More energetic than I've seen her in years," Vita answered. "Which is saying a lot, considering what a ball of fire that woman has always been. But even so, it's easy to see that Felicia has made a world of difference in her life. There's a certain kind of sparkle about your mother these last couple of weeks that I have to confess I haven't seen in years."

Aaron knew that Vita wasn't given to exaggerations, either, which was why the observation she had just made pleased him quite a bit. Not for the first time he found himself really thankful that he had been overridden that first day about Felicia and that she had wound up staying on despite all of his objections.

"Where is Mom?" he asked, then before his aunt could answer, he guessed, "Up in that bedroom that she's turned into a gym, right?"

"Yes," Vita confirmed. Then, as he turned to go upstairs, she put her hand on her nephew's arm. "Can I talk to you for a minute?"

His aunt was still smiling, but something in her tone

alarmed him. She knew she could always talk to him. Why was she even asking? Something was up.

"What's wrong?" he asked her.

Vita bit her lower lip. "That's just it. I'm not sure— but I think that something might be."

He immediately jumped to a conclusion. "With Mom?" he asked.

"No." She paused, then said, "With Felicia. Have you noticed her being a little...how shall I say this... jumpy, of late?"

He thought back to the reason he had taught Felicia those self-defense moves. "Well, now that you mention it, I did," he admitted. Out of courtesy to Felicia, he had kept that to himself. Needlessly, it seemed now. "She displayed a lot of the signs I've seen in some of my at-risk kids. The ones that had been abused. That was when I decided to show her a few self-defense moves she could use so that she'd feel more secure."

Vita thought that over and then shrugged. "Maybe she *is* feeling more secure and I'm just reading things into her actions that really aren't there."

And then she switched subjects. "The good news is that your mother is better than ever." She flashed him a smile. "Maybe I should just quit while I'm ahead. Rick says I worry too much," she said, referring to her second husband. Not a day went by that she didn't thank her lucky stars that she had married Rick Yates.

Aaron raised his eyebrows, feigning shock. "You, Aunt Vita? Never," he told her with a broad grin. It was followed by a quick wink. And then he decided to press on and ask his aunt something. It couldn't hurt, right? "Let me run something by you."

"Go ahead," Vita urged, waiting.

"What would you think if I offered to take Felicia out to dinner? You know, just to thank her for everything that she's been doing for Mom—and to apologize for giving her a hard time about her background to begin with."

Vita smiled. She didn't have to think about her answer. It was automatic. "Well, I think that would be very nice. Quite honestly, I don't get the feeling that she has very many friends here. As a matter of fact, I'm not sure if she has any. Felicia doesn't talk very much about herself. This might be a good way to loosen her up.

"I hear that one of your 'other set of cousins' runs a really popular restaurant and that the food is excellent—not as good as what Nicole is capable of whipping up on her own of course, but still good," Vita said. "And this way, Felicia has an opportunity to go out on the town, so to speak, with a very nice young man escorting her."

Aaron grinned. "I was the one who thought of taking her out, Aunt Vita. I don't need to be sold on the idea."

"I know, dear. I'm just going the extra mile." She patted his cheek affectionately. "Now go upstairs and do what you do best—spread some sunshine."

"What are you going to do?" Aaron asked, curious. Since her main reason for visiting was to check on his mother's progress, he assumed that she would accompany him.

"I'm going to go and check on that meal that your mother was working on, make sure that it's all packed up and ready to go," Vita told him cheerfully, as she left the room.

Aaron made his way over to the stairs and hurried up to the second floor. His mother had temporarily converted the second bedroom there. It was slightly larger than the other three—only the master bedroom on the main floor was larger. Under Felicia's watchful eye it had been converted into the gym that was now being used to get her to do her physical therapy exercises.

The door was open, allowing, among other things, the unobstructed flow of air. Rather than verbally announce his presence, Aaron decided to stand back for a moment and observe both his mother and Felicia in action.

As he watched, he realized that his aunt was right. His mother seemed to not just be as good as new when she moved, but she seemed to have actually reached a new plateau.

He had to admit that in all honesty, it was watching Felicia go through her paces that really captured his attention. Her movements seemed to be almost lyrical. Aaron couldn't help being slowly drawn in.

It was like watching poetry in motion, he thought.

And then the words replayed themselves in his head, and he grinned. Wow, talk about being corny, he chided himself.

Felicia was utterly and completely wrapped up in what she was doing. So much so that when she finally finished a set and turned around, she was surprised to see that they weren't alone the way she thought they were. Not only that, but that the person in the doorway observing them was *not* Vita.

A small shriek escaped Felicia's lips. It would have been larger, but somehow she managed to stifle it at the last moment.

The sound startled all three of them—but only Felicia looked as if she was ready to jump out of her skin.

Concerned, Aaron was quick to hurry into the room. "Are you all right?" he asked her, doing a quick scrutiny of the young woman from top to bottom.

Felicia took in a covert, deep breath, willing her heart to settle down as she tried to hide her embarrassment.

Unsuccessfully.

She waved away his question. "You just surprised me, that's all," she said, trying hard to cover up her reaction. "I didn't expect to see anyone standing there watching—except for maybe Vita," she allowed. "And you're not Vita."

Nicole felt bad for Felicia. "Not that I don't love seeing you, Aaron, but you should know better than to sneak up on people when they're in the middle of doing something."

Nicole blew out a deep breath as she picked up her towel and began wiping away the perspiration along her forehead.

"Sorry," Aaron apologized absently. At this point he was really concerned about Felicia. Why was she so exceedingly nervous? It wasn't right. There was definitely something going on here and he intended to get to the bottom of it for Felicia's sake.

He made up an excuse for not making himself known and startling her.

"You both seemed to be doing so well I didn't want

to interrupt you," he told his mother, referring to the exercise. "But now that I seemed to have marched right into the middle of this, can I interest you in going out to dinner with me after you get my mother all squared away?"

Felicia's first reaction was to happily agree. But that was immediately followed by a wave of nervous self-preservation. Convinced that there was someone following her, she didn't want to pull Aaron into this. Neither did she want to get entangled with him. She felt that he had the ability to get her to focus on him, which in turn made her drop her guard. That could easily make her vulnerable. Not when it came to Aaron—that could even have pleasant possibilities—but just possibly to Greg, if he actually were somewhere in the area, stalking her.

"I'm sure you have better things to do than to spend time and money on me," Felicia told Aaron, attempting to dismiss the idea of going out to dinner with him without being rude.

Better not take chances, she told herself.

But instead, Aaron looked at her and innocently replied, "Nope, not a one."

She felt like a drowning woman, going down for the second time as she made one last protest.

"Besides, your mother's a fantastic cook and just eating the meals that she's been preparing has utterly spoiled me for anything else," Felicia told him in all honesty.

"Oh, Mom's great," he admitted, giving his mother a quick wink. "But I happen to know other, almost equally great cooks."

"Oh?"

"Yes," he confirmed. "For instance, there's my cousin. She just opened up her restaurant a couple of years ago. It's called True. She belongs to a side of the family that we didn't even know existed until a few months ago," Aaron admitted. "We—meaning my brothers and Aunt Vita's kids," he said with a nod in his aunt's direction as she chose that moment to walk in, "are trying to cement relations with them." He saw that he had Felicia's attention, so he pressed on. "It seems that they're part of my grandfather's first family."

Felicia's eyes widened in curiosity, so he backtracked and told her, "My dad and his twin brother were born first, but my grandfather was already legally married to the woman who gave birth to her own set of twin sons shortly after that." He grinned. "Have I lost you?"

"No," she answered. It was a lie, but she was struggling to try to make sense of everything he was telling her. His life definitely had more going on in it than hers did. "But I think that I'm getting this killer headache trying to make sense out of all this."

"Well, if you do wind up making sense out of it, then maybe you can guide me through it," he teased. "In the meantime, we can go out and have dinner at True."

Felicia still appeared rather undecided as her eyes looked over toward Nicole.

The latter didn't wait for Felicia to say anything. Instead, the older woman coaxed, "Go. You deserve an evening out, dear. As a matter of fact, I couldn't think of anyone who deserves it more."

"But I don't like leaving you alone," Felicia told Nicole honestly.

"I'm never alone," Nicole assured her. "Besides, if I want company, Vita will stay here until Aaron brings you home." She smiled at her sister-in-law. "You can invite that sweetheart of a husband of yours to come over and we can make an evening of it. It's been a while since he came over to regale me with his ever-increasing knowledge of plants." She turned to Felicia. "So, see? You're free to leave. Now go, before I'm accused of breaking some little-known labor law by working you to death."

To explain what she meant, Nicole glanced at her son. "Do you know that when I'm not looking, this one insists on cleaning my house?" she asked, gesturing toward Felicia. "She claims it keeps her fit." She gave Felicia a pointed look. "I told her if I wanted a housekeeper, my sons would have hired one for me, but there's no talking to this one," she pretended to complain, shaking her head. "So take her out to dinner and show her the sum total of both of our appreciations."

Aaron nodded at his mother. "You got it, boss."

Felicia eyed him uncertainly and tried one last excuse. "I'm going to need to take a shower first."

Aaron saw nothing wrong with that. "Take all the time you need. I'm taking the rest of the day off."

That meant that Aaron would be with her for at least part of that time, she thought. The information both excited Felicia as well as scared her just a little.

For her own peace of mind, she dismissed both emotions and just hurried out of the gym to her own room. She had a shower to take—quickly.

Chapter Twelve

"What are you grinning about?" Aaron asked as he turned around and saw his mother. She had opted to come downstairs and keep him company while he waited for Felicia to get ready.

His mother's eyes were sparkling as she continued to smile at him. "Must be that inner glow I feel right after doing a round of physical therapy, dear."

He knew damn well that wasn't it and that she was pulling his leg, but he played along, at least for now. If this was a fairy tale, part of him would be watching his mother's nose to see if it was beginning to grow.

"Then I'm glad she's making such a difference in your life, Mom."

"She is, dear," Nicole told him with a pleased laugh. "She has this way about her that actually makes me happy to sweat as she puts me through my paces—and there are a *lot* of paces. We're lucky to have found her."

"I get it, Mom. *You're* lucky to have found her and I'm lucky that I didn't manage to talk you out of having her come work with you," he willingly admitted. He was a big enough man to own up to his mistakes when he realized that he'd made them; he always had been.

His mother looked at him with an indulgent smile. "Oh, honey, when have you *ever* managed to talk me out of doing something when I've set my mind to it?"

Aaron nodded his head with a grin. "Point taken." He saw his mother looking at something behind him, just to his left. Curious as to what had caught her attention, he turned around.

For a moment, his entire train of thought came to a screeching halt as he stared at the woman who had entered the room.

Rather than one of the utilitarian outfits she normally wore, Felicia was dressed in a soft, light blue summer dress that lovingly adhered to her curves. While she usually preferred sneakers or sandals when she wasn't overseeing his mother's physical therapy routine or working out with her, she now sported what appeared to be four-inch-high heels that flattered her legs. The mere sight of them caused Aaron's gaze to linger longer than he knew it should.

But he made no apologies. Instead, a single word managed to escape his lips.

"Wow."

Nicole smiled at the young woman she had welcomed into her home and was in the process of welcoming into her heart. There was just something about Felicia that spoke to Aaron's mother. "I think that's Aaron's inarticulate way of saying that he approves of your outfit, dear."

Felicia's eyes appeared to look that much bluer because of her dress. They crinkled as she smiled at what her client's son had just expressed. "I think that 'wow' said that and more," she replied.

Clearing his throat, Aaron forced himself to snap out of the dazed state that had descended on his brain.

"Shall we go?" he asked even as part of him was surprised that he was actually able to form words, since his mouth had temporarily gone bone-dry.

"So you like the dress?" Felicia asked him. She didn't need his stamp of approval, but she did want him to like what she was wearing.

"I think if he liked it any more, you might have trouble leaving the house," Nicole told her, amused.

"Mom," Aaron admonished.

"Just saying it how I see it." Nicole shrugged innocently. "By the way, where is it that you're planning on taking her?"

He had been up-front with his mother about the Coltons he and his brothers and cousins had recently stumbled across. He was aware that his mother and aunt knew about them now, but until recently, his branch of the family had no clue that the other branch existed—and vice versa. Getting to know them had certainly been an education on all of their parts.

"Like I said, one of our 'newly discovered' cousins—Tatum—runs this restaurant. It's caught on really fast. They say the food there is fantastic. Not as good as yours," he injected diplomatically, "but still fantastic. I thought I'd take Felicia there. I've heard from several people who have eaten there and they all raved about it." He looked at Felicia, not wanting her to feel as if he was making an arbitrary decision that she had no say in. "If you find that the food is not to your liking, we can always go somewhere else."

Felicia wasn't accustomed to having someone be

so thoughtful about her likes and dislikes. As a matter of fact, she couldn't remember the last time she had gone out to eat with a man. Greg had ruined that for her, and she had no desire to be subjected to anything like that ever again.

Or so she had thought. Aaron made her want to take another chance at it.

"I'm sure it'll be fine," Felicia assured him, then added as an afterthought, "I'm easy. It doesn't really take much to please me."

A second later, she replayed her words in her head and wound up flushing a bright red. Not looking at Aaron, Felicia pushed onward, doing her best to ignore her own words.

However, Aaron couldn't quite get himself to do that, at least not altogether. "Nice to know," he told her with a wide smile that sent butterflies fluttering through her stomach.

"Okay," he told her. "I made reservations while you were getting ready, so we should get going."

"Don't keep her out too late," his mother told Aaron as she walked both of them to the front door. And then she paused. "On second thought, keep her out for as long as you want," she amended with a soft laugh. "Felicia's been working much too hard and she could definitely use a night out."

Felicia smiled as she passed Aaron's mother and went out the door he was holding open for her. "I guess I have no say in the matter," she said.

"Sure you do," Aaron told her. "You can say yes." And then he lowered his head so that only Felicia could hear what he had to say. "It'll make my mother happy."

Felicia glanced back over her shoulder. "Well, then, by all means. I wouldn't want to miss the opportunity to make Nicole happy. She deserves the best."

Aaron nodded. He liked what she said, liked the fact that Felicia genuinely seemed to have a bond with his mother and that she obviously liked her. He had always prided himself on his ability to be able to spot a phony a mile away. And he was willing to bet any amount of money that Felicia Wagner wasn't a phony. Quite the opposite. She was very, very genuine.

But at the same time, there was something about Felicia that he couldn't quite put his finger on. He sensed that she was holding back something that made her uncomfortable to talk about it.

The simplest thing would be to come right out and ask her about it, but he guessed that it wouldn't get him anywhere. Aaron knew that he needed to be patient, which wasn't all that easy for him.

But patience was something he needed, to get Felicia to trust him and let him in on what was going on with her.

Maybe not today or tomorrow, he thought, but eventually.

He opened the passenger door for her, and after she got in, he closed her door and rounded the rear of his vehicle to get in on the driver's side. He started up his car and guided it onto the main thoroughfare.

"I think you'll like my cousins," he told her, slowly engaging her in conversation.

She took in a breath, as if bracing herself for something. "How many of them are there?" she asked, wondering if these cousins he mentioned were going to sit in judgment of her and if taking her to eat at this cousin's restaurant was just an excuse to get her to drop her guard.

The next moment, Felicia upbraided herself for being so suspicious. This was all Greg's fault. Greg was the one who had gotten her to a place where she couldn't relax or take anything just at face value.

Aaron wasn't like that, she silently insisted. Maybe he really did just want to take her out to say thank-you for what she'd done for his mother.

"Not too many cousins," he assured her, turning on a corner. "Tatum is the one who owns the restaurant. It's been open for a little more than two years and reservations are really hard to come by—unless you're related to the owner, which, luckily, I am," he told her with a wide smile.

It seemed to her that Aaron had gone through a great deal of trouble to take her here. There had to be other restaurants that were easier to go to, she thought. "You do know that I would have been happy getting a burger at a fast-food place."

"But I wouldn't have been," he told her. "Besides, then I wouldn't have gotten to see you all dressed up and that—" he glanced in her direction to underscore his point "—is something I wouldn't have missed for the world."

Felicia caught herself blushing again even though she knew that he really didn't mean anything by the comment. It was just harmless flirtation on his part, nothing more.

Distracted, she didn't realize that Aaron was pulling into a parking lot until he turned off the engine.

"We're here," he announced.

There was a valet, but Aaron had always been a man who did everything for himself. He saw no reason to surrender his vehicle to someone else just to park it when he knew that he was perfectly capable of doing so himself.

Rounding his car, he was at the passenger side before Felicia had removed her seat belt. Ever mindful of the manners that his mother had made such a point of drumming into his head at a very young age, Aaron opened her door, offered Felicia his arm and helped her out, then closed the door for her.

Felicia couldn't remember the last time she had been escorted like this, the last time she had felt special, even for a moment.

"You know, I can walk," she told him, not wanting him to feel as if he had to go out of his way like this.

"I know," he told her with a smile that managed to swirl right into the pit of her stomach. "I've seen you do it. But, between you and me, for the most part I spend my days training a bunch of sweaty guys. This is a really nice change of pace." He swept his free hand around to take in the entire scene. "Let me enjoy it."

The way he had put it tickled her. "I guess that seems like a simple enough request," she agreed.

As they entered True, she found the restaurant warm and inviting. If the food was anything like the atmosphere, she was instantly glad Aaron had brought her here.

He had no sooner given his name at the reservation desk than a vivacious young woman came forward, waving away the hostess who was about to show them to their table.

"I'll take them, Rachel. You show the next couple to their table," she said, then turned toward Aaron. "I wasn't sure if you were actually going to show up, cousin," she told him in a warm, friendly voice. "It's been a while since you graced us with your presence." Her eyes turned toward Felicia. Interest flickered in them. "And this is?"

"A miracle worker," Aaron volunteered without pausing. "It's only been a little while since she started my mother on a physical therapy program and she's practically got her doing handstands," he told the blonde woman as she led them to a table located just off the main path.

"Oh, that's right. I heard that your mother broke her hip," Tatum said. With everything she had going on, not the least of which was running the restaurant, she had temporarily forgotten that. "So how is she doing?" There was genuine interest and concern in Tatum's voice.

"Much better since Felicia started working with her," he told his newfound cousin.

"I can't take all the credit," Felicia protested with feeling. "Your mother would have done fine on her own—just perhaps not as quickly because it does take the right set of exercises to get on the right path."

"Pretty and modest," Tatum said, nodding her head with approval at the other woman's words. "Excellent combination, cousin," she told Aaron. "You seem to have found the right person for the job."

She gestured toward the table. "Here you go. Best table in the house. Glad you came when you did, Aaron. I wasn't sure how much longer I was going to be able to hold it for you. Latecomers get pushy at times," she confided. "Your server will be here in a minute with your menus." She looked at Felicia. "I hope you enjoy your dining experience," she said with feeling. "And if there's anything I can do to make it better for you, please don't hesitate to let me know."

Then, flashing a smile at her cousin and his guest, Tatum withdrew.

"She seems very nice," Felicia told Aaron once they were alone, or as alone as they could be in a crowded restaurant.

"That's because she is," Aaron assured her. "From what I can see, this whole branch of the Colton family is."

"You sound surprised," Felicia commented, observing his face.

"Not surprised, exactly," Aaron told her. "Just... well, *relieved* probably describes it best. Considering what my grandmother is like, Tatum's family could have very easily looked down their noses at my branch of the family and treated us like we were pariahs—if not worse."

His answer wasn't what she was expecting. She didn't quite understand why he would say that. Granted, she didn't know his family, but his mother and aunt seemed to be exceedingly nice.

"What does your grandmother have to do with it?" Felicia asked.

He had opened his menu, but his mind wasn't on making his selection. An ironic smile twisted his lips at her question. "My grandmother is the kind of woman who, if you suddenly found yourself drowning, would happily hand you a big anchor instead of a life preserver."

He was kidding, right? "You're exaggerating," Felicia laughed.

"No, I'm not," he told her. "If anything I'm being kind. You have to understand that she was convinced that my grandfather was going to leave his wife and marry her, especially when she told him that she was pregnant with twins. My grandfather had always wanted a family and he had every intention of marrying my grandmother," he explained. "But when my grandfather went to tell his wife that it was over between them and he was leaving her, his wife surprised him by saying she was pregnant with twins, as well. Nothing for all those years and then he suddenly hit the jackpot. Since he still really loved her—I gather that their only point of contention was that she hadn't been interested in having a family—my grandfather decided to stay married to her.

"Being an honorable man in his own way, he told *my* grandmother, the mother of his illegitimate twins, that he would always provide for her and the twins, as well as take care of any and all bills that might come up. As you can imagine, that wasn't good enough for her, but she made her peace with it—or so it appeared for the time being.

"Meanwhile, she waited to exact her revenge. Not because she loved him—or any of us as we came along in due time—but because she just felt as if she had been wronged, and she was determined to make him pay for it."

For the first time, Felicia found herself feeling sorry for Nicole and her family. "That sounds positively terrible," she cried.

"It could have easily been, if my mother and Aunt Vita hadn't turned out to be such good, loving and honorable women. They were the ones who made my life and the lives of my cousins not just tolerable but good and decent."

Realizing that he had gone off on a tangent, Aaron cleared his throat as he waved his hand to clear the air. "Sorry, I didn't mean to go on and on like that."

"Well, I'm not," she told him. "It helps me understand why you behaved like a protective pit bull when you first met me—you were looking out for your mother."

"About that," he began, then told her simply, "I was wrong."

But she shook her head. "No, don't apologize." She now knew what had driven him to behave the way he initially had. "It's really nice to meet someone who is so protective of his mother. I find it refreshing and admirable. That's why when you finally wound up approving of what I was doing, it meant so much more."

Because he had just shared so much about his family, for the first time Felicia felt as if she had become part of that intimate circle, just the way Nicole had told her time and again that she was.

Chapter Thirteen

Felicia had to admit that part of her was still amazed to find herself sitting here opposite Aaron Colton in a fancy restaurant, having what amounted to an exceptional meal.

"This is really good," she said, leaning over her serving so that Aaron could hear her over the general din in the main dining area. She had only needed to sample a single forkful to come to this conclusion. The chicken parmesan she had ordered was probably the best she had ever had.

Aaron seemed amused by her declaration. "You didn't think that it would be?"

"Oh, no, I expected it to be good," she quickly assured him. She didn't want to accidentally insult him or anyone in his family, since this was his cousin Tatum's restaurant. "I just didn't think that it was going to be *this* good. This is absolutely fabulous."

"I'm sure that Tatum will be happy to hear that—I think," he qualified, thinking of the way Felicia had worded her compliment.

Felicia caught her lower lip between her teeth. She realized that she hadn't said that correctly. "I guess I should have left out that last part, you know, about not thinking that the meal would be *this* good."

The next moment, she found herself caught up in the smile she saw entering his eyes. Aaron wasn't exactly laughing at her, she realized. Instead, he seemed to be enjoying her.

She found the thought warming her.

"That's probably a good idea," he agreed. And then he leaned back in his chair for a moment, growing quiet as he studied her.

"So, tell me, is everything all right?" he asked Felicia out of the blue.

She looked at Aaron sharply. "Why wouldn't it be all right?" she asked uneasily. Had he heard something, or noticed something? Worse, was he aware that she was being followed?

The expression on her face troubled him for a moment. He really wanted to get to the bottom of this and there was no way to approach this except honestly and directly. So he leaped in.

"My aunt seems to think that you've been a little jumpy lately—her words," he qualified. "And she and my mother are concerned about you."

Guilt washed over Felicia immediately. The last thing she wanted was to cause the two women any sort of concern or worry.

"I'm not jumpy," Felicia denied. Then, because she had always found lying uncomfortable, she amended her protest a little. "Well, maybe just a little," she admitted.

His interest was immediately piqued. Now he was getting somewhere, he thought. "Mind if I ask why?

You can tell me that it's none of my business if you want," he told her. "Although I hope you won't."

Up until that moment, that was exactly what she was debating saying, just not in those exact words. But now that Aaron had opened up the door to that excuse, Felicia found she just couldn't use it. She found the words to be too dismissive and blunt. He was obviously concerned about her, and she really was grateful for that, even if it put her in an awkward position.

But at the same time, she didn't want to tell him about Greg, her defunct marriage and the abuse the man had subjected her to. Most of all, she was ashamed of the fact that she had been a victim at his hands.

Maybe she would be able to talk about that someday, but not at this point.

Still, she could see that Aaron was waiting and she knew she had to say something to him, so Felicia fell back on something she felt was credible and believable. "I'm just trying to make plans for my next job when that time finally comes."

"Your next job?" Aaron questioned. At this point, he hadn't thought that far ahead. Felicia had quickly become a fixture in his mother's life and that was where the situation stood at this point.

"Well, yes." Felicia felt that the term she had used was self-explanatory. "Your mother's progress is going extremely well, a lot better than I had even anticipated," she admitted. "If she keeps this up, she's most likely going to be finished with her physical therapy routine sooner than later, and I've got to be prepared for that eventuality. After all, I can't just have her doing her physical therapy exercises forever."

An amused smile played on Aaron's lips. Felicia caught herself feeling warm all over. The man's effect on her seemed to be intensifying steadily.

"Why not?" he asked innocently.

Felicia wasn't sure if he was just teasing her—or baiting her. In either case, she gave him an honest answer. "Well, for one thing, I would be guilty of milking the situation."

Aaron's eyes met hers. "What if my mother wants the situation milked?" He was asking the question in all seriousness.

Felicia blinked, speechless. "Excuse me?"

Aaron almost couldn't believe he was saying this, since he had been so against having Felicia take over his mother's care to begin with, but now he was looking at the situation from a completely different angle. At this point, he viewed having Felicia stay on as his mother's therapist as something that would be beneficial for his mother as well as for Felicia.

And for him, he thought with a smile.

To make the explanation as simple as possible, Aaron drew on what he knew best. "You know how there are some people who have personal trainers?"

"A personal trainer," she repeated. "You mean like what you're doing?"

"Yes, in a way, although there isn't a big match riding on the outcome," he allowed. "You could see continuing here, working with my mother, as just keeping her in the best shape she has ever been in."

Although she really liked the idea of staying on in Nicole's beautiful, Victorian-style home, she felt it wouldn't be honest of her to remain indefinitely—or even much longer.

"But I've already given her all the tools to be able to accomplish that," Felicia protested. "She's not going to need me, or she won't very soon."

Aaron shook his head in amazement. "You have *got* to be the most honest person to have ever walked the earth, bar none. Look, simply put, my mother likes your company. You're doing her a lot of good motivating her with this physical therapy program. And unless I miss my guess, you don't exactly hate the fact that you have a large house to stay in right now—do you?"

"No, of course not. Your mother has a lovely home." There was no arguing with that. "But I can't be there indefinitely. That would be taking advantage of her. That's not something I want to be guilty of doing."

Aaron raised a point. "What if she didn't see it that way?"

Finished with her meal, she retired her silverware and looked up at him. Hope was dueling it out with disbelief. She found herself rooting for hope. "Excuse me?"

He rephrased his question. "What if she didn't think of your being there as you taking advantage of the situation? What if, in my mother's all-seeing eyes, you are both getting something out of this?"

She couldn't see how he could view it that way. "Such as?"

"Such as you get a place to stay." He had looked into her background to some extent. Aaron was aware that she had traveled from one place to another, making temporary arrangements rather than permanent ones—

and she didn't strike him as someone who was really satisfied living that way. "And I get to have the reassurance of having someone looking out for my mother without making her feel as if she's an inept little old lady who needs to be taken care of."

Felicia felt called upon to come to Nicole's defense. "Your mother is definitely not anyone's idea of an inept little old lady."

"No, but you can understand that I do worry about her, and having you here, at least for the time being," he qualified, to lay that argument aside temporarily, "takes away that concern."

Felicia frowned slightly as she delicately wiped her fingers on her napkin. "I still feel as if I'm not being honest."

He couldn't understand why she would feel that way. "Felicia, if anything, you're the most honest one here," he pointed out. "Most people in your position would jump at the chance to continue making money doing what they were hired to do. They'd do whatever they could to prolong the situation, not attempt to put it to rest." He paused for second, then asked, "You like my mother, don't you?"

"Oh, very much." How could he even think to ask that? From the bottom of her heart, she could only wish that she'd had a mother like Nicole Colton. "She's a self-made woman who, despite the blows that life gave her, picked herself up and refused to be beaten down by her circumstances." Admiration throbbed in her voice. "She's just like your aunt, except that Vita found a life partner to be at her side while your mother had to forge this life for herself and her sons all on her own. I really respect your mother a great deal."

"So it doesn't sound as if you'd mind staying on awhile longer," he assumed.

"Of course I wouldn't mind. Your mother's a dream client and a terrific person. But, like I said, I just feel guilty taking her money."

"Actually," Aaron pointed out, "it's not her money. It's mine. When this all started, I told her I'd pay for everything for as long as she needed it."

Felicia focused on what he had just said. "That makes it even worse, because she's quickly approaching a point where she won't be needing it anymore."

Again, he shook his head in awed disbelief. "You are the most stubborn woman I have ever met—outside of my mother," he qualified—and even that was actually a compliment. "Stop fighting this, Felicia. One way or the other, you're staying on for now." Aaron put it that way to placate her. "It's a given. I believe that my mother really needs this."

She opened her mouth and he knew she was going to continue arguing with him about this, so in an attempt to point her in a different direction, Aaron asked her, "What made you get into physical therapy in the first place?"

That caught Felicia off guard for a moment, but only for a moment. "I wanted to help people and, very honestly, I didn't have the time or money to go to medical school, so this was the fastest way that I could accomplish my goal."

She had almost blurted out that she had met Greg that first year while taking classes in physical therapy, but she managed to catch herself just in time. So instead, what she said was, "Taking those classes and making a difference in people's lives was the calling I was looking for. And, most noteworthy, if I hadn't taken those classes, I wouldn't have met your mother or been able to, in some small way, help her."

He had listened to her without interrupting, but now he felt he had to say something. "Do you realize that you have a habit of diminishing what you accomplish?" he asked her.

She didn't see it that way. Her throat dry, she took a sip from her water glass before answering. "I don't want to come across as if I think too much of myself."

That was partially due to Greg, who had ripped into her at one point, accusing her of being conceited.

Heaven knew there was no way she would ever come across as thinking too much of herself, Aaron thought. "A little self-confidence never hurt," he said.

Felicia smiled at him. There was no point in arguing. And she did like his interpretation. "You're probably right," she agreed.

He caught himself thinking, out of the blue, that when she smiled like that, her whole face lit up, and he found himself totally captivated by her. He wondered about her, about things that went far deeper than just her background and her education.

He wondered about Felicia the woman.

"So," he asked, switching subjects as he looked at her empty plate, "are you up for dessert?"

It had been a long time since eating represented something more than just survival to her. This had been the most leisurely meal she could remember having in a very long time. Oh, meals at Nicole's table had been welcome and appetizing, but they had been a means to an end, something she grabbed quickly in order to get on to the next thing on her agenda.

Tonight it had been more of an event, a very tasty event.

"Yes," she replied, not really wanting this experience to end just yet. "I think so."

"Good," Aaron said, thinking that she was in for a real treat. To him dessert had always been the best part of the meal.

Turning in his seat, he held up his hand to attract their server's attention.

But instead of their server, it was Tatum who waved the woman away and made her way over to them. Apparently, Aaron thought, his cousin had been keeping an eye on them.

"I gather from the looks on your faces that you enjoyed your meal," Tatum surmised, pleased, as she looked from her cousin to his guest.

"Oh, very much so," Felicia answered enthusiastically.

"Good," Tatum declared. "Could I interest either one of you in dessert?" she asked, tapping the dessert menus she had brought with her and was now holding out to them.

"Oh, I think you might be able to talk us into it." Aaron put his hand out for the menus and handed one to Felicia. "What do you think, Felicia?"

Her eyes darted across the menu quickly. One thing looked more tempting than the next. Making up her mind was going to be hard.

"Oh, definitely," she agreed.

"Tell you what, why don't I make a choice for you?" Tatum proposed, her eyes sweeping over the two of them.

"Sounds good to me," Aaron told her, then turned toward Felicia. "Fee?"

Having Aaron use her nickname had a wave of heat washing over Felicia. Although it fit in as a substitute for the name she was using, it was actually short for her real name. A name she hadn't used or heard since she had fled home and taken on this identity for her own protection.

Fiona.

Pulling herself together, Felicia smiled a little too quickly at the two people looking at her. "My mouth is watering already."

"Be right back," Tatum promised just before she turned on her heel and made her way into the kitchen.

Desperate to have something to say that would draw Aaron's attention away from what she felt might be her flushed face, Felicia asked, "What do you think she's going to bring back?"

Aaron laughed. "From what I've come to gather about Tatum, it'll be something sinfully delicious and way too fattening."

Felicia said, "Then maybe I should take a pass on dessert."

"Why?"

"Well, if you think that whatever your cousin picks is going to be fattening…" Felicia's voice trailed off, her meaning clear.

He almost laughed at her for that. "If there's *any-*

one who could stand to consume a few extra hundred calories, trust me, it's you."

A blush blossomed on her cheeks. "You're just being nice," she said.

"No," he told her seriously, "I'm being accurate and honest. Besides, from what I hear, it'll be well worth it. My own mother paid her the ultimate compliment by saying that Tatum can do unimaginably wonderful things with food," he told Felicia. "As for dessert, it's probably as close as you'll come to going to heaven while still being on this mortal coil."

Felicia had her doubts about that, but she wasn't about to argue with him, especially since he was paying for the meal.

When Tatum returned a few minutes later, she was carrying two slices of spumoni ice cream cake, which, put together, looked as if they could form a healthy-sized cake.

"There you go," Tatum declared, placing one slice of the colorful ice cream cake in front of each of them.

Felicia looked at the plate, then at Tatum. "This is unbelievable."

Tatum's eyes crinkled as she smiled. "I'll be sure to pass your comment on to the chef," she told her cousin's companion. "For Suzanne, I know that cooking and baking are both art forms, but she never gets tired of hearing compliments. Well, enjoy," she told the duo, gesturing at the plates of dessert. "And remember, dinner was on the house."

Aaron shook his head. "Tatum, that's not how you make money."

"If I can't pick up the occasional check for a family

member, what's the point of having my own restaurant?" she asked. Glancing over her shoulder, Tatum realized that there was somewhere that she had to be at this moment.

"All right, I need to go right now," she told them, "but remember, we're family and have finally all found one another. Don't be such a stranger," she told Aaron. She turned to Felicia. "Same goes for you. If nothing else, one never knows when one can use the skills of a physical therapist," Tatum said with a wink just before she melded back into the crowd.

Aaron saw that Felicia had her fork in her hand, but it wasn't moving. "You're not eating," he noted. Was there something wrong?

"I'm not sure how to approach this," she confided, studying the thick piece of cake.

"My guess would be one forkful at a time." Aaron was already digging into his slice.

"I guess I can't argue with that."

"Good, because the way I see it from here, it's already beginning to melt," he told her, nodding at the slice on her plate.

Felicia began to eat more quickly.

Chapter Fourteen

"I'm so full I'm not sure I can move," Felicia said, suppressing a groan as she finally rose from the table.

Aaron had gotten to his feet moments ago. He went around to the back of her chair and pulled it from the table in order to facilitate her exit. Since Tatum had flatly refused to allow him to pay for their meal, Aaron took out his wallet and left a large tip tucked against his plate for the server.

Amused by Felicia's comment, Aaron promised, "We'll walk slowly. Besides, there's no real hurry to get you back quickly to my mother's as long as I have you there before midnight."

She thought that was an interesting way for him to put it. It made her think of the familiar children's fairy tale.

"Which one of us is going to turn into a pumpkin, you or me?" she asked him.

"Mom didn't specify," Aaron said, keeping a straight face. "You do know that she thinks of you as the daughter she never had. Right now, I think that she's exercising her right to dote on you."

As he said that, Aaron could remember what that

was like when he was in his early teens and his mother insisted on knowing where he was and when he was going to get home. If she wasn't happy about his answer—and admittedly, he was flippant—she said as much, while he felt stifled, to say the least.

Felicia didn't strike him as the type to resent having his mother insert herself into her life, but then anything was possible.

"Don't let it bother you," he advised her as he unlocked his car doors. He watched her get in, then got in on his side himself.

"Oh, it doesn't," Felicia quickly assured him with more than a little feeling. She fastened her seat belt and shifted in her seat to look at him. "As a matter of fact, it's kind of nice in a way. I never had anyone worrying about me."

It was true. Her mother had taken off when she had still been a little girl, and her father, between working long hours and losing himself in a bottle when he was home, had never worked at having any sort of a real relationship with his daughter. That was why when Greg came along, sweet and attentive, she had been so ready to take up with him.

But ultimately, Greg had only wanted to control her, making sure to keep a tight rein on every part of her life to the point that she felt as if she was being strangled.

"Well, just remember that she does mean well," Aaron was saying. "But if you start to feel that she's overstepping her bounds, venturing into areas where she has no place being, don't hesitate to tell her so. I guarantee that she'll back off."

A nostalgic smile curved his mouth. "She's good

that way. Sometimes she gets a little too carried away, being protective, and she forgets that she's dealing with an adult."

"I take it that you're speaking from experience," Felicia surmised with a smile.

"Oh, yeah," Aaron said, laughing. "We butted heads quite a lot when I was a know-it-all teenager years ago."

"Well, you don't seem to be any the worse for wear," Felicia observed. To his credit, he had his own business, handling four gyms in all. And he seemed totally well adjusted. Whatever had gone down between his mother and him during those years hadn't affected him badly, Felicia thought.

"Oh, I'm not," he agreed. "Compromise is a great thing. And, to be very honest, I have to give Mom a lot of credit for putting up with me. I was determined to get my way come hell or high water, and for the most part, Mom stepped aside and let me do my thing, even though my 'thing' had her sitting up nights, worried sick. To be honest, I'm surprised that her hair didn't go entirely gray."

Aaron glanced at her as he stopped at a light. "Mom did put up with a lot," he admitted. "Not many other mothers would have gone along with the career path I picked for myself. She not only put up with it, she was very supportive."

Felicia could easily see that happening, given the relationship that existed between Aaron and his mother now. "Maybe she was proud of you."

"Oh, she was," he assured her with a note of pride in his own voice.

"Then how do you know that it was hard on her?" she asked.

His smile was slightly lopsided as he thought back to that day.

"Because the day I decided that maybe I should give up being a human punching bag, my mother cried. It was the first and only time I ever saw her do that. And then she threw a huge party. To be very honest, I have never seen her looking happier," he confided. "Except maybe the day you helped get her back on her feet and walking comfortably."

Felicia laughed at the image he had projected of his younger self. "Having her cry would have definitely been a sign."

"Actually, looking back, I think my brother Nash is the only one of the three of us who didn't give her any reason for concern. He's an architect now and was always known as the calm one."

Felicia was trying to keep his family members straight. "You have another brother, right?"

Aaron nodded. "Damon. He works for the DEA." He refrained from telling Felicia that a good deal of Damon's work lately had involved being undercover. What that ultimately meant was that at any moment, Damon could wind up being exposed and ran the very real risk of being instantly in danger.

No one in the family had come out and said as much to his mother, but Aaron knew how her mind worked. Nicole had intuited that fact shortly after Damon had told her that he had taken the job. He had referred to it as a desk job, but Nicole seemed to know better.

Felicia put her own interpretation into the silence that had passed between them. "Given what two of her sons are, or 'were' involved in," she said, referring to his boxing career, "your mother seems incredibly calm and laid-back. At least on the outside," Felicia qualified, thinking that the woman might just be good at hiding things. "In her place, I think I would be a total wreck."

"I know. Sometimes I worry that she's actually a ticking time bomb and that she could go off at any moment." He looked at Felicia intently. "That's why I want to do whatever I can to make sure that she's happy."

The next moment, the light turned green again and he took his foot off the brake.

She couldn't explain exactly why Aaron's words about his feelings concerning his mother created such a warm, vibrant feeling within her, a feeling that seemed to spread and encompass everything that it touched, but it did.

Felicia decided to not try to analyze it. She just wanted to enjoy it while it lasted.

"Looks like we're here," Aaron told her.

They had reached their destination without her realizing it. He pulled up in front of the old Victorian house he had called home, parking to the side so his vehicle wasn't blocking the entrance to the front door. Turning off the engine, he sat back in his seat for a moment and needlessly repeated, "We're here, and it's not even midnight."

He winked at her, sending another unnerving, warm wave undulating through her stomach. It was all she could do not to press her hand against it to try to make it calm down.

"No, it's not," she finally said, the words hardly a whisper.

Felicia realized that she was tired, but at the same time, she also felt an excitement stirring in her.

She recalled that feeling. It was the same one she had experienced when she had first begun dating Greg. A nervous-down-to-the-tip-of-her-fingers feeling, she remembered, that continued for almost the first two years of her marriage—until it suddenly came to a screeching halt.

Because that was when Greg started changing.

The memory of those days nearly caused her to shiver before she could put a lid on those feelings.

"Are you all right?" she heard Aaron suddenly ask, concerned. He was looking at her.

"Sure," Felicia answered a bit too quickly, hoping that Aaron wouldn't notice that her voice had also gone up by an octave. Clearing her throat, she asked, "Why would you ask that?"

"Because," he told her, his voice low, soothing as he crooked his index finger and ran it slowly along her cheek, "your complexion just turned really pale."

She willed herself to breathe, damning Greg's memory and the way he kept infiltrating her mind. "Must be your imagination," she told him, trying to sound offhanded. But she was all but whispering the words.

She could feel her scalp growing warm. The entire world had just shrunk down to include only the two of them.

Just Aaron and her.

She could hear her heartbeat resonating in her ears. And her skin continued to feel as if it was growing progressively warmer as anticipation seemed to take possession of her entire being.

"And now," he told her, never taking his eyes off her face, "it seems to be growing a very interesting shade of pink."

"Maybe you need glasses," she told him, her mouth growing drier by the moment. She could hardly breathe now and she was unable to look away.

"Maybe I just need to take a closer look," he told her, managing to shift even closer to her despite the bucket seats.

"Maybe," she heard herself agreeing just before his lips touched hers.

And then the whole world suddenly went spinning totally out of control.

Felicia's heart was pounding now and her pulse raced wildly through her entire body. Arching closer to him, Felicia realized she had woven her arms around Aaron's neck.

The kiss grew stronger, more demanding, and she fell headlong into it.

It didn't even occur to her to resist.

For his part, Aaron wasn't quite sure how it all happened. It almost felt beyond his control. Granted he was attracted to her. He had felt that subtle pull almost from the very beginning. But attracted or not, he had always been able to exercise restraint and control over himself before now. That meant being able to clamp down on his inner desires if they flared up.

Up until this point, he had been able to isolate them

and keep them separate so that his thought process wasn't affected.

But no such restraint was there for him to draw on right now, no inner strength that he could exercise. There was just this wave of desire that had washed over him and taken over his very soul, loudly urging him on.

And growing stronger.

Although it wasn't comfortable for them, sitting in the front seat like that, he had his arms around Felicia, holding her. And as he kissed her, he could feel her melding into his heart.

His kiss grew stronger in its intensity, as if there was no end in sight.

Any moment now, he knew this feeling would explode, propelling him to another plateau. He wanted her with an overwhelming desire that nearly stole away not just his breath, but every part of him.

For a very long moment, he entertained the idea of taking her over to his loft and showing her just how much he truly wanted her.

But then a very small part of his brain realized how making love with her would wind up complicating things. That working part of his brain told him he needed to back off for now, even though he didn't want to.

Besides, he reasoned, if this was meant to be, then it would happen. All in due time. For now, he would savor this kiss and think about where it would lead them—eventually.

Aching for her, Aaron forced himself to draw back and then look at her.

"It is true what they say," he finally murmured.

She struggled to get her longing under wraps, stunned at what had very nearly transpired just now.

"About what?"

"About still waters running deep," Aaron told her with effort. There was a great deal of affection in his eyes as they washed over her. And then he smiled. "I'd better take you in before Mom calls Damon and asks him to go looking for you."

For just a fleeting, intense moment, Felicia felt bereft. She had come so very close to making love with Aaron just now. But then she told herself that it was better this way. There was no future for her with Aaron, no matter how attracted she was to him.

Still, she let out a long, shaky breath before she finally nodded and told him, "I wouldn't want to worry her."

"Neither do I," Aaron said as he walked with her up to the massive front door.

Felicia took out the key that Nicole had insisted she accept and inserted it into the lock. Before turning it, she looked at Aaron. "Do you want to come in?"

The question struck her as odd the moment it was out of her mouth. She was asking him if he wanted to come into his own house, a house he had more right to be in than she had. He probably thought she was a little strange, if nothing else, asking him that.

He looked as if he really wanted to say yes, but instead, he said, "No, I'd better not. I've got an early day tomorrow and if I go in with you, I've got a very strong feeling that my mother is going to want to ask a lot of questions about the food, Tatum's restaurant and the evening in general. Once my mother gets going, she can go on endlessly, and while I do like her company a great deal, I really don't have that much time to spare tonight."

Felicia grinned, seeing the humor in the situation. "So you're throwing me to the wolves—so to speak."

"Mom won't get carried away with you. And even if she does, all you have to do is yawn and she'll quickly take that as her cue to let you go upstairs to your room. That's not to say that she might not want to interrogate you come morning," he added, "but at least you'll get a break."

She looked at him. "You seem to have this all down pat," she marveled. "I take it you've been through this drill before."

"No." He didn't want Felicia thinking that his mother questioned him about his romantic activities on some sort of a regular basis. "But I do know how her mind works," he told Felicia. "She used to do this kind of thing before every one of my bouts. You see, Mom likes getting a handle on everything."

Felicia nodded. "So I guess this is good-night," she said, trying to find a way to politely extricate herself before she gave in to the growing desire to talk him into coming in and staying with her a little longer.

He smiled into her eyes, thinking he could easily get lost in them. "It is."

She squared her shoulders. "Well, I had a lovely time, so thank you."

"Don't thank me, thank Tatum," he told her. "She was the one who covered the meal."

"Yes, but you were the one who thought to take me out for the evening in the first place," she reminded him. "And I don't mind telling you that it's been a very long time since I've been out for pleasure anywhere. Thank you for making me go."

He smiled at her warmly. "My pleasure," he told her. And then he added, "If you don't make good your escape into the house this minute, I'm going to be sorely tempted to kiss you good-night again."

What makes you think that I wouldn't want you to? Felicia silently asked. But then, as much as she wanted a repeat performance of what had transpired earlier in his car, she knew that would be a mistake—and asking for trouble.

So, offering Aaron a wide smile, Felicia told him, "Good night," and, opening the front door, quickly went inside before she wound up weakening.

He watched her wistfully, then forced himself to go. Quickly.

Chapter Fifteen

Aaron hadn't expected his mother to be the one to open the door when he rang the bell around noon the next day, especially since he could see from Felicia's and Vita's parked cars that they were both home. He had actually been hoping that Felicia would be the one on the other side of the door, opening it to admit him inside.

Still, Aaron didn't lose a beat as he smiled at the woman who had given him life. "Hi, Mom. How are you doing?" he asked cheerfully.

Nicole gestured for Aaron to come on in. "I'm fine, dear. I must say that I haven't seen this much of you since you were in elementary school. Give it to me honestly, Aaron," she said, pretending to be serious as she closed the door behind her and turned around to confront him. "Am I dying?"

The question caught him completely off guard. "What? No," he denied with verve. "Why would you even ask that?"

"Well, like I said. I haven't seen this much of you—and so often—since you were a little guy and hanging around your mother was acceptable. When you got a little older, you were always more interested in going your own way. And now you've been stopping by the house more times than I have fingers. I was just wondering if something dire was motivating you."

She wasn't really wondering. She was fairly certain that she knew why her son had become such a frequent visitor, but she wanted to hear Aaron admit it. They both knew he wasn't coming by just to check on her. Although Aaron was a loving son, that was only a secondary excuse he was using. The real reason he kept coming by was because of Felicia, and Nicole couldn't have been more thrilled about it.

The only thing that would make this whole situation better in her book was to hear Aaron come out and actually admit it.

But she wasn't greedy, Nicole told herself. She felt that would all come in good time. Just as Aaron had come around when it came to giving up boxing for a living and had turned to training contenders instead.

Aaron eyed his mother and said seriously, "Maybe finding you on the floor on your hands and knees made me aware that I shouldn't take having you around for granted."

He sounded so sincere that Nicole could feel her heart responding. "Oh, Aaron, don't make me cry now."

"Wouldn't dream of it, Mom. So—" he looked around the area "—where is everyone?" he asked, trying to sound as casual as possible.

Nicole's eyes narrowed slightly. Aaron could all but hear his mother declaring, "Aha." Wanting to avoid discussing the obvious, he quickly followed up his question by saying, "I thought I saw Aunt Vita's car in

front of the house. I thought she might be down here
with you."

"As a matter of fact, she is here," his mother told
him with a pleased smile. "And your aunt Vita brought
someone with her."

"Uncle Rick?" he asked. It seemed like the logical choice.

Unlike his father's twin brother, the amoral Uncle
Axel, who had been Vita's first husband and the father
of his cousins Myles and Lila, Vita's second husband
was adored by everyone in the family. Right from the
beginning, Rick had made a real effort to be a father
not just to his wife's children, but also to him and his
two brothers. Aaron and his brothers all knew that if
they had a problem or needed help dealing with anything at all, Rick would always be there for them. Rick
was a true family man in every sense of the word.

And just as Aaron asked his mother if Rick was the
one who had come with his aunt, it occurred to him
that he hadn't seen the man for a while. He realized that
he was allowing the management of his four gyms to
take up all of his time. It had taken his mother's accident to finally wake him up to the fact that he wasn't
interacting with the rest of the family—and this newest addition, he thought, his thoughts straying toward
Felicia again.

Things definitely needed to change, he decided.

"Actually, no, dear," his mother said, answering his
question. "It's not Rick. Your uncle Rick is stuck at the
nursery, insisting, since he is one man down, on overseeing all the details—something that doesn't exactly
make Vita very happy. She swears she's going to force

Rick to hire some extra help for the office so that he can get out a little more," she said. And then she smiled brightly. "No, this is an actual surprise."

Aaron studied her for a moment. "Is this your attempt at being mysterious, Mom?"

"Not at all," she replied innocently. "This is my way of getting you to follow me to the family room," Nicole said, leading the way into that room.

The next moment, he no longer had to ask any more questions as to just who the surprise visitor was. He saw Vita's daughter, his cousin Lila, sitting on the sofa between his aunt and Felicia. All three women were laughing.

Aaron quickly walked over to the sofa and gave his cousin a warm, welcoming hug.

"Lila, when did you get back?" he asked as he released her.

"Late yesterday," the pretty, dark-haired twenty-nine-year-old answered. "The minute I got past my jet lag I went right over to see my mom," she said, glancing at Vita, "only to find out that she was over here, so here I am."

And then she turned to look at Nicole. "You have no idea how upset I was to find out about Aunt Nikki and her broken hip," she told her cousin. There was compassion in her eyes as she looked at Aaron's mother.

"My hip isn't broken anymore," Nicole pointed out. "It's better than new—thanks to Felicia here." Lila's aunt put her arm around Felicia's shoulders and gave the young woman a quick, warm hug.

Felicia had no intentions of taking what she considered undue credit. "The doctor put you together, Nicole," she told the woman. "I just did my part to help get you back in working order."

"See?" Nicole asked, looking over at her niece. "What did I tell you? Not only is she great when it comes to physical therapy, but the woman is also pathologically modest."

"Accurate," Felicia corrected. "The word is *accurate*, not pathologically modest."

Nicole sighed. "Have it your way if it makes you happy, dear," she said, patting Felicia's hand. "The rest of us know the truth. Don't we, Aaron?" She turned toward her son.

He could see that all this extra attention was making Felicia look very uncomfortable, so he decided to change the subject. He asked his cousin, "So how did your trip to meet up with that recluse Homer Tinsley go? Did you get him to part with any of his paintings to put them on exhibit at the gallery?"

Lila knew her cousin was just being polite. Paintings held absolutely no interest for him. But she obliged with an answer anyway. It was actually her way of blowing off steam after what she had just been put through.

"Well, Tinsley continues to be a mystery man," she said. She knew artists were a breed unto themselves, but she definitely didn't appreciate this artist's hide-and-seek personality.

"You mean he didn't meet with you?" Felicia asked, surprised that a renowned artist would behave in this fashion.

"That's what I mean," Lila said wearily, doing her best to hold on to her irritation. After all, she had gone out of her way to meet with the man the way she had been directed, and then, after all that, he'd made himself unavailable. "Homer Tinsley usually communicates through his agent, Walter Fox, but this time Fox was a no-show, too."

Vita took umbrage at the treatment her daughter had received at the so-called artist's hands.

"How extremely rude," she declared. "If you have an address where to get in contact with this impolite man, I'll pass it on to your stepfather. Rick can teach that barbarian some manners if anyone can."

"No need, Mom, although I appreciate the offer," Lila told her mother. "Just when I got back to my new town house last night, there was a message waiting for me that Mr. Tinsley will be sending several of his pieces for exhibition at the Weston Street Gallery next month," she said, referring to the gallery that she managed. Lila shrugged and shook her head at the way things had turned out. "I guess I could have saved myself the trip."

"Don't you think that his behavior was a little odd?" Felicia asked, referring to the way things had played out. "To have the artist say he was going to meet with you, then not show up, but still send word that he would lend out his works to be put on exhibition?"

To Felicia, that had all the earmarks of someone who was trying to hide from the public at large. She should know, Felicia thought, being an expert when it came to hiding behind another identity.

Further questions came to mind regarding the artist's behavior, but for now, she decided to leave the matter alone. Especially since Aaron's cousin seemed to be content with the way things had ultimately turned out. Besides, if she did raise further questions based on her own experiences, they might just pique Aaron's curiosity, something she definitely didn't want.

No, this was a case she should leave well enough alone, Felicia silently lectured herself.

Meanwhile, Lila was telling the others how surprised she'd been that Walter Fox, Tinsley's agent, hadn't shown up, as well. She would have expected, especially after the note about the exhibition had arrived, that at the very least Fox would have contacted her in person. But he hadn't.

Something was definitely up, Lila thought. But what?

"I'm beginning to think that not only are artists strange creatures, but that evaluation goes for their agents, too," Lila said. "But I guess when you have all that talent going for you, something else has to perforce be out of whack in another area." She looked at her mother. "Being completely normal requires being ordinary, I suppose."

"I disagree, Lila," Nicole told her niece, speaking up. "I happen to know very talented people who are perfectly normal. Well, maybe not 'perfectly,'" she amended with a wide grin, "but very close to it. I think people like Tinsley just use their talent like a shield to cover up their odd behavior." She shook her head in disapproval.

Aaron agreed with his mother. There was no excuse for that sort of behavior. "You know, you might be right, Mom."

"Of course I'm right," she stated flatly. "Talent doesn't give anyone the right to be rude like that."

Vita clapped her hands together in approval. "Hear!

Hear!" she declared. Resting her hands in her lap, she looked at Nicole's son and Felicia. "And this is why I really like this woman. Your mother makes a great deal of sense."

Lila turned toward Aaron. "So, how's everything going with you, cousin? Turn out any boxing champions since I left town on my fruitless expedition?"

"Off the top of my head, there're a couple of guys at the gym who look like they have a lot of potential," he answered. "But you have to remember, training potential champion boxers is not my primary focus. I'm training fighters so I can put that money into my charitable programs. I want to help keep at-risk teens off the streets and out of trouble. If I can teach them to channel the energy that's building up inside them into something productive, then that will be my main contribution to society."

"Lord, if anything," Lila declared, pretending to roll her eyes, "I see you've gotten even more noble-sounding than the last time we talked."

Aaron merely smiled at her assessment. "Fish got to swim, birds got to fly," he said with a wink.

Lila laughed. "You know, I think I'll have that made into a sign and hung up on a wall at the gallery," she teased.

"If it was mine to give away, you'd be the one I'd give it to," Aaron told her. Then he turned toward Felicia. "Can I talk to you for a minute, Fee?"

The request, coming out of the blue the way it did just now, took Felicia by surprise. He sounded almost serious, she thought, immediately wondering if there was anything wrong.

"Sure," she agreed after a beat.

Aaron nodded. However, he didn't want to talk to Felicia here, in front of his mother, his aunt and his cousin. He knew that would just give them ammunition to tease one or both of them later.

"In the next room," he prompted, nodding toward the doorway.

These days, uneasiness was always Felicia's first reaction. So much had happened to her in the last four years that she hadn't been able to anticipate or foresee. It felt as if her mind always went to the worst-possibility scenario first.

But she saw no way around going along with his request.

"Of course," Felicia agreed the way a prisoner agreed to having the warden take them aside for a private word that was far from welcome.

Aaron caught the way his mother was watching him as well as the smile on her face. Nicole Colton looked a little like the proverbial cat that had swallowed the canary. It took everything he had to refrain from commenting on his mother's expression. But he was grateful that at least she didn't either egg him on or say anything about the situation as she saw it.

"Right over here," Aaron told Felicia, leading the way into the next room.

"Take your time, dear," his mother said, raising her voice, unable to keep her peace any longer.

"Mom," Lila began, turning toward Vita, "is there something going on here that I don't know about?"

"That, my dear daughter," Vita replied, glancing

at her sister-in-law before answering Lila, "remains to be seen."

For her part, Nicole put a finger to her lips and shushed Vita. When Vita looked at her, somewhat offended, Nicole told her, "Don't jinx it, Vita."

"Jinx what?" Lila asked, now thoroughly curious and feeling totally left out of the loop, a situation she found irritating, especially coming on the heels of previous events.

"Your cousin finally seeing what's right in front of his nose and acting on it," Nicole replied vaguely.

"Okay, that settles it," Lila declared. "I am never going out of town ever again. Too much seems to happen when I'm not around."

"Don't feel bad, dear," her mother told her, placing her hand over Lila's. "If anything worthwhile had happened, I would have called you and let you know about it."

"In plain English," Nicole said, lowering her voice as she addressed her niece, "what your mother is trying to say is that we believe Aaron has opened his eyes to some very real possibilities when it comes to Felicia." She added with a beatific smile, "You fill in the blanks. It shouldn't be all that hard."

Chapter Sixteen

Felicia looked back toward the family room. She could hear the voices of the others as they talked.

"I think your aunt might think we're being rude," she told Aaron, not completely comfortable about walking away from the others like this.

"Don't worry, this won't take long," Aaron promised. Damn, but he felt as if he was lighting up inside just because he was standing so close to Felicia. Why hadn't he noticed this before? "Besides," he went on, trying to keep his mind on the conversation and not the woman in front of him who was stirring his blood, "Aunt Vita is crazy about me. As far as she's concerned, I walk on water."

Felicia couldn't help smiling at the imagery he had just projected. "I think that you're overselling it a tiny bit."

"Okay, she thinks I walk on puddles," he amended. "Deep ones." He grinned. "Anyway—" he got down to the main reason he had drawn her away from the others "—I wanted to run something by you."

Felicia could feel herself bracing, not knowing what to expect. Was he going to talk to her about his mother's physical therapy program? Or was he going to bring up the fact that his aunt had noticed she seemed jumpy at times, and he wanted to ask her what was causing it?

Or was this about something entirely different? Felicia was at a complete loss as to what to anticipate.

All she knew was that she had let her guard down yesterday and allowed herself to experience what had to be the most exciting kiss of her life.

A kiss she had no right to experience because she wasn't here for a romantic interlude, she reminded herself. This was all strictly business and just for a while, and she had allowed herself to forget that.

"Go ahead," Felicia heard herself saying even as she felt her throat tightening. Not only that, but it felt as if air was having a great deal of difficulty going in and out of her chest.

"It has come to my attention, thanks to my mother, that I've been working almost nonstop lately and I really need to slow down a bit and take some time to—how did my mother put it?" And then it came to him. "Smell the carnations."

Maybe this wasn't going to be as bad as she had imagined, Felicia thought. "Don't you mean roses, not carnations?"

"No, carnations. My mother is partial to carnations, not roses. One of the reasons for that is because they last a lot longer. She's practical that way," he said with a grin.

Felicia laughed. "If she's interested in longevity, she should look into chrysanthemums. Those things seem to last *forever*," she emphasized. "You can wind up getting sick of them and they're still hanging on, still alive." Felicia shrugged. "I suppose another way to look at it is that you really get your money's worth with chrysanthemums."

"I'll keep that in mind the next time I send flowers," he said, smiling. And then he looked at her. "I'm getting off the point I was trying to make."

Felicia glanced over her shoulder toward the room they had just left. Apparently, the others were still talking and no one looked as if they were going to come out looking for them.

"Sorry," she apologized. "I didn't mean to distract you. What were you going to say?" she asked him, bracing herself again.

"I was going to ask you if you wanted to go on a picnic with me," Aaron told her.

Felicia blinked. She had definitely not seen that one coming. "A picnic," she repeated uncertainly, not really sure what to make of his request or just how to respond. Was he being serious?

"Yes, you know, one of those things where you spread out a tablecloth on the grass and eat food that was packed up in a basket—hopefully before the insects can get to it. Does any of that sound as if it might be appealing to you?"

She took so long to answer that Aaron was forced to draw his own conclusion. "It doesn't, does it?"

Felicia quickly shook her head. That wasn't it. He had just stunned her. "I've never been on a picnic before," she told him.

Aaron stared at her, not sure if she was pulling his leg. "You're kidding."

Why would she kid about something like that? "No,"

she told him. "I've never had the time to go on one." *Or anyone to go with*, she added silently.

She could just guess what Greg would have said to that if she had suggested going on a picnic to him. Most likely he would have said something to the effect that it struck him as childish—if anything it was a juvenile way to pass an afternoon.

When she had admitted that she'd never been on a picnic, Aaron arbitrarily made the decision for her.

"Well, now you have to go," he told her. "Think of it as a rite of passage."

His choice of words made her laugh, which in turn mercifully helped Felicia relax again. "Well, then I guess I'll have to go. Tomorrow?" she asked to make sure.

He nodded. "Unless there's something you have to do with my mother," he qualified, not wanting to interfere with the program she had instituted for his mother.

"I'm sure if I explain this to your mother, she'd be willing to let me work her therapy around the picnic." Felicia smiled at him, her eyes sparkling. "Your mother's very accommodating that way. As a matter of fact, your mother's got to be the nicest person I've ever had the good fortune to work with."

Her assessment brought back memories for Aaron. "When I was a kid, everyone was always telling me how much they really loved my mother. Hell, even after I stopped being a kid, everyone I knew was crazy about her." He laughed. "It made complaining about her really hard for me."

She frowned. "Why would you complain about your mother?" she asked him, mystified. By his own admission, he really didn't have anything to complain about. She had to be the most easygoing mother ever created.

Aaron shrugged. "Oh, you know. The usual teenage angst," he explained. "But that's why my friends had no patience with me when I went looking for a sympathetic ear. Every one of them said they would have given their eyeteeth to trade places with me. When I was growing up, my mother was always known as 'the cool mom' and she never even had to do anything out of the ordinary to earn that title. It was just a given. She was always the cool one," he said with a note of nostalgia.

"How about your mom?" he asked Felicia, thinking he had monopolized the conversation long enough. Besides, he found himself wanting to learn something about her background. This was as good a place as any to start. "What was she like?"

She shrugged. "Not overly sure," she admitted honestly. "I don't really have a clear memory of her. She took off when I was five. I'm not even sure if she's still alive." She had tried looking her up once but had gotten nowhere.

He had really walked right into that one, Aaron thought. He hadn't meant to bring up anything so painful.

"I'm sorry," he apologized. "I didn't know."

"Why should you know?" she asked. "It's not something that I advertise exactly. But thank you."

"What about your father?" he asked, then quickly qualified, "Was he in the picture?" He knew that in a lot of cases the father was absent from the scene. There was no way that Aaron wanted to be guilty of making the same mistake twice.

"Only in a negative way," she said, playing off the image of a "picture" that he had just raised. "My father worked for a living at a job he absolutely hated, so every night, when he came home, he drank to forget." An ironic smile played on her lips. "Unfortunately," Felicia told him with a philosophical shrug, "one of the things my father forgot was me most of the time."

As he listened, Aaron could feel his heart going out to her. It sounded as if she definitely had a terrible childhood.

"Wasn't there anyone else around to take care of you?"

She drew back her shoulders in an almost defensive manner. "I learned to take care of myself at an early age."

He thought of some of the stories he had heard about. There were some that sent a chill down his spine, but there were others that had turned out well.

"What about social services?" he asked.

"What about them?" She asked the question so flippantly, Aaron felt as if he had his answer. But he pushed on anyway just in case he had guessed wrong.

"Didn't anyone call them on your behalf?"

"You have to understand that my dad didn't mingle with people. Hardly anyone knew that he had a daughter who was raising herself while he lost himself inside of a vodka bottle with a fair amount of regularity. So there was no real reason for anyone to call about my circumstances."

"Didn't you go to school?" he asked, thinking that

her situation should have caught someone's attention during those years.

"I did," she answered. "But I kept to myself, did all my schoolwork because, aside from everything else, it made me feel normal and gave me a sense of purpose. And, in addition," she added with a smile, "I got fairly good at forging signatures at a very young age."

"And no one questioned anything?" he asked in disbelief.

"What can I say? It was a very crowded school, and with a little bit of effort—and self-preservation—I got lost in the shuffle." She smiled at him. "Added to that, my report cards were pretty good," she said with a touch of pride.

He didn't doubt it, Aaron thought. Still, he was having a great deal of trouble picturing what she was telling him. It sounded as if she had somehow fallen through the cracks.

"So there was no one for you to turn to?" he asked again with compassion.

That's just the trouble. I turned to the first person who showed me the slightest bit of kindness and I wound up paying for that dearly, she thought. But there was no point in her going into that. Or telling him even the slightest details about that life she had lived. Her ex's abuse had just continued to escalate, growing harsher and harsher each time he lashed out at her, until she had finally escaped and made a new life for herself somewhere else.

But she wasn't about to tell Aaron any of that because she didn't want him thinking of her as a victim. Nothing would erase that look from his eyes faster than telling him about what she had gone through, and she wouldn't be able to bear that.

Felicia still lived in fear, waiting for Greg to suddenly pop up and make her "pay" for all the imagined wrongs. But she had managed to convince herself that it was just that, nothing more than fear taunting her. There was no reason for Greg to pop up here.

He had no way of knowing where she had gone. She had been very careful about that. After all, it was a large country and people could still get lost if they exercised the proper caution.

The way she had.

"No," Felicia finally said, answering Aaron's question. "There was no one." She hated lying, but the truth was far more complicated. "Anything else?" she asked him brightly.

Felicia wasn't saying it, but he had a feeling he knew what she was secretly telling him by that look on her face. That he was asking too many questions.

"I didn't mean to pry," he told her.

"And yet, you did," she replied. "Sorry, that just slipped out," she apologized, realizing how harsh that must have sounded.

"I just wanted to get to know you," Aaron explained. "Maybe that was wrong of me." And then he smiled at her. It wasn't a sexy smile, but it disarmed her. "I couldn't help myself."

This was how it started with Greg, she remembered. Somehow, he managed to work his way under her defenses. She hadn't even realized what was happening—until it did. She needed to be wary and stay alert, she told herself.

"Why is that?" she asked, her voice cool, distant.

"Because..." His eyes held hers, and suddenly, she had no way to hold him at bay. "I think I'm falling in love with you, Felicia Wagner. And I want to learn everything there is to know about you."

She was quiet for a long moment, her eyes delving into his, searching for some indication that he was lying to her. But there was no evidence of that. He was being honest.

Still, she had learned the hard way that she was too trusting.

"Every woman likes to maintain a little mystery about herself," Felicia finally told him.

"Mysteries are for people who like playing games," he answered. "I don't want to play games, Felicia. I want us to be honest with one another and get to know the real person beneath all the rhetoric."

Oh, Lord, she could feel herself melting despite all her efforts to keep up a barricade. "You sound so serious," she said, doing her best to sound just the opposite.

There was something in Felicia's eyes that spoke to him, something that told him she had been hurt very, very badly. By the mother who deserted her, by the father who abandoned her morally and by someone else, someone he couldn't put his finger on right now, Aaron thought. But he intended to, eventually.

Right now, he wanted her to know that she could count on him and that he would always be there for her, heaven help him—if she would just let him.

"I'll be serious—or not," he told her. "In short, I will be anything that you want me to be," he promised, and she had a feeling that he actually meant it.

It was her turn to call the shots, Felicia thought. Her turn to lighten the moment because if it were anything else, anything more serious than that, Felicia was afraid that she wouldn't be able to handle that, not feeling vulnerable the way she did.

"Then just be happy," she told him in reference to his offer to be anything that she wanted him to be. "Otherwise, you'll ruin the picnic with that gloomy face—and we wouldn't want that."

"Then you will come with me tomorrow?" Aaron asked. He had to admit that she had him wondering whether or not she would. For a woman who seemed so simple on the surface, she was very complex beneath it all.

Felicia smiled at him, reacting to the surprised look in his eyes. "Did you have any doubt that I would?"

"I have to admit that it did cross my mind," he told her honestly. "You seem to be very straightforward, but underneath all that, you are an extremely complicated lady, Felicia."

No, I'm really not. Just very wary. Felicia took his hand in hers. He looked at her in surprise. Somehow, this felt more personal, although he couldn't quite say why. "Call me Fee," she told him.

"Why? Do you like that better?" Aaron asked, curious.

"Yes, I do," she answered. *Because it's my nickname*, she told him in her mind. It was short for the name she was born with. The name she had abandoned when she moved to Chicago to elude Greg. But out loud she answered, "I think it's kind of cute."

"No," Aaron corrected, putting his hands on her

shoulders and drawing her closer to him. "You're cute. And you'd still be cute if you answered to 'Dolphin' or 'Pecan' or any one of a whole slew of nicknames."

She almost laughed out loud. "Pecan?" she questioned in wonder.

"The point is, the name doesn't matter. *You*, however, do." He combed his fingers through her hair, framing her face with his hands. "I just wanted you to know that."

"Okay." She inclined her head. "Consider me educated." A noise from the other room caught her attention and she glanced over her shoulder again. "Shouldn't we be getting back before your mother gets suspicious?"

"My mother doesn't 'get' suspicious. As far as I know, she was actually made that way. But it's a good kind of suspicion," Aaron told Felicia with a wink. And then he added, "Trust me."

"I guess I have to." When he looked at her curiously, she added, "Since we're going to be going on a picnic together."

Aaron grinned at her. "Yes, we are," he agreed. And with that he took her hand in his and brought her back into the family room.

Chapter Seventeen

"Are you sure you don't mind?" Felicia asked Nicole uncertainly.

While she was looking forward to the idea of going on a picnic with Aaron, she didn't want to leave the woman she'd come to care for alone for half a day.

What if Nicole suddenly had a relapse and needed her? she thought.

"Mind?" Nicole scoffed at the mere suggestion. "I'm thrilled to death that both you and Aaron are going to be taking some well-deserved time off." She placed a hand on the young woman's shoulder. "If you want my opinion, dear, you both work much too hard. I think it's a toss-up as to which of you are the most guilty of that."

Felicia couldn't help laughing. "Said the woman whose middle initial is *W* for workaholic."

Nicole's eyes narrowed. She wasn't annoyed; she just wasn't used to having her words used against her.

"We're not talking about me, dear, we're talking about you and Aaron," her client reminded her. "Now, since you've fulfilled your morning obligation and practically run me into the ground with those new ex- ercises you've come up with, you going out on that picnic in the park will give us *both* a chance to regroup for tonight's extravaganza. Although, if you decide that it's perfectly fine to cut back on my PT for one day and turn that picnic into a night out with Aaron, I would be very agreeable with that decision," she added cheerfully.

Felicia blinked and then shook her head. "You really must be getting better, Nicole. You didn't leave me any space to get in a word edgewise," she said with a laugh.

"Are you trying to hurt my feelings?" Nicole deadpanned.

Felicia wasn't sure if the woman was being serious or just pulling her leg, but she was taking no chances.

"No, no, of course not," Felicia denied quickly. "I'm just making the point that you've never been this energized before. At least, not since I began working with you," she qualified. She took the woman's behavior as a sign that she was returning to her old self. "I guess this means that you won't be needing me much longer."

Nicole looked at her, appalled. "It means nothing of the sort. I'm just thinking about possibilities."

"Possibilities?" Felicia questioned.

Nicole waved away the topic. She realized that she had already said too much.

"Never mind, dear. That's a conversation for another day. Right now, you have a picnic to get ready for," she told Felicia. "And, to that end, since you mentioned going on a picnic yesterday, I took the liberty of preparing a little something for the two of you." With that, she led Felicia over to the spare refrigerator in her garage.

Opening the door, she took out the picnic basket

she had packed that morning before she had begun her morning exercises with Felicia.

Felicia stared at the picnic basket. That had to be the largest basket she had ever seen. "Oh, Nicole, you didn't have to do that."

Nicole gave her a patient, although somewhat long-suffering look.

"You're missing the point, dear. This is something that I *wanted* to do. Preparing special meals is, very plainly, what I do. It's what kept me going in the early days," she told the younger woman. "And since you mentioned that this is your very first picnic, I wanted it to be memorable—something special," she emphasized with a smile.

"Now, go get ready," Nicole urged in the next breath. "You have a perfect day for it and we don't have all that many perfect days in Chicago. It's usually too hot, too humid or just too rainy. My advice is to take advantage of it before the weather suddenly decides to reverse itself. Now shoo," she said, waving Felicia up to her room.

She was treating her like a daughter, Felicia thought with a smile, finding the idea exceedingly pleasing.

Felicia quickly ran up the stairs to get ready. The last thing she wanted to do was to keep Aaron waiting. That was way too predictable. Besides, she was very excited about this adventure and wanted to be ready for Aaron when he rang the bell.

Also, Nicole was getting better at an incredible rate, she noted. Who knew how much time she had left in this house? She felt she had to make the most of it while she could.

Since it was summer and the weather was definitely leaning toward being hot right now, Felicia decided to wear a pair of navy blue shorts, a white tank top and a pair of sandals.

She thought about putting her long blond hair up in a ponytail, then decided against it. Looking at her reflection in the mirror, she thought leaving her hair down made her look more at ease.

Ready, she was on her way downstairs when she thought she heard the doorbell ring.

Her heart jumped.

Aaron.

He still wasn't using his key, she thought. She knew he had one and wondered if his refraining from using it was his idea, or his mother's. She had a feeling it was probably his.

Rather than speed up, she decided to come down the stairs a little more slowly, as if deliberately making an entrance.

And maybe, in a way, that was what she was doing— because she wanted to make an impression on Aaron.

If she was in any way undecided as to whether or not she had chosen the right outfit, the expression on Aaron's face settled the matter for her.

He had been speaking to his mother when, hearing Felicia come down the stairs, he looked over toward her.

"Wow," he whispered, unaware that he had said anything as his mouth dropped open in awe.

Nicole took in his reaction as well as the outfit that Felicia was wearing in one quick, sweeping glance. She smiled to herself, pleased on several counts.

"Careful, darling," she whispered with a laugh to her son. "You're drooling."

Aaron's head popped up as he quickly snapped out of his trance. It took him a bit longer to locate his tongue. When he finally did, he told Felicia, "I like your outfit."

Nicole laughed and glanced at Felicia. "Aaron always had this gift for understatement," she told the physical therapist affectionately. "All right, you two, I suggest you get started. The weather is practically perfect and, for all intents and purposes, accommodating right now, but it's as unpredictable as a fickle woman with her first taste of freedom. Which means that it's liable to change without warning."

The woman was really trying to get them to go out the door, Felicia thought. "That's a little simplistic and stereotypical, don't you think?" she asked Nicole.

"Possibly," Nicole admitted. "You two better get going."

Aaron lingered for a moment longer. "I asked Damon to look in on you later," he told his mother.

His words were not met with the reaction he had expected. His mother was frowning and didn't look at all pleased by his actions. "Aaron, I told you, I'm fine. I certainly don't need a keeper."

"Not a keeper, Mom," he protested. "Think of it as a drive-by."

She didn't follow that at all. "That sounds more like a shooting," she told her son. "In any event, call your brother off, dear. If I find I need someone for any reason, I can call your aunt Vita and she can come over. She likes the excuse."

Aaron gave his mother a skeptical look and then laughed at the scenario she was attempting to sell to him. "Like I really believe that."

Nicole glared at her son impatiently. "Look, are you going to take this lovely creature out for her first picnic, or are you going to stand here and waste your time arguing with me?"

He sighed. "Okay, you win—as usual."

Nicole smiled. "That's what makes me the mom and you the kid. Now go!" she ordered. "I outdid myself with the lunch I prepared for the two of you. Don't let it go to waste." She looked at Felicia. "Help me out here, Fee."

Felicia glanced at Aaron. "She's right, you know. We should get going before we run out of daylight and it's suddenly time to get back to our regular lives."

"Hear that? She's making sense. See if she can get some of that to rub off on you," Nicole said, walking them to the door.

"You know, for a little thing," he told his mother, "you certainly are bossy."

"I have to be," Nicole informed him, humor curving her mouth. "My sons don't listen to me the first half a dozen times I say something." Placing her hands against Aaron's back, she all but pushed him out the door. "Now go and have fun. That's a command."

And with that, Nicole closed the door on both of them.

"I do still have a key, Mom," Aaron called out, raising his voice to goad her.

"And you know better than to use it," Nicole countered.

His mother had made her point. Aaron looked at Felicia. "I guess that's our cue to go."

She laughed. "Short of both of us getting the bum's rush, I would say that you are right."

"Bum's rush?" Aaron repeated. He hadn't heard the expression in years. "Just how old are you, Felicia?" he asked her with a laugh.

"I've never heard anyone ever actually use that expression," she told him. "I just read a lot—and watch old movies."

Well, that certainly sounded like a well-rounded, if somewhat vicarious, life, Aaron thought. "And yet you've never been on a picnic," he marveled.

"I said I read a lot. I didn't say that I experienced a lot of things," she pointed out.

Aaron nodded, opening the passenger door for her. "No, you did not," he agreed. As she got into the car, his eyes skimmed over her shorts, which hugged her body and drew attention to her legs. Definitely arousing, he thought before he shut down his reaction.

"All right," he declared, "let your education begin." With that, he slid in behind the wheel and started up the engine. The car purred to life.

"You make it sound so pragmatic," Felicia said, referring to what he had just said to her.

"Don't worry, Felicia. I promise you that you'll have fun. My mother would have my head if she thought you weren't enjoying yourself immensely. You know, I've never seen her take to anyone as quickly as she has taken to you."

Felicia smiled broadly. "That goes both ways," she told him. "I've never enjoyed my work as much as I have in these last few weeks. Don't get me wrong, the people I've dealt with were all very nice." She didn't want Aaron to think she was attempting to slant this. "But your mother, well, she's in a class all by herself."

Aaron laughed softly. "She is that."

Because he hadn't opened up a car window yet, the aroma coming from the picnic basket swiftly wafted around them, filling up the inside of the vehicle with warm, delicious smells.

"Mmm..." He inhaled appreciatively. "Just what did my mother prepare?"

"A feast fit for the gods, from what I gather. How long has she had her catering company?" Felicia asked. "And what made her get into that field in the first place?"

That was actually simple enough to answer, he thought as he began to drive to the park he hadn't been to in years.

"Mom always had a knack for whipping up really fantastic meals, practically out of nothing. Money started being a problem—my father wasn't exactly timely with his payments," he confided matter-of-factly. "He was juggling two families at the time and doing a really poor job of it. Mom decided it might be time to try to supplement her income. She gave it a shot and it turned out to be successful. That was when it occurred to her that it wouldn't be a bad idea to just do catering for a living, feeling she could depend on herself far more than she could depend on my father to make those regular alimony payments.

"Over time she turned it into a business. Word of mouth naturally spread like wildfire because she's such a great cook. Pretty soon she had as much business as she could handle," he told Felicia proudly. He took in a deep breath, glancing at the picnic basket on the floor between them. "That smells like my mother's Southern fried chicken," he said, "and her deep-dish apple pie—with cinnamon."

"If your days training fighters ever dry up, you can always make a living substituting as a bloodhound," she told him with a wide grin.

"I can just see the business cards," he commented, laughing.

She looked at him and suddenly envisioned him as a lovable, sexy-looking bloodhound. Felicia started to laugh. The image struck her as being so funny, she couldn't stop laughing.

The sound was infectious and Aaron found himself joining in, even if he wasn't 100 percent sure as to why he was laughing so hard.

Taking a deep, cleansing breath to get a hold of himself, Aaron brought his vehicle up to a welcoming, semishady area. They had driven into a public park that also doubled as a picnic area. It was a perfect place for people to spend some private time away from what some could call "a madding crowd."

"We're here," Aaron needlessly announced, pulling his vehicle into a small parking area. There were trees lining three sides of it, creating a very peaceful oasis.

"This is really nice," she said as she got out on her side. Closing the door, she looked at Aaron. "Do you come here often?"

"I did when I was a kid," he answered. "But not for a long time lately. I've forgotten how pretty it was."

Seeing that she was reaching in for the picnic basket, Aaron gently moved her aside and reached into the vehicle to take out the basket. "Let me show you my favorite spot," he told her.

"I'd like that," Felicia said. She went with him happily, feeling as if she was about to get a glimpse into his childhood.

Chapter Eighteen

Felicia had no idea how the afternoon managed to get away from her, but it did. One moment, she and Aaron were spreading out the tablecloth on the grass, and the next, they were finishing up the last of the feast that his mother had packed for them, no small feat in its own right.

It struck her that for the first time in a very long time, she had enjoyed an afternoon that was totally devoid of responsibility. Not just that, but it was an afternoon devoted to enjoying the weather, the spectacular meal and being with such an attractive man. There was a rapport between them that went beyond words. That brought with it its own form of contentment and communication.

Considering how nice the weather was, Felicia noticed that there weren't really very many people in the entire park.

There was one family who had come to the park apparently with the same intentions they had—to just enjoy a day outside. The young, somewhat harried parents had come with a boy and a girl, who looked to be approximately four and five years old.

Felicia couldn't help noticing that the kids behaved as if they were a living, breathing advertisement for an energy drink, one that their parents should have definitely consumed, as well.

She found herself fascinated with the two little people, mesmerized as they went whizzing around nonstop through that section of the park.

"If you ask me, I think that those kids' parents are going to be worn out long before the kids are," she commented to Aaron.

Aaron had been busy observing Felicia watching the children. She looked almost enthralled. He threw back his head and laughed now at her comment.

"I think you're probably right," he agreed. An amused glint entered his eyes. "Think there's any chance that those kids are battery powered?"

"At this point, I'd think just about anything was possible." She didn't think either had paused for more than a moment before flying around again.

Aaron turned to look at her just as the little girl went sailing by their tablecloth, narrowly avoiding leaving her footprint where one of their dishes had been. To his credit and her surprise, Aaron looked unfazed.

"Have you ever thought about having kids?" he asked her.

Felicia nodded. "I did," she admitted just as the little girl's brother raced after her. "Once."

Aaron thought he detected an odd note in her voice. "Once," he repeated. "What happened?" he asked, curious.

That was when she'd just married Greg, Felicia recalled. Back then, wildly in love, she had envisioned the perfect future for him and herself. At that time, she had planned to work for a little while, get accustomed to the idea of being a married lady before she went on to the next logical step, trying to have a baby.

But by then Greg had begun to show his true colors. Scaring her. So much so that she'd been really relieved she hadn't gotten pregnant.

The more time that went by, the more convinced she became that Greg's temper made him a terrible candidate for fatherhood. He had put a stranglehold on her bank account, doling out a tiny allowance for her so she could buy her lunch and pay for her parking. And even that she had to beg for. No, having a child with this man would have been a terrible idea.

Out loud Felicia simply replied, "The timing just wasn't right."

Her reply raised more questions in Aaron's mind than it answered. He found himself wanting to know more about this sweet, competent woman, but he didn't want her feeling that he was attempting to invade her privacy, or worse, interrogate her.

But there was something there. He could sense it. Something that kept her from sharing, from opening up. Aaron really wanted to be able to find out what that was. In short, he wanted her to be honest with him. For that to happen, Felicia had to be able to trust him.

One small step at a time. That was all he could do, Aaron thought philosophically. He had resigned himself to playing the waiting game.

"Maybe you just hadn't found the right man at the time," Aaron said.

The family with the two overactive children was

packing up their leftovers. Looking at them, Felicia decided that the adults appeared to be even more wiped out than the kids. But frankly, it was pretty close. As she looked on, she still couldn't help envying the parents.

Felicia suddenly realized that Aaron had said something to her that needed a response. Turning toward him, she found his eyes skimming over her, making her feel warm and alive in a very intimate way.

She looked up, her eyes meeting his. Taking a breath, she replied, "Maybe."

Her pulse began to race. No amount of deep breaths she took managed to steady it. She had never felt like this. Not even with Greg. She needed to get control over herself.

"Are you all right?" he asked her in a whisper that only managed to further unsettle her.

"I'm not sure," she answered honestly, watching his mouth and growing progressively more enticed by the man.

Rather than press her to elaborate, he made a simple observation. "Looks like everyone's left." He looked at her, letting her call the shots. "Do you want me to take you home?"

Felicia didn't want the day to end, not yet. She raised her eyes to his. "No."

Her voice was low, sultry, sounding almost like a siren's song. He couldn't help being incredibly drawn to her. He leaned in, and his lips found hers. And when he kissed her, he discovered that somehow, without meaning to, they had managed to rise up to a whole new level.

The sweet, gentle kiss they had just shared ignited, and suddenly there was fire erupting between them. Aaron closed his arms around her, enveloping Felicia as he drew her even closer to him than before.

It was almost as if their very souls were touching.

The more he kissed her, the more he wanted of her, and he knew that if he didn't attempt to put a stop to this right now, they would wind up going a great deal further than either one of them had counted on when this "harmless" picnic had begun.

His heart slamming against his rib cage, Aaron forced himself to draw back. It was the hardest thing he had ever done.

"I'd better take you home," he told her in a low voice.

It took her a moment to catch her breath. When she did, she asked, "Your place?"

Aaron realized that he wanted that with a passion that took him completely by surprise. But he wasn't about to impose his needs and desires on her no matter how much he found himself wanting her.

Taking a breath to steady himself, Aaron asked, "Is that what you want?"

Felicia knew she should say no, but because Aaron wasn't attempting to push himself on her, because he was giving her a chance to say no, she wanted Aaron Colton more than she would have ever thought was humanly possible.

"Yes," she whispered without hesitation.

Aaron wasn't able to resist her any longer. He kissed her then, long and hard, with enough passion to ignite his soul. And it was extremely hard for him to pull back at this point, but somehow, he did.

Taking her hand, he looked into Felicia's eyes as longing filled him. "All right, if you're sure," he said, giving her one final opportunity to draw back. But, to Aaron's relief, she didn't. "Then let's put the leftovers and the tablecloth back into the basket and go," he told her, already feeling anticipation flooding his veins.

Part of Felicia wished he would take her right here, where they had had their picnic. It appeared that everyone had already cleared out and gone home. But he didn't.

Aaron refused to press his advantage. He was determined that the first time between them was going to be special. But he did help her put everything into the basket in what seemed like record time.

Taking her back to his car, Aaron drove them to the gym. Felicia had been there before, of course, when he'd brought her to show her some self-defense moves, which she still practiced. But everything looked different to her as night enveloped the area.

Or maybe it looked different because anticipation had wrapped itself around her, whispering in her ear and promising wonderful things.

When he parked his vehicle to the rear of the gym and used the back entrance to go into the building, Felicia could literally feel her pulse speeding up.

Taking her hand, he went up to his loft and unlocked the door. The whole building sounded almost eerily quiet to her.

"I guess the gym's closed now," she commented,

hoping he would confirm that. The last thing she wanted now was for someone to interrupt them.

"It's the middle of the week. Unless other arrangements have been made, I usually make sure the doors are closed by seven," he told her. It was a little past that now. "For all intents and purposes, we're alone," Aaron told her. "That doesn't bother you, does it?" he asked.

She couldn't believe that Aaron was concerned about her state of mind. This was why she was so attracted to him.

"I think if I could make out the sounds of someone punching a boxing bag, that might bother me right now," she admitted. "But you said the gym was all closed up."

"It is." Walking into the loft, Aaron turned on the light and closed the door behind him. "Can I get you anything?" he offered.

Her eyes washed over him. "Just you," she heard herself saying.

The smile that touched Aaron's lips began in his eyes.

"That I can do," he told her as he drew her into his arms again. It felt so right having Felicia there.

The fireworks began the second his lips touched hers. It was as if the flames ignited themselves immediately. At the same time, her breath totally vanished. Although she hadn't realized it, her whole body had been waiting for this very moment.

She could feel herself trembling as his mouth touched her everywhere, setting off fireworks in every part of her body, making her crave him even more.

Felicia kissed him over and over again, each time with increasing passion.

Part of Aaron had thought he knew what to expect. His anticipation of that was what had initially driven him.

But once he found himself confronting this moment, savoring it and instantly reacting to it, he discovered that there were no words to begin to describe it.

His expectations had been much too low.

Aaron learned that no matter how much he kissed her, touched her, relished her, he still couldn't get enough of her. Desire drove him like a hot poker stroked against his skin.

He undressed Felicia with hands that were almost trembling with anticipation. The sensation made him feel like a teenager, not like a man who had had his share of women and truly enjoyed the act of lovemaking. He had never reacted like a teen who just couldn't get enough of a woman—until now.

When Aaron felt Felicia's hands gliding along his skin, felt her fingers as they removed the barriers that still remained between them, the anticipation all but shot through his body.

There was a sofa in one corner of the loft and eventually he made his way over to it with her. Once on the sofa, he marked a clear path along her body with his lips, branding every single part of her that he wanted.

And he wanted all of it.

The sound of Felicia's heavy breathing stirred him and spurred him on, enticing him more than he thought was possible.

When Felicia moaned, shifting and moving beneath

him as his mouth methodically claimed every part of her, the sound just fanned his desire, sending it up to another level.

He couldn't stop himself. As he anointed every part of her, his desire grew increasingly more urgent.

Felicia twisted and purred. The explosions that went off within her body as climax after climax vibrated through her were almost more than she could bear. He teased her and kept her at bay for almost longer than she thought possible.

"Now," she whispered hoarsely. "Please, now."

Aaron understood what she was telling him, and he was more than happy to oblige. Quite honestly, he wasn't all that sure how much longer he could have held off if she hadn't been ready for him.

Mercifully, there was no need to find out.

Sliding his damp body along her heaving torso, he slipped his fingers through hers, joining their hands before he rose above her and completed the act by joining their bodies together, as well.

He felt her hips rising in a silent invitation just before he began to move. At first slowly, then with more urgency, each time going faster than before until it felt as if the ride toward paradise had both of them racing ever more quickly until the explosion finally came, drenching them in a shower of stars and unimaginable passion.

Felicia could hardly catch her breath. She could feel Aaron's heart pounding against her chest, compounding the ecstasy that had found and seized them until it finally and slowly abated, fading into the shadows like a treasured memory.

She vainly struggled to catch her breath as she lay with her cheek resting against his chest. Felicia was more than a little convinced that she would never be able to breathe normally again. But that was all right because she had been able to experience something indescribably wonderful just now. Something she had never even thought possible in her wildest dreams.

She realized now that she had never known true lovemaking before.

Not until now.

Joy radiated through every part of her, even as she told herself not to get used to it.

Aaron stroked her hair, doing his best to breathe normally. But it wasn't easy.

"I'm going to have to take you home, you know." When she raised her head to look at him, he clarified, "My mother's house." He would have loved to have her spend the night, keeping her locked in his arms, but that just wasn't possible.

At least, not yet.

"I know," she murmured, doing her best to ignore the wave of sadness that washed over her.

His arms tightened around her just a little. "You were incredible, you know."

He felt her smile forming against his chest. "You don't have to say that."

"I know. But you were. And I'd really like to have you spend the night," he told her honestly. "But we're not the only ones involved here," he needlessly pointed out. And then he laughed softly to himself. "I don't want my mother thinking that I seduced her physical therapist."

Felicia raised herself up on her elbow and looked at him, a smile in her eyes. "Instead of the other way around?"

"Oh?" He feigned surprise. "Are you saying that you seduced me?"

"Well, didn't I?" she asked, pinning him down with her eyes on his. Her smile couldn't have been wider.

"Tell you what, why don't we call it a draw?" he suggested. "Or, we could do it again to see who seduced who."

"You can do it again?" she asked in surprise. Greg had always claimed that once a night was his absolute limit, saying that it was every man's limit.

Aaron's grin grew wider. "Properly inspired, I can." He ran his finger along the outline of her lips. "I promise not to linger so we will get you back to Mom's before midnight."

"Midnight again," Felicia said with a laugh, slipping her arms around his neck. "Definitely getting a Cinderella complex here," she told him just before she sealed her lips to his.

Chapter Nineteen

"Did you have a good time?"

Felicia swallowed the scream that had instantly risen to her lips as she swung around, her heart hammering wildly in her chest.

Less than two minutes ago, she had walked into Nicole's house. She was doing her best to quietly ease the front door closed after Aaron had dropped her off.

Given the hour—it was after eleven—Felicia assumed that Nicole was in bed and if not asleep, then pretty close to getting there. Felicia had entered the house trying not to make any noise. The last thing she wanted to do was wake Aaron's mother up.

Obviously she had miscalculated.

Pressing her hand against her chest, as if that would somehow slow down the rapid pounding—it didn't—Felicia took in several deep breaths. Sadly, even that didn't help all that much.

For her part, Nicole looked extremely apologetic when she looked at Felicia.

"Felicia, I am *so* sorry. I had no intentions of scaring you like that," she told the young woman. "I just wanted to ask you if you had a good time and if the food I prepared for your picnic was to your liking. You poor dear." Nicole felt terrible for having frightened Felicia this way.

Instinctively, Nicole rubbed her hands up and down Felicia's arms—as if that would somehow restore the color back into the young woman's face. Right now, Felicia looked as white as a sheet.

"That's all right," Felicia assured her, doing her best to force a smile to her lips. She needed to get better control over herself and stop being so jumpy, she silently lectured herself.

She didn't want Aaron's mother feeling guilty, especially not over the fact that she had—to her embarrassment—overreacted. Again. After all, Nicole had no way of knowing that her reaction was due to years of having Greg suddenly pop out of the shadows. He would grab her by her hair and, shouting into her face, accuse her of all sorts of terrible things, none of which she was ever guilty of.

But that somehow never seemed to matter to Greg. It was enough that he believed those things to be true at the time, despite the fact that she had never once done anything to make him suspicious of her.

And now, it was happening again. Or at least it felt that way to her. She couldn't get away from the feeling that someone was following her, even though she tried to convince herself that it was absurd.

Desperate to come up with an excuse for her behavior, Felicia grabbed the first one she could think of.

"I guess I was so fixated on not making any noise and waking you up, I somehow didn't hear you coming up behind me." Felicia smiled at the woman, trying to make a joke. "You'd make a good ninja."

She took a breath, doing her best to sound normal. "Everything was wonderful, just the way every meal you've ever prepared has been. As a matter of fact, it was so good we ate everything except the napkins and the knives and forks." A little calmer now, Felicia couldn't help smiling. "That was really very nice of you, to go through all that trouble to prepare that picnic basket full of all those great things to eat for us."

Nicole was not thoroughly convinced that there was nothing more behind what Felicia was saying. Ordinarily, she might work in a question or two to get to the bottom of things. But it was late and she was not about to press the matter at this point.

She had a feeling that the young woman would tell her what was bothering her in her own time, when she was ready to do so—although she really was quite worried about Felicia. Her instincts were telling her that something was wrong.

Something that went beyond just a case of jittery nerves.

So she patted Felicia's shoulder and said, "Well, I won't keep you, dear. I have to go to bed and get my rest." She lowered her voice as if sharing a secret. "My physical therapist probably has some new, really difficult exercises planned to spring on me in the morning." She winked at Felicia. "Glad you enjoyed the meal."

"Thank you," Felicia called after the woman, who had turned to go to her room.

"My pleasure, dear," Nicole responded. "My pleasure." And she meant that in more ways than one.

Felicia had already won her heart, and her mother's intuition told her that the young woman and her son belonged together. They made a very good pair.

She just hoped that they would see that for themselves.

Nicole was convinced that Felicia needed to feel protected, and Aaron, well, he was definitely the man for the job.

With a sigh, Nicole got comfortable and settled back in her bed. Tomorrow, after she had more time to think about this, she was going to start setting the wheels in motion so that there was more of a reason to keep bringing Aaron and Felicia together, Nicole promised herself.

She fell asleep creating a variety of new, different menus.

"You know, I have never seen anyone making so much progress so rapidly as you have," Felicia told Nicole the next day after she wound up their morning session. "You should be very proud of yourself."

"The only reason I've made so much progress is because I have such a wonderful teacher," Nicole told her happily.

Felicia still had trouble accepting compliments. "Thank you, but be that as it may, I feel guilty taking your money when you clearly really don't need me anymore."

Nicole appeared disturbed by the very suggestion. "Of course I need you. Do you know what will happen if you sign off and leave me?"

"You'll go on doing your exercises," she told Nicole

with the confidence of someone who was fairly certain she knew the person she was speaking to.

But Nicole smiled almost sadly as she shook her head. "That's just the point. No, I won't." Felicia began to protest the woman's reply, but Nicole stopped her right there. "Oh, I'll have all these wonderful intentions of continuing to do them, but you know what they say about the road to hell—that it's paved with good intentions. I will really intend to do the exercises religiously, but something will come up. Something *always* comes up," she emphasized with a sigh. "And what will actually happen is that I'll eventually stop doing them altogether—or even thinking about doing them," she added before Felicia could say anything.

"Don't you understand, dear?" she asked the young woman. "I need you here to keep cracking the whip—figuratively if not literally."

Felicia looked at the older woman thoughtfully. She had a feeling that Nicole was not just making this up. Nicole was being serious. Maybe the woman actually did need to have someone standing over her to make sure that the exercises were being done rather than put off.

She rethought her initial words to Nicole. "Well, maybe if I cut back on my rates," Felicia began. It didn't seem quite fair to keep charging Nicole the full amount if she knew which exercises to do.

And if the woman continued to have her living on the premises, well, that would take care of a large part of her regular expenses. Maybe they could come to some sort of an understanding or arrangement after all.

But Nicole apparently had other thoughts. She

draped the towel around her neck, wiping away the perspiration that had formed along her forehead while doing her exercises.

"Absolutely not. You're not going to cut back on your efforts, so I'm not about to cut back on your normal rates. Now, no more discussion about cutting, all right?" she told Felicia. And with that, she deftly changed the subject. "I hope you don't have any plans for tonight."

That caught her off guard, because she did—sort of. Felicia was really hoping to hear from Aaron today about the possibility of getting together with him again. He had said something to that effect when he dropped her off at the house last night, but so far, she hadn't heard from him.

Don't call us, we'll call you, right? she mocked herself.

C'mon, Fee. You know better than to get carried away like this. You know what happens when you get carried away. One way or another, you're going to be disappointed, Felicia cautioned herself.

Out loud she said brightly to Aaron's mother, "No, I don't have any plans."

Nicole beamed happily at the response. This morning, even before she began her exercise regimen with Felicia, she had already gotten in contact with her son about coming over for dinner. She had discovered, to her relief, that it didn't take any arm-twisting on her part at all. As a matter of fact, Aaron seemed extremely amenable to the idea.

"Good," she declared. "That means you can come to my impromptu dinner party tonight. I'm going to be trying out a few new recipes and I'm going to need some willing guinea pigs."

"Guinea pigs?" Felicia questioned a bit uneasily, not sure exactly what that meant.

"Yes," Nicole confirmed. "You, Aaron and Lila, as well as Vita and that sweetheart of her husband—if we can tear him away from the nursery before midnight. Dinner will be at six." She patted Felicia's arm. "Thank you for indulging me."

Nicole was a firm believer in striking while the iron was hot and she had a definite feeling that things were heating up between Aaron and Felicia. "It means a lot to me to get fully back into the game."

It was clear that the woman considered resuming her catering business as being part of her entire healing process.

Felicia understood where Nicole was coming from. She had dealt with workaholics before and knew that they considered their work as defining who they were. But even so, she still worried about the woman. She didn't want Nicole getting carried away. That could ultimately do more harm than good.

"As long as you promise not to overdo things. You've made so much progress in these last few weeks, I wouldn't want to risk you suddenly backsliding. I realize you think of yourself as a superwoman, but you still have to take it a little easy just awhile longer. Deal?"

"Deal," Nicole said, a smile playing on her lips as she elaborately crossed her heart. "Now, if you don't mind, I think I'll go grab a shower. That last workout left me feeling particularly pungent."

"You smell like a rose," Felicia told the woman innocently.

"And you lie really badly," Nicole told her with a laugh. She paused for a moment in the doorway, thinking. She had an idea. "Say, would you like to help me, Felicia?"

"Sure, what do you want me to do?" she asked, ready to do whatever Aaron's mother asked her to.

"Would you lend me a hand preparing tonight's dinner?" Nicole asked. She looked at Felicia hopefully.

"Lend you a hand preparing the dinner?" Felicia echoed. "Isn't that usually something you'd ask Vita to do? I wouldn't want to step on anyone's toes. Especially not hers."

She really liked Nicole's ex-sister-in-law. The two women had a relationship that she really envied and could only wish she had. She wouldn't accidentally insult Vita for the world.

"Oh no, you wouldn't be," Nicole quickly assured Felicia. "Right now, she's committed to helping Rick finish his end-of-the-month inventory at the nursery. He's bound and determined to get it finished, and on his own, it'll take the man until midnight, so Vita's pitching in whether Rick likes it or not."

Nicole shook her head. "You know, I never saw a man so dedicated to living up to *all* his responsibilities. When my boys were growing up, Rick was so good with them. My ex never had any time for any of them, but any time the boys or I needed anything at all, Vita's husband never even thought about saying no. Instead, he was always right there. The same went for Vita's own two kids.

"Sometimes," she continued, "a second husband acts as if he wants to have nothing to do with his wife's kids, but not Rick. He adopted Lila and Myles and, for all intents and purposes, acted as if he had adopted mine, as well. I really can't say enough about the man. I only wish I had been able to find someone like him myself.

"Anyway, if you're willing to help me with the preparations, we can get started right after we both take our showers. Is it a deal?" she asked.

Felicia smiled. "How can I possibly say no?" she teased.

Nicole thought about her ex-husband—and especially his mother. Carin didn't have a maternal bone in her body—or any kindness at all, for that matter. She doubted that either one of them would have any trouble saying no.

"You would be surprised what an easy word that is to say," she murmured. Snapping out of it, she promised, "Meet you in the kitchen in fifteen minutes."

"It's going to take us all day to prepare?" Felicia asked, surprised.

"Oh, no. But I thought you might want to grab something to eat for lunch before we get started."

Felicia smiled. "If you're making it, then I'm happily eating it." The woman had yet to prepare anything that was less than spectacular. "I'll be quick," she promised.

TRUE TO HER WORD, Nicole was ready in record time. Rather than blow-drying her hair, Aaron's mother decided to just air-dry it, using a towel to get rid of the major dampness.

She came downstairs dressed in cutoff shorts, a

fresh, smaller bandage on the leg that had had the hip replacement surgery.

Felicia came down several minutes later, surprised that Aaron's mother had beaten her downstairs.

"Boy, you certainly are fast," Felicia commented.

"When you're a mother juggling raising three boys and holding down a couple of jobs in order to provide for them, you learn how to be extremely fast getting ready," Nicole told her.

That didn't sound quite fair to her. "Maybe it's none of my business, but wasn't your ex-husband supposed to at least pay a good part of the alimony and child support?" she asked.

A long-suffering look came over Nicole's face. "Ah, the difference between what he was supposed to do and what he actually did do was always worlds apart. Erik didn't let so-called responsibilities get in his way. But at least I got the house so the boys and I always had a place to stay."

These were the Coltons they were talking about. Felicia would have thought that there was a different set of circumstances governing their actions. "Didn't the boys' grandmother feel any sort of responsibility to help provide for her grandsons?" Felicia asked.

Nicole affectionately slid her hand along Felicia's cheek and laughed softly. "You are adorable, Fee. Truthfully, I doubt if Carin felt an iota of responsibility toward anyone but herself. Her own needs and desires always came first and foremost." Wanting to get away from the subject, Nicole declared, "All right, let's

get you fed so you're not tempted to nibble on any of
the new dishes before I serve them."

And with that, Nicole turned her attention toward
making lunch.

Chapter Twenty

With a contented sigh, Aaron retired his knife and fork, placing them in the form of an X in the middle of his plate.

"Well, I have to say that you've truly outdone yourself, Mom. This had to be in the top five—no, make that the top *three* meals that you've ever made," he said with a grin. "And I remember all of them very fondly."

He, Felicia, his uncle and aunt along with Lila were all sitting around the dining room table. As for his mother, she more or less alighted in her chair for short periods of time rather than sat. For the most part she was a picture of perpetual motion.

Nicole laughed. "You know, if you were ten years younger, I would have said that you were buttering me up for a reason." Smiling at him, she sat back for a moment and took a sip of the single glass of white wine she occasionally allowed herself.

"I never tried to butter you up, Mom," Aaron protested, feigning surprise. "I knew you were too smart for me."

"Yeah, yeah," Nicole murmured, rolling her eyes as she waved her hand at her son. "You know, your acting hasn't improved, either," she told her son with affection. "I just wish your brothers could be here, but Nash has that out-of-town meeting for his company and Damon, who knows where he is these days?" she said, addressing her words to Rick and Vita.

Aaron glanced over toward his mother. That was her way of pretending that she really wasn't worried, he thought. Apparently, he wasn't the only one in the family who needed to brush up on his acting lessons.

"Don't worry. He'll turn up, Mom. He always does," Aaron assured her. In his opinion, there was no other way to view the situation. Anything else was just too unnerving.

It was Vita who spoke up, sympathizing with her ex-sister-in-law. "It doesn't matter," she told her nephew as well as the other young people seated at the table. "A mother always worries."

"Worrying never helps or changes anything," Aaron told the two women.

Rick shook his head. "Don't waste your breath. There's no talking your mother or my wife out of that frame of mind. How about you, Felicia?" he asked good-naturedly, turning his attention toward the young woman that his wife had raved was doing wonders for her former sister-in-law. "Are you a worrier?"

"I don't have any children," Felicia answered, deftly sidestepping the question.

There was no point in admitting that yes, she was worried. Constantly. Worried that, somehow, Greg had managed to find out where she had gone and was in the process of looking for her.

"You know, Aaron was right on the money," she told

Nicole. "This has to be the very best meal you've ever made. But then, I haven't been sampling your creations for as long as everyone else has. Is this for a special occasion?" she asked her patient, doing her best to redirect the conversation.

"Are you trying to say that you don't consider having most of my family over and making dinner for them a special occasion?" Nicole questioned, wide-eyed.

Felicia looked a little flustered. "Nicole, I didn't mean to imply—"

Vita leaned over and patted Felicia's hand. "She's just teasing you, honey." She turned to look at her former sister-in-law. "Shame on you for messing with the girl, Nicole," Vita chided. "There's no need to draw this out. You know that we all think you're a fabulous cook, bar none." She smiled as she looked at her husband. "Just one look at Rick's expanding waistline is all the evidence you need."

"What expanding waistline?" Rick asked, feigning indignation as he looked down at his belt.

Vita laughed and patted her husband's stomach. "That one, dear," she told him innocently. "I don't think you can miss it."

Rick sighed. "I guess I did get a little carried away," he said, patting his waistline, too, but willingly, to suggest that this was temporary. "But then I don't get to attend these gatherings as much as the rest of you do," he pointed out. "I just got carried away."

Nicole clapped her hands together, calling an end to this line of conversation. There was something more important to discuss. "All right now, who's up for dessert?"

There wasn't a single refusal in the lot.

"How's that fancy new artist showing coming along?" Rick asked his adopted daughter as he and the others consumed Nicole's latest, delicious rendition of chocolate meringue pie. "What was his name again?" His forehead wrinkled as he tried to remember.

"Homer Tinsley," Lila said, wrinkling her nose as she recalled her last experience. "And it's still stuck in first gear, but the showing isn't for another few weeks, so I'm hopeful that the man stops playing hide-and-seek and comes through in the long run."

"Well, my offer still stands to teach that man some manners," Rick told her, his eyes meeting Lila's.

"First you need to find him," Vita told her husband, recalling what her daughter had said about the artist being a ghost.

Lila laughed dryly at the comment. "I wish you better luck than I had."

"Well, just say the word," Rick said, sounding totally sincere, "and I'll go looking for that conceited so-and-so."

Lila smiled at the man she had loved and admired from the first moment he had entered her and Myles's lives. To her, he was the perfect stepfather. "Thanks, but I think I'll give it a little while longer."

"I understand. But just remember, the offer's on the table," Rick said.

The meal and banter continued in this vein for close to another hour. When it was finally over and no one could eat another bite, cleanup was a communal affair with everyone pitching in. It went much faster that way.

And when it was over and everything was put away, Rick and Vita begged off. There was still a little more inventory at the nursery to take care of. For her part, Lila said she had a few people at the gallery she needed to get in touch with.

"And you?" Nicole asked her son. "What's your excuse for beating a fast retreat out of here?"

"Three hours is hardly *fast*, Mom," Aaron pointed out. "But to answer your question, I thought I'd take Felicia over to the gym so we can work off some of those delicious extra calories we just both consumed."

A smile highlighted Nicole's eyes. Whether she was smiling in response to the compliment Aaron had just given her or because she had put her own interpretation as to why he and Felicia were really leaving was anyone's guess. He decided that it was in everyone's best interest not to ask about that for now.

"You do that, dear," Nicole said to her oldest son. "You do that."

With that she shooed the duo out the door. "As for me, I'm going to enjoy some well-deserved peace and quiet," she told them as she closed the door behind Aaron and Felicia.

Felicia turned to look at Aaron as they went down the front steps. He had parked his car only a short distance away.

"The gym?" she questioned, not completely buying his excuse. "Really?"

Aaron grinned as he pressed his key fob. All four doors opened when he pressed the button a second time. "Well, the gym *is* there," he said innocently. "And we're going to have to pass it in order to go up to the loft."

"Ah, the loft," she responded, trying hard not to

grin. She had really been hoping for a repeat performance of last night. "Are you kidnapping me, Aaron?"

"It's only kidnapping if you don't want to go," he pointed out. Glancing in her direction, he asked, "Do you?"

If her smile was any wider, she was fairly certain that her face would crack. "What do you think?"

One look into her eyes and he had his answer. "I think that I'm going to be looking forward to my real dessert," Aaron told her. Putting his key into the ignition, he turned it and his vehicle suddenly purred to life.

Pulling out, he guided his car to the main road. Once he was on his way to the loft, he glanced in her direction for a moment. He debated saying something, then decided why not? This had been bothering him since dinner.

"I'm sorry you didn't get much of a chance to get a word in edgewise tonight," Aaron apologized as he drove.

"Are you kidding?" she asked, totally surprising him. "I loved it."

He hadn't been expecting that. "You loved not being able to talk?" Aaron questioned. He didn't know if she was being serious or not.

"No, not that," she said dismissively. "I loved listening to the rest of you talk," Felicia explained. "You all sounded like a really warm, loving family that cared about one another. That's not as common as you might think."

It didn't take a genius to interpret her comment. "I

take it you didn't experience that very much growing up?" Aaron asked.

"No, I did not," Felicia answered. There was a note of finality in her voice as she deliberately brought the subject to a close. Aaron had pulled into the gym parking lot. "Looks like we're here," she needlessly announced. The next moment, she was getting out of his car.

The gym that loomed before them was almost completely dark except for a couple of lights on the first floor, a sure sign that it was closed down for the night.

"Looks like everyone's gone," Felicia observed.

"If the gym's closed, how are we going to work off those calories we just consumed?" she asked, pretending she was asking a serious question.

Aaron unlocked the door that led up to the second floor and his loft, then ushered her inside.

"Well, if you're interested, I've got another way to work off those extra calories," he told her, doing his best to suppress the grin that was attempting to curve his lips.

Felicia walked up the stairs just ahead of him. For his part, Aaron was enjoying the view as he followed her up.

"Oh?" Felicia asked innocently, glancing over her shoulder to look at him. "And what way is that?"

Aaron laughed, thinking, not for the first time, that she was adorable.

"I think it's better if I just show you," Aaron told her.

Felicia turned at the top of the stairs just before his door. She smiled into his eyes. "Sounds promising," she murmured in a low voice that undulated right under his skin.

His smile widened. "I certainly hope so."

He unlocked the door quickly and the very next moment, they were inside his loft. Aaron reached over inside and turned on the light, then closed the door behind him.

After that, things happened rather quickly. They were in each other's arms, eagerly kissing and reigniting the flame that hadn't completely gone out last night.

Any concerns she had harbored that now that they had consummated their attraction Aaron was willing to walk away from her were quickly smothered. If anything, he was more eager to take her than he had been the first time around.

The moment their lips touched, it was as if they couldn't get enough of one another. Nor did they want to. The more they kissed, the more they caressed, the higher their desire to continue making love grew.

It occurred to Aaron that he could go on like this forever.

Until the other day, he had gone through life believing that he was never destined to meet the one woman that he wanted to spend the rest of his life with. But now, as they made love again with a verve that just went on and on, Aaron couldn't bring himself to imagine a day without her.

As Aaron covered her face and her body with kisses over and over again, quickly divesting her of her clothing, which landed in a heap on the floor next to his own, he realized that he had been waiting for this from the moment he had opened his eyes this morning.

He had certainly fantasized about this throughout the entire meal. Mentally, he had been counting off the minutes, even as he interacted with his family. He might have been talking to them, but deep down, all he had wanted was to be alone with her. So that he could make love with her again.

And again.

It was as if his very soul had been renewed.

Aaron would have been more than happy to have her in his bed for the entire night so that he could make love with her each and every time he had the occasion to open his eyes again.

But he knew that doing so would be tantamount to making their situation open knowledge as far as his mother was concerned.

He had a strong feeling that his mother probably already saw through this charade and was undoubtedly on to them. He could tell by the way she had smiled at them during dinner that she felt that they had discovered one another in that special way. There was way too much electricity vibrating between Felicia and him to believe that anything else was happening.

Still, he felt that Felicia wanted to continue to keep this a secret for a little longer, and for his part, he really wanted to make her happy. So, if this was what it took to do it, it was little enough for him to go along with.

Her happiness really mattered to him.

He kissed the top of her head, thinking that her hair smelled really, really good.

"We're going to have to be getting back," he told Felicia, however reluctantly the words came to his lips right now.

"I know," she replied with a sigh, moving just a little away from him so she could look up into his face. And then she said, "Just a minute longer."

This was like a dream come true, and part of her was afraid that if she blinked, she would realize that it *was* a dream. And all dreams ended, she reasoned. It was inevitable, no matter how much she fought against that notion.

"You know, we don't *have* to go home tonight," he told her. "I could call and tell my mother that we got a flat tire on the way back. We can say that we're getting it repaired."

"Right. Like she is going to believe that," Felicia responded. "At the very least, she'll send Rick to come get us—for that matter, *she* would come get us. You know that."

Nicole was definitely a hands-on woman who didn't wait for someone else to come to the rescue. *She* was the cavalry.

He laughed as he drew Felicia closer to him, reveling in the warmth of her body and the very real urges that created within him.

"Yes, I know that," he agreed. "You're right. We should start getting ready to go."

But as he spoke, his lips brushed against hers. And, as expected, one kiss led to another, creating yet another fire within her as well as within him.

"You know," he told her. "There's no *real* hurry. Mom would probably welcome a late start on her exercise regimen…"

She put her hand against his lips, stopping him from

kissing her. She was weakening and if he did that again, she wasn't going to want to leave.

"Aaron, I can't do that," Felicia told him, struggling against the urges and desires firing all through her.

"Yes, I know," he confessed. "But you can't kill a guy for trying. You are so damn desirable..." His voice trailed off.

Aaron couldn't have said anything more flattering and alluring to her if he had deliberately planned it that way.

She kissed him back.

And predictably, that led to another kiss. And then another.

Within moments, the dance between them began again.

Chapter Twenty-One

Despite the best intentions, Felicia didn't get back to Nicole's house until a little after midnight. The only reason she had made it back at all was because she had exercised extreme control rather than giving in to her own overwhelming longing. Aaron had made it oh-so-easy for her to stay where she was, nestled in the shelter of his arms, the light scent of his cologne teasing her senses. She knew that all she had to do was just hint at wanting to remain and he would be more than willing to oblige her.

But she knew that she couldn't. It wouldn't be right for so many reasons, not the least of which was that she just couldn't allow herself to get used to this. In her heart she knew that being with Aaron this way, wonderful though it was, had an incredibly short life expectancy. It was destined to end.

Oh, maybe not tomorrow or the next day, but soon, and the more often she gave in to this desire, the harder it was going to be on her when the time came that she would have to do without him.

Tiptoeing into the living room and making her way to the stairs, Felicia stopped for a moment just to absorb everything, thinking how normal it felt to be part of this family, if only for a little while.

And wishing with all her heart that it could go on forever.

But she didn't believe in forever, she reminded herself. She had once, but not anymore. Greg had taught her that. Felicia now believed that she had to pay a price for every bit of happiness that came her way, knowing full well that when it did, it wouldn't last.

But for however long this did last, she thought as she took a breath, Felicia was determined to enjoy it, because even a little bit was better than the alternative—which was nothing at all.

With a sad smile playing on her lips, she made her way up to her room.

WHEN SHE FINALLY went to bed, Felicia had had absolutely no intentions of sleeping in; it just somehow seemed to happen. If she were to make a guess, it was because she had enjoyed herself so much last night. For the first time in a very long time, she had actually felt content and yes, even a little relaxed.

So when she woke up and saw that it was after seven, Felicia sat bolt upright in her bed. This was late for her. Her feet hit the floor before she was even aware of swinging them over the side of the bed.

She needed to get ready, she told herself sternly. Nicole's physical therapy class was set for eight. She knew the woman would insist that she have breakfast before they got started so that would eat up more time, and time was a very precious commodity not to be wasted.

Upbraiding herself, Felicia hurried into the bathroom, where she took what was probably a five-minute shower. Drying off quickly, she hurried into her clothes and got dressed.

She didn't bother with her hair, leaving it damp and curling around her face like someone who had been caught in a sudden rainfall. But she could worry about drying it properly and styling it after she and Nicole had finished with the physical therapy program for the morning.

Felicia was particularly anxious to get to it since they had skipped the second part of that program yesterday because of the dinner that Nicole had prepared for everyone.

Making her way downstairs quickly, Felicia called out a greeting before she even saw Nicole.

"Hi, Nicole. Are you down here?" she asked. Since it was morning, she just assumed that the woman would be moving around the kitchen and waiting for her to join her.

And then she stopped dead before she reached the last step.

Her mouth dropped open.

It looked as if a hurricane had passed through the lower rooms. Everything appeared as if it had been ransacked.

Panicking, Felicia ran down the rest of the way. "Nicole!" she called, her voice rising as she tried not to panic. "Are you here?"

"Yes, I'm here," the woman answered. Her voice was oddly bewildered as she stepped out of the kitchen and into the small foyer. Her face was the picture of disbelief.

Felicia was quick to join the woman and put her arm around Nicole's shoulders. She still couldn't believe what she was looking at. "Nicole, what happened here?" she asked.

"I don't know," the older woman answered honestly, looking around again as if she expected everything to go back to normal and that this was just a bad, momentary hallucination.

But it wasn't. It was real.

"When I got up to make coffee this morning, I found it like this." Nicole looked quizzically at the young woman beside her. "When you came in last night, Felicia, did you—"

"I came in a little after midnight," she told Nicole, trying to be precise. "And it certainly wasn't like this. Everything was neat and tidy, the way it always is," Felicia reported. Whoever was responsible for this had to have made some sort of noise. This hadn't happened in a vacuum. "Did you hear anything? Any kind of noise that sounded as if something was falling or being thrown?" she asked the woman.

But Nicole shook her head. "No." And then she reconsidered her response. "You know, I did think I heard something around one or so, but I thought it was part of my dream, so I went back to sleep." Her hands were on her hips as she looked around again, completely stunned at the chaos she saw. "I guess it wasn't a dream," she concluded in a resigned tone.

She didn't like this, Felicia thought as she surveyed the damage. She didn't like this one little bit. Someone had deliberately broken in and ransacked Nicole's place. But why? What were they looking for?

A cold chill ran down her spine.

"Can you tell if anything was taken?" she asked the woman.

Nicole moved her head from side to side. "Not that I can see." None of this made any sense to her. "Who would do something like this?" she asked, stunned and overwhelmed.

Felicia could feel her stomach tightening. As much as she didn't want to believe it, she thought she had an answer to that.

Greg.

Somehow, Greg had found her and was now attempting to upend her life. There was no logical reason for what had happened here, but Greg never needed a logical reason. He just created havoc for its own sake, to throw her life into complete turmoil.

The next moment, she realized that the very fact that she was here could very well put Nicole's life in danger. She could feel nerves eating away at her stomach.

Felicia was doing her best not to let her imagination run away with her. But she found it really hard not to panic. Logically, she knew that it didn't *have* to be Greg. Houses were broken into all the time, and there could still be another explanation for what had happened here. But in her heart, she knew there was no other explanation.

This was all Greg's work.

He couldn't be allowed to do this, Felicia thought angrily. With that, she began to head toward the rear of the house.

Moving toward her, Nicole blocked her. "Where are you going?" she asked.

"I'm going to see if whoever is responsible for this is still in the house," Felicia answered, her feisty spirit returning.

"No, you will not," Nicole told her sharply. "You will stay right here and wait until Aaron arrives."

"Aaron's coming?" she asked. Had Nicole called him? When had that happened?

"Just as soon as he gets this call," Nicole told her, reaching into her pocket for the cell phone she religiously carried around with her. It hadn't been out of her sight since that morning when she had broken her hip.

Felicia was leery about pulling Aaron into this. Leery about what he would have to say about the situation. "Maybe you should call Rick," she suggested to his mother. When Nicole looked at her quizzically for an explanation, Felicia said, "You know Aaron. He'll immediately think the worst and maybe there might be some sort a logical explanation for this. I just thought you might want to consider everything before you called him."

The look on Nicole's face told Felicia that she thought that was crazy. "What sort of logical explanation could there be for a break-in?" Nicole asked.

Felicia sighed. "You're right. There isn't one." She nodded her head. "Call Aaron. If he hears your voice, at least he'll know that you're all right."

Nicole began pressing the keys on her phone. When Aaron picked up, she put it on speakerphone so Felicia could hear what her son said, as well.

"Honey, could you come over?" Nicole asked.

Aaron's mother was trying to sound as calm as she

could but she sensed that she wasn't really fooling her son. As she spoke, she watched Felicia methodically going through the various piles that had been tossed around the room. There didn't seem to be any rhyme or reason to the mess. It was as if someone was attempting to create chaos and stir up fear for its own sake through their actions.

"I was going to swing by later today," Aaron told her. And then his tone changed as suspicion took over. "What's wrong, Mom?"

"There's nothing wrong, exactly," she told him, hedging. She was trying to find the best way to word this for her son and failing badly.

"Mom—" There was a warning note in his voice. It indicated that Aaron was not in the mood for games; he just needed straightforward answers.

As she listened to the exchange, Felicia decided that it was time for her to speak up. Rather than raise her voice, she took the phone from Nicole to level with Aaron before he started interrogating his mother.

"Aaron, it's Felicia. There's been a break-in," she told him matter-of-factly, trying to divorce herself from what had taken place.

"A break-in?" Aaron echoed. "What do you mean there's been a break-in?" He couldn't believe he was actually saying the words.

Felicia pressed her lips together and closed her eyes, before she pushed on. "I mean someone broke into your mother's house sometime after midnight."

She could almost feel his anger telegraphing itself through the air. "Did you see him—or her?" he finally questioned.

"No, I did not. But it was sometime after you dropped me off early this morning and before seven a.m.," she told him.

If he was furious, he was containing the emotion well. "What was taken?" he asked.

"That's just it. We don't know if anything *was* taken," she answered. "Everything in the area looks like it was haphazardly tossed, like whoever did this was looking for something. But so far, we can't determine what that was."

"And you're sure that Mom wasn't hurt?" he questioned, his tone indicating that he wouldn't appreciate any attempt at covering up the truth.

"No, thank heavens. She's just a bit shaken up," Felicia said with sincerity. "But she's totally unharmed. Trust me."

She heard him blow out a sigh of relief. "And you?" he asked. "Are you okay?"

She dismissed any concern or attention shifted in her direction. "Don't worry about me," she told him. "I'm fine. But I think your mother would really appreciate it if you got here."

"I'm on my way," Aaron said just before the connection terminated.

Felicia handed the cell phone back to Nicole. In case the woman had missed that, she told her, "Aaron said he'd be right over."

Nicole nodded. Now that Aaron was en route, she was having second thoughts about having him come. The woman frowned.

"Maybe I shouldn't have called him," she said. "I know Aaron. He's just going to start worrying about me again. I just got him to calm down that I wasn't going to have another accident and hurt my hip again. This is going to set us back to square one."

Felicia had continued going through the mess, trying to figure out just what the person—if it wasn't Greg—had been looking for.

However, if it *was* Greg, then he didn't need an excuse and he wasn't necessarily looking for something. He was just trying to create havoc for its own sake and frighten away anyone who might have befriended her. Just like he had done before, he was out to isolate her.

"You had to tell him," she told Nicole, trying to alleviate any guilt the woman might have been feeling. "You know he would *never* forgive you if you didn't call him and he wound up finding out about it accidentally," Felicia told her.

Nicole nodded her head. "You're right."

NICOLE HAD JUST finished drinking her cup of coffee when Aaron came all but barreling in. "Mom!" he called out, worry stamped into his handsome features. "Mom!"

"We're in the kitchen, dear," Nicole called out.

Her voice sounded infinitely calmer to Felicia than it had less than a few minutes ago. She was right, Felicia thought. Cooking really did relax Aaron's mother.

Aaron entered the kitchen like a man struggling to keep his heart from leaping into his throat and choking him.

"Mom!" he cried, embracing his mother. He was the personification of immense concern. Holding her at arm's length for a moment, he searched every inch of his mother's face. "You're absolutely certain that you're all right?"

"Yes, dear, I'm absolutely certain. For all I know, someone broke in looking for food," she said, trying to calm Aaron down. "You know how my reputation is getting around." She was doing her best to reassure her son and make him laugh.

"Then he's a mental midget because he certainly doesn't know what food looks like," Aaron said, looking around at the mess. And then he looked at Felicia. "How about you?" he asked. "Are you sure you're all right?"

He was concerned about her, as well, but somehow, he felt confident that Felicia was far more able to take care of herself than his mother was, even though he had seen how very self-sufficient his mother could be. Still, this was his *mother*, and he couldn't help being inordinately concerned about her reaction to all this.

Felicia waved away his question. Her guilt was increasing by leaps and bounds. The more she thought about it, the more convinced she became that Greg was responsible for all this somehow.

"I'm fine," she replied stoically.

"And nothing was taken?" Aaron asked, turning toward his mother.

"Not as far as I can see," she answered. "It almost looks like whoever did this was playing 'one-two-three, pick up,' that old children's game I used to play with you, before your brothers came to live with us." Nicole allowed herself a fond memory for a moment.

"Well, this isn't a children's game," Aaron told his mother, frowning intently as he looked around. "This is really serious. Someone's trying to frighten you, or send a message, or—"

Aaron abruptly stopped talking. When he had turned toward the two women, he had caught a glimpse of the expression that crossed Felicia's face.

Something he had just said had sparked something in kind in her head. He could see it in her face.

"Felicia," Aaron said sharply, calling for her attention.

Her stomach tightened. *Oh, Lord, here it comes*, she thought, bracing herself. She had every intention of telling Aaron about Greg and the role he had played in her life, even if they never got together. But on her own time, not now.

She pressed her lips together. "Yes?" The word came out almost breathlessly.

Aaron drew closer to her, looking into her eyes as he searched them for some sort of an answer. "What is it you know, Felicia?" he asked. "Tell me."

"Aaron, what are you accusing her of?" Nicole asked, coming to Felicia's defense just as she had the first time he had met her.

He continued looking pointedly at Felicia. "I think Felicia knows. I'm accusing her of holding something back. Something I think she should have told us about."

Chapter Twenty-Two

The look on Nicole's face told Aaron she knew where he was coming from, but she still wanted him to back off a little. It was obvious that she felt for the young woman, just as she had the first time Aaron questioned Felicia's ability to administer her physical therapy sessions. Granted this was more serious, but she still felt just as protective as she had then.

"I think Felicia will tell us when she's ready to share, Aaron."

Aaron was frowning as he shook his head. Ordinarily, he would agree with his mother and just back off. But what had happened could have very well endangered his mother's safety—as a matter of fact, it still could—and he could damn well be adamant about it.

"Not good enough," he told his mother. "Felicia?" he asked expectantly. "Do you know who broke into my mother's house?"

"How could she know that?" Nicole asked defensively. She thought of Felicia as a daughter now and she was determined to protect her. Why was her son accusing her like this?

Felicia refused to have the two people she had come

to care about a great deal get into an argument because of her.

"Because I think I do," she answered in a small voice that seemed almost devoid of emotion.

The next moment, she looked at Nicole, distraught over the very idea that she might have actually put the woman she had come to think of as a second mother in harm's way.

Stunned, Nicole looked at her. "How could you know that?"

He knew it! "Who was it, Felicia?" Aaron demanded sharply.

"I think the person who did all this might have been my ex," Felicia told Aaron and his mother. Every word cost her.

"Your ex? Your ex what?" Nicole asked, stunned. And then it seemed to hit her. "Felicia, you were married? Honey, why didn't you say anything?" she asked. Rather than feel betrayed, Nicole was clearly concerned about Felicia. It was evident from her tone that the woman was convinced Felicia was afraid of someone and needed protecting.

"It's not something I'm proud of." Felicia pressed her lips together.

She caught a glimpse of the way Aaron was looking at her in her peripheral vision, like he didn't even know who she was. Wounded, she tried to avoid making eye contact with him.

"How long were you married?" Nicole asked, her tone compassionate.

"Four years," Felicia answered. "The first two years were everything I had always imagined a good marriage would be like." Sadness entered her eyes. "And then he began to change. He became angrier and more and more abusive. The slightest thing would set him off."

"Did he beat you?" Aaron asked. He sounded angry and unapproachable.

Felicia couldn't read the expression on his face. Was Aaron taking umbrage in her defense, or was he disgusted by the fact that she had been a victim? She was unable to tell, but she was afraid it was the latter.

Now that she had started this, Felicia knew she had to tell them the truth, but the words refused to come out. So she said, "No, but even after the divorce, Greg kept behaving as if he had every right to just come into my life any time he felt like it."

"Did he beat you?" Aaron asked again, his expression darker than before.

Again, she couldn't tell if he was disgusted or furious at the thought and at Greg.

And her.

"No," Felicia answered, refusing to make eye contact. "Oh, he shoved me a few times, and even left a couple of scars, but he never went so far as to double up his fists and beat on me. But the last time he shoved me, it was hard enough to come close to breaking something. That was when I decided it was time to get away because the next time, it could get even worse." She took a breath. That much was true, she thought. "I packed up just what I needed and moved to Chicago in the middle of the night. I made sure I didn't leave a trail he could follow." She saw the skeptical look on Aaron's face. "And no, I didn't leave any kind of a parting note for him. I just left."

"I wouldn't have left one, either," Nicole told her. "Although he really deserves to be made to pay for the way he treated you."

Felicia looked at the woman. "My word against his," she said simply. Since she had said this much, she felt she had to go the extra mile. "I think I should tell you that my name isn't Felicia Wagner. It's Fiona. Fiona Harper."

It was hard to tell who looked more surprised by this last revelation, Aaron or his mother.

"Was any of it real?" Aaron demanded coldly.

His tone really hurt, Felicia thought. "My credentials are real. I really do have a degree in physical therapy," she told him. "And the way I feel about...your mother is real." She felt completely at a loss, stripped of anything she could use to defend herself.

Nicole looked at her, grappling with this newest revelation. "This is a lot to take in," she told Felicia honestly.

Felicia put her own interpretation to the woman's words. "I understand if you want me to leave..."

"Leave?" Nicole cried, stunned. "Why would I want you to do that?" she questioned. "I'm just saying that there's a lot to wrap my head around, but it's not impossible. I can certainly do it." She looked at Felicia compassionately, aching for what she must have gone through and not having anyone to share it with. "If I could take in my ex-husband's sons without blinking an eye when he abandoned them to take up with yet another woman, this is a piece of cake."

Patting Felicia's hand, she told her, "Don't worry, we'll get through this." Ever resourceful, Nicole turned toward her son. "Aaron, why don't you call Damon? I'm sure he can refer us to one of his connections so you can look into this further."

Aaron was surprised by the request but managed to collect himself almost immediately. "And by look into you mean…?"

She gave her son a knowing look as she answered, "Who actually broke into my house. Maybe we're jumping to conclusions," she said hopefully, turning toward Felicia. "Would your ex-husband actually have any way of knowing where you are?"

She wouldn't put anything past Greg, Felicia thought. "Not that I know of," she admitted out loud, but saying as much didn't do anything to make her feel any better about the situation.

"So maybe it wasn't him," Nicole said. "Let's not jump to any conclusions yet." The woman slipped her arm around Felicia's shoulders, giving her a quick hug. "And smile, dear. Other than this mess we need to clean up, there hasn't been any real damage done."

Yet, Felicia thought, although she kept that word to herself.

Aaron had learned not to say anything when he was really angry, so he said nothing in response. Instead, turning away, he placed the call to his brother. Damon had given him a special number to use in case of emergencies when he was undercover. It was the same number he had used when their mother had taken that spill and broken her hip. As he had before, Aaron left a coded message.

"I've got a special order I'd like to discuss with you at your earliest convenience."

While Aaron was placing the call to his younger brother, Nicole took Felicia aside. It didn't take much insight for her to see that the young woman was really upset by Aaron's cold reaction.

"Don't worry, dear," she told Felicia warmly. "Aaron will get over it. He doesn't mean to sound as if he's angry with you. He's not. He's just angry at the situation. I know my boy," Nicole whispered to her confidently.

"But in Aaron's mind, I'm the one who caused the situation—and he's right, I did."

"Cut yourself some slack, Felicia," Nicole advised the young woman. "Say, what do I call you now? Felicia? Fiona? Which would you prefer?"

Bless Nicole, she was worried about her feelings. Felicia was touched beyond words. "You can keep calling me Felicia, since we're both used to that. But 'Fee' works, if you prefer," Felicia told her. "It goes with both names, and besides, I've been 'Felicia' for so long that 'Fiona' sounds like someone from another lifetime."

"In a way, it is," Nicole told her. "A lifetime ago when you didn't have enough courage to stand up to that bully of an ex-husband. But now you do—you left him and began a whole new life for yourself." There was pride in Nicole's words. "If you ask me, that's pretty courageous of you." She cupped Felicia's chin in her hand. "I know that 'Fee' isn't going to be taken advantage of," she told Felicia with feeling.

Finished sending texts and making calls, Aaron

closed his cell phone, put it away and came over to join Felicia and his mother.

"I'm going to sack out on the sofa down here tonight," he told his mother. He left no room for argument. "Until all this is resolved, I'm not taking a chance on whoever redecorated your ground floor coming back for another shot at it—no matter who he is."

Nicole hated seeing Aaron so worried. "I really appreciate that, dear, but I doubt whoever it was will be back."

He was not about to be argued out of it. This didn't involve him; it involved his mother—and Felicia. "Well, I'm not that sure," he told her, pointedly glancing in Felicia's direction.

"Did Damon give you the name of someone to call?" Nicole asked, changing the subject to some extent. He needed to calm down.

"I didn't get a hold of him, but I left him a message. Don't worry, Mom. Damon will get back to me when he gets it. Sometimes it just takes a while, that's all. But I'll hear from Damon before the end of the day," Aaron assured her.

She gave her son a look. "That all sounds very cloak-and-dagger to me," Nicole commented, tongue in cheek.

Aaron looked at his mother. It was one of those cases where he knew that she knew about Damon's double life, and she knew that he knew about it, but neither one of them would say the actual words out loud, making it an open secret.

Nicole clapped her hands together, as if signaling an end to the conversation. "All right, why don't I make breakfast for the three of us? After that, Felicia and I are going to get started on that cruel PT regimen she insists on putting me through." She smiled brightly at him. "You're welcome to join us."

He almost laughed then. "No, thanks," he told his mother, and then, given everything that had happened and was still unresolved, he asked her, "You can actually focus on doing those exercises?"

Nicole gave him a look that seemed to say, *How could he ask her something like that?* "Aaron, I focused on getting things done and earning a living while embroiled in heated divorce proceedings with your father, plus having two new members added to my family I needed to provide for—I can do absolutely anything," she informed him with no little pride.

Aaron laughed and kissed her cheek. "Yes, you can," he agreed. "Okay, I'll stay for breakfast, but I'll take a pass on the PT. I'll just hang around until Uncle Rick comes over."

"Uncle Rick?" his mother echoed, surprised. "Don't tell me you bothered him about this." If there was a problem—which she still wasn't convinced there was—she didn't want to bother her sons' step-uncle. She wanted as few people involved as possible.

"Okay, I won't tell you," Aaron said. "But you should know that I called Aunt Vita and she immediately volunteered Uncle Rick. Until Damon calls back with the name of his friend and I can get some answers, you are going to have company one way or another."

Nicole was about to say something in protest, but Felicia spoke up first. "Aaron's right, Nicole. It wouldn't hurt to make sure that someone is here just in case."

"But someone *is* here 'just in case,'" Nicole said to Felicia. "You are." Saying that, she looked at her son. "You said that you taught her some of your self-defense moves, didn't you, Aaron?"

"Yes, I did," he said, and then, belatedly, he looked at Felicia. Guilt was beginning to nibble away at his conscience. "Look, I'm sorry if I snapped at you earlier," he apologized.

In Felicia's opinion, even though he said the words, Aaron didn't look all that contrite—not that she could really blame him. This was all her fault, and she really hated the idea that she had brought a very real threat into Nicole's home.

"You did," Nicole said to her son. "But lucky for us, Fee has a forgiving heart." She looked at her son, a warning look in her eyes. "Just don't let it happen again, Aaron."

Aaron knew his mother was only half kidding.

The next moment, Nicole shifted gears. "All right, enough lecturing," she declared. "Time for breakfast." With that, she turned her attention to the stove. And then, because she heard no movement, Nicole glanced over her shoulder. Felicia and Aaron were both still standing there, looking like statues in her opinion. "Sit," she ordered, then added, "please."

That got them to move, she noted. They both took a seat facing each other, neither one of them appearing to be at ease with the other.

Especially not Felicia.

Felicia could suddenly feel her heart sinking as it became vividly clear to her that she had lost Aaron. She had made her peace with the fact that she would, eventually, but she hadn't thought it would happen so soon. It brought with it this terrible, oppressive feeling of finality and almost doom.

Felicia had never thought she would fall in love again, but she had. And this time, it had turned out to be far better, far deeper, than the only other time it had happened before. That first time didn't even compare to what she was experiencing now. It hadn't even scratched the surface.

But this feeling with Aaron had been nothing short of magnificent—and now it was over.

She could feel tears stinging her eyes, although somehow she managed to keep them back. Her fault, she thought again. This was all her fault. She should have never let her guard down the way she had, never allowed Aaron in. Now she felt totally at a loss and there was nothing she could do about it. And the worst part of it was that she had possibly put Nicole in danger.

Well, she just couldn't risk taking another chance that Greg might come back. When it came to Greg, things only escalated whenever he did anything, and the idea terrified her that the next time things might wind up being fatal.

Felicia made up her mind, doing her best to look cheerful as she dug into the breakfast that Nicole placed before her.

She was going to have to leave.

As soon as possible.

FOR THE NEXT few hours, it was very difficult maintaining a front. She had a feeling that Nicole suspected something was wrong. Several times, the woman would ask her if she was all right. And each time she did, she would tell Nicole that she was fine. She didn't want to admit that she was concerned that Greg might come back. With all her heart, she sincerely regretted putting Nicole and everyone else through this.

Sensing this unspoken guilt, Nicole was quick to try to set her mind at ease, assuring Felicia that nothing that happened was her fault. By that time, Rick and Vita had come over.

"How can you both be here?" Felicia asked Rick. "Did you finally find a new person to hire for the nursery?"

He shook his head. "No, not yet."

Puzzled—and feeling guiltier by the moment—she asked, "Then how—"

She didn't get to finish. Vita explained, "We put up a Closed for Family Emergency sign on the nursery door, promising to be back within the day. Not to worry. You mean more to us than the nursery does," she told Nicole as well as Felicia.

That was another thing that Felicia felt bad about. Much as she had come to care for everyone within Aaron's family, she knew that she had carelessly put everyone in danger just because she had wanted to steal a little extra time with people she wished with all her heart were her family.

But they weren't her family, and she couldn't risk ever seeing them again once she left. She knew that.

For the remainder of the time, she acted as if nothing was really wrong. The first chance she got, she slipped away and quickly made sure her belongings were all packed up in the battered suitcase she had initially brought with her. Because Nicole had insisted on buying her a few things, saying that they had her name written all over them, Felicia had to stuff the suitcase practically to the breaking point.

But she couldn't bear to leave anything behind. There was a memory attached to every item the woman had given her. Memories she treasured and couldn't bring herself to give up.

It wasn't until after the second set of physical therapy exercises that Felicia finally had her chance to put her plan into action. Vita and Rick had talked Nicole into going out in the backyard to enjoy a little peace and quiet. A welcome cooling trend was just beginning to embrace the area.

Making certain that they were all occupied, Felicia made her move. She quickly slipped out the front, clutching her suitcase and doing her best not to cry.

She told herself that this was the best thing for all of them.

Felicia kept repeating that to herself like a mantra until she was clear of the house and driving away from it. Only then did the tears fall.

Chapter Twenty-Three

She hated him.

Felicia had never really hated anyone before, especially not like this. But she had reached the point that she hated Greg Harper with a nearly overwhelming, red-hot passion.

She hadn't even hated her ex-husband when he had turned abusive and several of his outbursts had landed her in the emergency room. And she hadn't even hated him when she was forced to pack up and flee to another state because he had begun stalking her and turning up on her doorstep.

But she certainly hated him now.

Hated him for bringing fear into Nicole's life. Hated him for the angry expression that had risen in Aaron's eyes when he looked at her. And really hated Greg for destroying the one bit of happiness she had ever had.

Hated him because, just like the last time, he had left her no choice. She had to leave the state.

Again.

Felicia knew that she had no real recourse open to her. She would have to leave the area on the first bus bound for another state. It didn't matter which one, just as long as it took the threat of something unforeseen and dangerous happening to Aaron and his family away from here.

With a sinking heart and a sick feeling in the pit of her stomach, Felicia made her way to the bus depot. She still couldn't shake the feeling that she was being followed, but at this point, she felt that she had become permanently paranoid.

Again, because of Greg.

She damned the day she had ever met him.

"HI, MOM," AARON called out, for once using his old house key to let himself into the house. "I came over early so that Uncle Rick and Aunt Vita can get back to their lives again," he told his mother, closing the door behind him. Seeing Rick and Vita, he nodded at them and then looked around. "Where's Felicia?" he asked. "I didn't see her car outside."

That came as a surprise. Nicole glanced at Aaron's aunt and uncle. On their way out, they both stopped and looked at one another.

"I don't know," Aaron's mother said quite honestly. "She didn't say anything about going out." Nicole looked at Vita and Rick. "Did she say anything to either one of you?"

They both shook their heads. Vita glanced at her nephew. "No. Are you sure her car is gone?" she asked Aaron.

But Aaron was already heading for the stairs and Felicia's room. "Maybe she parked it somewhere else." It was a shot in the dark at best, but he really doubted it.

Taking the stairs two at a time, Aaron made it up to

her room in record time. Felicia's bedroom door was closed. Containing his frustration, he knocked on it.

"Felicia? Fee, are you in there?" he asked. When there was no answer, he knocked again. Not waiting this time, he tried the doorknob.

It gave in his hand, opening. He had a bad feeling about this as he walked slowly into the room.

The bad feeling only grew worse when he saw that the single closet door was standing wide open. A quick check into the closet showed no trace of Felicia's things.

She was gone.

Trying not to dwell on the sinking feeling in his gut, Aaron went over to the bureau and pulled opened the drawers. Just as he had anticipated, there was nothing there, either.

She was really gone.

Holding on to a shred of hope that he could still find her, he took out his cell phone and called Felicia.

"C'mon, c'mon," he muttered impatiently as he listened to the phone ring against his ear.

Her phone rang a total of four times and then he heard her voice. "This is Felicia. I can't come to the phone right now, but if you leave your name and number and a short message, I promise I'll get back to you as soon as I can. Have a nice day."

"C'mon, Felicia, pick up. Pick up," he coaxed. But she didn't. "Look, I'm sorry. I shouldn't have said what I said to you earlier. And I shouldn't have put any pressure on you to tell me about your past. That's your business. I should have let you tell me when you were ready to let me into your life." He was pacing as he spoke into the phone, willing her to pick up. "But you have to understand, I was just worried. About you, about Mom. Just come back and we can work this all out—"

That was when he heard her cell phone disconnecting against his ear.

"Damn it," he muttered, utterly frustrated.

Nicole was waiting for him at the bottom of the stairs when he came out of the room. "Did you get her?" she asked hopefully.

He shook his head as he came down. "She's gone, Mom. She took her things. I tried calling her, but she's not picking up."

"I guess maybe she's too angry to talk to you right now," Nicole told him.

That made the most amount of sense, he thought. "Maybe if you call her," he suggested. He just asked that she was all right and that nothing had happened to her. Until he heard the sound of Felicia's voice, that was still up in the air.

"I'm way ahead of you, dear," Nicole said as she took her phone out of her pocket. She quickly tapped out Felicia's number.

The moment Felicia's cell phone connected with hers, Nicole found herself on the receiving end of the same message that Aaron had listened to.

Growing concerned, Nicole pressed her lips together. "Fee, please call us," she said. "We're all very worried about you."

Saying that, Aaron's mother closed her phone and addressed her son. "She's not picking up."

"I can see her ignoring me. She's angry with me, but she wouldn't just ignore you," he told his mother.

"Something's definitely wrong. Do you have any idea where she went?"

But Nicole shook her head, feeling helpless. "No, I don't. I really wish that I did, but she never talked about any place but here."

Aaron was back on his phone. This time he was calling the number that Damon had given him, getting in contact with the person Damon had said could do some research for him by looking on the dark web. His brother had sworn that the man could find things out that weren't normally available or even known to the average computer tech.

He crossed his fingers that Damon's contact was as good as his brother had said and that he could locate Greg's whereabouts for him.

Aaron had a feeling that somehow, Greg was at the bottom of all this.

The only thing that his brother had told him was that the contact's name was Ryan. If "Ryan" was a first name or a last name or just a code name in this case, Aaron had absolutely no idea, nor did he care. He just wanted help—as fast as possible.

The phone on the other end rang an inordinate number of times.

Where the hell is this Ryan? Aaron thought impatiently. He was about to hang up and try again, thinking maybe he had misdialed.

And then Aaron heard the phone being picked up.

He began talking immediately. "Ryan, this is Aaron Colton. I got your number from Damon. He thought you might be able to help me."

In contrast to Aaron, the voice on the other end was

exceedingly calm and soft-spoken. "Yes, Damon explained the situation to me."

The man had a slight accent, but Aaron couldn't really place it. Again, that didn't matter. All that mattered was getting results. And the faster he could get those results, the better.

"I've taken the liberty of doing a little research into this Greg Harper that you're trying to locate," Ryan was saying.

"And?" Aaron asked, trying not to sound too impatient, although he really couldn't help himself. Truthfully, he had no idea what to expect or what he was actually hoping for. But if Ryan could give him a location where he could get his hands on Felicia's abusive ex-husband, then he felt he had a very real chance of saving her.

Because he really believed it had come down to that and he damned himself for not being more careful when it came to watching out for Felicia. He had dealt with at-risk kids on a regular basis, and he of all people should have seen the signs much earlier and been protective of her.

He tried not to dwell on the fact that he had failed her. What mattered was that he intended to find a way to save her.

"He's here," Ryan told him simply.

Even though he was really hoping that Ryan could provide him with a location, the fact that Ryan actually did stunned him.

"Here?" Aaron repeated incredulously. Could it actually have been just that easy?

"Yes. I've tracked this Greg Harper down and he's

registered in a motel on the outskirts of Chicago. It's not all that far away from where Damon said your old home is located," he informed Aaron. "From what I managed to find out about your guy, he hasn't held down a job for any length of time in about three and a half years." He was silent for a moment, as if reviewing something. "There's something here about charges being brought up against him, but nothing seemed to stick and eventually the charges were dropped. Tell you one thing, he doesn't sound like a nice guy," Ryan commented.

Aaron could feel his jaw clenching. "He's not. That's why I need to find him as soon as possible. What's the address of the motel?"

"It's really a hole in the wall," Ryan told him. "You know, one of those places where you pay by the hour, or by day, or occasionally, by week. Even by those standards, it comes across like a real hole," he added, then rattled off the address for him. "You got that? I can repeat it if you need me to," Ryan offered.

"No, thanks, I got it. I owe you," Aaron told him in all sincerity. "Big-time."

"No, you don't. I'm just paying Damon back what I owe him. The guy saved my life," Ryan said matter-of-factly as if it was an everyday occurrence. "Anything else?"

"Not unless you have something more to add," Aaron told him.

"Nope. I'm good. Tell Damon the debt's paid."

And with that, the connection terminated.

Only then did Nicole say anything to her son. "So,

did you get an address for where this worthless waste of flesh is staying?"

"Yes, I got an address for that lowlife," he confirmed. He really looked angry with himself.

Nicole saw his expression. "What's wrong?"

"Felicia kept behaving as if she was being stalked. If she actually was—" and he now had no reason to believe that she wasn't "—then this Greg character knows where she is. If he doesn't, I can still make sure that he stops bothering her."

Nicole knew that tone of voice and what was behind it. "Aaron, Nash is back in town. Take him with you."

"No, Mom," he told her, rejecting her suggestion, "I need to handle this on my own. Don't worry. One way or another, I'll find Felicia and bring her home."

"You said you had the address of the motel where her ex was staying. What is it?" she asked him.

"The Highland Inn," he told her. Aaron realized that his mother was picking up her purse. Worried, he moved directly in front of her. "Hold it, where do you think you're going?"

"With you," Nicole answered simply.

"Oh no, you're not," he told her. "Mom, I don't need to worry about you, too. If Felicia was right, then this Greg character is capable of anything. I need to know you're safe, do you understand? I promise I'll call you the minute I know where she is."

Nicole looked at her son doubtfully. "Do you promise?" she asked him even though Aaron had said as much.

"I promise," he told her solemnly. And with that, he was gone.

AARON'S HEART WAS in his throat the entire way to the run-down motel. If anything happened to Felicia because he had been inaccessible and put pressure on her, he would never forgive himself.

When he'd gotten behind the wheel of his car, he was barely aware of driving to the motel. All he knew was that it was taking him too long to get there.

DAMN IT, SHE had let her guard down. Knowing everything that Greg was capable of, she hadn't been nearly alert enough. Focused on getting to the bus depot and getting the first bus leaving the state, she had somehow allowed him to come up behind her when she parked her vehicle in the bus depot parking lot. Part of her inattention was due to the fact that her car was on its last legs and she was just praying that it lasted long enough for her to get to the depot.

If she hadn't been that preoccupied, she was certain that she would have heard Greg coming up behind her.

But she hadn't.

She had parked in the first available space she could find, got out and grabbed her suitcase. She hadn't even been aware that there was someone directly behind her until she felt Greg grabbing her roughly by the waist.

She gasped, ready to fight him off, knowing in her heart it had to be Greg. But he'd caught her so tightly that he stole her very breath away.

"Finally!" she heard Greg declare. "Thought you could get away, didn't you, you little bitch? Haven't you learned by now that I'm cleverer than you?" he asked maliciously.

Felicia tried to pull away, but he had pinned her

arms against her, tightening his hold. And then, the next moment, he yanked her almost savagely over in front of him.

Suddenly, she was being shoved into the trunk of a car.

His car, she guessed, although she didn't recognize it.

"Now you'll stay put, won't you?" Greg laughed in satisfaction, mocking her. The next moment, the lid of the trunk slammed shut on her and she was completely encased in darkness.

For a second she panicked, unable to breathe.

Calm down, Fee, calm down.

She knew that she had to calm down. Otherwise, it would all be over with far too quickly—and then Greg would finally win this confrontation.

She hadn't come this far just to give up, Felicia told herself. She refused to die here in Greg's dirty trunk, refused to give him the satisfaction that he had won. That he had finally gotten the best of her.

He wasn't a winner. Greg was a loser and he would lose this battle. She just needed to keep her head.

Calm, stay calm, Felicia told herself. *Deep breaths.*

It took some doing, but she managed to reach into her pocket and extract her cell phone. Holding on to it tightly—because if she dropped it, it would be over with—she managed to turn it on.

If Aaron was trying to find her, she needed to give him a signal to track.

Now all she had to do was pray that he *was* trying to track her and that he hadn't just decided to write her off as a lost cause, a ship that had crossed him in the dead of night and then sailed away.

With effort, shifting carefully, she put the cell phone back into her pocket.

Now start looking for me, Aaron.

Please.

Chapter Twenty-Four

Felicia realized that the car had stopped moving.

She braced herself, knowing she would have only a split second to react once Greg opened the trunk again.

Even so, when the lid popped open, light came flooding in. Felicia felt as if she was temporarily blinded. So much so that she couldn't react immediately.

The next second she felt Greg grabbing her arm and roughly hauling her out of the car's interior.

Desperate to focus, she thought she made out the glint of a rifle barrel in the trunk, but she wasn't sure. It had felt like she had been lying on something exceedingly hard and unyielding.

Greg had almost wrenched her shoulder as he got her out of the trunk. It took everything for her not to gasp out loud in pain.

Mind over matter, she told herself.

Her ex-husband looked disappointed. He'd obviously expected her to cry out. "You've gotten tougher in the last two years, Fee. Did your new boyfriend give you an education in working out?" Greg taunted her.

He was still holding on to her arm tightly, all but cutting off her circulation. He was giving every indication that he wasn't about to let her get away, not this time.

"There *is* no new boyfriend," she told him through clenched teeth.

There was no way Felicia would admit anything to Greg. She knew him, or at least the man that Greg had turned into, and there was no way she would give him an excuse to hurt Aaron, or any of the members of his family.

"Don't give me that," he snarled. He had parked his car on the far side of a rear lot, deliberately out of sight. It was obvious that he wasn't going to allow anyone to rob him of this. "I know you. I've got eyes. You get your claws into a man and then just suck him dry, like you tried to do with me," he mocked. "I'm tired of putting up with that, tired of seeing you use men for your perverted purposes. Well, no more Mr. Nice Guy. This time, there's not going to be any forgiveness. This time, you're going to pay for making a fool out of me."

Felicia had no idea what he was talking about. Somehow, in his mind, he'd switched their roles, made himself her victim instead of the other way around. She had absolutely no idea how to begin to bridge the chasm he had created between reality and what he believed was reality.

"I never made a fool out of you, Greg," she told him. But she could see that her words had no effect. They didn't even penetrate. She wanted to add that if he felt like a fool, that was his own doing, but if anything, that would only incense him and there was no point in doing that.

Greg couldn't see reason anymore, much less be reasoned with.

He was bending her arm behind her back as he pushed her toward a run-down building. A motel, she realized. Leaning forward, he whispered a warning into her ear just before they entered.

"Don't get any ideas about asking the guy behind the desk for help. I've got a gun in my pocket and the minute you call out to him, he's a dead man, understand? Your choice," he all but barked, punctuating it with a nasty laugh.

She would have said he was bluffing. He didn't have a gun on him. When she was with him, he hadn't even known which end of the gun to point. But those were definitely weapons in the trunk of his car. She could have sworn that there was more than one because she had lain on them. She couldn't risk some man's life on the supposition that Greg was lying. So she said nothing as they walked by the front desk.

Greg continued holding on to her arm, shoving Felicia ahead of him and walking her toward the stairs that led to the motel's second floor.

"Smart girl," he told her nastily.

The man behind the desk barely looked up from the magazine he was reading.

For just a second, despite her best intentions, Felicia debated crying out to the short, overweight man, asking him to call the police. But if Greg did have a gun on him the way he claimed, she knew he wouldn't hesitate to use it. She just couldn't risk that.

Reaching the landing and out of the desk clerk's earshot, Greg laughed nastily at her restraint.

"Still the bleeding heart," he mocked. "I guess that some things never change."

The way he said it, she was almost certain Greg had been lying about the gun. And even if he wasn't, she didn't care. They were out of the clerk's range and if Greg did have a gun on him and shot her, that was still preferable to allowing herself to be tortured at his hands, and she was certain that Greg had escalated to that point.

That was behind her, Felicia thought. She was not about to be that accommodating, meek little victim ever again.

She saw that Greg was momentarily distracted as he tried to fish his key out of his pocket in order to open the door to his room.

Felicia seized her opportunity and twisted around, wrenching her arm away as she got away from him. Cursing, Greg grabbed her by her hair, yanking her back to him.

Tears of pain filled her eyes, but she still managed to sink her teeth into his arm, biting down so hard that she actually drew blood.

Greg hollered in pain, letting out a string of vicious curses. Rather than try to get away, Felicia swung around, doubled up her fist and drove it straight to his throat.

Caught by surprise, Greg began choking and coughing violently. She used the opportunity to drive her fingers into his eye sockets. It wasn't easy for her because the very act turned her stomach, but she knew it was a matter of Greg or her and she had sworn to herself that it wasn't going to be her ever again.

Another string of curses emerged from his lips as, breathing hard, Greg tried to grab her hair again. But this time, because his eyes were tearing up, he missed.

Spinning around on her heel, Felicia took off and ran back toward the stairs. It was the only way out of the motel. With one hand on the railing to steady herself, she flew down the steps.

Greg was directly behind her.

"You're going to pay for this, bitch!" he promised angrily, determined to make her regret attempting to fight back.

Felicia's heart sank when she didn't see the desk clerk behind his desk. He had obviously gone somewhere, maybe on a food break. This wasn't the kind of high-class place that had employees subbing for one another because they were leery of leaving the front desk unattended.

It didn't matter, she told herself. She didn't need the desk clerk. She could make it out of the motel on her own.

She could, she swore. She could. While it was true that Greg had been on the track team in high school—or so he had said—a lot of years had passed since then and he had obviously been neglecting his workouts. What that meant was that it had caused him to lose some of his speed since then.

Felicia was so laser-focused on making her getaway she didn't even realize that the man she had run past was Aaron, until she was almost behind him.

"Aaron!" she cried in disbelief, practically doing a one-eighty.

Overjoyed at finding her, Aaron quickly shoved Felicia directly behind him. He wanted to pull her into his arms, but now wasn't the time. He had to be sure she was all right,

Aaron swung around to face the bellowing man who was running after her.

"Did he hurt you?" Aaron demanded, ready to make her ex-husband pay if he had harmed so much as a single hair on her head.

She was relieved beyond words to have Aaron suddenly appear out of the blue like this. "I'm all right."

She still couldn't believe that Aaron had somehow managed to find her just in time. She had left her phone on, but she had no way of knowing if he could actually track her.

"But she's not going to be for long," Greg boasted, his expression ugly. "Listen, you SOB, this is none of your business," he shouted at Aaron. "So unless you're asking for a few new holes to be put in your body, I'd get the hell out of here if I were you."

"But you're not me," Aaron told him in a taunting, belittling voice. "You're a sniveling, craven coward who gets off on brutalizing women."

In response to Aaron's jeer, Greg's face turned to an angry shade of crimson red.

"He said he's got a gun, Aaron," Felicia cried, terrified that her ex actually did and would carry out the threat he'd made earlier.

What if he shot Aaron?

If anything happened to Aaron because of her, Felicia knew that she wouldn't be able to ever live with herself. That was why she had left Nicole's house in the first place. To spare everyone, not to get anyone shot—especially not Aaron.

"Don't worry. Cowards always make empty threats," Aaron told her. His eyes met Greg's, all but penetrating the man's soul—if he even had one. "He doesn't have a gun. He doesn't have anything."

"Oh, you think that? You think that?" Greg repeated, practically shrieking.

Wild-eyed, the man took one step toward Aaron, his intention to harm him and then take his fury out on Felicia infinitely clear. With a savage yell, he ran up to Aaron—and wound up walking right into Aaron's powerful right hook.

It took Aaron just two swings to bring Greg down for the count. The man was knocked out cold.

Unable to believe that Aaron was safe and that he had actually managed to save her, as well, Felicia threw herself into his arms. She held on to him tightly, as if she was never going to let him go.

She was shaking and on the verge of tears as she cried, "You found me! You actually found me!"

"Damon's friend gets part of the credit," Aaron told her, holding her to him and feeling incredibly relieved to actually be able to do so. He was not about to release her. "That was pretty clever thinking," he told her, "leaving your cell phone on so we could trace the signal to that car outside of the motel."

Felicia smiled at him through her tears. "What can I tell you?" she sniffed. "I like spy novels."

Laughing, Aaron hugged her even closer to him.

Just then, they heard the sounds of an approaching police car as a siren cut through the air.

The siren grew louder, obviously coming closer.

Felicia looked at Aaron quizzically. "Did you call the police, too?" she asked, surprised that he would think to do something like that.

She had just naturally assumed that Aaron would have waited until he had gotten here and then just handled the situation himself. When it came to things like that, he struck her as a loner.

"I didn't call them," he admitted, "but I've got a feeling that my mother did," Aaron said. "As soon as Damon's friend gave me the name and address of the motel where your ex was staying, I told my mother. There was no other way she was going to let me leave without her unless I told her where I was going."

Still shaking, Felicia was grinning from ear to ear. In Nicole's place, she would have done the same thing. "I love your mother," Felicia told him with feeling.

"Yeah," Aaron said, finally giving in to the temptation he had been dealing with and kissing her briefly, "I know."

Aaron glanced over toward the crumpled heap on the floor. "Your ex is going to go away for a long, long time."

"He's not *my* anything," Felicia firmly informed Aaron. "And as for his going away for a long time, it's going to be longer than you think."

He thought her words were motivated by wishful thinking and animosity, but Aaron discovered it was otherwise when the two policemen who had responded to his mother's call entered.

"Mr. Colton, your mother filled us in on what was going on here." Hogan, the older of the two policemen, told Aaron. "We're going to need you both to come down with us and give us a statement."

"We will, but I think you might want to look into this man's vehicle first," Felicia told the two responding police officers.

Both men and Aaron looked at her quizzically, waiting for a further explanation of what had prompted her to say that.

"When Greg had me locked in the trunk of his car, I thought I could smell drugs—he had something floral and chemical in there, and flowers were definitely not in there," she told them.

The two officers exchanged looks. "Sounds like it might be drugs," Wilson guessed.

Felicia nodded. That sounded right. The smell had made her head hurt by the time the trunk was opened. "If I know him, Greg has turned to supplementing his income with what he once referred to as easy money."

"Go check it out, Wilson," Hogan directed.

"Would you happen to know where he keeps his car keys?" Wilson asked.

"I think he should still have it on him," Felicia answered.

Wilson began to pat Greg down and made another discovery. Finding a handgun on Greg's person, he pulled it out and held it up. "My guess is that he doesn't have a permit for this," he speculated.

Felicia stared at the gun, horrified and stunned. "For once, he was actually telling the truth," she cried, looking at Aaron. "He really did have a gun." She looked at Officer Hogan. "He said he did, but I didn't believe him."

"Well, if what I just found in his closet is any indication, this guy's going to go away forever," the younger policeman told the couple.

Thank God.

It was over, Felicia thought. The nightmare she had been living for the last four and a half years was finally over.

She blinked back tears as she looked at the two police officers. "It can't be long enough for me," she told them honestly.

Putting his arm around Felicia, Aaron pulled her to him. "That scum is never going to bother or try to hurt you again," he promised and meant it from the bottom of his heart. Even if Harper wasn't going to prison.

Hogan, meanwhile, had handcuffed Greg's hands behind his back. Coming to, Greg moaned.

"That's it, Sleeping Beauty. Time to wake up," Hogan told him. But Greg had passed out again. "Hey, this guy's really out cold," he commented, taking a closer look at Greg. "What did you hit him with?" he asked, curious.

"A right hook," Aaron said simply.

The policeman grinned at him in admiration. "Good for you," he said. "A lowlife like this guy had it coming to him. Drugs, guns and abusing women. That's a trifecta if I ever heard one. Don't worry, ma'am," he told Felicia. "This guy's going to go away for a long, long time."

"Hear that, Fee?" Aaron asked, pressing a kiss to her temple.

She beamed at him. He had called her "Fee," she

thought, instantly feeling closer to him. "I heard,"
she replied.

The sigh of relief she breathed echoed in her very
soul as she leaned against Aaron and watched the two
policemen half walk, half carry Greg out of the motel.

She was finally safe, finally free.

Epilogue

The moment Felicia opened the front door and she and Aaron walked into the house, Nicole immediately flew into the foyer. She was wearing the widest smile possible as she greeted them. Blinking back tears, she threw her arms around Felicia as if the young woman was, at the very least, her long-lost daughter.

"Oh, thank goodness!" she cried as she looked up at her son. Nicole extended her hand toward him so that she could touch him, as well. "I was so worried about you two. Did the police get there in time?" she asked. She had spent the last hour imagining everything that could have happened to them, worrying herself sick.

"Not for Greg. Aaron had already knocked him out cold," Felicia told his mother.

She was looking at Aaron and smiling as she thought about him coming to save her.

Nicole released Felicia as she assessed her son. "I guess all those boxing championships of yours did come in handy," she told Aaron with no small amount of pride.

Aaron, never one to bask in credit, whether justifiably or not, merely shrugged off her words. "I guess," he said.

"Come," Nicole beckoned, leading them into the family room. Sitting down on the sofa, she patted the places beside her, indicating that they should both take a seat next to her. "Tell me everything." And then she interrupted herself. "I take it that the police arrested your ex," she said hopefully.

Aaron turned toward Felicia. This was her story and he felt she should be the one to tell his mother what actually happened.

"That they did," Felicia assured the woman. "And they'll be throwing the book at him, seeing as how they found drugs and a cache of firearms both in his car *and* his motel room."

Nicole looked incredibly relieved as well as concerned at what *could* have happened. She shook her head. "Guns and drugs! Thank heavens he's off the streets. You're right. They *are* going to throw the book at him."

Felicia nodded. "If there's any justice, they will," she agreed.

Nicole paused to kiss Felicia and then her son. "There still is," she said with the confidence of a woman who had lived long enough to actually witness justice in action a number of times.

BECAUSE THEY WERE all wound up thanks to the events that had transpired, Aaron and Felicia stayed up and talked with Nicole for more than an hour. But eventually, because it was getting late, Nicole begged off, saying that she was going to bed. Her parting words to the two of them were, "I am so happy that everything turned out the way it should have."

"Yeah, me, too." Aaron was sitting on the sofa, his arm resting comfortably around Felicia's shoulders. "You tired?" he asked her, not seeing how she couldn't be.

"Yes," Felicia admitted. "But I'm also wired. Besides, I don't want you to go yet."

He smiled at her. "Who said anything about my going?"

Felicia caught the inviting note in his voice. "Oh? Does that mean you're staying the night?" She could feel hope budding within her. What she had gone through with Greg had been awful, but if it got her to this place, then it had all been worth it.

"That all depends."

She raised an eyebrow. Maybe everything hadn't been resolved.

"On what?" she asked.

"On whether or not you want me to," Aaron said.

She looked at him, elated that he would want to stay and surprised that he actually thought she might not want him to.

Rising, Felicia wrapped her fingers around his hand and tugged. Taking the hint, Aaron rose to his feet.

"Why would you even think that?" she asked him as they went up to her room.

"Because I acted like a horse's rear end," he told her with all sincerity.

They reached her room and went in. The sound of the door closing behind them was strangely intimate and inviting, Felicia thought.

Aaron began to undress her and Felicia responded in kind.

"I should have realized that you had a good reason for keeping your past to yourself," he said. Aaron kissed her neck softly, sending shock waves of anticipation vibrating all through her. "I had no right to press you the way I did."

"You're right," she told him, breathing heavily. It was getting hard for her to think. "I did have a good reason for not telling you. I was ashamed that I allowed myself to be treated like such a victim," she admitted. "I thought once you knew that about me, that I let myself be abused, you wouldn't want to have anything to do with me anymore." There were tears in Felicia's eyes as she looked up at him. "That you wouldn't want to be with such a loser."

"Such a loser?" Aaron echoed in disbelief. By now, their clothes were all discarded in a heap on the floor. "Are you kidding me?" he asked her incredulously, slowly running his hands along her body. He loved the way she reacted, loved the way she twisted beneath his touch. He had come too close to losing her and he never intended to run that risk again. "You are the strongest woman I know," he told her, kissing the hollow of her throat. "And that includes my mother."

He couldn't have said anything more endearing and arousing to her if he tried.

Felicia sealed her mouth to his, feeling as if, at long last, she had finally, finally come home.

*   *   *   *   *

COMING SOON!

We really hope you enjoyed reading this book.
If you're looking for more romance, be sure to
head to the shops when new books are
available on

Thursday 5th August

MILLS & BOON

THE HEART OF ROMANCE

A ROMANCE FOR EVERY READER

MODERN

Prepare to be swept off your feet by sophisticated, sexy and seductive heroes, in some of the world's most glamourous and romanti locations, where power and passion collide.

HISTORICAL

Escape with historical heroes from time gone by. Whether your passion for wicked Regency Rakes, muscled Vikings or rugged Highlanders, aw the romance of the past.

MEDICAL

Set your pulse racing with dedicated, delectable doctors in the high-pre sure world of medicine, where emotions run high and passion, comfort love are the best medicine.

True Love

Celebrate true love with tender stories of heartfelt romance, from the rush of falling in love to the joy a new baby can bring, and a focus on emotional heart of a relationship.

Desire

Indulge in secrets and scandal, intense drama and plenty of sizzling ho action with powerful and passionate heroes who have it all: wealth, stat good looks…everything but the right woman.

HEROES

Experience all the excitement of a gripping thriller, with an intense ro mance at its heart. Resourceful, true-to-life women and strong, fearless face danger and desire - a killer combination!

To see which titles are coming soon, please visit

millsandboon.co.uk/nextmonth

LET'S TALK
Romance

For exclusive extracts, competitions
and special offers, find us online:

facebook.com/millsandboon

@MillsandBoon

@MillsandBoonUK

Get in touch on 01413 063232

For all the latest titles coming soon, visit
millsandboon.co.uk/nextmonth

JOIN US ON SOCIAL MEDIA!

Stay up to date with our latest releases, author news and gossip, special offers and discounts, and all the behind-the-scenes action from Mills & Boon...

 millsandboon

 millsandboonuk

 millsandboon

It might just be true love...

GET YOUR ROMANCE FIX!

MILLS & BOON
— *blog* —

Get the latest romance news, exclusive author
interviews, story extracts and much more!

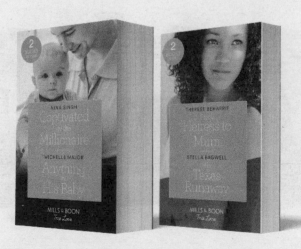

MILLS & BOON
MEDICAL
Pulse-Racing Passion

Set your pulse racing with dedicated, delectable doctors in the high-pressure world of medicine, where emotions run high and passion, comfort and love are the best medicine.